More B

UNDYING MERCENARIES
Steel World
Dust World
Tech World
Machine World
Death World
Home World
Rogue World

STAR FORCE SERIES
Swarm
Extinction
Rebellion
Conquest
Battle Station
Empire
Annihilation
Storm Assault
The Dead Sun
Outcast
Exile
Demon Star

Visit BVLarson.com for more information

ALPHA FLEET

(Rebel Fleet Series #3)
by
B. V. Larson

REBEL FLEET SERIES
Rebel Fleet
Orion Fleet
Alpha Fleet

ISBN-13:   978-1521879672
BISAC: Fiction / Science Fiction / Military

Cover Illustration © Tom Edwards
TomEdwardsDesign.com

=1=

After all the excitement of battle and adventure among the stars, coming home to Earth was... well... kind of boring. At first, the crew of my ship *Hammerhead* didn't see it that way. They were glad to relax and answer countless questions in countless debriefings. As the crew of Earth's only space-going warship, we were pretty important to the brass on our homeworld.

It didn't take long for the novelty to wear off, however, and Dalton was the first man to ask me about it.

"When are we going out there again, Captain? I can't bear to be stuck on this dull ball of dirt much longer. I'm going to go bonkers soon."

"They haven't issued me any orders yet. In fact... we might not be crewmen anymore."

"What's this?" he demanded with outrage. "Which cock-up got us blacklisted? I have to admit, it could have been anything—there were plenty."

"No, no, we didn't screw the galactic space-pooch. But *Hammerhead's* crew is considered a planetary treasure now. A resource of experience that is unique on Earth. In short, they want to turn us into instructors."

Dalton squinted at me for a moment, and I got the feeling he was trying to discern whether I was joking or not. When he made his decision, he gave me a dirty laugh.

"Me? An instructor? I'll give them both barrels, as you Yanks like to say."

He left then, chuckling evilly and shaking his head in amusement. I wasn't quite sure what he had in mind, but knowing Dalton, I was certain no one else was going to enjoy it.

The number of staffers at Space Command had grown over the last year. The old NORAD tunnels were too small to contain our swelling ranks. Most of the personnel were now housed outside the mountain in a freshly constructed series of imposing, government-looking buildings. They were growing like weeds all over the slopes of Cheyenne Mountain, with new roads being carved into the rocky slopes.

There was something like a moat in front of the citadel-like base, with a lone road crossing it. The entire thing resembled a fortress. Guard towers, still freshly painted a tan color, were being assembled and placed all along the moat.

I was standing on the top floor in the new executive building, and let me tell you, it was pretty nice. Big-budget features were in evidence everywhere. There were marble columns, statues, visiting politicians taking near-constant tours, and God-knew-what else in this formerly lonesome region of the Rocky Mountains.

Without question, Space Command was where the action was these days. It was early spring, and as I stared through massive windows at the snow-topped peaks surrounding the base, I knew I should be feeling elated. But somehow, my eyes kept drifting up from the moat, the construction traffic and the marching lines of troops.

Above it all was the sky. Beyond the streaky clouds the atmosphere thinned and turned a sheer blue, a color that was deceptive. Space was really black and white for the most part. It was a glittering river of white stars on a background made up of endless night.

"Leo?" a feminine voiced asked me. "Am I disturbing you?"

It was Gwen, and I turned to flash her a smile. She'd clearly been talking to me, and I hadn't been listening.

"No," I said, "of course not. I'm just reminiscing about the stars. Do you ever miss them?"

"What? Fighting and dying in that frozen void?"

"Yeah."

She was quiet for a second, then she sighed. "Yes, sometimes. Down here, everything seems so small. I remember when the Imperials first retreated. Commander Shaw and the rest of them were all depressed."

"Right. No more glory points for anyone after the war ended. Everyone going home, and the few professionals left in the Rebel Fleet were all stuck in dead-end jobs."

Gwen stepped to my side and gazed upward, standing with her hands clasped behind her back.

"It's been nearly a year," she said. "People are beginning to think the Imperials won't be back for another millennium. Did you hear they want to disband our whole crew and turn us into instructors?"

"I did hear that," I said. "That's what the meeting here in this conference room is about."

She looked around, startled. "That's why you're here early, isn't it? You're *never* early."

"This is a big one."

"What are you going to ask for?"

I glanced at her. "You mean in terms of rank?"

She nodded.

I turned back to the window and shrugged. "I don't care. If they think it's the best way I can serve the build-up effort, I guess I'll go along."

"Going along to get along? That's not like you."

Heaving a sigh, I gave her another shrug. If the truth were to be told, I was a little torn up about it. Earth had built more than twenty phase-ships like *Hammerhead* over the last year—but I'd been passed over for an appointment to command any of them.

The new vessels were sleeker, faster and more deadly than my ship had been—but there were certain elements aboard the original ship that our techs had yet to duplicate. There were

3

characteristics of the ship's hull and equipment that were still beyond human engineering.

That was because parts of *Hammerhead* had been cannibalized from the alien-built heavy fighter I'd brought home to Earth. There were some things Dr. Abrams and his team had yet to figure out.

The thought made me smile. The technical challenge was probably driving Abrams mad.

"You two need some time alone?" a booming voice asked from behind us.

We turned to see General Vega. He was the base commander, and we'd never gotten along very well.

He was laughing at his own joke, messing around with a laptop as he set up a station at the front of the room. Gwen and I had been a romantic couple once—but that was all in the past. Some people, like Vega, still liked to bring it up whenever they found us together even today.

"We're just the early birds, sir," Gwen said. Her tone wasn't as light as her words. I could tell she was pissed off about Vega's innuendos, but she was trying to hide it. "I'll go check on the staffers," she said. "They should have been here by now."

She hustled away, and Vega's eyes lingered on her as she passed by.

When his eyes swiveled back to me, he shook his head. "I don't see why you pissed that away for some furry thing with a tail."

That comment made me suck in a breath. I wanted to let go with some shouting, but I held back.

"We all have our private lives, sir," I said.

He shook his head, tapping at his computer. "Don't know what's wrong with a human woman," he muttered. "But that's not what we're talking about today, is it?"

"No sir."

"I hear your bucking for a promotion."

I blinked in confusion. "Not that I'm aware of, General."

He chuckled again and shook his head. He tapped at a screen to open a file. A memo was displayed in the midst of the conference table. From any angle, it appeared to face the viewer. It was a nice trick they'd gleaned off the alien perception gear we'd captured over the years.

"Right here," he said. "On August 2nd and again in November—and lastly in March. You've put off entreaties to join the ranks of our instructional staff here at the Mountain."

"Uh... that's true, sir. But nowhere did I mention a promotion."

"Only a fool would put it in print, and whatever people say Blake, you're no fool. Why would a man resist a transfer into an easy life on the most important military base on Earth? No one would, of course. Only a man who's holding out for a better offer would even pretend. So, what's your next move?"

Startled, I shrugged. "I was hoping for a command position, General. On one of the ships we've been commissioning every three weeks."

"Right..." he said, nodding and tapping at his computer. "I knew you'd try that play. What's next? Threatening to resign if we don't give you your due...? That's the endpoint of this negotiation, isn't it? Maybe we should jump ahead to that moment right now."

I was finally beginning to frown. Vega was the kind of man who grew more irritating the longer you talked to him—about anything.

"Nowhere in those documents did I threaten to resign," I pointed out.

"No—and again, you're playing this masterfully, boy. You know how important you are to Earth's defense efforts. If it was anyone else other than the great Leo Blake, we'd have simply ordered you to a new post. If they'd wanted to bail out, we'd have let them. But you and your people are special. You know we need you, and you're squeezing. I can hardly blame you for that—even if it's somewhat unethical."

My frown grew. Before I could reply, however, I heard the swelling sound of voices in the hallway outside. I paused, eyeing the entrance. I expected a gaggle of staffers to join us, but they kept on walking. They sounded excited.

"Um..." I said, gesturing toward the hallway. "What's going on, General? Isn't this supposed to be a larger meeting? Why are we the only two people in here?"

"It's all nonsense," Vega said, waving away my words as if they stank. "After the last war, everyone is jumping at shadows."

"What kind of shadows?"

5

"Some nerd spotted a few shimmers out in far orbit, a few million kilometers out. Some say it's a breach opening, but I say that's nonsense. We know now that events like this appear naturally once in a while."

"I see..."

"Back to the matter at hand," he continued. "Will you or won't you accept a position under my command as a full-fledged instructor?"

"I didn't return to Earth's service in order to teach."

"Come on, man," he said earnestly, leaning forward. "We need you. We need your experience. I can't have just one experienced crew the next time war heats up. I want a hundred teams who've been trained by that one experienced crew."

"Yeah..." I said, turning back toward the window again. "I get that. Normally, I'd try to weasel out of your trap. But you're right. I can better serve Earth by training new crewmen. Just tell me this, General. If I take the job, will you put me back into command service someday later on?"

"Of course!" he purred happily. "That's always been assumed! No one is putting a tiger like you out to pasture, Blake. You have too many fine qualities as a line officer."

"That's what I thought," I said, knowing he was lying. As an accomplished bender of facts myself, it wasn't hard to detect false statements coming from another.

"Well then," Vega said with delight in his voice. "The rest of this meeting will focus on how we get the other key members of your team to join us. What do you think would be the best—?"

He broke off, as an excited group of staffers spilled into the conference room. There were five of them, and Gwen was in the lead.

"Sirs?" she asked breathlessly. "I tried to contact you both, but you're syms are blocking me out."

"That's what I always do when I have an important meeting," General Vega said stiffly. "I hate interruptions while I'm handling people who are physically present. I don't even see how you young people can get anything done with your syms buzzing in your brains all the time."

One key piece of tech Earth had spread around their armed services was the sym. Our "syms" were symbiotic life forms that lived inside our bodies and linked us to technology around us. The original form of the biological implants weren't entirely innocuous, as they could be influenced by any high-ranking member of the Rebel Kher. My sym was one of those original versions.

For the benefit of the standard soldier, Dr. Abrams had managed to clone my sym and perform gene-splicing alterations upon it. According to him, his modern Earth-grown syms were immune to outside influences. I wondered if that was really true, as the Rebel Kher had never returned to challenge his assertions.

"The techs think it's an arrival event," Gwen explained. "A breach."

"Confirmation?" Vega asked. "Ship sightings?"

"Not yet, General."

"No, I thought not. False alarms every day. Why was I put in command of such an excitable bunch of kids?"

The staffers took offense to this, and they began to argue with General Vega about the importance of their news, but I ignored them all. I opened up my sym and used it to reach toward the sensor arrays surrounding the base.

I still had the clearances needed to pass security. My mind reached effortlessly through the radio waves, then deeper to the physical wires, then lastly out to the instruments themselves. Collecting all the latest data of significance, I let my sym absorb the raw stream for perhaps five seconds before urging it to formulate a grand overview. A big-picture took another few seconds to coalesce.

When it did, I staggered and gasped. Everyone looked at me.

With a tossing motion of my hand, I cast what I was seeing to the conference table, which dutifully transformed it into a hanging, three-dimensional image in our midst.

The final image rapidly filled in and sharpened as my sym kept collating details. A spinning rift was growing in far orbit. It had appeared between the Earth and her sole loyal companion, the Moon.

Everyone stopped chattering. They all stared in fascination. Someone—something—was coming to visit us. No one could deny it when they saw the rift—not even General Vega.

A starship was about to arrive. Would it be friendly or hostile? There was no way of knowing.

=2=

It didn't take long for the techs to perform the same analysis I'd done, and they quickly came to the same conclusions.

Alarm spread quickly over the base. Air raid sirens wound up, singing their long, low, mournful note from a dozen towers. The noise reverberated off the granite walls of the mountains surrounding us until it was almost unbearable.

"You'd better hope these visitors nuke this place, Blake," Vega told me as he rushed out of the conference room to the control center. "Because that's the only way you're getting out of your new duties."

Before I could assure him I had no intention of resisting his plans, he was gone. Without an official role in the operation of the base—I'd been a glorified PR rep for months—I moved back to the windows and stared upward. With the naked eye, I couldn't make out anything unusual.

The temptation to use my sym again to monitor the situation proved unbearable. I closed my eyes, cast outward with my mind, and watched events unfold in space beyond the clouds.

At first, the situation was unclear. I could see the swirling rift, a riot of colors painted with dusted, gauzy lights. It wasn't until I overlaid our own naval positioning that I got the picture.

Our tiny ships were moving in. They were all phase-ships, invisible because they weren't entirely located in our dimension of space. Using their only advantage, stealth, they crept toward the rift from multiple angles.

My mind raced as I watched. Three of our ships were close enough to reach the region. Earth's new fleet wasn't much, not by the standards of the more established Rebel Kher worlds. Some of our older siblings could field hundreds of large vessels. All we had was a score of sneaky ships that employed tech we barely understood.

The breach widened, and I could see stars through it. I gasped aloud, and I wasn't the only one. Another voice gasped behind me at the same moment.

I opened my eyes and turned to find someone behind me. I also saw I'd left the streaming feed open, and it was still being relayed to the conference table. The rift was there, spinning in a ghostly fashion above the flat glassy surface.

"Blake," Lt. Commander Jones said, "tell me this isn't really happening."

"Sorry," I said, "but it's real. That feed is from space—that's what our sensors are picking up right now."

"A rift is opening? How far out?"

"Maybe three hundred thousand kilometers above us. Just beyond the orbit of the Moon."

"Why would they do that? Why would they choose to come out right there?"

I hesitated. I had an idea—but everything I knew about enemy behavior was classified. There had been secrecy breaches here at the base, enough of them for me to take secrecy seriously.

"Dammit, man!" Jones said. "I know I'm only the base goon around here—no one tells me anything. But I deserve to know I'm going to die, if that's how this is about to go down."

I narrowed my eyes at him. He was my friend. I'd saved his life, and he'd saved mine in the past. But to see him here, now... it was odd. He was the security chief of the interior tunnels. Not here on the general external base.

"What are you doing here?" I asked him. "Why aren't you down in the tunnels watching the transmat?"

He looked startled. "I thought you knew," he said. "They brought me up here to help convince you to take that base job Vega wants to place you in so badly. You know... an old friend talking up a shit assignment."

I almost laughed, and I relaxed. Walking over to stand beside him, I looked at the table. The rift had widened like a dilating eye.

"You recognize those stars?" I asked. "Seen through the rift? That one is red—and damned big."

9

"Uh..." he said. "You think it's Antares?"

I nodded. Over the recent years, everyone had gotten pretty good at astronomy. Antares was a red supergiant. It was so large our sun would look like a dot of light if the two were close enough to compare. Located about five hundred lightyears from us, it was used as a beacon for navigation during long jumps.

"That means they're coming from a beacon point," Jones said thoughtfully. "They're probably from an even more distant starting location, if they had to use the beacon as a first step to get into our neighborhood."

"That's right," I said.

"But you haven't told me who you think—" Jones said.

That's when I clocked him. A hard right to the jaw. It was a sucker-punch, and I felt bad about it the moment I'd launched it.

Jones was my friend, as I said, but I was pretty sure this wasn't Jones.

The man fell, knocking aside a few chairs. He was on his hands and knees, not quite flattened.

"How did you know?" the man asked.

"I just knew," I said.

"Liar. I gave myself away somehow."

I didn't know his real name—but I knew who he was. To me, he'd always been Godwin.

"Godwin," I said, putting my hands on my knees and leaning over him, "are those your ships up there? Are you invading my world?"

He shook his head and rubbed at the blood dripping from his face. Already, the pigment of his skin was changing. His head was shifting shape, becoming smaller. It was an amazing process to watch.

"Can I get up?" he asked. "Or are you in a punchy mood today?"

"I am, but you can get up."

I backed up a wary step, and he rose to his feet. "I'm not going to let you do that again," he told me. "That's the third time you've struck me without warning."

"As I recall," I said, "you came at me with a knife the first time."

"Yeah... well okay. Two times, then."

His transformation continued as he spoke. It caused him to slur his words somewhat. Lt. Commander Jones was an older, black guy.

He was large, but not flabby. This new figure, Godwin, was Caucasian and average in build, height—everything. Right then, that struck through to me. Perhaps if Godwin could change his shape, he'd chosen a very average appearance in order to blend in.

"You're still playing the spy?" I asked him. "While some kind of armada is about to violate our local space? Can't you understand why I might be jumpy?"

Godwin—because he was Godwin now—eyed the display hanging over the conference table.

"You're scared," he said. "You hit me out of fear?"

"Yes, I guess I did—but I'd call it caution mixed with outrage at your attempt to fool me."

He tore his eyes from the display and looked at me. "Do you know that you're the only human who's ever spotted me? You've done it three times, too."

"You're a spy," I said. "You can change your appearance, but you can't change who and what you are. I know you now. I'll always know you."

"Disconcerting... but anyway, I'm here to help, not hurt. The ships coming to visit aren't from my worlds."

"Ships? More than one?"

"A handful at first. Many more if you won't comply."

I stared at him. "And what demands will these ships present us with?"

He shrugged. "The usual, I guess. Surrender of sovereignty. Perhaps a regular tribute of wealth. Political and military obedience, at the very least."

As he spoke easily of unthinkable humiliation for my planet, my blood ran cold.

"How did you know they were coming?" I demanded.

"We know what's happening in this system. We watch you constantly. Normally, we don't interfere—but this could be big."

I frowned at him, trying to think. "So you *are* the Nomads? The people the Imperial Kher ran out of the galaxy?"

His eyes flashed in anger then. I'd struck a nerve. That impressed me, as I'd injured this being on several occasions, and he'd never seemed to be overly angered at any of those moments.

"That's what they call us," he said in a low tone. "Your ancestors were our friends, long ago. Trading partners. But they violated every deal we ever made and stabbed our backs when we were weak. We retreated—but we've never been beaten."

I nodded, absorbing this. I'd already begun recording the conversation with my sym. I knew it would be considered valuable intel by our spooks.

"The Imperials aren't my people," I pointed out. "We Rebel Kher—we're different. You've said it yourself. Besides, they'd slaughter us just as soon as they would you."

He nodded slowly. "All right then, I'll give you some information. The ships coming today are Rebel Kher—like you. They were friends when the Imperials came against you, but now, they think the Imperials are in retreat. They think they can dominate you, and they will most likely succeed."

"We have ships," I said. "We're not helpless."

He shook his head. "They have more."

I frowned. "What should we do?"

He shrugged. "What all conquered peoples do. Fall on your knees, pretend obedience, and plot for the day the tide turns. Survive so that your children may—"

I wanted to hit him again. Perhaps he sensed that, because he flinched away and stopped talking.

"Never!" I told him. "We'll not bend a knee when threatened. You should know us well enough to be aware of that by now."

He shrugged, stepping back. "My message has been delivered. I came to try to get you to see reason, but I failed. My work is done here..."

He turned to go, but I reached out and hauled him back. He looked me up and down in irritation.

"Why should I let you leave?" I asked. "Why shouldn't I march you to the stockade right now?"

"I doubt you have a prison on this planet that could hold me," he said with a hint of arrogant pride. "But I'll give you a reason to save us both the inconvenience. Think about it, Blake: I came here to find you. I gave you valuable information. What did you give me in return? Pig-headed boasting and a bloody mouth."

"Yeah..." I admitted, "that's pretty much how it went."

"Well then, can you imagine a situation in the future where I might know something Earth would like to hear about?"

I nodded slowly. "Yes, I guess so. You're offering to come find me and pass me intel? As a back-channel?"

"I'm promising nothing. I'm pointing out facts that should be more than obvious."

"All right," I said, letting go of him. "One more question, and you can be on your way. I won't sound the alarm for ten minutes."

"You don't have that long."

I blinked, and I glanced at the projection of the rift that still spun over the conference table. It hadn't changed, but I had the feeling the lull wouldn't last long.

"Why'd you choose me?" I asked him. "Why me, Godwin?"

"You have more imagination than most of your kind," he said. "And besides, when the invaders come, they're going to ask to talk to you. I thought it would be best to communicate with you because you're about to become directly involved in this interstellar confrontation."

Interstellar confrontation? That sounded suspiciously close to *war* to my ear.

Were we about to go to war? The thought was grim. I'd seen dozens of scorched worlds with exterminated populations turned to ash.

"Go then," I said. "I have to think. You've got one minute to..."

I glanced back, but he was already gone. Had he stepped out into the corridor? Gone invisible?

It hardly mattered. Godwin had left me with a giant pile of shit, and I knew that my recording of his statements wasn't going to solve anything. No one was going to want to surrender on the advice of one ghostly alien.

=3=

Striding out into the hallways, I found the place deserted. People had all moved to their battle stations. The base was on full alert, and no one had been assigned to stand around in the conference room on the top floor.

I felt a little left out. I wanted to find *Hammerhead*, gather my crew and scramble—but that wasn't going to happen. *Hammerhead* was parked in orbit now, at a station in geosynchronous freefall over Europe. I still felt like she was my ship, but very few people seemed to agree with me.

It was frustrating, but all I could do was walk to the nerve center of the base and look around for a way in. Tactical Operations was for approved personnel only, especially when we were on a war-footing, but I figured if I showed up, someone might invite me into the party.

Being able to watch the events unfolding above me via my sym was no comfort. I wasn't able to take *action*. Knowing nothing would have been better. Sometimes, ignorance truly was blissful.

"What are you doing here, Captain Blake?" a twitchy serviceman asked me as I approached the building.

"That depends on General Vega," I told him. "We were in a private meeting when all this broke. Is he inside?"

The man flinched when I mentioned Vega's name. The General had a reputation for chewing on people who got in his way. I could tell the guard was trying to figure out his next move. If he stopped me, he might have to deal with Vega if I was in fact supposed to go inside. On the other hand, if I was just another unauthorized tourist in the command center, things may go even worse.

In the end, he decided to play it safe. He shook his head.

"I can't let you in, sir. We're under lock-down. Sorry."

"No problem," I told him, giving him a nod.

Turning away, I stepped out to the concrete columns along the narrow, curving drive out front and leaned against one of them.

"Uh... sir?" the guard called out. "Don't you have somewhere else to be?"

"Not right now," I admitted. "I don't have an official post in an emergency on this base. My post is up there, aboard *Hammerhead*... but they aren't letting me fly her today, either."

The guard fell silent for a moment, but I could almost hear him fidgeting.

"What's going on, sir?" he blurted at last. "What's really happening? Are there alien ships up there? Above the clouds?"

I closed my eyes and sent my perception up through an army of computers and satellites. At last, I found one that had optics focused on the rift.

A ship had appeared since the last time I'd looked. As I watched, another ghosted into view behind it.

They were big vessels—heavy cruisers by the look of it—but they were moving in cautiously. Perhaps they knew we had a few ships of our own.

"They've shown themselves," I told the guard, turning to look at him. "I can see them with my sym. Two ships have just arrived. More might be coming."

He looked like he might shit himself, but I didn't think this was the time to comfort him or laugh at him. This was go-time.

The guy took in two panicked breaths, glancing upward then flicking his eyes back down to me.

"Go in, Captain Blake," he said at last. "You know these aliens better than anyone on Earth. *Do* something. Stop them, blow them up—anything!"

I gave him a reassuring smile and nodded as I walked past. He had an inflated view of my capabilities, but I wasn't going to tell him that.

"I'll do what I can," I said.

Inside, the command center was a genuine charley-foxtrot. Everyone was tense, nearly panicked, but they couldn't really do anything other than shout at each other demanding more information.

The base commanders at Cheyenne didn't have any direct authority over our collection of phase-ships, that team was inside the mountain itself, but we were in the loop as far as current events went.

Glimmering imagery hung over our heads, displaying the scene I'd already formulated in my mind with the help of my sym, but their version was much higher resolution. There were numbers—ranges, velocities, course vectors—superimposed on everything.

Three of our phase-ships were already within reach, and six more were inbound. Within minutes, the intruders would be surrounded.

But it might not matter. The alien ships outclassed us. If they brought in more—even just a second full squadron—we'd be hopelessly outmatched.

None of this seemed to impinge on the circle of staffers surrounding the projected scene. They were working up fresh numbers, reporting anomalies and waiting to see if they would be called upon to act.

"Not much we can do about it if they start shooting," I offered, stepping up to the projection table and standing there nonchalantly.

Several officers glanced my way.

"Captain Blake?" Gwen said. She'd been assigned here months ago, as she hadn't been holding out for space duty. Right now, that fact made me envy her. "When were you called in?" she asked.

"A couple of years ago," I said. "By the Rebel Kher."

She released a little puff of air. "You think that's who they are? How can we be sure?"

"Those aren't Imperial ships," I pointed out. "They're some kind of independent. Either they're Rebel Kher from another nearby world—or we're really in trouble."

"What will they do, sir?" another staffer asked me.

"How should I know, Lieutenant? I'm a spacer, not a mind-reader."

They stopped asking questions then, and I was glad they'd skipped over asking me if I belonged here. They'd all assumed someone had brought me in—and that was true, but I didn't think any of them would respect Godwin's authority to give orders.

Gwen pointed at the projection then, making a hissing sound of worry between her teeth. A third ship had appeared. The third ship took its place in a line with the other two. Together, they moved toward Earth at a stately pace.

I felt a tickling droplet of sweat under my arms. How many more ships were coming to this party? Already, they had more firepower than all twenty of our phase-ships combined. All we had was the surprise factor, as our ships could maintain stealth until they engaged. But for all we knew, these aliens could see us anyway. There was no way to tell from their actions so far.

"Are they pinging at us?" I asked.

"Negative," Gwen said. "It's all quiet up there. Maybe they have no idea we have ships of our own."

"Why would they send three heavy cruisers, then?" I asked. "Why not just one ship loaded with bombs?"

Several sets of alarmed eyes fixated on me.

"You think they're going to do that, Captain?" the watch officer asked.

"I'd have to know what world they came from to divine their intentions."

The officer looked me over. "I'm not sure you're cleared for this—but I don't know if that matters anymore, either. Here's what we've got so far: They're Kwok ships, manned by Grefs—at least, that's who they usually use. I understand this particular group of primates refuse to serve as anything other than officers."

"Kwok ships..." I said, thinking hard. "That's Admiral Fex's homeworld..."

All of a sudden, I got a sick feeling. Before my ship had been mustered out of the Rebel Kher navy, one of the last things I'd done involved Admiral Fex. Secretary Shug had placed him aboard a ship full of Grefs... That decision had been made based on my accusations against Fex.

"Hmm..." I said, watching the ships as they approached. "If I were you guys, I'd assume these vessels are hostile."

"You do know something, then?"

"Just Admiral Fex, his people the Kwok, and the Grefs themselves... well, they don't like humans too much. The last time we were in contact with them—it went badly."

Memories flooded over me. We'd shot Grefs with disrupters until the smell of their burnt hair lingered for days.

17

The watch officer stared at me for a moment, then he contacted General Vega.

That made me wince, as he mentioned my name during his report.

"General, it's the considered opinion of this ops team, including the expert you sent us, that they're hostile. What's that, sir? What expert...? Why... I'm talking about Captain Blake, sir."

My smile lingered, but it was pasted on by now. The watch officer listening closely, then turned slowly to frown at me.

"General Vega would like a word, Captain."

"I bet he would," Gwen commented.

I shot her a glance and tapped into the conversation via my sym.

General Vega seemed pissed off about something.

"Blake? What are you doing away from your post? A war is about to start—"

"I don't have a post on this base, sir," I said, "but I'm technically still *Hammerhead*'s captain. If you wish, I'll scramble to Geneva and—"

"Your post is a faculty office!" the General boomed in my ear. "Now, get out of my control room and toss me back to Commander Tenet."

"Immediately, sir. I'm sure you have Fex and his ships under control."

"Fex?"

"Admiral Fex, sir. The alien commanding this squadron of cruisers."

"How do you know it's Fex?"

Glibly, I repeated back the information the watch officer had provided. The conclusion seemed obvious to me, but I had to explain a few details to the General.

"And now sir, as I'm sure you have this matter in hand, I'll be—"

"Shut up," he said. "Stand your post. You're not to leave that tactical table until I relieve you personally."

"As you say, General."

After he closed the channel, I didn't bother to glance at the staring audience around me. They'd shifted in their opinion of me, I could tell. They'd gone from assuming I was an expert liaison to wondering what the hell was going on.

It was a situation I was familiar with.

General Vega arrived in a shockingly short amount of time. He barged through security and demanded I follow him. He had two MPs at his back, so I didn't argue.

Gwen gave me an alarmed, private look. I shrugged in return. Perhaps it would be the firing squad this time—but I didn't think so.

General Vega loaded me into a Humvee, and we roared away toward the mountain. He didn't bother to explain anything, and I didn't ask.

Clearly, I was going down to the real command center. To the ops table that really mattered.

=4=

We rushed down into the cool tunnels. The wind and roar of the engine thrumming powerfully in my ears. The MP sergeant at the wheel was driving at triple the government posted speed limit, but I wasn't about to be the first to whine about it.

Things had changed at the old NORAD base since it had been the active center of the US defensive systems. If anything, it'd become more impressive and secretive.

The mission of the installation was essentially the same, but it had been expanded. Space Command governed all the skies over Earth these days, and the threats they dealt with here were much greater in scope than the Soviet Union had ever been.

The tunnels were larger, the vaults sculpted and reinforced. The computers had been modernized intensively, as had the general tech level of the place. Once we reached the command center, I knew there were many new levels unseen under our feet. They seemed to be drilling deeper all the time.

With miles of rock surrounding the ops center, the place was cool, but it still needed air conditioning due to the impressive amount of equipment and the bodies crammed into the limited space.

After some brief introductions, I was allowed to stand at the central ops table. Even though I was surrounded by brass, I felt right at home. After all, I knew the approaching enemy aliens better than almost anyone on Earth. I belonged here.

"Captain Blake," General Vega said, waving his hand in my direction. "I'm sure everyone here knows you—and your rep."

"Thank you, General," I said firmly, taking his comments in the best possible light.

"We certainly do know him," Dr. Abrams said, stepping out of the shadows to the table's edge. He planted two long-fingered hands on the rim and leaned forward. His eyebrows bristled in disapproval. "I was assured he was not to be present at this meeting."

"We've got no time for petty jealousies, Doctor," Vega said.

Abrams made a sound that reminded me of a choking cat—but he shut up.

"All right then," Vega said. "Blake believes these alien vessels are loaded with Grefs. What do we know about these aliens?"

"Preposterous!" Dr. Abrams said. "Grefs aren't capable of launching such sleek vessels. All their ships are like secondhand junkyard garbage!"

"I never said the Grefs built the ships," I pointed out. "I said they manned them—as mercenary crewmen. It's my belief that the Kwok built the ships."

Abrams narrowed his eyes at me.

I knew him well, and I figured he'd been the chief advisor on aliens until I showed up. He was knowledgeable—but not as experienced as I was.

But such facts wouldn't matter to Abrams. There could be only one supreme know-it-all when he was involved, and that title had to belong to Abrams himself. Anyone else who offered a different opinion was either a fool—or something worse, like a saboteur.

"Why have you inserted yourself into events once again, Blake?" Abrams demanded. "The last time it was a disaster."

This startled me. To my mind, I'd been a hero the last time the Imperials had faced off with the Rebel Kher.

Before I could answer, Abrams turned smoothly toward General Vega. "I beg you to reconsider. This man set our technological efforts back years due to negligence."

Now, finally, I knew what his problem was. He'd never been happy with me after I'd jettisoned his prototype Hunter-attraction device. He'd developed it to attract and repel Hunters at will. Since then, I knew, he'd never quite managed to build another one that satisfied him.

Vega threw up his hands. "Shut up. Both of you."

I wanted to protest, as I hadn't been speaking, but I figured that wouldn't buy me any points. I stood with my arms crossed, looking at Vega.

"The rest of you talk to me," Vega continued. "Does it add up? Are these ships built by some kind of smarter monkeys—what are they called?"

"The Kwok," Abrams prompted. "And technically, General, they're *not* monkeys. They're primates, to be sure, but I'd classify them—"

"I don't care," Vega said, shutting him down. "Has anyone gotten them to answer our hails? Can you transmit in their native language?"

"They're hearing us, General," one of the com people assured him. "But they aren't answering."

"They've made no demands? Nothing?"

"No sir."

General Vega massaged his chin and eyed the layout on the projected map. The enemy ships looked relatively small in comparison to Earth, but I knew they'd be gigantic lined up beside regular shipping. Any one of them outweighed a fully loaded supertanker.

"Blake..." Vega said. "Listen to me closely. This is very important. In your opinion, do these ships represent a clear and present danger to the security of Earth?"

"I feel I can safely say that much, General."

He nodded slowly. "I agree. Why aren't they talking to us? Why are they sliding forward slowly, without saying a word?"

I shrugged. "I can only conjecture on that point, General—"

"That's right!" Abrams blurted out. "Pure theory. We *must* get some hard data before we take action, General."

Vega put up a hand. "I know that, Doctor. Blake, continue. Why are they coming in quietly like this?"

I shrugged. "Isn't that how predators behave? Maybe they want to get in close, sneaking up like a cat in the tall grass. Tigers don't give a battle cry when they attack you. They simply work their way into range and pounce from behind without warning."

"Tigers?" Abrams questioned. "Ah yes, you're an expert on such beasts, aren't you?"

I shot him a glare. He was making a rude comment about my girlfriend, Mia.

Vega ignored Abrams and nodded at me slowly. "You're right. We have no choice. Order the phase-ships to strike at their engines first. I'll inform the Joint Chiefs personally."

This statement alarmed me. The staffers seemed to have been waiting for his command, and they huddled and began buzzing.

Stepping around the table I closed with Vega before he could leave the room.

"Sir—? General? Isn't that a hasty decision?"

"You really think so, Blake?" he asked. "You said it yourself. These beings are stalking us. They're not here to make friends. Friends don't come uninvited with three warships and move directly into attack range over our cities."

"We have to talk to them," I insisted.

"They aren't interested in talking, Blake. They've made that abundantly clear."

"Are you really the one calling the shots on all this?" I asked. "What about the Joint Chiefs? The politicians?"

"You can't run a planet-wide war in space from a parliament chamber. I've been given the authority I need to defend our world."

I stared at him, letting that soak in. "So... you're in command of our entire fleet?"

"In peacetime, I run this base. It was decided privately that in dire times of war, my role would change suitably."

"Why would your position be a secret?"

"There are alien spies here, Blake. Surely you know that."

Thinking of Godwin, I nodded.

"We're not supposed to have a large space fleet, remember? Our phase-ships have been built in secret, against Rebel Kher edicts."

"So..." I said, catching on, "you're in charge of a harmless base most of the time—until war breaks out? Surprising the enemy, just like our phase-ships?"

"That's right, and God help us all, it looks like the worst is about to happen."

"At least try to warn them off first, General," I insisted. "Tell them they have to halt their advance or you'll order their destruction."

He looked at me thoughtfully, then shook his head. "It's a good idea, but it's impractical. Those ships might destroy a dozen of our cities while we stand around with our thumbs in our butts. Which city are you willing to risk to talk to them?"

23

It was a tough question, and it made me doubt myself. Vega was facing a grim level of responsibility. It was his job to defend Earth. In such a situation, a commander couldn't take chances.

"Look," he said watching my face, "I appreciate your input—even if it doesn't look like we're going to need a liaison. But I didn't choose today to show up at their planet and come parading toward their civilians. They've invaded our space."

"Just try," I insisted. "Warn them off first."

"Our ships are tiny stealth vessels, Blake. The whole point of a phase-ship is to sneak up and strike without warning. Threats will only give away our single ace card. You should know that."

"I do, sir," I said, "but part of the power of any stealth tech is the uncertainty the enemy feels when facing it. If you talk big, like you can wipe them out with a single order, they might back down. Fex and his kind aren't the brave types. That's why they're stalking us, feeling their way. They want to do this without a loss."

"Hmm..." he said thoughtfully. "You've changed my thinking somewhat."

Feeling relieved, I followed him back to the ops table. The moment passed quickly as I listened to his new orders.

"The first ship to enter," he said. "Take it out. Everything we have must hit it at once—forget about just crippling it. Tell our captains to blow her out of the sky then phase-out again."

The staffers looked as shocked as I did.

"But sir," dared one of them, "we're sure to lose some of our vessels that way. We can't knock out a cruiser in one volley—we'll have to stand and do battle at close range. It won't be a hit-and-run, it will be a fight."

"I know," Vega said. "And I'm hoping that will scare them."

24

=5=

There was no talking General Vega out of starting a war this time. Somehow, I couldn't help but feel responsible. If our ships were wiped out up there... I would bear some of the guilt for that.

Grimly, the command group watched the battle unfold. The alien ships continued to close in. They seemed to be in no hurry, and they maintained a tight formation. The only good news was that there were only three of them. One of my fears had been that another dozen cruisers would appear and join this spearhead.

Our phase ships gathered strength until there were eleven of them in range. They circled the enemy like ghosts. Not even we knew exactly where they were. Their displayed positions were based on conjecture, rather than hard data. We knew where they'd been *ordered* to move—but we could only hope they'd reached their designated positions.

The lead ship started off the ambush. Since none of the phase-ships knew where their sister ships were any more than we did, the leader moved into position and struck first. That was designed to be a go-signal to the rest.

"That captain has balls of brass," Vega muttered. "Whether he lives or not, I want him up for a commendation."

"Noted, General."

I stared at the displays, yearning to be out there with them. I felt I belonged on the line. During the final seconds before the attack began, I noticed that Vega was watching me.

"You wish you were out there, Blake?" he asked.

"Yes."

He nodded, and he thumped me on the back. "I take back all shit I spouted about you when you weren't around. Whatever else you are, you're a dedicated defender of Earth."

"Uh... thanks, General."

"There it is!" a staffer shouted, pointing to a spark of fire on the projection. "Our lead ship has phased-in—they're firing, General."

A gout of energy, highlighted into visibility by our computer systems, streaked out and connected the tiny phase-ship with the stern of its victim. The shields flashed and buckled, but they didn't go down.

"A hard kick in the ass!" Vega shouted, thumping his closed fist on the table. The image shimmered in reaction, but he didn't seem to notice or care.

"No penetration, General—"

"There! Another one!"

A second phase-ship appeared, even as the big cruiser began to rotate to face her first attacker. The other two cruisers reacted a moment later, coming about and focusing their guns on the initial assailant.

The second ship was quickly joined by a third. Together, they struck the cruiser's flank. The shields went down this time. Overloaded by beams from different angles, and unable to predict the direction of the next attack quickly enough, the cruiser took damage.

"A hit!" Vega laughed. "Look, she's venting! Is that fuel?"

"Radioactive gas, by the spectrometer."

I kept expecting the lead phase-ship to fade away again and run—but of course, that wasn't their orders. They stayed in sight, evading, but not retreating.

The ship fired again, and this time the nose of the cruiser was scarred by hot energies.

"Looks like one of the enemy's forward batteries was knocked out."

That's when things shifted, as I knew they must. The cruiser finally had a lock on her tormentor, and she lashed out. Three converging beams struck the tiny phase-ship and obliterated her.

A gasp of dismay swept through the group. All the bravado drained out of us. No one gasped or cried out in anguish—but we were feeling it.

"Two more of our ships—no, three of them—have engaged the cruiser now."

"Good..." Vega said in a quiet tone.

We watched tensely as the three ships lit up the cruiser's stern again. The attack was well-coordinated. The bulk of our forces had been placed in front of the cruiser, while the lead ship attacked the stern. When the big ship wheeled to blast the leader, that naturally placed the others behind her. They struck together and delivered a fierce shock to the target.

She was wounded badly, but not out.

"Come on," Vega said, "come on... Die, damn you!"

He'd ordered our ships to stay in the fight until the cruiser was destroyed. If she hung on long enough...

"The other two cruisers have locked on, General. Do we tell them to withdraw?"

"No!" he shouted. "No... Stick to the plan."

Right then, I had respect for him. He was in charge, he was living it, and he was going to suffer right along with our best crews as they died executing his orders. But still, he wasn't backing down.

The two cruisers, the enemy's wingmen, blasted two more of our phase-ships out of existence. But then, all of our ships revealed themselves. It occurred to me that they weren't perfectly coordinated. That if they had been, ten would have struck the moment the cruiser had wheeled to face the lead ship—destroying it.

But it didn't matter. The last eight had taken the field, and they pounded the cruiser to fragments and slipped away, phasing out of sight again.

The remaining two cruisers spun this way and that, laying down patterns of fire on predictive paths to catch more of our smaller ships. We watched tensely for another ten minutes—but there were no more hits.

"They've escaped, General."

Vega nodded, staring blankly at the field of battle. Radiation, swirling pools of gas and twirling bits of metal were still expanding from the epicenter. Hours from now, debris would shower down into Earth's atmosphere, burning like falling stars.

"Seventeen ships left," he said, turning to me. "Plus your outdated wagon. Earth might need to put *Hammerhead* back into action again."

"Ready to serve, General."

He nodded vaguely. "All right," he said. "Contact the invading fleet again. Make a statement in their language—the language of these Kwok people. Tell them they've been warned. That if they don't turn away, they'll all be destroyed in our next attack."

The translation team worked on it, and transmitted it. We waited in the dim light, watching the glowing aftermath of battle in space as it dissipated like smoke from a dying fire.

"Do you think they got our message, Blake?" Vega asked me.

"I don't see how Admiral Fex could have missed it."

There was a wait that seemed overly long. Still, the enemy made no move to acknowledge our message.

But then, finally, a reply came back.

"This is Admiral Fex. Your unprovoked attack upon the Rebel Kher has placed you in the category of a rogue planet. You are now considered outlaws, outside the horde, outside the governance of the Central Council. Not even Secretary Shug can save you now."

A chill ran through me. Could he be right? Had we made a horrible error?

I began to think through Fex's behavior. Had he come in stalking us, looking as menacing as possible, in order to provoke just such a rash action from us?

Dr. Abrams, who'd had the good sense to stay quiet while the battle unfolded, took this moment step forward again.

"That's what you get, General, when you listen to Blake. He's a warmonger. A danger to all. Every time I saw him interact with the Rebel Kher, the result was misunderstanding and bloodshed."

There was some truth to Abrams' words, which made them hurt all the more.

But General Vega shook his head. "I made the call," he said. "The responsibility is mine, right or wrong."

Dr. Abrams had an insufferable smirk on his face.

"And you," Vega barked at him. "You'd better hope you're wrong and Blake is right. Because your ass is on the line now, too. We're all in this together—live or die."

This seemed to strike through Abrams' smugness. His expression faltered, and he frowned at the tactical screens.

"Well," he said. "At least their ships aren't advancing any closer to Earth."

We snapped back to the projection, and we took note of the velocity measurements.

"He's right," I said. "They're braking. They're practically dead in space."

Vega thumped me again between the shoulder blades. "Maybe you didn't get us all killed Blake—not yet."

I grinned at him. "That's the best damned news I've heard all day."

=6=

"I'm going to get demoted for this," Vega said, "but I no longer care about that. I'm going to answer these hairy bastards."

We watched him with wide eyes. The fledgling ops group at Space Command had been given tactical control of any battle that arose on short notice—but now, we were stepping into diplomatic territory.

Already, a horde of brass was on the way to our lonely mountain stronghold. I was sure at least two dozen admirals, generals and chiefs-of-staff were kicking themselves about not being here when all hell broke loose. Soon, they would be. At that point, Vega would lose his authority, and the crowd would take over.

"This is still very much a live-fire situation," Vega announced. "The enemy has not retreated. They are still within range of Earth. They could change their minds and move back in—or they could simply launch missiles at our cities from where they stand now. Do we have any effective defense against such a straightforward attack?"

The staffers shook their heads. Their faces were ashen. We'd spent so much time building our phase-ships and organizing ourselves, Earth had kind of forgotten to cover the basics.

"I guess no one really thought we'd be faced with an outright invasion, General," I said.

"Idiocy," Vega said. "The last two times, Kher ships came here to pick up crewmen. The Imperials never came here at all. So, we built a small navy capable of defense in space. But we didn't build

30

fortresses on the Moon, or orbital platforms bristling with missiles. Just the ships."

"What are your orders, General?" one of the staffers asked. She looked frightened, but she was also determined.

"Let's open a dialog. Let's find out why they're here."

She transmitted the request to the two remaining cruisers, and we waited. At last, a transmission came back.

"It's a live feed," she said. "Shall I—"

"Yes, dammit. Put him on screen."

The imagery of space and ships faded. Instead an alien face, just the head and shoulders, looked back at us.

It was none other than Admiral Fex. I'd know him anywhere. He was a tall, lanky, ape-like being. His appearance belied his intelligence and natural cunning.

"Admiral Fex," Vega said. "I'm sorry we had to meet under such circumstances."

"As am I," Fex said sternly through his translation device. "What's the purpose of your call?"

"Well, I'd think that would be obvious. We've warned you off, and you ignored us. We were forced to attack to defend ourselves, and we warned you again. I'm at a loss to understand why you're still lingering in our star system."

Fex looked surprised. "*Your* star system? You've made an error—many of them. You were once Rebel Kher who provided excellent crews to aid the war effort against the Imperials. Perhaps that fact went to your head."

"I don't know what you're talking about, Fex," Vega snapped. "I want you out of our space, pronto."

"I'm afraid the situation has changed. I've applied to become the protector of your planet and this entire star system. It's clear you can't fend for yourselves against predatory neighbors. Secretary Shug awarded me the contract."

"What contract?" Vega demanded, confused.

"Why, the same basic contract all undefended planets operate under. We, the Kwok, will provide local defense. There will be no raids from your neighbors any longer."

"We've never been raided by our neighbors," Vega complained. "Unless you count your ships coming and abducting crewmen to fight the Imperials."

"I most certainly would not," Fex said stiffly. "Service in the fleet was offered as an honor to your backwater planet. It's offensive you would suggest otherwise."

Vega erased the conversation with his hands. "All right, whatever. The situation is as it now stands. We are not helpless. We are not in need of your protection. We will not give any portion of our sovereignty away to the likes of you."

"This is pointless," Fex said. "Do you have anyone else available that I can talk to? Anyone in authority?"

"I'm in charge here," Vega stated flatly.

"No, I mean someone with standing among the Rebel Kher— wait, I see a familiar face. Aren't you the notorious outlaw known as Blake?"

I stepped forward into the camera pickup. "I'm Leo Blake."

"Excellent!" Fex said. "At last, someone I can talk to. You have served in the Rebel Fleet. You are worth a thousand—no, a *million* buffoons like this general of yours. Please explain that to him, Blake."

"Um..." I said, looking at General Vega. He glowered back unhappily.

One of the things about dealing with the Rebel Kher that was never well understood by Earth governments is that the Kher considered all local military establishments to be illegitimate. Only service against the Imperials in war brought status. Every general, admiral, king or president on Earth was no more important than the lowest recruit in the Rebel Fleet to them—possibly less so.

"General Vega," I said. "He's not insulting you—well, not intentionally. The Kher only recognize their own ranks. They only recognize military people who've worked their way up in the Kher command structure."

"Let me ask you something, Fex," Vega said angrily. "Did your cruiser's crew die in space or not? We've got an effective military force, and we know how to use it. We're a power. I insist you deal with us as equals."

Fex laughed at that. "You destroyed a single ship. As we observed, that effort required the loss of nearly a third of your absurd navy. Let's not have any repeats of such tragedy. Accept your annexation and let us all be done with this nonsense."

"Annexation?!" Vega boomed. "Are you mad? We've just defeated *you* in battle, Fex."

"If you had a hundred more ships, you would have destroyed all three of mine. We have counted your fleet, and we find it unimpressive. Even though you're clearly a misinformed, primitive planet, we're still willing to offer you—"

"I'm done talking to this crazy alien," Vega said, and his staff moved to cut the channel.

"Wait!" Fex said. "Let Blake talk. Him, I respect."

Vega gave me a reluctant nod.

"Admiral Fex," I said, "let's not shed any more blood. We destroyed a single ship so you would take us seriously. We can, and we will, destroy you all. Not all our phase-ships have revealed themselves. You are surrounded, sir."

Fex was quiet for just a moment. I thought he was taken by surprise.

"Threats..." he said at last in a quiet voice. "Threats and invective. I'd expected better from a loyal officer of the Rebel Fleet."

"I'm loyal to Earth first, Admiral," I told him firmly. "Especially now, since the war with the Imperials is over."

Fex threw up his hairy hands in a gesture I found surprisingly human.

"I've done my best!" he declared. "I must withdraw. We've offered you our help, and we've been refused most rudely. You Earthers are like feral beasts. You bite the hand of your only friend. I would not be surprised if Shug orders that you all be put down."

"We'll be ready for you," Vega shouted over my shoulder, "if you come back to try."

"The alien ships are retreating, General," one of the staffers said quietly.

We glanced at the projections, and we saw it was true. Fex was pulling out. He was moving slowly, but determinedly, back toward the breach where he'd arrived in our system.

Vega nodded to me, indicating I should keep talking to Fex.

"Admiral," I said, "it would be best for both our peoples that this misunderstanding be left out of the history books. We don't want war, but we can't allow foreign warships to orbit Earth without so much as an invitation. The next time you come, please arrive at least ten light-hours from Earth. Contact us politely, and we'll arrange for permission for a single vessel to—"

"Preposterous!" Fex interrupted. "You don't know your place, Blake. You never did. It shall be a shame to burn you and your world away to ash, if it comes down to that. But you *will* be protected! That I can assure you!"

Then, a new rift spun open beyond the retreating cruisers. It twisted and shone with wispy colors. Silver, pink and blood-red disturbances rotated just ahead of the retreating ships.

"General," the ops officer running the fleet assets said in a low voice. "We have several ships in position. We might be able to stop one—possibly both of them—from retreating."

"No..." Vega said, closing the channel to Fex's ship. "Let that pompous ass withdraw. We smacked him down hard enough. Besides, I don't want to lose any more ships today."

There was a general sigh of relief that swept the room. We watched as the two remaining cruisers entered the rift and winked out. They were gone, and the crisis was over.

Unfortunately, the recriminations had yet to begin.

=7=

The rift spun on the screen for several minutes, and I watched it closely. Wherever Fex's escape route had taken him, I could tell he wasn't going back to Antares. The color of the star on the other side was all wrong. Rather than being a huge, swollen red ball of fire the star was quiet, blue-white, and of normal dimensions. Antares was a supergiant in its death throes, enjoying its last few million years of life, destined to explode into a supernova someday soon. The star we glimpsed through the rift was relatively young and stable.

"Aren't we sending a ship after them, General?" I prompted, watching the assembled group.

They seemed startled by the idea.

"Ah, right," Dr. Abrams said before Vega could answer. "You did that, didn't you, Blake? Risking *Hammerhead*, Earth's only vessel, on the off-chance you'd learn more about the enemy. An insane gamble then and now."

"It was our mission to learn all we could," I said calmly.

General Vega watched the interplay between Abrams and I, but at last he shook his head. "I can't do it. I'd like to see where they went, but what would we do if we found out?"

"Perhaps the rift leads to their homeworld," I suggested. "It might be good to know where retaliation could be delivered."

"The information wouldn't offer any immediate advantage," Vega argued, "as we've got no starships of our own capable of opening a rift."

35

Dr. Abrams rumbled something in his throat at that point. I wasn't sure if he was coughing up a hairball or commenting. In any case, he said nothing intelligible. He simply looked pleased that Vega had sided with him this time.

"We've only got seventeen ships left—plus *Hammerhead*," Vega explained to me. "That's it, the sum total of our defensive forces in space. I can't risk six percent of our minuscule navy on a scouting mission right now."

I shook my head and spread my hands. "All right, sir. It's your call."

The staff remained tense and on station until the rift closed behind the retreating starships. Earth's skies once again belonged to us.

It was a vast relief, but my day wasn't over with yet. Brass soon began to swoop in from various headquarters locations around the country and the world. There seemed to be more of them every hour.

As we were debriefed and questioned on every decision and detail of our actions, I could tell the brass wasn't happy to have been left out of the command decisions. They'd collectively assumed Earth's fledgling Space Command was a gambit for the future. Few of them had wanted to commit and lay their reputations on the line by taking charge of Space Command's operational status—therefore, they'd left the dirty work to Vega.

Not everyone was satisfied with our choices, but they couldn't argue with the final outcome. Their consensus was we'd taken desperate gambles and won the day.

When the briefings mercifully paused, the head of Earth's Joint Chiefs asked Vega and I to attend him in a private meeting at around ten pm.

The man was a British Admiral named Clemens. He was old for an active admiral, pushing seventy if I had to guess. He had two matching tufts of white hair partly covering each ear. They weren't really lamb chops, mind you, but the thought was there.

"Gentlemen," Clemens began, "I'm past my prime when it comes to running battles—especially ones that occur in space."

Neither Vega nor I moved a muscle. There was nothing to be gained by agreeing or arguing with Clemens' statement—the truth of it was self-evident.

"But I *am*," he continued, "still a good judge of character. While you were being poked and prodded all afternoon by my colleagues like specimens on a plate, I stood back and attempted to apply that judgment. Do you want to know what my conclusions were?"

"We'd love to hear them, Admiral," Vega said.

Clemens chuckled and shook his head. "You even lie with enthusiasm, Vega. But in any case, what I saw was real competence. I viewed some of the live vid recordings of the interaction at the ops table—and I liked what I saw. You two make a good team. Most of the rest of the staffers looked like someone had run over their cocks."

"Uh... crudely put, sir," Vega said. "But accurate, I guess. In their defense, my team is made up of good people. They've just never had to run a battle in space before."

"Right... but *you* have done so, Captain Blake? Am I right?"

"On several occasions, Admiral."

"Exactly. That competence shone through all the bollocks when the battle fell into your lap. I *need* that competence, Blake. I need your shine."

I felt a sinking feeling in my gut. I'd been entertaining thoughts of wangling a command at last out of this event—but those hopes were fading fast.

"Thank you, sir," I mumbled.

"Here's how this is going to go," Clemens said. "I'm going to get push-back, but I'm also going to get my way in the end. You're going to be reaffirmed as Space Command's operational leader, Vega. You'll be pushed up in rank a notch, effectively making you the highest ranking officer in this new service of ours."

Vega's mouth sagged for a second, but he snapped it shut again. "I've been Air Force my entire career, sir."

"I know that, but as I said, we need you. When the U. S. Marines broke off from your Navy—or the Air Force from your Army—where do you think the first officers came from?"

"I'm well aware of the historic precedents, Admiral," Vega said. "It's just that... I guess it's a shock."

"Well, get over it. Immediately. Earth was nearly fried today. That's my impression, anyway."

We didn't argue with him. He could well be right. It was my opinion that Fex had come to dominate Earth, rather than hurt us, but the threat had been real enough either way.

"There will be push-back," the Admiral repeated, "but that's how it's going to be. And you, Blake. I heard you were taking a post here as an instructor. Is that true?"

"Uh... that idea has been proposed, Admiral."

"What a crime. You're no desk-jockey. You're a line officer in a new service. You worked well with Vega at every step. Until I can get you a worthy command of your own, I want you at his side. Guide him the way you did today. Rely on each other, gentlemen. You make a good team under fire."

Vega and I exchanged surprised glances. We hadn't expected these changes to our relationship.

Vega nodded his head slowly. "All right," he said. "I can live with that. Blake showed real maturity today. He was a serious helper. But my idea was to pass his knowledge on to others, Admiral, rather than getting Blake killed in space. We lost three ships today—in a single action."

"I'm well aware of our losses," Clemens said. "But right now Earth needs her best at the helm. What would you have done if Blake had been in a classroom instead of at your side today?"

General Vega's face went blank for a moment. "Probably about the same thing..." he answered at last.

"Rubbish!" Clemens boomed. "Don't try to feed me nonsense, Admiral. You're not good enough to get away with it."

After that announcement, he stood up. We shook hands all around and stayed standing until he was gone.

Vega looked at me in irritation when the door had closed. "Looks like we both got our cards punched today, Blake. Welcome to my staff."

"Thank you, *Admiral*," I said, emphasizing his new rank.

He winced, but then he nodded and walked out. I followed and headed home to Mia. I wanted a drink and bed. A few people tried to accost me, but I dodged them smoothly.

The key to giving staffers the slip was to keep walking. They could follow, and they could chatter—but under no circumstances would I pause and let them dominate my time. Once you stopped moving, a talented bureaucrat could keep you in his sights for ten minutes or more. With a pasted-on smile and bland comments, I managed to get untangled and out the door.

To my good fortune, Mia was still awake and in a fine mood.

"You're a hero," she told me. "Everyone says so."

"Someone should tell Dr. Abrams."

She made a rumbling sound of displeasure. "I heard one of his staffers call him a name recently. They said he was a donkey-dick. Is that accurate?"

I laughed, and she laughed, and we had a drink together.

It had been a long, hard day, but I still had enough energy left over for my girlfriend. We made love and slept bare without so much as a sheet on top of us.

=8=

I awoke shivering. It was close to dawn, and the temperature in the room had plummeted. That was a problem when living in the mountains: the temperature swings could be brutal.

Throwing a sheet over Mia, I got up and padded to the bathroom. On the way, I paused in the kitchenette.

It was base housing, and the base was cramped. An officer's quarters were usually better than this, but here in the Rockies we had to stack up in what amounted to one-bedroom apartments. At least I wasn't commuting every day from Colorado Springs.

I closed the fridge with a slice of sausage in my mouth and a beer in my hand—and that's when I saw him.

"Godwin?" I demanded. The slice of sausage hit the tile floor with an audible slap.

He raised his hands in the universal sign of surrender. His hands were empty—but that didn't mean much with a being like him.

Reacting viscerally, I slammed the door of my fridge into his chest. He grunted and staggered back.

"Shhh..." he said. "You'll wake up Mia."

"I'm going to kill you this time."

"Is that the way you thank an ally?" he demanded. "I put it all on the line to come talk to you, to warn you about Fex. Where's the gratitude?"

Wearing nothing but boxers, I dragged him out of my apartment and into the hallway. I felt better outside my door.

"You can't go sneaking around like this," I told him. "Humans are territorial. One day, I'll kill you—maybe by accident."

He rubbed at his ribs where I'd slammed him with the fridge door.

"You certainly are. Your actions today were—unexpected."

"Are you here to state your disapproval?" I asked him.

"Would it matter?"

"Not to me."

"Well," he said, "the situation has shifted. I counselled you earlier to surrender to Fex. That would have been the prudent course. But that easy exit has closed. You'll have to take a much more difficult path now."

I frowned at him. "How did you get in here, anyway?"

Godwin shrugged. "Humans built their first primitive transmat only recently," he said. "Do you really think a race that's had such technology for centuries couldn't have improved upon it?"

"So... you used some kind of personal transmat?"

"No..." he said. "It's more complex than that. But please, let's not get lost in the weeds, as you like to say. Let's stick to the reason I'm here."

I crossed my arms and leaned against the wall. I was still within easy striking distance if he tried anything, but he looked relieved anyway.

"Reason prevails," he said, nodding. "It's never your first choice, but you can be persuaded. In any case, I'm here to give you new instructions."

Snorting, I waved for him to continue.

"When Fex returns with a full fleet, you *must* surrender," he said. "There won't be any second chances at that point. His hand will be forced if you resist."

I listened to him with growing concern. "He's coming back?"

"Of course. His mission has not yet been completed."

"His mission being the subjugation of Earth?"

"As I stated last time we spoke, that is his goal."

My mind raced. For some reason, I'd thought this crisis had been averted—or at least that we'd been given a breather.

"How long until he comes back?" I asked him.

"You would call it... a month? Maybe less."

"We can't build a fleet big enough to stop him in a month."

Godwin spread his hands and smiled thinly. "No, you can't. That's why I'm here. That's why you must follow my suggestions."

"What do you care?" I asked him. "Why do the Nomads want Earth to survive?"

"Because your breed is unlike the other Rebel Kher. There's something different about you... We've been studying your DNA for several years now, but we've yet to reach a firm conclusion. But whatever our researchers discover, the real point is you've managed to turn back the Imperial Kher twice now."

"Ah," I said, catching on. "We beat the Imperials, so you want us to be around the next time they come?"

He laughed quietly at me. "You did not *defeat* the Imperials. You caused them to retreat and reconsider. That is an amazing feat, but it isn't victory. Winning the conflict you're caught up in will take many generations—if it's possible at all."

"Okay, whatever. You were impressed by Earth, so you're helping us out. You're playing the long game."

"There is no other kind of game for a beaten people to play. We're outcasts here in your Galaxy, chased from our homeworlds by force and driven into the dark. We live in clustered star groups, places surrounded by nothingness. It's like living on a lonely handful of islands."

"Huh," I said, thinking about it. "And yet you come and go here with ease. Why not use your transmat tech to invade the Imperials directly and spoil their plans?"

"Would that it were so easy... They have ways to block us, to keep us out."

"But not us. Not Earth. Here, you come and go as you please."

Godwin shrugged.

His attitude kind of pissed me off. I frowned at him.

"Just what *are* you, anyway?" I asked him. "I mean underneath, when you aren't pretending to be human. Do you look like a wasp, or an earthworm or maybe some kind of spider?"

"My form is as you see it," he said. "It's my consciousness that's been transferred into this body. The current form of my person is relatively unimportant. This shape was chosen to put you at ease."

"Huh..." I mused. "That's really weird. So, is there some other version of Godwin elsewhere? Sleeping, maybe?"

"No, spare bodies aren't usually kept alive when remote transmission of consciousness occurs. It simplifies things to dispose of it, then construct another suitable receptacle at the next destination."

I squinted at him, frankly amazed. What he was describing was beyond my knowledge. Could these creatures really travel the cosmos by transmitting their minds from one body to another? The more I thought about it, however, the more sense it began to make.

"That's how you were able to look like Jones, and now you're back to being Godwin again, right? You must use the transmat, or something like it."

"Precisely. You *do* realize there's no such thing as an instant transference of matter, don't you? Not without a phenomenal usage of power and advanced equipment. What a transmat really does is send a long-distance signal that uses tricks of quantum physics to beat the speed of light. The booth you step into doesn't really transmit a person, it breaks down a body then another rebuilds a copy of it at a remote location."

"That's horrifying."

"Not when you get used to it. To me, it's no more disturbing than a haircut. That process is also a painless removal of excess body matter, is it not?"

The more I thought about it, the more upsetting his revelation became. The people who used the transmats believed they were being transported over a great distance—but it was a lie. They were being disintegrated and reconstituted elsewhere.

"So... you don't have a single solid form you call home? Did you *ever* have one?"

"Yes, of course," Godwin said, "but that was long ago. We're called Nomads, after all. We have no homes—even our bodies are temporary."

The very thought of how these aliens lived made my skin crawl—but I forced a smile.

"That's terribly interesting," I told him, "but since you're in an informative mood, I'd like to know why you're here. Why do you keep showing up and bothering me in particular?"

"Among the billions on this planet, very few are worthy of note. You happen to be one of them. My masters hope Earth can cause even greater distraction for the Imperials in the future."

I was beginning to catch on. We weren't expected to win the war with the Imperials—we were expected to irritate them.

"So..." I said, "the Nomads are plotting something big..."

43

Godwin looked startled, but he quickly recovered. "We're always plotting. We're always looking for a path, a way to regain a foothold among our home stars again. Is that so wrong?"

"Not at all. Very understandable. But I'm not sure you're really an ally from Earth's point of view."

Godwin took a deep breath. "Blake, for the good of your people and mine, you should realize that the stakes in this war are very high. No one is truly your friend. Not even the Rebel Kher who you trust most."

I didn't totally buy his opinion because I knew that some of the Rebel Kher put honor and friendship above death itself—then again, others like Fex shifted loyalties like the wind.

Would any of them risk their homeworlds for friendship? I wasn't sure about that.

Godwin left after having delivered his new "instructions" concerning our next meeting with Fex. I'd assured him I'd pass his wisdom on to the brass, but I didn't guarantee Earth would surrender—in fact, I told him I rather doubted that we would.

"Such a waste," he said, shaking his head.

Going back into my apartment, I couldn't sleep the rest of the night.

Was Godwin right? Was it the right move to surrender our sovereignty and allow Fex to "protect" us? It was hard to know, and a bitter pill to swallow.

=9=

As had been so often the case in history, Earth's governments were slow to open their treasuries without witnessing a direct threat. Over the last several years, frightening ships had come and gone in our home space, but few people had actually died. Some individuals, such as myself, had been abducted and sent into battle among the stars, but even among those few most had returned alive.

Everything felt different now. Earth had witnessed a space battle. Three huge ships had appeared, approached aggressively, and our tiny vessels had attacked them. We'd driven them off, but no one could now feel comfortable.

The following weeks were understandably full of frenetic activity. Earth had moved from a slow state of peacetime build-up to fully gearing for war.

"This is *war*," Admiral Vega told a circle of grim-faced officers. "Let there be no mistake about it. They came here, they threatened us, and we defended ourselves. But that wasn't the end of it. Far from it."

He was being dramatic, but I had to agree with him. After a few more doom-laden pronouncements, Vega turned to me.

"You all know Captain Blake, at least by reputation. He's our most experienced space fleet officer. He'll guide you through the rest of this seminar."

He passed me by as he left the room, and he gave me a stern look. "If anyone falls asleep, I want them shot."

"Yes sir," I said. "I won't even give a warning."

The officers glanced at one another. A few chuckled, but no one felt certain we were joking. We gave no hint in our expressions.

Vega left then, and the new trainees were my problem. I'd become an instructor after all, and that ground my teeth for me. Vega had gotten his way.

But the arrangement wasn't exactly as Vega had imagined. I wasn't a permanent prof in some dingy office whiling away the hours. My role was to give three-day, intensive seminars covering tactics and providing detailed information on the enemy. How they thought, how they may be expected to react to various actions— exactly the sort of thing only I'd experienced.

The compressed format suited me. Each seminar's attendance was limited to the command staff of a single phase-ship. I spent only a few days with each group. They listened intently, got what they could from me, and then went right back up into space to patrol again. No one was left with the impression we were wasting time.

The beauty of a real war was that it cleared the minds of the participants. We were all on the same page. We all wanted to survive, to keep the citizens of Earth breathing. Loyalty and respect were at a fevered pitch. I doubted it would last for years—but I also doubted Admiral Fex would take that long to come back to visit us again.

After talking to each crew about scenarios and watching live action vids with them, my favorite part of the training began. I put them through some scenarios I'd picked up from the Rebel Kher themselves.

Now, some may think me cruel to place young officers inside a dome-like arena and give them simplistic weaponry. But I knew better. These spacers weren't just learning how to fight, they were learning to think like the Kher.

The first round always began with the entire group arranged in a circle. Usually, there were about fifteen of us. The phase-ship crews operated with three groups of bridge crewmen, standing watch in eight hour shifts around the clock. That was an improvement when compared to how we'd run *Hammerhead*. Due to the ship's design restrictions, we'd lived with two twelve-hour shifts, and fatigue had set in after weeks in space.

To kick off each event, I had everyone strip down to a pair of coveralls. Then I handed each person a stick, and I gave them a little speech.

"All right," I said, "you're not on Earth anymore. You're in the Kher fleet. They operate very differently than we do here at home. Discipline is laxer, more immediate. They don't fight in a perfect line like we've learned to do—not usually."

They were all watching me closely. They'd heard about this—but no details. I'd worked hard to keep the whole thing secretive and mysterious. In my opinion, it made the experience more realistic.

"Only one man or woman is going to step out of this bubble on their own," I told them, eyeing each one sternly. "Why is that? Because you're all about to beat hell out of each other once I give the signal."

Warily, they eyed one another. That was an early stage, sizing up opponents. It was only natural.

But there was a certain hesitancy in the group. I recognized it right off. Our troops were used to obeying officers of higher rank. How was an ensign supposed to treat the commander standing next to him in a dogfight?

"Don't worry about ranks here. You're in the Kher fleet now—all of you have to earn your ranks from the bottom. Once we're past this training, you'll go back to your prior status, but you'll be wiser. I've got commitments from the senior staff that there will be no hard feelings. No recriminations for what happens here."

The oldest man in the group, a commander by rank, nodded when my eyes landed on him. He had a paunch, but there was a hard look in his eye. You could never tell who was the meanest until the action started.

I nodded back to the commander, and I continued walking around the group. I moved with my eyes cast down, just in case someone decided brain me from behind during my speech. It had never happened yet—but there was always a first time.

"So, take up your weapons—both hands, now."

They lifted their sticks, which had padded tips. The pads were something of a trick, however. The fighting sticks were weighted at the ends. A thin layer of vinyl and foam rubber should stop anyone from being cut badly, but a good hard blow could still knock out teeth or crack a bone.

47

"See the floor? How it's lit up green? That means there's no fighting allowed. When it goes yellow—ah, there it goes!"

A few men backed up in alarm. One of them touched his head to the domed surface and cried out, dropping his stick.

"Hold on!" I shouted. "Yellow is a transition point, a warning. Red means you're in battle. Also," I continued, pointing toward the cursing man who'd backed into the curving walls, "the walls are charged. Don't run into one unless you feel the need for some additional incentive."

They looked over their shoulders in alarm. They were breathing hard now, eyes wide.

"Any questions?" I asked, circling around to my starting point again.

No one spoke. That was good, because the floor went red at that moment.

At the same time, our syms began to agitate us. It wasn't a full-on murderous frenzy they induced, not today. The sensation that swept the group was more like waking up with a hangover on a sunny morning. We were all suddenly feeling itchy and easily angered.

Most of the troops spread out and paired off across the red deck—clacking together their sticks. One man went down, but he sprang back up again.

It was a lackluster performance. They were going through the motions without real bloodlust—not yet.

I stood apart with my stick in my hand, watching with a disapproving glare.

"Downright embarrassing..." I said. "You want to hold hands and sing instead?"

The commander had been left alone up until this point, but he was a man who understood the importance of an exercise. He stepped up behind a sparring pair and clocked the man who was facing the other way with his stick.

We all heard two audible cracks. The first one was the stick hitting an unsuspecting skull, and the second was that same skull hitting the floor—hard.

A whisper of a smile crept over the old man. Right then and there, I marked him as one of the mean ones. Like I said, you never could tell.

The man who'd been sparring with the fellow who was no longer conscious nodded to the old man warily—as if he'd been done a favor.

But the mean old commander wasn't having any of that. He had blood in his eye now. He'd tasted glory, and he meant to have more.

Syms affected people differently, causing reactions of various intensities. I, myself, was still able to think clearly and easily. It was a quirk of my personality, I guess.

But the commander wasn't like that. He was losing it. He was going animal. I'd seen it many times before.

His next victim saw it, too. He backed up a step, catching hard, smashing blows with his stick. He was faster, but probably not stronger.

The old man became angrier with every block. He was grunting and showing his teeth. His breath puffed out of his open mouth, and the look in his eyes began to seem unhinged.

Desperately, his victim turned his stick and held it like a spear. He thrust repeatedly, the way a man might work a bayonet. I could see he'd been trained in that ancient art. Feet apart, leaning forward, knees bent, keeping the tip of his weapon aimed at the commander.

Unfortunately, there was no sharp tip at the end of his stick. The commander lunged at him, catching a glancing blow to the cheek which slid off. He got in close, whipping the two weighted ends and slamming them repeatedly into the man's skull. About the third time, the bayonet guy fell on his face.

That didn't stop the old man. He'd lost it. He beat on the fallen man, and we all heard ribs crack.

"Commander!" shouted a female lieutenant—but she was no lieutenant here. She was just another fighter. "You're killing him!"

The old guy didn't respond. He thumped his stick on the fallen man's back.

The woman looked at me in horror. I shrugged, and pointed out that the commander's back was facing her. It was a perfect opportunity.

A change overcame her features. She went a little animal herself. Snarling, she rushed the commander and swung a roundhouse loop for his head.

He might have been enjoying his beat-down, but he was still able to think. He heard her coming, side-stepped and tripped her.

She fell over the fallen man and rolled into the barrier. There, she began to buzz and sizzle. The commander cackled and held her there with one foot.

That was it, I think. Everyone lost whatever was left of their minds. They'd prepared, they'd thought it through, they'd said their prayers and done their push-ups—but none of that mattered now. They went for each other all around the ring, slamming, biting, kicking and screaming.

The old man finally went down with two others beating on him. The girl was out, the old man was out—most of them were down and motionless.

Two final troops turned to face off. They'd taken down the commander together, and now they'd decide who was the best.

Before they were able to take their first shot, however, the man who had his back to me went down in a heap.

The second man looked at me in confusion for a second.

"I never said I wasn't in this fight," I told him. "A love-tap. That's all it was."

Snarling, he charged me with wordless rage.

What followed was the hardest challenge of my day. I was ready and unhurt, but this guy was a powerhouse. He knew how to fight, too.

We slammed our sticks together. Lunge, block, sweep, counter—it went on for maybe thirty seconds.

Then, I managed to catch his fingers with my stick. That was a legal tactic—because there weren't really any rules.

Broken, twisting fingers clutched his stick anyway. But his grip was weak. The next time he blocked me, he lost hold of his stick, and the weighted end of my weapon found his temple.

He went down in a heap, and the floor slowly changed from red to yellow, then at last to green.

Breathing deeply, I saluted those who could still move.

"Well done," I said. "This exercise, and this class, has reached its conclusion. You all passed with flying colors. As I promised, the final three combatants have been awarded one status point in the Rebel Kher Fleet."

There were a few groans, but no one thanked me.

"One last thing," I said. "Don't tell anyone else how this ends. Don't let some other crew off easy. Let them take their training, the same as you did."

"Damn straight..." mumbled a voice from the floor.

To my surprise, I realized the words had come from the bloodied mouth of the commander.

Hell, that man was part dinosaur.

=10=

A few more weeks passed, and the month long deadline Godwin had given us came and went. We didn't relax, however. Somehow, knowing that the enemy was late made everything worse. Tension was so thick around Space Command you could cut it with a knife.

Vega called me into his office—which was now underground in the operations facility—seven weeks after Godwin had come and gone.

"You still haven't seen him again?" he demanded. "You're friend, the freak?"

"No sir," I told him. "Godwin has sent no word, no message. There have been no midnight knocks on my door."

Godwin had long been a sore point with the officers here. He possessed the ability to make people forget seeing him, and only hard evidence had proven to my superiors I wasn't crazy.

Needless to say, the fact some alien power was moving freely about our most critical base had set them all on edge.

"We'll catch this sneaky alien of yours eventually, you know," Vega said.

"He's not *my* alien, sir."

"As far as I'm concerned, he's your baby."

"How so?"

"You were the first to bring him to our attention. If you break it, you get to fix it."

"Excellent, sir. How do I go about doing that?"

"We have sensors now," he explained, "automated ones that track individuals as they move around this base. We've also set up automated briefings for every security chief. They're reminded of Godwin's existence soon after they wake up, just to make sure that bastard doesn't erase anyone's mind again."

I wasn't sure these measures would work, but I didn't think they could hurt, so I nodded as if I was impressed.

Vega looked at me with narrowed eyes. "Why do you think he confides in you? Why not me, or someone else with more authority?"

"Originally, I discovered him and captured him," I explained. "I think that impressed him. He decided he could use a man to communicate with Earth, rather than to merely sneak around spying. He chose me for that purpose."

"Good enough, then," he said. "I brought you here to tell you we've decided to bring Godwin in—to question him."

I frowned at this idea. "You want to capture him, Admiral? I'm not sure that's a good idea diplomatically."

"You said yourself he's a spy. The stakes are very high now, Blake. We can't allow an alien to wander our most sensitive base at will."

"But look, sir, the Nomads are on our side."

"Really? What proof do you have of that? Can they lend us a few battleships?"

"Uh... I don't think they can, sir."

Vega nodded. "Exactly. He can't do anything to help. He gives you suggestions, steals information, and God knows what else. We're through putting up with it."

"But sir—"

"The matter is closed, Captain. I just wanted you to be in the loop so you aren't overly alarmed when our trap is sprung."

As he spoke, I realized I had to be the bait in this trap. Godwin had appeared and talked to me several times. If they wanted to catch him, they had to watch me to do it.

"On another, more positive note," Vega continued, "we're christening a new ship tomorrow."

"Another phase-ship, sir?" I asked brightly. My old dreams of flying my own ship flared again in my heart. I couldn't help it. Hope truly was eternal.

"There was a phase-ship commissioned last week," Vega said. "This is something new and experimental."

"Oh... what is she, then?"

"Meet me at the transmat just before noon tomorrow," he said, "and you'll find out."

"Will do."

I tried to get more details out of Vega, but I failed. Our meeting broke up shortly after he'd asked me to the launching of this new ship. I found he'd left me wondering about this mysterious new vessel. Could Abrams be behind the project? I'd gotten a certain vibe from him lately...

Dr. Abrams could keep a secret when he was forced to, but he didn't really like staying quiet for long. His idea of a good time was proving to everyone that he was a genuine genius. How could you do that by working on projects no one knew about?

As evidence of this problem, Abrams had made smug comments around me that suggested he'd been working on something big. Something *so* big I was too unimportant to be briefed about it. I'd assumed his hints were all fantasy and fluff—but now I wasn't so sure.

All that night and the next morning I thought about Abrams and the new ship, and by noon when I let my latest class go early for the day, I could think of little else.

Arriving at the transmat a full ten minutes early, I found myself eying the booth with a queasy feeling in my guts. Was it really about to kill me? Was I really going to step into that thing and allow myself to be blasted apart and reformed elsewhere, like a mosquito flying innocently in bug-zapper?

"What are you doing here, Blake?" Dr. Abrams demanded from behind me.

I spun around, tearing my eyes from the transmat. "Ah, Doctor. I'm waiting for you and Vega, apparently."

He frowned. "I haven't been briefed on your involvement."

"My involvement? Some would say the whole thing was my idea. What surprises me is seeing you here on the big day. I knew someone was doing the grunt work on our designs, but I didn't think they'd burdened you with something so mundane."

Dr. Abrams' mouth fell open. It was always so satisfying when he did that. I was pushing his buttons, and it really wasn't fair, but I couldn't help myself. The guy could be hard to take sometimes.

"*Your* idea?" he demanded, scandalized. "The ship's design is *mine*, Blake. You've had nothing to do with it! Frankly, I don't think you have the background to grasp even the basics of this ship's capabilities."

"Let's talk about it when we get up there," I said, making the supposition that ship was in orbit. My bullshit was running thin, but I was having a great time. "Vega will straighten everything out, I'm sure."

He stared at me with squinting eyes for a moment. "You're having me on, aren't you?" he demanded at last. "Is this all some kind of prank? Some kind of schoolboy entertainment of yours?"

"Not at all. Vega ordered me to be here today. Doesn't that tell you something?"

Abrams stopped talking and fell to muttering incoherently. His brows knit together in a petulant, angry frown. He gazed at the deck, the transmat—anywhere except at me.

At last, after three uncomfortable minutes of this, Vega arrived.

"Excellent," he said. "You're both here, and early."

"Admiral Vega," Abrams said loudly. "This man has made a number of alarming—"

Vega put up both his hands in surrender. "Doctor, let's just get on with the inspection. I know you don't get along with Blake, but today, that's just tough. We're going up."

The transmat hummed as it activated. My mood concerning the system had shifted. I was so annoyed with Abrams, I grinned as I stepped into its glowing, intertwined fields.

For just a second, I had the distinct sensation I was in two places at once, even though I knew that was impossible.

What had really happened was I'd been destroyed and converted to nonexistence for a few moments, then rebuilt at the far end. The very thought was enough to make one's mind and stomach churn.

=11=

When I arrived at the other end, I stepped out of a transmat booth that was identical in all respects to the one I'd entered down on Earth. The place where it stood, however, was quite different. Right off, I knew I was in space. There was a tug of artificial gravity, but it was much less powerful than the glue-like pull of my home planet.

The walls of the ship stretched out around me. I could tell it was big. Our phase-ships were built on a smaller scale. Aboard a vessel like *Hammerhead*, the walls curved in visibly in most chambers, as you were always close to the hull everywhere you went. On this vessel, there were no curved walls in sight.

Vega stepped out of the transmat next. I watched the shimmer, and I watched him give himself a shake.

"How big is it?" I asked immediately.

"Not as big as those cruisers Fex was driving," he admitted. "But she's a good two hundred meters long and thirty thick."

My mind whirled. That was a large volume of space. In the Earth's antiquated surface navy, a heavy cruiser would have been about the equivalent.

But spacecraft tended to be larger. They had to carry much more powerful engines, life support systems and power sources. Moving a ship over an earthly sea at thirty knots took some large turbines, but sea-going vessels weren't expected to push a ship to a million kilometers an hour. Nor were their weapons expected to reach a million kilometers out and damage an enemy. That kind of push and reach took massive amounts of power.

"What class is she?" I asked, almost whispering.

"Ah-ha!" Abrams shouted, eyeing me with gleeful triumph. "You don't know *anything* about this ship! She's a work of art, Blake. That's all you really need to know. The jewel in Earth's crown."

"She's a destroyer—or maybe a light cruiser at best," Vega said, ignoring Abrams. "But her size isn't the most important thing about her."

"She's a *starship!*" Dr. Abrams announced, stepping close to me and putting his face into mine. "Our first. *My baby.* My greatest achievement. And you—you had nothing to do with her creation. Nothing!"

I smiled. "That's right, Doc," I said. "She's all yours, and she's beautiful."

I ran my hands over sleek walls and gentle curves at the bulkheads. She *was* a work of art. Abrams was three-quarters mad on a good day, but I had to admit, he'd outdone himself.

Vega was talking about something, but I didn't hear him. My ears had stopped working shortly after Abrams had said: *Starship.*

I whirled around to face the two of them. "Did you say... starship?"

"That's right," Abrams said smugly.

"As in... she can open her own rifts in space? She can travel to other star systems?"

"In theory, yes," Vega said.

"Theory?" Dr. Abrams snapped. "What are you talking about? She's a *starship*—dammit man, that's settled science. She'll fly anywhere you want to go. You can be sure of that, Admiral."

Vega looked at me. "She can make a rift—we hope."

"I've already done it in the lab—twice!" Abrams said, speaking as if he was offended by any doubters.

I eyed Abrams, then Vega. I understood. Abrams was a man who always oversold his creations. He'd invented many amazing things, but often, they failed to deliver as promised.

Immediately, my mind dredged up images of his star-shot project that misfired at a quarter of the promised speed, and then of his gravity-wave generator that had twisted up the guts of everyone aboard *Hammerhead* the first time we turned it on.

In short, there was no telling what this ship was really capable of until we flew her, and Vega's attitude indicated he knew this was the case as well.

"Why am I here, sir?" I asked Vega.

"Yes," Dr. Abrams said. "I want to know the answer to that as well. Why are you here, aboard my ship?"

"Because we want you to be her captain, Blake," Vega told me, his eyes locked with mine.

Abrams made a choking sound, but no intelligible words exited his throat. He was too upset for that.

"A challenge," I said. "An immense responsibility... I accept, of course."

"Do you need a glass of water, Dr. Abrams?" Admiral Vega asked him.

"I need something stronger. Tell me this is a joke. Tell me you're not putting this engine of destruction in charge of my greatest achievement!"

"I'm sorry," Vega said, "but you two are just going to have to find a way to work together."

"I've got a question, too," I said. "Why the secrecy? Why did you let me think you wanted me to be some kind of school teacher?"

Dr. Abrams face twitched. It wasn't a smile. Not even a half-smile. But the left corner of his mouth did jump upward for a second or two.

"Don't play the fool," Abrams said. "You're a security risk. You've been followed around by a ghost for two years. Why would we tell you anything? In fact, it baffles me that you've been allowed to set foot on this vessel!"

I turned back to Vega, snapping my fingers. "That's why I've been passed over for every commission? Someone wanted me to command *this* ship? All the while you've been building it, you've been torturing me, Admiral?"

Vega shrugged. "Not my call. You met Clemens. He didn't want you to know anything."

"He knows about Godwin?"

"Of course he does. A security breach of that magnitude? Everyone knows about it. Some people wanted to blackball you permanently."

I nodded, feeling that many pieces were fitting together in my mind. Contemplating being in space again was a relief, a terror in my guts, and a sensation of exhilaration all at the same time.

Spinning around in the low gravity, I turned to Abrams again. He was red-faced and looking defeated.

"Doc," I said, "please show me around your masterpiece."

One great thing about Dr. Abrams was he could be easily mollified with compliments. He might fly into rages, demand insane things, or deny failures that everyone else could see plainly. But if you just told him he was the greatest for a while, in a manner that was justified and believable, you could turn him back into a calm happy man again.

That became my immediate goal once I'd learned what was really going on here. I followed Abrams and swooned over every gizmo, attribute and design feature he showed us.

The tour was magnificent in any regard. I barely needed to ham it up for Abrams' sake. The ship was sleek, unlike anything else Earth had produced. Instead of looking like a bunch of modules we'd hammered together in space, it was a single hull of planes with rounded curves joining them.

"Why is every angle gentle?" I asked. "There's nothing boxy aboard."

"It's a defensive design feature," Abrams said. "Space has no friction—or at least, very little. Nothing to run into like air or water on a planet. That normally allows designers to make sharp angles the rule, as they're easier to manufacture."

I glanced at Vega, but he just shrugged. I guess he knew he was out of his element when it came to starship design.

"But," Abrams said dramatically, caressing a bulkhead with his tapered fingertips. "This is a *warship*. She'll see plenty of matter and energy thrown at her hull. Like a stealthy aircraft, softer edges are harder to detect and harder to damage with particles or blasts of energy."

I nodded thoughtfully. "I guess that makes sense. You've tested these theories, right—?"

"Of course I have! Extensively!" he exclaimed, instantly defensive and angry again.

"Great... Let's see the bridge next, Doc."

Abrams marched off, and we followed. He grumbled about being insulted and taken for a fool the whole way up the spine of the ship.

For some reason, I'd expected to find the bridge to be designed along the lines of *Hammerhead*, my first command. Nothing could be further from the truth. The bridge was multi-level and spherical

59

in configuration. Padded cages, rather than true seats, were suspended here and there in front of various workstations.

"This is a marvel of modern design," Abrams informed me.

"Sure looks like it."

He looked at me suspiciously, correctly presuming sarcasm. I kept a blank face, and eventually he continued.

"Why arrange stations in a flat plane?" Abrams asked rhetorically. "There's no need for such restrictions. We've placed seven stations strategically around the spherical bridge. What's more, the purpose of each station is malleable. Any one of them can pull up and take over the tasks of any other. That way, if a person is injured or absent in an emergency, anyone else can take over their function."

I nodded thoughtfully. A frown had crept over my face, however, and Vega wore the same expression.

"Doubters..." Abrams said, putting his hands on his hips. "I'm plagued by this sort of thing. All my life, it's been a constant. You're like animals exploring new feed and immediately disliking—"

"It tastes fine, Doc," I said. "Please go on."

His eyes darted back and forth between the two of us. We kept our faces neutral, not wanting to distract him further, so he went on.

"All right then... The stations are interchangeable. I imagine that in practice, certain officers will be deemed best suited to a defined group of tasks. There's nothing preventing that arrangement. You've got freedom and flexibility here, not some new obstacle to worry about."

"Are there passwords, at least, protecting critical functions?" Vega asked.

I glanced at him. I'd been about to ask the same question.

Dr. Abrams glared again. "My team isn't made up of fools! Yes, there are permissions for each interface. A given crewman can't pull up the helm controls from engineering, for example, without the proper login credentials."

"From engineering?" I asked.

"Perhaps I didn't make myself clear," Abrams said. "Each function has a unique interface. Each interface can be accessed from anywhere aboard. This chamber—the bridge, as we'll call it for the sake of tradition—exists to allow command personnel a single location to gather. They could do all their work from disparate locations around the ship, if they wanted to."

Now I *was* alarmed. So was Vega.

"Can you work with that?" Vega asked me. "Or do we need to make changes?"

A gargling sound came out of Abrams, but he didn't shout at us.

"I can..." I said, figuring I'd lock out remote access except in special override cases. "I can work with this. It's not a problem."

Abrams breathed a sigh of relief.

"Far from a problem," he said loudly, "you'll find it's a dramatic advance in efficiency."

"I'm sure I will."

"Good... Now let's get down to details. When you shepherd a flock of phase-ships through a rift, they'll need to hug quite close. This ship is too small to make a rift of dramatic size. The anomaly will be small, but it will still be stable and effective."

I frowned, thinking about it. Earth's first starship looked good, but functionally it was starting to sound like a cut-rate affair compared to the vessels produced by our more experienced star-faring brothers.

"How close will they have to be?" I asked.

Abrams went over the numbers, and the display screens reproduced simulations. It was going to be tight. It was a good thing most of our ships *were* small.

In interstellar travel, ships traveled in groups. Usually a capital ship of real size opened a rift. The others following it had no star drives themselves. The smaller ships operated as screens to protect the starship, and they generally did the heavy fighting and dying. Only the biggest ships could do both tasks effectively.

The most surprising thing Abrams had managed with this vessel was a balanced combination of lean displacement, respectable weaponry, and the capacity to create a minimal rift.

"Wait a minute," I said, "what about this ship? Can she phase-out like the ships she shepherds?"

Abrams blanched. "No, sadly. The design elements won't allow it. A phase-ship generates a field that forms a bubble around the hull. That's a continuous energy drain. This ship has the capacity to summon a stable, but temporary rift at a single location. The technology and the math are entirely different."

I shrugged. "Why not just add a module to phase-out? They aren't very big. Then our entire fleet could operate together."

For once, Abrams didn't get angry.

"The main problem has to do with energy and size requirements," he said. "A phase-ship needs to be small in order to maintain a continuous effect. A true starship needs to be larger in order to generate enough power to create a stable rift all at once."

I nodded. "Then you *have* done something remarkable," I said. "This is the smallest starship I've ever seen. Even an Imperial destroyer is a bit larger."

For some reason, this statement made Dr. Abrams puff up with pride.

"I've been saying as much for months. I'm glad you can see reality in this instance, Blake—I know it doesn't come naturally to you."

I forced a smile. There it was again. Even when Abrams was complimenting you, he was also insulting you at the same time. I wondered if he even realized he was doing it. My honest impression was that he had no idea how others perceived his words.

Somehow, knowing he was clueless made it easier to put up with him.

=12=

Returning to Earth, I felt triumphant. I was going into space again. The ship up there—it was marvelous. As much as Dr. Abrams bugged me, I had to admit, we all owed him our thanks. He'd created technological marvels that moved Earth far ahead in the armament race.

There were problems, of course. The greatest of these was the imminent arrival of Admiral Fex's fleet. Had we built this wonderful light cruiser only to see it destroyed in its first action against invaders? Was it too little, too late?

I refused to entertain such thoughts of disaster and gloom today. Whatever happened, I was going into space again. It was only a matter of time. The ship was ready, even though a hundred elements weren't quite finished yet.

Admiral Vega didn't care. He'd ordered me to assemble a crew and get them aboard the new ship as soon as possible.

"Who can I take with me?" I asked.

He shrugged. "Give me some names. I'll get them approved. We have to move fast, however. It won't do us any good to have a starship that's sitting up there in dry-dock, empty and lifeless."

"Shakedown cruise?"

"As soon as you can get her underway."

The ship itself, I'd learned, wasn't in orbit over Earth. If she had been, it was likely Admiral Fex would have seen it. Possibly, they'd even have destroyed her.

The new ship was in orbit over Mars, rather than Earth. We'd taken that enormous leap due to the availability of materials that could be mined easily from Mars' moons and Mars herself. Also, we'd gambled the ship would go undetected there.

With the transmat allowing instant transport out to the vessel and back, most of our logistical problems had been defeated.

"What is the range of a transmat, anyway?" I asked Vega.

He looked at me sternly. "That's classified, Blake."

"Oh come on. Godwin doesn't care about our transmat technology."

"We don't know what he cares about. Here's my answer: one meter farther out than Mars. That's how far it can go."

I rolled my eyes, but I didn't argue. They'd given me the command I'd dreamed of. Respect and trust were implicit in that decision, even if Godwin was still freaking everyone out.

Frowning, I had another thought. "What do you think Godwin will do when I take this ship out for a test drive? If he comes back, I mean?"

"Hopefully, he won't be able to find you," Vega said. "You know him better than I do. What do you think he'll do?"

I shook my head blankly. "The guy is a mystery to me."

"That's what I hate about him."

We went back to planning the ship's maiden voyage and working up a crew roster. I put forward some names from my old crew, and they were accepted, but that was nowhere near enough people. *Hammerhead* had supported only a tiny complement compared to this monster. A crew roster of five hundred names had to be worked up. It was quite a task.

"I've got authorization for a big boost," Vega told me as we worked through long lists of personnel.

"I could sure use it," I told him.

"This ship can't be entirely manned by rookies. We understand that. Unfortunately, there are precious few service people who've manned a spacecraft of any kind."

"Don't I know it..." I said, scrolling on my tablet past lists of people from various aircraft carrier groups and the like.

"What we *can* do is sign on a portion of the people from each phase-ship."

I stared at him for a second. "That would be excellent—but I don't want to disrupt the rest of our fledgling navy."

"Right. At most, we'll allow you one of the three shifts from each phase-ship. They'll have to make due with two experienced crews, and one group of moonlighters."

"Ten people from each phase-ship?" I asked.

"We can do that."

"Great... that'll give me nearly two hundred experienced hands. That's a huge relief, Admiral."

He stood up, smiling, and clasped my shoulder. "Excellent. Take a first cut at those names. I'll meet with you again tomorrow."

"What's pressing?"

He shrugged. "I told them it would be no more than five from each phase-ship. I've got some arm-twisting to do."

He left, and I got to work. After my own list of familiar reliables, like Samson, Dalton, Gwen and Mia, I reached for the list of phase-ship people.

Looking at the names, I realized I knew a lot of them. I'd been giving these same people private trainings for weeks.

Frowning and cocking my head to one side, I looked after Admiral Vega suspiciously. Had he planned all this? Had he cooked up a scheme that would get me into contact with the phase-ship crews all the while knowing I would draw upon them for my initial crew?

I'm not a man who generally believes in coincidences—and this was too big of one to be an accident.

"Sly bastard..." I said, moving Vega up a notch in my estimation.

"Who, me?"

My head snapped back the other way.

The office had been empty the moment before, but it did have a small private bathroom attached.

The bathroom doorway swung open and Godwin stood there. A wisp of steam followed him, like he'd just gotten finished with a shower, but he was bone-dry and dressed.

"Godwin...?" I said, shocked.

Jolted into action, I grabbed up all the documents and tablets scattered over the desk. I flipped over each tablet and shuffled the hardcopy into a rumpled pile.

"Relax," he said, chuckling. "I know all about your starship."

I stared at him, then glowered. "What do you want? Give me a reason not to shoot you right now."

"Well, first off, it would be a diplomatic incident."

"You're a spy, not a diplomat."

"Is there any difference? Really?"

"Yes. One is officially sanctioned and accepted. The other is free game."

"Hmm..." he said. "Such ingratitude. Who do you think gave Abrams the tech to build that pretty ship of his? Did you really think he pulled it all out of his twisted mind? In two short years?"

I blinked, taken by surprise. I recalled then having had lingering doubts. Abrams had said he had been unable to figure out how to create a stable breach. Hell, many of the components of our original ship had been cannibalized from the Rebel Kher ship I'd brought home to Earth. To expect such advancement so quickly—it did defy logic.

"Okay," I said. "I can believe you helped. Why the hell doesn't Abrams remember you, then?"

"Because I don't want him to."

"And me?"

"You've been hard to control—the hardest on this world. Several times, I've tried to nudge you, and you've resisted. I decided to use different techniques with you than I've used with the others."

My mouth sagged. He was giving so much away. So much was implied. He'd "nudged" people. Did that include Vega? Or Clemens? Was my grooming for this position not an accident of fate, not a plan hatched by my superiors, but rather a plot backed by aliens I barely understood?

"I can see my words are disturbing you," Godwin said. "I apologize. Let me start again."

"If you 'nudge' me, and I figure it out... I'll kill you, Godwin."

He blinked then. I could tell I'd troubled him. Probably that was because he knew that I meant it, and that I might be able to figure it out.

"What would you prefer the basis of our relationship to be, then?" he asked.

"An exchange of information and suggestions."

He nodded and spread his hands. "That's all I've ever wanted! The problem has always been the natural resistance of your species. You don't trust outsiders."

"With good reason."

66

"But I've proven myself over and over again."

I made a farting sound with my mouth. "You warned me about Fex even as he was actually showing up. For all I knew, you were aboard his ship when he got here. You've constantly advised me to surrender, all the while claiming you're helping us to arm ourselves. Which is it?"

"There's no conflict," he said. "Just misperception. We want you to arm yourselves. We want to you to be victorious. But we don't want you to fight the Rebel Kher."

Frowning, I thought that over. Godwin came closer and took a seat across the desk from me. I stopped clutching the papers I'd been hiding and dropped them on the desk. There was no point in hiding things from this spook.

"Think of it from our point of view," Godwin said. "You're a project. One of many. A seed has been planted here. We hope you'll blossom and eventually grow into a great power to face the Imperials. If you fight Fex, you'll be wrecking our work."

I nodded slowly. "So, you council surrender, but we're supposed to keep building in the meantime, right? What if Fex doesn't like that? What if Fex outlaws an Earth navy?"

Godwin smiled oddly. "Let us worry about that. We'll talk to him, the same way we talk to your people. Eventually, he'll see reason."

My mouth squirmed but I said nothing. He was talking in the plural now. As if Nomads were crawling out of the woodwork.

"How many Godwins are there?" I asked him. "On Earth, I mean."

He laughed. "That's classified."

=13=

I reported Godwin's visit. That didn't make anyone happy—but at least they didn't try to take my command away from me.

"Why didn't your team catch him?" I asked Vega.

He glared at the desk, his hands on his hips. He was fuming.

"He was right *here*? That's what you're telling me? Right here in my damned office?"

"Yes. Check the vids. You have this area under surveillance, I'm sure."

"We have *you* under surveillance. Nothing was tripped. We got no signal that time. He must know we're on to him. He must have countermeasures."

"Aren't you going to bring up the recordings and—?"

He made an angry gesture, and I shut up. "Doesn't matter," he said. "We have an army of geeks watching it all right now, I'm sure. Maybe the problem is we were talking about classified information. The investigation team isn't entirely cleared on the new ship— that's a mistake."

I nodded. "By the way, I've got a name for her."

"No you don't. She's SCL-1. That's her name."

Making a derisive noise, I tossed him a tablet full of names. One was in bigger font and bold letters at the top.

"That doesn't sell well in the sticks, Admiral. I would suggest you check out this list."

"Florida class?" he asked. "This ship doesn't have a class, really, she's the only one we've got."

I almost rolled my eyes, but I managed to stop myself. "I'm a Navy man, sir," I said. "Ships have classes. In the Air Force, I know you guys like letters and numbers, but names are better for large vessels. We're making rapid advances, so we need a way to distinguish this design from others. We need to give her a class, and then we need to name her something with human appeal."

He heaved a sigh and grumbled.

"*Devilfish*," he said thoughtfully. "I like that one."

"That's at the bottom of the list," I complained. "Smaller ships get names like that—*Devilfish* would be good for a phase-ship, maybe."

"All right then, dammit. What's your name? Just tell me."

"It's right there in bold at the top."

"*Naples?* Are you kidding me?"

"It's a city in Florida, sir. Florida class, Florida—"

"I get it. The problem is, Blake, it sucks. Did your ghost Godwin give you that stinker?"

"No sir..."

"Starship *Naples*... people will think the Italians built it. That's a no-go."

Crossing my arms, I leaned back. "Okay then. What do we call her?"

He tapped the screen firmly. A word jumped up.

"*Devilfish*," he said. "That's the name. Take it, or shove it, and we'll go with SCL-1."

With a sigh, I nodded. I felt naval traditions were being violated, but that was nothing new around here. The good thing was the name was reminiscent of Rebel Fleet ship names. They were often references to local predators on their various planets of origin.

"*Devilfish* it is," I said, "care to help me work up my roster?"

"No," he said. "I'm going downstairs to abuse the spook-team that was supposed to detect Godwin."

"Give them my best."

He left, and I went back to the rosters. Notices were going out already. People who were active-duty and not already on a mission-critical assignment had begun to get their summons. The speed was shocking for the military, but also it was gratifying. It showed how much they valued me and my ship.

Emails were starting to flood into my inbox. They wanted to know why they'd been suddenly reassigned and ordered to report to me as their new CO. Apparently, they were getting no details.

After my talk with Vega, I decided to answer them all with a boilerplate statement.

Welcome to Project Devilfish, my note said. *This is a classified project. Don't tell anyone of your involvement. You're appointment date with Captain Blake is...*

After that, I customized it to the recipient. Most of them were officers—the first people alerted, and officers with balls enough to ask questions.

Thoughtfully, I decided to meet with one man before all the others. He was none other than the commander I'd beaten down in my arena just yesterday. Commander Hagen was his name. I wanted a good XO, a job he'd already been performing aboard one of the phase-ships. I might have asked for Gwen, but she'd become a staffer here on base and was off limits. Miller, my old XO, had been given command of a phase-ship of his own.

That left me with a hole in my roster. A big one. I hoped Commander Hagen could fill it.

Later that same day after lunch, Hagen came to see me. He had a wary look on his face—which was kind of swollen up after our last meeting.

"Good to see you again, Captain," he said, and we shook hands.

His words were a little mushy. His lips were purple, taped and sewn together, and they didn't quite form words right.

"You too, Commander. Take a seat."

He did so. "Captain, what is Project Devilfish?"

I paused for a moment. "I can't tell you that. Not until you agree to serve under me."

His eyes narrowed. They were dark and puffy, with red crescents under each one.

"Captain, is this some kind of test? Another one? Should I prepare to defend myself?"

I chuckled. "Nah. No beat-downs today. I need a sidekick. An experienced man I can trust."

"It seems like you don't need my approval. This reassign—it's airtight. My captain has been complaining to anyone who'll listen all morning. He got nowhere."

"Yeah... Listen, Hagen. I know you're a good XO on a phase-ship. You're a tough bastard with a pugil stick, too."

"That's another thing," he said, leaning forward. "Those pugil sticks weren't regulation. They were weighted."

"Do you feel abused? Are you going to lodge a formal complaint, Hagen?"

"What...? No sir."

"Good. If you'd given me any other answer, I'd kick you out of here right now. The Rebel Kher operate on the basis of status. We have to compete with them, and in order to do that we have to understand them. That was the purpose of the exercise."

"I get all that, Captain. It's just—never mind."

"Ah..." I said, catching on. "You're annoyed you didn't win."

His eyes flashed up to meet mine, then he studied my littered desk again. "I'm not that petty."

"Sure you are! That's what I like about you. You wanted to cream all those young punks. You almost did it, too. I'm beginning to think I made the right choice after all."

"Captain... what is Project Devilfish?" he repeated.

I shook my head. "I can't tell you. Not until you've signed on. I'm not going to force you, either, as the position I have in mind for you requires full commitment."

"How can I fully commit to something if I don't even know what the hell it is?"

"You have to believe in me. You have to believe in Space Command as an entity. You have to be willing to risk it all. I can tell you the project is a big deal, and it's critical to Earth's defense."

Hagen nodded slowly. "Well sir... in that case, I accept. Sign me on. I'll dive off this cliff with my blindfold on."

He made me smile. I knew I could count on him. He was tough, competitive, and a risk-taker. Making him commit blind-folded was a trick, of course, designed to put him in the right frame of mind.

But it was more than that. It had proved something about him to me.

After that, I laid out the whole story. I showed him pictures of the ship. Stills and video taken during my first tour.

"This is all absolutely classified. Top secret."

"I get it, Captain—and I can see why."

His eyes were alight. He'd had no idea. If I'd shown him the ship first, he would have certainly signed on without hesitation. But that wouldn't have proven much, as anyone could have seen it was a wise career move.

Commander Hagen was much more committed than that. He wasn't thinking about his career path. He was thinking about the defense of Earth.

71

That's just where I wanted his mind to be.

=14=

It was nearly a week later by the time I had my crew assembled and took them aboard *Devilfish*. There were still nearly a hundred unfilled positions, but all the key spots were taken.

Some of my choices had been met with resistance. Others were on missions that they couldn't be recalled from yet. Still other posts we hadn't yet found a suitable spacer to fill.

But I didn't care about any of that today. I'd moved permanently aboard *Devilfish* and taken up residence there. It was a glorious feeling—and she was a glorious ship.

My first surprise came less than an hour after I'd made the transfer. A tap came at my new office door, and I ordered the door to let them in.

It was Dr. Abrams. He had another surprising face behind him—Mia.

"Um..." I said. "This is unexpected."

"You have a new girl, don't you?" Mia demanded. "Several, if I'm right."

Dr. Abrams appeared pained. "I told you, creature," he said. "Blake has been celibate for a week."

"You don't know everything," she said. "You don't know how a male is supposed to act. Ra-tikh would never go a week without mating—not willingly, anyway."

"Uh..." I said. "What's going on, Abrams? How did you even get Mia up here?"

"We're both part of your crew now, Captain Blake."

I frowned. "I didn't sign any such orders."

The truth was, I'd kind of hoped to ditch Abrams on Earth. He was a pain, and I knew he'd question everything I did up here on our maiden voyage with his ship. Devilfish was his baby, and I didn't want him whining about how I treated her.

"You've been overruled," Abrams said with a faintly smug expression. "Admiral Vega decided—"

"Okay," I said cutting him off. "I get it. You went right over my head and told him you had to be on the ship. But how did you get Mia up here?"

"I told you," she said, crossing her arms and glaring at the floor. "He's taken up with others. I've seen several young females walking about unattached, and we've only been on this ship for ten minutes."

"Mia," I said, "I haven't replaced you. Have a little faith."

"I do have faith—in the disloyal nature of males."

Abrams raised his skinny arms in exasperation. "You should be greeting one another as a mated pair! Don't fight! I brought Mia here to calm your nerves, Captain. This is going to be a very long trip. It's best that your libido is quenched right from the start."

"That's beyond presumptuous of you," I told him.

He shrugged. "I'm the chief technical officer on this ship. You represent the military side, while I represent the researchers. Long term deployment in space is an experiment, one among many. Social and psychological—"

"What station?" I demanded.

"What's that?"

"What post did you get her assigned to? I'm assuming you got Admiral Vega to assign her to *Devilfish* without my consent."

He cleared his throat. "That's essentially correct. She'll be rotated into the aft gunnery shifts. She can serve from anywhere aboard—even your chambers."

I looked around at the workstation in my quarters, which also served as my office. It was a strange design. Abrams had compressed functionality wherever he could, including here. I wasn't entirely sold on the idea.

"She'll serve on the bridge or in the gun operator's room. Not here."

He smiled and lifted his hands to display his palms. "It's up to you, Captain. It's *all* up to you."

"No, apparently it isn't. But I'll accept your interference in this case, if you'll promise to keep out of my private life."

"Naturally! I never wanted to impose."

"And," I said, "I want you to run ideas like this one through me first. I'm the captain of this ship. I can't serve with someone who undermines me."

"That was never my intent, but I will *of course* submit to your will."

I glared at him for a moment, knowing he was full of shit, then gestured for him to get out. He did so wordlessly.

Mia was pouting by this time. She'd assumed wrongly that all my anger had been due to her arrival.

"I should never have come here," she said. "I knew it was over when you vanished for days at a time. I knew—"

"Come here," I said, outstretching my arms.

She wandered over reluctantly.

Without warning, I reached around behind her, grabbed her tail and gave it a firm yank.

Her eyes widened in surprise. "Here?" she asked. "Now?"

"Yes."

She melted, and we were happy again. We made love like we hadn't done for months.

When it was over, I had to wonder if Dr. Abrams had known more about my mental state than I wanted to give him credit for.

The days flew by, and I worked from the moment my eyes opened until I couldn't keep them from sagging closed. I didn't even keep regular shifts. I worked all shifts, for as long as I could keep going effectively.

My XO, Commander Hagen, was usually the one to order me off the bridge. He had purposefully taken over the "night" shift, and he would tolerate my lingering for an extra hour or two. But finally, he requested a private word and demanded I go to bed.

Mia was likewise engaged, always trying to test me and fuss over my habits. Between the two of them, I felt like I hardly needed Dr. Abrams at all.

* * *

It was on the ninth day that everything changed.

75

Events unfolded rapidly, beginning with a horrible noise that rang off the metal walls in my quarters. My eyes snapped open, and I sought the source of it.

After a moment, I knew it to be a klaxon, one of those nasty ones that sounds like an air horn gone mad.

"Captain, please log in," an artificial and vaguely feminine voice said. "Captain, please log in."

The klaxon kept warbling, and I was up and scrambling for clothing. The clothes helped with this, wrapping me up and crawling over my skin. Less than a minute later I was stumbling into the hallway, forcing my service cap onto my head.

"Captain, please log in," the calm voice said again. It seemed to be following me.

"I'm on my way to the bridge!" I shouted at the walls. "I'll log in when I get there. I promise."

"Acknowledged."

The voice shut up, but the klaxons weren't so easily put off. When I reached the bridge, I found it overflowing with freaked-out officers.

One of them was Commander Hagen. "It's the AI, sir, it's gone ape. We've got nothing from Command. Nothing."

"Who's analyzing the sensor data?" I demanded.

I soon had a wealth of information blasted to my console. I ordered the computer to turn off the sirens, and it did so. With irritation, I realized I had to log into a console to get it to take commands from me.

"This ship isn't like *Hammerhead* at all," I said.

"No, it isn't," said a voice from behind me. "It's infinitely superior."

I turned to see Abrams standing there, looking down at me over his imperious nose.

"Get strapped in, Doc," I told him. "We might have to perform sudden maneuvers."

He did as I asked with poor grace.

"Now," I asked, "why is your computer demanding we all wake up and move to battle stations?"

He shrugged. "Why don't you ask her?"

"Ship?" I asked. "What's the reason for this alert?"

"Long range sensors indicate a tear in localized space-time."

"A rift is forming?" I asked. "Where?"

"The visual mapping data is already—"

"Zoom in for me. Show me the affected area."

The central display, which amounted to a lingering holograph in the center of the chamber, lit up. I could see a rift forming now, just as the computer had said. I didn't see anything around it other than empty space.

"Zoom out slowly. Give me a point of reference with enhanced imagery."

The names of constellations appeared in the background as the image zoomed out. At last, I could see Jupiter. Then, as it continued to expand the range of the image, Mars appeared. Our ship was in orbit over Mars, so a tiny sliver of green with the label *Devilfish* appeared there as well.

"Okay, give me a range estimate."

A staggering figure appeared.

"Sixty-one *million* kilometers?" I demanded. "That's hardly an emergency."

"Predictive calculations place the arriving ships within striking range of Earth in forty hours."

"Two days...? How long until we could make it back, if we shift to full burn to get home starting now?"

"Ninety-two hours."

I took a deep breath. "Great. We're out of range. Who the hell placed us out here at Mars? We can't even help—"

"Captain," Abrams said gently. "Are you satisfied with the ship's reasoning in waking you up? Or do you, perhaps, want to go back to bed?"

I flashed him an ugly stare. "No, Abrams. I get it, the ship is worried we can't get back home fast enough to aid in the defensive effort."

"Precisely so," Abrams said with an insufferably pleased expression on his face. He'd gladly let a billion souls die if it proved him right about something.

"Plot an intercept course," I ordered the AI.

Immediately, the charts shifted and the arcing curves connected our two ships, not at Earth, but in the middle of the ocean of nothing between Mars and our home planet.

"We can do it..." I said. "Just barely."

"We'd have no support, Captain," Commander Hagen pointed out.

I glanced at him. In a way, it was his first real moment as my XO. I didn't resent his input—but I hoped he wouldn't turn into a problem.

"Do you have a better option, XO?" I asked him.

"Hmm... Maybe. Can we jump to get there? Instead of using our standard drive?"

Abrams made that choking-cat sound again.

"No!" he said. "We can't do that. It's not—we're not designed for precision jumps."

Hagen and I both frowned at him. "Precision jumps?" I asked. "There's not much out there to run into between Earth and Mars, Abrams."

He shrugged and crossed his arms, grabbing his own knobby elbows with each hand.

"Regardless, I can't condone it. My star drive works, Blake—but the targeting isn't very exact."

"You mean we might scatter? Jumping about an AU, we'll scatter?"

He didn't meet my eye. "We might, yes."

"How many tests have we successfully performed on this drive of yours?"

"One hundred and seventy-three," he said.

"Well then, what—ah..." I broke off, catching on. "You're talking about simulated tests, aren't you? Computer models and all that?"

"Obviously," he snapped. "We only just assembled the ship over the last few months. How could we have performed live flight tests?"

I nodded slowly. I'd known the drive wasn't well-tested—but this was madness. For all I knew I was test-flying a stick of dynamite.

"Have we alerted Command yet?"

"Yes," Lieutenant Chang answered me, "but the round trip for a blip of light at this point is about ten minutes between the planets. We haven't gotten a response yet."

"We can wait another five minutes. They must be reviewing the same information we are."

Commander Hagen cleared his throat.

"Something to say, XO?" I asked him. "Speak up."

"If we want to make the choice ourselves, we have to do it now."

"Right... Dr. Abrams? Can you prep the star drive for a short hop? I think it would be good to know if we're a starship or a new kind of bomb."

He looked a little green at the suggestion, but he nodded and quickly left the bridge without word. I had the feeling we'd finally called his bluff.

Commander Hagen sidled closer after he'd gone. "Are you going to do it, sir?" he asked. "Are we jumping?"

"I'm waiting for Command to make that call. It did me good to see Abrams get sick over it, though. He always oversells his gizmos."

Hagen laughed uncertainly. He was new to my distinct brand of leadership.

Those among the bridge crew who were veterans on my bridge weren't laughing. They could remember the hard times—the days when they'd wished they'd never signed up with this newborn space navy.

I looked around at the bridge people, frowning. "Commander, except for Chang, I don't know anyone on your shift."

"Yes sir... sorry sir. I picked them from my own associations."

"Right, well, no offense, but if we're about to go into combat in an untested ship, I don't want to do it with a green crew. Get my people up here. I want Samson, Dalton and Mia."

Hagen didn't sputter or argue. I liked that. I simply began walking from station to station, contacting the replacement crewmen and tapping those who were being mothballed on the shoulders. They got up and left without so much as an angrily muttered curse.

"Very professional crewmen," I said. "I'll give them their shot the next time we fly this ship into battle—if there is a next time."

Hagen looked mollified. He greeted each newcomer from my old bridge crew and seated them personally. He made sure they knew how to operate their consoles—and he soon found that they did.

"Somehow I knew I'd end up dying on this bridge the moment I saw it," Dalton said cheerily. "Thanks for proving me right, Captain."

"My pleasure. Where's Samson?"

"He's probably lost himself in a bag of hammers somewhere."

About then Samson showed up. He looked wide-eyed at the consoles and the central depiction of our tactical position.

"How many of them are out there, Captain?" he asked.

"Just one ship so far. Looks like a carrier. We're still at long range, and Earth's sensor network isn't as good as we're used to in the Rebel Fleet."

"A carrier... we're not big enough."

"We're not going to attack alone, fool," Dalton told him. "The captain has a flotilla of phase-ships to back us up. Right, Captain?"

I eyed them both for second. "We'll see."

"Oh... it's like that, is it?" Dalton asked, shaking his head. "Is that a wet spot on your trousers, Samson? Already?"

Smiling, I shook my head at the two of them. It was hard to understand how they could remain friends. Samson took a daily ration of shit from Dalton whenever they served together, but he rarely got seriously mad about it. Now and then, he lost his mind with the smaller man's jabs, but I could hardly blame him for that. I tried to turn away whenever it happened and let them sort it out. They'd made a good, if non-traditional, team for years.

Mia arrived next. Her eyes were inhumanly big. That happened whenever she got excited. Most of the time, I think, she was bored with Earth. She'd seen little action since arriving. I'd gathered that on her homeworld of Ral, things were much more lively. Her people tended to get into physical fights and displayed emotional outbursts on a daily basis.

"This is fantastic," she told me. "How do I kill things?"

"Strap in, Ensign. You've been trained on these consoles, right?"

"Yes, of course. Extremely dull. All a simulated blasting of pixels—I want to kill something real. Something with blood inside."

"Right... well, you might get your chance today."

Mia took her spot and began testing her guns. She didn't fire them, but she swiveled the main batteries on manual control.

"Hold on," Commander Hagen protested in alarm. "Those are automatic. Gunners just choose targets on this ship."

"There's a manual override right here," Mia said. "I've selected it."

"Uh... I can see that. Captain, can you explain?"

"Mia, this isn't a fighter. These guns don't swing completely around."

"Why not?"

"The shock of the recoil would throw us off course. We have to fire along the centerline of the ship for the most part."

"That's no fun."

"If you hit something, you'll be happy," I told her. "Let the computer do the targeting. You select hit location priority, and range to fire. The numbers will move fast, giving you hit probabilities."

"I don't aim the guns?"

"Usually not," I admitted. "We'll be too far from the enemy. You won't be able to even see them. But, you won't fire unless I've given the all-clear anyway. At that point, select and wait for the guns to line up. See these crosshairs? The reticle will light up when—"

"Yes, yes," she said. "I went through the training... sir."

"Good."

I caught Commander Hagen shaking his head. I was sure he thought by now that his crew was a thousand times more disciplined and qualified to man these stations than my people were. Possibly, he was right.

But to my mind experience really counted out here in space. Things rarely went down in an orderly fashion. When the shit really hit the fan—well, that's when my ragtag group would show their true worth.

=15=

Command answered our queries eleven minutes after we'd transmitted everything we knew about this crisis to Earth. I was impressed by their promptness. They'd managed to formulate a plan in about ninety seconds, if my estimates were correct.

"Vega's people are on the ball," I said, skimming over a wall of text.

As we all reviewed the orders, however, I began to squint. Then Dalton produced a dirty chuckle.

"It's all on *you*, Captain!" he said. "Those cowards..."

I took in a deep breath. "As you can see, our orders are to deal with this emergency in deep space—on our own. We're not to allow any hostile force within ten million kilometers of Earth."

"Pretty big territorial waters," Commander Hagen muttered.

"Yes... well then, I'm taking this as good news."

Dalton, Mia and Samson craned their necks around from their seats to look at me. Their expressions ranged from confused on Samson's part to suspicion from Mia and outright mirth from Dalton.

"Good news? How so, Captain?" Hagen asked in confusion.

"If Earth Command thought this was a serious threat, they'd send in everything they had. Instead, they're only sending us. That's because—"

"Because we're expendable," Dalton complained. "Because they're holding our phase-ships in Earth orbit as a final line of defense."

Hagen blinked at him, then turned to me. "Do your crewmen often talk so disrespectfully, sir?"

"Not on this ship. Shut up, Dalton."

"Yes sir. Zipping my mouth tighter than Samson's balls."

"See that you keep it that way. This isn't a heavy fighter with a crew of five. We've got five *hundred* people aboard. Order will be maintained, or you'll be dismissed from the bridge."

He knew I meant it, so he clammed up. Hagen nodded to me approvingly.

"Helm," I said, "go to full burn following the intercept course we've laid out—and Hagen, send someone below to jolt Dr. Abrams out of his lair. I want him to double-check the AI's numbers by hand."

"Aye, Captain."

Within a few minutes, we felt the thrusters push us back in our seats. It wasn't oppressive, no more than half a G of force. But that was only because our inertial dampeners were operating. We didn't have a full anti-grav system working on this larger vessel, it would have consumed too much power. Even so, the stress that powerful engines could exert upon the human body was reduced. Our actual acceleration was several Gs, but we felt only a fraction of it.

A slow, tense fifteen minutes went by. At last, Hagen returned with Abrams in tow. I got the feeling that the old buzzard wasn't happy.

"Preposterous!" he complained. "I'm doing critical work, and this interruption is going to cost everyone aboard! There will be breakage, mark my words!"

I had no idea what he was carrying on about, but I assumed a patient expression.

"Good of you to return to the bridge, Doc," I said. "What do you think of the AI's numbers?"

He rudely grabbed the tablet from my hand and peered for a few moments.

He snorted. "They're perfect, of course."

"Well then—"

"—perfectly *wrong.*"

"What is the source of the error?" the ship's computer voice asked. She sounded a trifle annoyed to me, but I might have been humanizing the AI.

83

"The course projection fails to take into account an intelligent response on the part of the enemy vessel," Abrams said. "Once they see our plume and spot our ship, they'll apply more thrust. That will throw off these projections and bring them to Earth before we can intercept."

"Why would they do that?" Commander Hagen asked.

"Why wouldn't they?" Abrams asked. "If they're nothing but innocent diplomats, they'll want to slide past whatever band of pirates we might be. If, on the other hand, they intend to bomb Earth, they won't want to fight with us first. In short, I can't envision a situation where this ship will simply glide along without varying their—"

"Captain," Chang interrupted. "I'm getting new sensor data. The unknown ship is accelerating."

"There!" Abrams barked in triumph. "You see? Child's-play. You should take that new AI and jettison it for the good of us all. Its only value is to provide a false sense of safety."

The AI took this abuse without comment. My eyes slid from Hagen to Chang and back again. Both men were frowning and working numbers on their computers.

I looked back at Dr. Abrams, uncertain. The AI was one of the major elements of the ship's systems that he had not developed himself. That made him scornful of its operation, due to his twisted personality. But now I wasn't sure who to trust.

"What's the verdict?" I asked Chang and Hagen. "Is he right?"

"Yes..." Chang said first. "The invading ship's acceleration arc is clear. They'll reach Earth long before we can intercept them."

"How long?"

"We now have... twenty-nine hours."

I nodded. The game was heating up. I didn't even know who the other player was—I doubted it was Fex, as only one ship had arrived and it wasn't of any known Kwok configuration. But their moves so far seemed hostile. They also weren't communicating with us, ignoring all Earth's transmissions.

Even more ominous, they were racing us to see who could get to our planet first.

"Okay..." I said. "It's time for plan B. You're the heart of that plan, Abrams."

"Me? I'm washing my hands of this debacle. We can't reach them in time. We should—"

84

"We can intercept them... if we jump. We have to open a rift in local space. Use Sol as a beacon. It shouldn't break your mind or the AI's to do the math."

"It isn't that simple, Blake. This ship wasn't designed for short-range jumps."

I snorted. "What's the difference?"

"For one thing, the error rate will be doubled. We're sure to scatter. Possibly, we'll end up farther from this invader than we were when we started."

"I don't get that."

"You didn't get an A in theoretical physics, did you Captain?"

My mouth took on an angry twist. I didn't feel like telling him I'd never had that class in college. He was already insufferable enough.

"Just spit it out, Abrams, before I space you."

Samson raised his hand enthusiastically, clearly volunteering for the task.

Abrams took on the voice of an exasperated professor lecturing a marginal student. "Jumps are usually done relative to a beacon star, using the star's large gravity-well as an anchor. In this case, we'll have to use the same star for both ends of the wormhole. That means if we get any of the data wrong once..."

"Hmm," I said. "I see. A bad measurement will have double the effect."

"Exactly. Add to that the reality that Sol isn't really a good candidate as a beacon star, and you have a grim situation."

"I thought short jumps were safer than long ones."

He put up a single finger and wagged it at me. "In general, that's true. But not when we're attempting to jump across a single star system."

Right then, I came to a fateful decision. I had my orders. We were to intercept this ship at all costs.

"Very well then," I said. "We're going to do this another way."

"What, pray tell, is that?"

"We're jumping to Alpha Centauri—farther if you like. Then, we'll turn around and jump back. We'll place ourselves directly in their path."

Abrams sputtered. "That's madness!"

"Can it be done?"

He thought about it for a moment or two. "We'd have to wait on the far side for the initial rift to close naturally. Then, we'd have to charge our engine long enough to safely open another..."

"Yes, but we have twenty-nine hours. Can it be done, Doctor?"

A startled look came over his features. "Yes..." he said wonderingly. "I do believe it can be, Captain. But we may not survive any errors. We're close to large masses here—and the drive is not thoroughly tested."

"Then don't make any," I told him.

I could tell he was worried. I didn't blame him, as I knew he'd only used simulations and the like to test the drive. Fortunately, the rest of the crew was in the dark about that.

"It can be done..." he said, as if speaking to himself. He wasn't even looking at me, I suspected his eyes were focused on some far-off conceptual twist of mathematics.

"You have less than an hour to arrange the first jump," I told him. "It hardly matters if we scatter a little. The trick will be to return here close enough to intercept them."

Abrams shook his head, staring off into space. There was a slight glitter of madness in his eyes as he contemplated the whole thing.

"The return will be the hardest part..." he mused, "but we'll learn from the first jump. I can recalibrate—assuming we survive the first leg of the journey, of course."

"Get us out there and back, Abrams," I told him. "Make it happen. That's an order."

He wandered off below decks. I could tell he wasn't really hearing me. He was muttering to himself about calculations and probabilities.

When he'd left the bridge, Hagen came up to my station and stared after him.

"Do we really have to trust our lives to that mad hatter?"

"Unfortunately, yes," I said. "On the bright side, we've been doing it for weeks already. He designed most of this ship, you know."

"Why's he so strange?"

I glanced at my XO. "Aristotle said thousands of years ago that no great mind has ever existed without a touch of madness."

Commander Hagen laughed. "There goes your proof, sir."

"Exactly..."

My own mind was whirling. Could Abrams pull it off? Was this sort of situation the very reason he was tolerated by Space Command?

I hoped the answer to both questions was "yes".

=16=

The hours crawled by. There wasn't much we could do other than eat, pray and triple-check every system aboard. The drama was all being played out inside Dr. Abrams' elastic mind. He had support, of course: the ground work of the navigational teams, and the AI's number-crunching—but really, it was all up to him.

For the rest of us, the wait was excruciating. In more typical cases I'd been able to sleep through days like this one—but the stakes were too high now. I felt singled out at the top of a newer, larger pyramid. Just having a large ship with five hundred souls relying on me was stressful enough. To top that off, I'd handed over their fate to the whimsy of Abrams and his machines.

It was nearly sixteen hours later when we finally made the first jump. I'd been complaining steadily by then for six hours. Earth Command had been riding my ass, wanting to know how I was going to pull off this amazing intercept. They could see the situation. They could do the math.

But I hadn't told them anything. Not even in code. I'd assured them we were taking appropriate action and insisted they allow me to continue.

We all knew our systems were compromised. The Nomads, the Imperials, Fex and his gang—anyone might be listening to our transmissions in space. Sure, you could use a focused, narrow beam from ship to satellite. You could also encode it all. But there was always a lingering doubt about the effectiveness of such measures. Godwin, for example, had ignored them many times.

For that reason, I believed, Earth never ordered me to reveal my plans. They were going crazy wanting to know what I was up to, but they accepted that I needed an element of surprise to pull it off. Admiral Vega, I imagined, had to be tearing up his desk down there in Colorado.

Finally, at the end of the sixth hour, Abrams came to me. His eyes were shot with red and they glistened with insanity.

"I've done it," he said. "I can get us out there."

"And back?" I asked.

"Maybe. We'll have to make the first jump to know for sure."

"Do it. Right away. I don't want to have a meeting or even think—"

"It's already done," he said.

"What?"

"We're in the countdown now. I assumed your permission had been given in advance, and since time is of the essence—"

"Fine," I said. "Let's go to the bridge and ride it out."

By the time we got there, the rift was already opening in front of *Devilfish*. We nosed toward it, and everyone aboard gasped to see the spiraling lights.

"Get strapped in," I ordered. "Samson, sound the alarm."

The klaxons began to howl all over the ship. The wailing sounds echoed down every metallic passageway, and no one could have missed what was coming.

Still, it seemed to take a long time. The rift got bigger. It was slightly ovoid in shape, rather than perfectly circular. I had no idea why, and didn't feel like enduring Abrams' scorn if I admitted any kind of ignorance.

The minutes turned into seconds, and at last, we merged with the rift.

The ride through hyperspace was brief, but bumpy. We soon slid out the far side, with every crewman aboard complaining about the experience.

"Oh, spare me," Abrams said. "Can your crew be so spoiled? They want humanity's first rift to not only deliver them to Heaven's Gate, they don't want to experience any jiggling along the way."

"They're just scared," I told him.

"They should have a little faith," Abrams sniffed.

89

We arrived at last. I looked at the incoming data pouring from the sensors. Stars were being painted pixel-by-pixel—but the stars were wrong. All wrong.

"We've scattered!" I said.

"That's impossible!" Abrams replied.

I walked over to him, and it was all I could do not to grab him and shake him.

"That's not Alpha-Centauri out there. It's not even a tri-star system."

He looked worried, but he was putting on a good front. "Allow me to work in peace, please," he huffed.

"I did that the last time—for six hours. You brought us here—wherever here is!"

He lowered his tablet and glared at me. "You forced me to jump before I was fully ready."

"I didn't force you to do anything."

"You ordered me to intercept that ship. We had to jump now in order to complete the operation."

Taking a deep breath, I looked around the scenery. "Where are we, *Devilfish*?"

The ship's AI didn't answer for nearly ten seconds. Dalton slapped the side of his console. "Has this thing locked up?"

But then, the AI came back. "Cygnus beacon star identified. Ninety-nine percent probability achieved."

We all swept our eyes to the central holo-projection, which zoomed out with sickening speed. We now saw our location in green, and Earth's in blue. A yellow line interconnected them.

"We're approximately three thousand seven hundred lightyears from Earth," the ship said calmly, "significantly outside the galactic mainstream of stars."

"Three thousand..." I breathed. "Abrams?"

I turned to him, but for once he was speechless. His face was slack, his mouth open, his skin drained of color. He stared at the map in abject horror.

The arms of the Milky Way were clearly visible in the image. We were so far out, you could see much of it on the map. After all, our entire galaxy was only about a hundred thousand lightyears across.

"*Abrams!*" I roared at him.

Still, he did not respond. He stared in shock.

"What do we do?" Commander Hagen asked. "Sir, the rift we came through is already fading."

"Go back through," I said. "Turn around, helm, and go back through. With luck, we'll get home."

Dalton spun the ship, and he applied full braking thrust. We'd been moving at a good clip, and it took nearly twenty minutes to turn around and get back to the rift. By then, it had dimmed and was beginning to fade away.

"Are we going to risk it, Captain?" Dalton asked me. "A decaying rift... We might not make it out again."

"We're clearly not going to get home with an easy jump. We're out in the middle of fucking nowhere—literally. Do it."

We plunged into the rift again, and as the swirl of darkening colors closed over us once again, everyone's heart was pounding.

=17=

The maiden hyper-jump ended with a small success. We were right back where we started, and no one had died. That put it in the category of a sub-disaster, and I kept up a tight smile no matter what I was thinking on the inside.

No one spoke for a time. They simply verified we were in our home star system and groaned aloud with relief.

"What *happened* out there?" Abrams croaked at last.

"We scattered, Doc," I said. "We went out to Neverland, but we managed to get back in one piece."

"Scattered...? Impossible. Not to such a degree. The AI—it must be compromised." He turned to me, his eyes bloodshot and bulging. His voice lowered to a paranoid whisper. "Is that Nomad creature of yours aboard? Could he have done this?"

I would have laughed, but I could tell he was serious.

"Doc," I said gently, "we scattered—badly. But we all lived. We got back home in one piece. Even Kher ships scatter now and then. They've been working these navigational problems for a thousand years, and they still make mistakes. It's acceptable to screw up your first time out."

"I made no mistake!" he shouted.

Furious, he stormed off the bridge. Dalton's mocking laughter followed him. It was a cackle, really. Dalton was gifted when it came to producing an irritating sound of mirth.

"What an insufferable wanker..." he muttered after Abrams disappeared.

I didn't admonish Dalton. He was more than correct.

Commander Hagen came to stand near my station. My smile was still pasted in place, but I was lost in thought.

"I don't know if we have enough time for a second attempt," he said. "But even if we do, I'd advise against trying it."

I glanced at him, then back at the maps. They depicted Sol, and our local planets. Two triangles of different colors raced together on converging courses. One was our ship, the other belonged to the invader. The only trouble was, the invader was going to reach Earth before we could reach them.

"We lost all our momentum with that jaunt into the blue," I said. "Even if we hadn't, we still couldn't have caught them. I'm thinking we have to try the two-jump strategy again."

Commander Hagen looked pained. "You think Abrams can get the numbers right this time?"

"Maybe. If we get lucky twice, we can still do it."

Hagen leaned closer. "I'm with you, Captain, but it's a long shot. *Two* long-shots. I mean, if he does a dramatically better job, he might get us to Alpha Centauri then pop us back home just beyond the orbit of Pluto."

I nodded, unable to deny the charge. "Really, I should have expected this."

"How so, Captain?"

"I'm accepting the truth as I review the situation. This ship is experimental. She needs months of shakedown cruises, testing and recalibration. Abrams isn't really to blame. Our technology is all new, and he's had no time to work out the kinks. It's really not fair to expect perfection."

"Yeah..." Hagen said, thinking it over. "When you put it that way, I see your point. It's amazing this ship hasn't sprung a leak and killed us all."

"The day is still young, Commander."

A dismal half-hour passed. We heard nothing from Abrams. Sighing, I got up from my command chair, intending to go down to his lab personally and pep-talk him. Mostly, I'd been feeling out the odds we'd have time to take another stab at it.

But I never made it to the hatch.

"Sir?" Chang said suddenly.

Something in his voice made me turn around and move to his station. Chang was an unflappable guy. He didn't sound concerned unless there was a damned good reason.

He sounded worried now.

"Sir...look at this, Captain."

He made a sweeping gesture that caused his console interface to throw his current view up to the central holo-projection system. Everyone on the bridge turned to look at what he was displaying publicly.

It wasn't an image of stars or rifts. Instead, it was a streak of moving light. As I watched, the light went from being a straight line to a gently arcing curve.

"Is that what I think it is?" Commander Hagen asked.

"That's right," Chang said. "It's the ship we're trying to intercept—she's changing course."

"Plot it," I said, "project it!"

"It's still changing, sir."

"AI," I said loudly. "Put up a predictive arc. Shade the possible course variations yellow."

"Unable to comply."

"Why not?"

"The vessel in question could go anywhere."

I rolled my eyes. "Assume it's made ninety percent of its course change. Project on that basis. Assume it will only change course on one axis—the one it's shifting on now."

The imagery shimmered and fuzzed. After a few seconds, it came back. A swath of yellow shot out like a widening ray between the orbital paths of Mars and Earth.

"We're inside that region, Captain," Commander Hagen said.

"That's right. We're right in the middle of it." Slowly, I began to smile. "Gentlemen, we've been given a gift. The enemy has taken interest in our activities. Maybe they're wondering why we opened a rift, went through it, then came back. Maybe they want to know if Earth has such technology, or if we're from somewhere else. In short, we've made them curious about us."

Dalton laughed. "Curiosity will kill this cat," he said with certainty.

Mia growled a little at that.

I wasn't so sure we would win the coming encounter, but I was certain of one thing: we were going to intercept the vessel after all. For good or for worse, the encounter was going to happen.

=18=

L ess than twenty minutes later, as our two ships drove toward one another on a definite intercept course, the game changed again.

"Captain? Earth Command is calling us."

"Let's hear it."

Honestly, I expected to hear a marveling message. One full of praise at our cleverness. They had to be watching, and they'd seen our two ships turn together and converge.

I was proud of that. We'd not only managed to get the interloper onto an intercept course, we'd also delayed its arrival at Earth. If nothing else, even if we'd failed to stop the invader, we'd given Earth more time to prepare her defenses.

But the message was entirely devoid of praise. It was voice-only, and it spoke with the familiar tones of Admiral Vega.

"Captain Blake," he said, "what are you doing? The enemy is no longer heading for Earth. Don't try to take it on alone if you don't have to. Let them chase you around a little. *Devilfish* is the only starship we have—don't lose it in a blaze glory!"

"Talk about ingratitude," Dalton complained.

"Yes... it's more than that, though. Commander Hagen? What do you think?"

"Me sir?"

"Tactical analysis, please."

He looked at the charts and squinted. He shook his head.

"I don't like the idea of breaking off now. That ship could just as easily turn back toward Earth. We couldn't catch her if she did so now—but that window is closing. Soon, we'll be able to force the encounter by altering our course to match them."

"Right," I said. "Get the navigational team on it. We'll drive straight toward them until they can't escape, then turn away to delay matters."

Commander Hagen shook his head and tapped at his screens.

I frowned. I trusted his judgment. Over his career, I'd been told that he'd been an accomplished navigator and tactician.

"What's wrong?" I asked him.

"Too many unknowns. We know how fast they can go, but we don't know if we've seen their best speed yet. If they turn away and accelerate... they could still slip past us."

Blinking, I considered what he was saying. Chang and the navigational team worked the projections with the help of the AI. It bore out. We couldn't be certain the plan would succeed.

There were other issues bothering me as well. Psychological ones.

"I know the Rebel Kher," I told them. "Hell, I know the Imperials pretty well, too. They aren't robots. If anything, they're more emotionally driven than we are. They might turn away just *because* they realize we're toying with them."

"No captain from my planet would accept such an insult," Mia said, confirming my statement. "They'd turn away in disgust, considering your cowardly ship to be without honor, and therefore with no value as a kill."

"Not worth any status points..." I said thoughtfully. "Hagen, formulate a message to Vega explaining our concerns. Let him know why we're not breaking off—yet."

"Me, sir?"

"I think he likes you better than he likes me."

Commander Hagen looked baffled at that, but he was too good of an officer, too accustomed to following commands, to argue with me about it.

Twenty quiet minutes here followed before Vega's response came in. It took that long for the radio message to reach Earth and his response to make the round trip.

Wisely, I took the message privately this time.

"Blake, I appreciate your concerns. But we have concerns of our own. Turn away from that ship! Drive a parallel course and see what he does. You can always correct if things go wrong—that's an order!"

That last part was the thing I'd been hoping not to hear. I was stuck now.

We changed our course, and we waited tensely to see what the enemy ship did. It took a few minutes—then we saw what I'd feared. They turned too, going back to their initial trajectory. They were now heading straight toward Earth again.

"Speed?" I demanded. "Timing? Will they beat us home?"

"Calculating..." Chang said.

It was then that Abrams made a fresh appearance on the command deck. He looked wilder than he had before—even less sane than usual.

"Blake? Why are you dodging and weaving my ship all over the cosmos?" he demanded.

"We've been ordered to break off by Earth Command."

He looked at me with a mad stare for a time. His mind was racing through all the ramifications.

"Good," he said at last. "Vega is an idiot—but I approve."

He did an about face and went below again.

I frowned after him in irritation. He knew the Kher would probably evade as well. Either calling our bluff or deciding we weren't worth it. Either way, this ship would survive another day.

That didn't sit right with me, however.

"Come about again," I ordered. "Helm, return to our original course."

"But sir... that won't intercept them anymore. They're on a new heading."

"I know that! Make the change."

They did so, and the navigational people shook their heads, muttering. The ship was run by a pack of madmen, as far as they were concerned. I couldn't argue against them, so I didn't try. I just watched and waited.

Ten tense minutes passed. I knew Vega had probably already sent off a barrage of complaints, but I intended to fully enjoy the grace-period before they reached my ears.

Before Vega's first squawk of complaint rolled into my inbox, the tactical situation shifted again.

"They've shifted course again," Chang said. There was a hint of a marveling tone in his voice. "We're going to intercept them again."

I nodded, and I couldn't help letting a smug smile appear on my lips.

"Captain?" Hagen asked me privately a few minutes later. "Why did that happen?"

"They're Kher," I said simply. "Most breeds can't back down from a challenge. They saw us return to our exact same course. That meant that if they didn't match us, they were now the cowards, not us."

He mulled that over for a few minutes. "So... you're saying we're out here in space playing an elaborate game of chicken with these aliens?"

"Yes. That's a pretty good analogy. The Kher would like that game—but they might all slam into one another and die every time they played."

Bemused, Hagen wandered off and went back to his station. He had a lot to learn about our rivals, but I had high hopes for him.

=19=

The following day, we approached the intercept point. Admiral Vega had given up on trying to get me to turn away—various xenopsychologists had managed to convince him I was playing it right.

The trouble was cultural, as always. When two peoples—much less two distantly related species—met one another for the first time, there were invariably misunderstandings. Sometimes, these misunderstanding ended in disaster for one side or both. Any number of explorers and missionaries who had ended their existence in stew-pots or propped up on spear points could attest to that.

"We really should study our own history more," Commander Hagen told me as we approached the point of no return—we were close to it now.

"How so?" I asked him.

"I'm sure there are valid parallels," he said. "How to greet native populations—people with widely varied societal norms."

"We have people to study such things in Space Command," I told him. "The trouble is, we've moved forward so fast, and with an understandable sense of paranoia, we haven't been able to let them have the room they need to learn."

He nodded slowly. "The stakes are always too high. We're talking extinction, not a clash with swords on a beach."

"Exactly. This time out, I think we're playing it well."

"Why haven't we attempted to contact the other ship directly?" he asked me. "All the transmissions have come from Earth."

"That's how I wanted it. We're building up curiosity. Mystique."

"Really? Seriously? That's your plan?"

"Part of it. Remember, the Rebel Kher aren't human. They're similar to humans, not totally alien, but then so is the behavior of a gorilla or a killer whale when compared to a microbe. We're in their territory out here and—"

"Hold on, sir," Samson said, turning his harness around in my direction. "This is *our* star system. Our territory. Don't they know that?"

"No," I said firmly. "At least, the Kher don't accept it. They ruled here until recently, even in the light of our own Sun. Remember how they came to Earth and plucked us up like animals? We have to earn their respect."

He turned back to his console thoughtfully.

"What's our next move then, Captain?" Hagen asked.

"When we get to a range of ten million kilometers, I'm going to open a dialog."

"What if they don't respond?"

"They will," I assured him.

We waited another half hour, and we crossed the line I'd mentioned. It was significant, because our longest range weapons could be detected at that distance. They weren't effective, of course, but a nearby ship could actually see we'd fired them.

"Open forward gun ports," I ordered.

Mia made an odd sound of excitement. She laid her quick hands on her console and did as I'd ordered.

"Aim our weapons to the starboard of the enemy ship. Fire a single shell."

She frowned and turned to look at me. "You want me to miss?"

"I want you to miss precisely. I want you to miss their flank by one kilometer. Then, ten seconds later, do it again."

"Miss again?" she asked in disappointment.

"Exactly."

"What's—"

"Are you able to follow the order, Ensign?" I asked her.

She stiffened and looked angry. "Of course!"

A burst of fire leapt out from our ship. On the tracking charts, the gauss-accelerated shell moved with shocking speed. It looked like it was right on target—and for just a wincing moment, I thought Mia had nailed the enemy amidships.

100

Surprised, they took evasive action, rolling to one side away from the projectile. As the shell was moving at several million kilometers an hour, the second shot had to be fired even as the first went past.

Mia didn't hesitate. She never did when killing was involved. She was, after all, a pure predator. Humans were gun-shy in comparison to her people.

The second shell was on a direct course for the ship. I could see that—everyone could.

"I didn't tell you to ram it right down their throats!" I told her.

"You told me to put it a kilometer off their flank—but they're moving!"

She had me. I'd been unclear. I'd meant to put the second round exactly where the first one had been. The idea had been to prove to the approaching ship we'd missed the first time on purpose. That was supposed to be an opener to possible negotiations.

Instead, she'd tracked and gotten in the second shot closer than the first had been. What kind of message was that?

Simple: we were trying to destroy them at long range.

The trouble was at this distance they would have time to dodge. We had to get closer to actually nail them. They knew that—and they knew it even more clearly after we'd demonstrated our primary offensive power.

Taking a deep breath, I decided to go with my next move anyway.

"Open a hailing channel," I ordered Chang, "and Mia, stop firing. I can see you prepping the next round."

She flopped back in her seat, arms crossed in disgust.

"Channel open—they're listening, but so far, they've never responded."

"To the unknown ship in our territorial space. This is Captain Blake of the Starship *Devilfish*. We wish to greet you and warn you at the—"

That was as far as I got. The central holoprojector lit up. They were responding.

Dalton turned to Samson with a grin. "See? The captain could train a dog to talk."

The image that swam into view, however, caused us all to suck in a breath.

I knew the face well, or at least, the type of face. I'd dealt with this particular branch of the Kher family on a number of occasions. Virtually all those encounters had been negative in nature.

"Captain Blake?" the Terrapinian asked. "Captain Leo Blake? From the Rebel Fleet?"

"The same," I said, staring at the leathery face. "Do I know you?"

Members of the Terrapinian species had a mottled look to their skins. They were lumpy and greenish, often with hints of gray. The skin was hairless and tended to wrinkle at every joint. Their big skulls were wedge-shaped and decidedly reptilian.

This individual looked older than most. His eyes were like black shiny marbles, and they regarded me with intelligence.

"You do not," he said, "but I know of you. I am Captain Verr. Why do you attempt to destroy us, then try to contact us a moment later? Is this a primate trick?"

"No," I said, "helm, slow down and come about. I suggest you do the same, Captain Verr."

"Cowardice?" Verr questioned. "You missed, and now you have second thoughts?"

"We didn't miss," I told him firmly. "We fired to warn you."

"Absurd behavior... but not implausible, considering the source."

"Will you break off and talk first?" I asked. "We can always honorably destroy one another afterward."

He stared at me distrustfully. We were slewing to one side, but he was plowing directly into our flank.

"It could be a tactic, Captain," Commander Hagen's voice buzzed to me privately through my sym. "He's edging closer to get into range."

"Three more seconds," I said, "and we must fire again."

The Terrapinian waited for two of them before leaning forward.

"Very well. We accept your invitation. As the challenged, we demand you come to our circle."

The connection broke, and everyone blinked in confusion at the abrupt end of the conversation.

"What did he mean?" Commander Hagen demanded. "We could blast him now, sir. We're still pretty far out. We might get a hit, and he seems to be out of range. They're using particle beams that diffuse to ineffectiveness at this distance."

"What's he doing?"

We watched as the projections showed the enemy ship's path. It had turned, as we had, and now we were both braking and veering off.

"He's opening a side hatch—a big one. It's either a weapon the size of an office building, or it's his main hold."

We zoomed in to watch the alien ship in fascination. We were close enough now to get excellent optics. They were still wavering, but you could make out a dark square on the enemy ship.

"What's the enemy vessel's estimated mass?" I asked.

"About four times ours. It's either a heavy cruiser or a small battleship—call it a battlecruiser."

"Right... she outclasses us. We outrange her, but she's already proven she has more speed. If she gets in close enough, we'll be destroyed for sure."

"So... we stand off and destroy her at a safe distance?" Hagen asked hopefully.

"No... we honor our invitation."

"What invitation?"

"Didn't you hear? I said we should break off hostilities and talk first. He took this as an invitation, and he's clearly accepted it."

Hagen squinted at me, not getting it. "But he's not talking. He cut off the channel."

"Right, but then he opened his main hold door. Now, if I'm right, we'll see him brake to a stop soon. We should do the same."

"Excuse me, Captain, but what the hell for?"

"Because we're going to go aboard their ship, that's why. The Terrapinians prefer to discuss things in person."

Commander Hagen's jaw sagged open and stayed there. He turned to look at the alien ship, which was still braking hard. We were doing the same now, as I'd directed Dalton to match their moves.

"This is a little gunboat diplomacy," I told Hagen. "You'll get used to it—if we don't all die first."

I gave him a grin which he didn't return.

=20=

Once we were fully stopped, I suited-up and launched a small pinnace toward the Terrapinian ship. I felt relatively relaxed in the cockpit. Commander Hagen, on the other hand, seemed agitated.

"Sir, I'm not comprehending this at all," he said via radio. "As your second in command, I understand why you left me in charge of *Devilfish*—but why go yourself? We have five hundred personnel aboard, any one of whom might have been volunteered for this duty."

"Not possible," I told him. "That would amount to an insult. Captain Verr and I spoke as equals and struck a deal. Any tricks would be seen in the worst light."

"Tricks? Sending a team of xenologists would be a trick?"

"Definitely. Kher society is highly status and honor-driven. Even the Imperial types can be shamed into following an honorable code of behavior. Let me remind you, Commander, that without honor in space, there can be nothing but violent death. It's a harsh place, and for any kind of diplomacy to exist, both sides must adhere to some basic rules. People are required to keep their word, for example. These traditions have evolved over thousands of years among the Kher due to necessity."

"Yeah... I get all that... but what do I do if you get into trouble? What if they kidnap you and hold you hostage?"

"They won't," I said firmly, "but if something like that did happen, you should do your best to destroy their ship with me inside it. They won't understand or expect anything less."

"Great... Is that all, sir?"

"Blake out."

Beside me, a hulking figure laughed quietly. It was Samson. He'd been my ace-in-the-hole before, and I thought he might serve in that capacity again today.

"Why am I coming along this time, Captain? Is it the usual? To play the part of your champion? To serve up honor with my fists?"

"If necessary," I said, "but they might not try to duel with us."

Samson shrugged and cracked his large knuckles. They popped loudly as he did so. "I kinda hope they do. It's been boring on Earth for the last year."

The Terrapinian ship loomed in our screens, then in our thick windows. Their main hold was still open, yawning like a mouth ready to swallow our smaller ship. Ice crystals grew over the rim of the windows as I watched.

"They must be venting a little," I said. "Do you think Mia caught them with one of her shots?"

Samson shrugged. "That wasn't what the sensors indicated at the time. Maybe they dodged so violently they sprung a leak."

Unable to determine the facts with the limited sensor array on the pinnace, I stopped trying. Scanning their ship too much at this point would seem rude to our hosts, anyway.

A few moments later, we plunged into the hold. It was dark inside—totally dark. This was unusual, as normally Kher ships were well illuminated.

"I don't like this," Samson complained.

"We're here, so don't show any fear. Walk tall, move with confidence. We can't let them know we're cowed if this is some kind of intimidation technique."

"If it is, it's working..." Samson muttered.

We landed the ship using our own lights. The interior of the hold was iced over with crystals on the deck, further evidence of venting. Escaped gases and water vapor had come in here from the exterior hull and frozen over into a crunchy, frosted surface.

The hold doors closed behind us, but no one came out to approach the ship.

"Let's go," I told Samson, putting on my helmet and checking the seals. "I'm not sitting here in the dark waiting around."

He followed me down the folding steps. We were met with mild gravity, just enough to allow easy movement, but no air. The frozen deck glittered like diamonds under the stabbing beams of our suit lights.

Finally, figures approached. There was an entire delegation of them. The Terrapinians were covered in thick suits. They hailed us only when they were standing right in front of me.

"Rebel Kher," the leader said, "you are permitted aboard our ship. Do no harm, and no harm will come to you from our captain."

I detected a loophole in that statement. It might just be a matter of custom, or a matter of translation error, but I felt I had to ask as we crunched over the frost toward an open passageway.

"Crewman," I said, as he'd never identified himself. "Are we guaranteed safety from all Terrapinians aboard this ship? Or only the captain himself?"

He stopped plodding along, and all of our escorts turned to look at me strangely.

"There is never a guarantee of safety among the Kher," he said. "Any real member of our alliance would know that. Are you truly Leo Blake, or another ape standing in his place? It is difficult for me to distinguish individuals among you."

"You all look like turtles who lost your shells to us, too," Samson retorted angrily.

I silenced him with a raised hand. "I am Leo Blake. I asked only for clarification of your statement. We are ready—proceed."

They kept marching, and we kept following. It wasn't until we reached the open passageway that I realized something was wrong.

I'd accepted that the hold was frozen and airless, and that there was some evidence of venting. But the passageway led into the heart of the ship. It too, was covered in ice. The doorway could barely be shut, having to grind and force its way through a thick layer of growing frost.

"Is your ship damaged, crewman?" I asked.

"Of course," he said. "Why else would we have come to such a lowly star system for help?"

I blinked twice, but I didn't say anything. The situation had taken a drastic turn—and I thought it was for the better.

Samson trudged with me, and he followed my lead by not talking about what he'd heard. His eyes were big, however, and he gave me a shrug of confusion when I glanced at him.

I could hardly blame him. We had countless unanswered questions. Sticking to my stoic strategy, I said nothing, and I avoided acting excited and concerned.

After all, if the Terrapinians were calm about the dying state of their life support system, who was I to panic?

=21=

We were led to a large, open chamber where another group of Terrapinians awaited us. To get into the room, we had to go through a makeshift airlock. I was grateful, however, to find the region pressurized and heated. I took off my helmet in relief, as did Samson and the Terrapinians.

"This is *not* a surrender," Captain Verr told us sternly. "It is not a plea for aid. It is an offer of comradeship."

"I get it," I said, smiling.

Samson was smiling too. We'd both come aboard thinking we'd have to fight our way out of some kind of situation, but we'd thought wrong. The Terrapinians were in a bad way, and they needed our help.

"Do you, then," Verr asked, "accept our offer of aid and protection? In return, we'll expect the same of your people. Your ships will be of great service helping us, and we'll do the same for you."

As he spoke, my smile faltered. A request for emergency assistance was one thing. A full-blown alliance that dragged Earth into whatever conflict they were involved in sounded dangerous.

"Well..." I began thoughtfully. "There are several problems with what you suggest. First off, I don't have the authority to commit Earth to an alliance. I'm just one ship's captain, I'm not a king."

Captain Verr was disappointed, but any human would be hard pressed to tell that from his expression. The only emotion I could read on their leathery faces was anger. He wasn't looking pissed off now, but he didn't look happy, either.

"So, you refuse my offer?"

"Let's keep talking, exchanging information before we get to any final decisions. There's so much we don't know about your people's political status."

Verr shifted in his chair. The furniture we were crouching on was really more like small slings or hammocks supported by some steel tubing than anything we'd call comfortable, but then, the reptilian Kher weren't known for cushy decor.

"I see," he said. "You wish to spy more completely before you refuse aid. Very clever—I would expect nothing less from a primate."

"You insult us?" I asked. "You ask for aid, then you spit on those who are considering it?"

This line caught him by surprise. He froze and thought about it for a moment.

"I will offer an explanation. We have been caught up in a struggle for dominance since the end of the last Imperial incursion."

"Did someone come to your star system and offer to 'protect' you by making you a vassal state?"

Again, the alien looked surprised.

"Yes," he said. "Has Admiral Fex come here too?"

"He has."

Captain Verr stood up suddenly. He reached for his sidearm, and Samson did the same. My hand snapped out to stop Samson from drawing his weapon.

"Hold on," I said to Verr. "Why are you upset?"

"I did not understand the situation until now," Verr said, his thick fingers caressing his weapon. He obviously wanted to pull it out and shoot us. "I now understand why your technology has advanced so quickly—you sold out to the Kwok, didn't you?"

"No," I said firmly. "We drove him away. In fact, the reason my ship came out here to intercept you was because I thought your ship was in the service of Admiral Fex. I assumed you were working for him."

Captain Verr mulled that over. At last, his lumpy fingers slid away from his weapon. "My apologies. It seems we have both made the same miscalculation. Your aggressive behavior makes more sense in this light—you were moving to defend your planet."

"That's right. We didn't consider ourselves to be the aggressor. We assumed you were."

Verr made a burbling sound. I took this to mean he was thinking hard.

"That brings us back to the topic of an alliance. We have the same foe already. Why would you refuse any offer of aid?"

"I have to explain all this to our political leaders," I told him, "but I think they might want to commit to an alliance. We're already at war with Fex. It's only a matter of time until he returns."

"What you say is true. But I find it disturbing you do not fully command your own ship. Among my people, a ship's captain has independence. Others surrendered to Fex. Some refused. Most of those ships were destroyed, but some, like mine, escaped into a rift."

"I see," I said, and I did see. Long ago, a Terrapinian leader had declared himself to be my vassal. That relationship had lasted for years.

These people weren't a single political entity. They were a loose feudal association. A given leader might owe allegiance to another, until he saw fit to shift that allegiance.

"Who do you owe loyalty to now?" I asked him.

"None," he said sadly. "I am alone."

"What kind of damage has your ship sustained?"

"We have weaponry, but we don't have the power to operate much of it. The hull leaks from several locations, and we've given up worrying about pressurizing the interior. We're living in suits, looking for help."

"I say again, Earth can render that help. But that doesn't mean we'll fight your wars for you."

"Tell me, Captain Blake, if Fex arrived here right now, would you fight his fleet?"

"Yes," I said firmly.

"We would do the same. You see? We are allies already, in his eyes."

I nodded, getting his point. We were all on the menu. Fex meant to subjugate the local minor powers, one way or another.

"Then this will not be difficult," I said. "Let's review the damage to your ship—if you don't mind. Let me assess how hard it will be to effect repairs."

He studied me for a moment before responding. "Or, you may be determining how best to destroy my vessel. To finish off a wounded opponent."

110

"That would make no sense. Earth has more than this one ship of mine. We could destroy you—I knew that right away. Fex and his fleet—they're the real problem."

Captain Verr agreed, and we began a tour. The situation was grim, but not terminal. The ship could fly with speed, but didn't have the power available to support both weapons and maneuverability.

The Terrapinians seemed to have prioritized their engines first, which made sense since they were on the run. Their secondary efforts had gone into weaponry, and they had a fair arsenal available to them. If they'd been whole, they could probably defeat *Devilfish* in a fair fight.

But, they had major power problems and enough holes in their hull that were leaking gases to cripple them. They basically had no life support other than their suits, and without more power and supplies, they probably could never fix the ship completely.

"They really do need our help, Captain," Samson told me on a private link.

"I know. They're in a bad way."

Samson's specialty was support systems. He'd put in years of service repairing oxygen recyclers, carbon dioxide scrubbers and a dozen other critical systems that kept a crew alive. I trusted his judgment on the topic more than my own assessment—which nearly matched his.

"Captain Verr," I said about an hour later. "I think we can help, but we'll have to take your ship to an orbital station at Mars."

"Agreed. We can't do it out here in space. We need mass, liquids, gasses... but there is something else we must sort out first."

"What is that?"

"Dominance."

I was surprised, but not too surprised, by his statement. I'd struggled with a Terrapinian leader back in my early days in the Rebel Fleet. We'd both been nothing more than two pilots driving heavy fighters back then. After many attempts on his part to beat us, the leader and his crew had accepted we were better fighters.

Then, an odd thing had happened. Most humans would have wandered off, angry but cowed. They'd probably live quietly at a respectful distance, always resentful but never daring to challenge their old enemies again.

That wasn't how the Terrapinians did things. Instead, they'd sworn allegiance to me—personally. They'd given me their loyalty and helped on a few occasions where it was critical.

Such a decision is what was on Captain Verr's mind. One of us had to be the master, one of us the follower. There could be no mutually beneficial trading of aid or goods. The Terrapinians didn't comprehend the concept of interacting as equals.

"I understand," I said evenly.

"Good. Not all primates comprehend the requirements of dominance. Unfortunately, I'm of great age. In Earth years, I'm over four hundred cycles old. I may, therefore, be forced to select a champion."

Again, I nodded evenly. None of what he was talking about phased me.

"Acceptable, if not optimal," I said. "I've also brought along a champion to decide this matter."

With a gesture, I indicated Samson.

For nearly the first time since we'd arrived, Captain Verr studied Samson.

"I understand now why you brought this servant. I'd been wondering if he was to be a gift of some kind—instead, you've wisely brought him along as a weapon. Already, I see why you have a reputation for great cunning."

This was all news to me, but I did my best to keep a poker face. Samson squirmed at being called a servant, and his eyes narrowed in anger.

"There it is!" Captain Verr continued. "A feral appearance on his face. He's building up his courage to fight. I'm impressed again."'

"Listen up, turtle-man—" Samson began, but I shook my head.

Samson stopped talking, but he continued to glower and curse under his breath.

Captain Verr turned to me. "I see I underestimated you again. You brought a champion, one who is no doubt your best human warrior. I will take the only possible route to advantage left to me—I will battle with you personally."

"At your age?" I asked.

He made a snorting sound. "I'm not so old I can't bring down a monkey."

"All right then. It's on. Where, when, and how?"

"Right now. No weapons. No preparation—"

He was going to keep talking, I could tell, but I'd already taken a step forward and landed a hard right on his thick jaw.

His inky-black eyes flared in surprise, but he didn't fall.

The fight was on.

=22=

Sucker punches aren't illegal in duels among the Rebel Kher. In fact, they're practically expected. So, when I laid a gloved fist on Captain Verr, rudely interrupting his speech, he was annoyed, but he wasn't scandalized.

His crewmen had circled around us by then. There was a general hiss of displeasure from the crowd. But when he came at me, arms out as if to bear-hug me, they thumped their feet in slow unison. This, I knew, meant they were excited and urging their captain onward.

The stakes were high, so I couldn't risk letting him close with me. I danced away and jabbed. A few kicks at the knees made him slow down, but he didn't stumble. Terrapinians were thick-skinned and built with heavy bones. Their knees were much more strongly built than the human equivalent, and therefore they took much more punishment than ours tended to.

However, what they'd gained in durability due to their structure, they'd lost in speed. I was able to keep away from him and continued tossing out attacks of my own. Each time, I skipped away before his powerful counter could slam into me.

I soon saw dark blood dripping from his face, and I dared to think this might go my way. Captain Verr had admitted he was old and slow, even for one of his kind—but he was determined, like all those of his race I'd fought before.

"I see your fear," he said in a raspy voice.

"I hear your labored lungs," I said. "Give it up—there's no shame in defeat old one."

He made that same bubbling snort he'd done earlier, and I realized he was laughing at me. "Other than defeat, dishonor is the greatest source of shame. Every time you retreat from me, you embarrass yourself further. Soon, my crew will never follow you, even if you do win."

That gave me pause. Could it be true? I'd defeated his brothers in a number of tricky ways in the past. They did follow me in the end, but maybe that was because we were part of the Rebel Fleet then. At the time, we were all following the customs laid down by Ursa on her ship.

"I'm not a coward. I'm using superior tactics."

Again, the burbling. "You fail in your task. You want to unite us, but you fear to do what is necessary. It is amusing to watch you repeatedly run. Listen to the others—they're laughing."

It was true. The burbling sounds were now coming from a dozen leathery throats.

Deciding to shift my approach, I danced in from the side, delivered two quick blows, then bounced away again—almost.

It was as if that big gray-green bastard had read my thoughts. His two arms formed a loop, which closed over my head and one shoulder when I came close. He let my blows land unimpeded, but when I tried to slip away again, the circle of his arms crushed down and caught me.

Being caught by one of these creatures was like being grabbed by a gigantic python. The arms were each as thick as my leg. They squeezed with inexorable strength. I felt my ribs shift and crackle.

I knew in that moment I'd lost. There was no way I could break his grip. All he had to do was crush me until I lost consciousness.

My instinct was to struggle. To wriggle and probe his body for a weak spot. Experience had taught me there was no such thing on a Terrapinian body. Even striking the genitals repeatedly did nothing more than anger them.

So, I decided to apply a bit of Judo. Rolling and pushing, I drove myself against him, rather than struggling to get away like a fish on a hook. He was forced to retreat a step, and his grip loosened almost imperceptibly.

At my action, the crowd woofed and thumped their feet again. They were impressed. Gone were the laughs and what I imagined were catcalls.

"You can do it, Leo!" Samson shouted. Even he admired my new vigor.

My struggle with the bigger creature was doomed to failure, I knew, no matter what the crowd wanted. My goal was different—I wanted to throw the Terrapinian off-balance.

I managed to shift in his grasp—hooking my ankle behind one of his legs. I grabbed the back of his thick knee, and heaved upward for all I was worth. Ramming upward with my legs, I managed to get one of his two stumpy feet of the ground. A sound like a gasp went up from the onlookers.

Scrambling with my faster feet, I pushed and pushed, feeling ribs crack under the larger Kher's squeezing grip. I ignored the pain, and kept pushing.

At last, like a tree that's spent a hundred years in a park, he finally fell over backward. He landed with a crash on his spine, but his arms didn't break their circle around me.

We were wrestling now, not boxing. It wasn't where I wanted to be, and it wasn't comfortable for Captain Verr, either.

"Foolish Earthman!" he complained. "Why do you seek to dishonor both of us this way?"

Already, as he'd indicated, the surrounding Terrapinians were laughing at us. They were exchanging glances and making odd gestures to one another. I could only imagine these were derogatory or obscene.

"I'm sorry, Captain," I grunted, "but you insisted on this conflict."

"Then I hereby end it!" he called out. "There is no honor in you. I will not serve you as your loyal vassal—and I would not have you serve me."

He released his grasp, and I rolled away. I got up on my feet, breathing hard and rubbing my sides. Captain Verr got to his feet as well, slowly and painfully.

I eyed him and the crowd. They were amused and insulted. This couldn't be good. I'd offended them.

"I'm not a Terrapinian," I said, "but I am Rebel Kher, the same as you are."

"You're an embarrassment. Get off my ship, monkey!"

Not knowing what else to do, I put my helmet back on, turned away and headed toward the main hold.

Captain Verr followed me. We did not speak for at least two minutes.

"Will you train your weapons on my ship now?" Verr asked finally. "After all that was said?"

"Would that better serve honor? Or would you prefer we leave you here in space to freeze?"

"That will not happen," he said. "Fex is trailing us. He'll be here within a hundred hours. At that point, we will be destroyed."

I felt stunned for a moment. I'd been quite angry with Verr and his hissing pack of reptiles. My ribs were aching, and it was all I could do not to cough. He might even have punctured my lung—but all that didn't matter. Not if Fex was returning soon.

"You refuse to accept my dominance?" I asked him. "Even though it means the death of your ship and crew?"

"I cannot."

"What if I apologized for dishonorable behavior?"

His big black eyes expanded fractionally in surprise. "That would only compound the problem. Being defeated by a mentally weak creature is an even greater embarrassment than losing to a vicious trickster."

"So, you want to die? Do you want your ship to be destroyed, caught helpless in our space?"

"No."

I nodded, thinking it over. "All right then. I'll see what I can do."

Captain Verr retreated. We climbed into our pinnace and fired up the engines. The frosty door of the hold rolled away silently, and we flew through it.

"What are we going to do, Leo?" Samson asked me. "These turtles are crazy."

"Yes... but I think I might know a way out. Get me a scrambled channel to Hagen."

"On it..."

Soon, I was talking to my XO. As I laid out my thoughts, I noticed that Samson's expression was becoming increasingly alarmed.

=23=

Returning to my own ship, I stumbled to Medical and laid down on a table. A few doctors surrounded me and began to operate machines. Needles shot cool liquids into my veins, and I barely felt the cold metal probes that began to rearrange my ribs.

Once I could breathe easily again, I used my sym to link with *Devilfish's* sensors. I reached out to perceive what the Terrapinian ship was up to.

My disappointment was bitter. They were just sitting in space, drifting, no doubt repairing whatever systems they could. It was almost beyond comprehension.

"Overly prideful, thick-skulled friggers..." I muttered to myself.

"What was that, Captain?" the ship's AI asked me. "Are you in discomfort?"

"Yes, but I wasn't talking to you, ship. I was talking to myself."

"Are you suffering mental anguish, or—?"

"No. I'm fine."

The ship shut up, and I groaned as I climbed off the medical table. A few crewmen watched me. A doctor in charge came to frown and cross his arms—but as I was the captain, he didn't quite dare to order me back to bed.

Putting on my best face, I marched up to the bridge. They were surprised to see me.

"Captain?" Hagen asked. "I was told you were out for the night at least."

"You were told wrong."

I got into my harness clumsily. I let the straps hang loosely, as I couldn't stand anything cinching up on my cracked ribs. They'd been glued together by the micro surgery units, but they still hurt like hell.

"Helm," I said, "set a course back for Mars."

"Course set."

"Apply thrust, ah, gently. No more than one G of force over the dampening effects for now."

The ship began wheeling around, and our engines thrummed. We were basically pulling a U-turn, heading back toward our docking point.

"Captain...?" Hagen said as he loomed next to my chair. "You don't look so good."

"I'm fine."

"Did those turtle-things really kick your ass, sir?"

I glanced over at Samson, who wouldn't meet my eye.

"I won the contest. They didn't see it as enough to admit full defeat, however. It was a point of honor, but not one great enough to allow Captain Verr to swear loyalty to me."

Hagen frowned. "That's why you went to their ship? To decide who had the bigger dick?"

"That's how most Rebel Kher think," I said. "That's what they understand."

"So... if he wouldn't follow you even after you beat him, what would it take?"

I shrugged. That was a mistake as the motion made me wince. "Probably several beat-downs over a long period. Maybe if we were fighting against Imperials, he'd follow then."

"Oh... now I understand the rest of your plan. But we're not really prepared to—"

"We're going to wing it," I said.

He backed away and continued the preparations I'd requested while still in the pinnace with Samson. Mia climbed down from her station and watched me curiously.

She soon came nearer to check on me. She reached out a soft hand and probed my side. I let her, because she was my girlfriend, but I wanted to push her away.

"Human bones are too brittle," she complained. "I can't understand how you would survive a fall of more than fifty meters."

I snorted and winced again. "We probably couldn't survive a drop of more than twenty."

119

Her eyes widened, and they moved oddly. She kept probing, however. "Does this hurt?"

"Yes."

"But you're allowing me to do it?"

"I thought maybe you were trying to comfort me."

She laughed. "No. I was testing to see how fit you are for battle. At least you're not howling and begging me to stop."

The next time her hand came toward my side, I caught it up and kissed it, rather than let her poke at me. The ruse worked, and she smiled.

"Mia," I said, "are you prepared to lie to the Terrapinians if they ask you any questions?"

For a moment, she hesitated. "It's not the way of Ral," she said. "We stalk, we ambush, we hide and wait for prey—but we don't tell falsehoods."

"Right... that's what I thought. Simply don't answer then, if the topic comes up. Be quiet, as if you're hunting."

"I can do that," she said, and I sent her back to her post.

Mia was the only Kher we had aboard ship, so I felt confident in ordering the rest of my crew to go along with my plans. They knew how to lie—they were, after all, humans.

When everything was prepared, I contacted Captain Verr. He answered politely.

"You are hereby required," I told him sternly, "to power up your ship and follow me."

"I thought our position was clear. You do not command my vessel."

"No," I said, "but I am an officer in the Rebel Fleet. I am in charge here, because we are of the same rank, and this star system is my home territory."

"There must be some confusion," Verr said. "The Rebel Fleet has disbanded. We are no longer—"

"Fex is working for the Imperials," I told him. "Admiral Fex is therefore a tool of the enemy. We are required by ancient accords to unite against him. Proceed to Mars, allow your ship to be repaired, and stop arguing."

"This is some kind of primate trick, isn't it?" Verr asked suspiciously. "You will destroy my ship, or sabotage it, or plant a bomb—"

"No," I said. "I came aboard your ship and fought you honorably. You should not dare to insult me now."

Verr hesitated for a moment, then he relented. "You're right. I apologize. It's just that—what you claim is unfounded. Unproven—impossible."

I signaled Hagen then. He sucked in a breath and transmitted what he had.

During our previous conversations with Admiral Fex, we'd recorded everything he'd said. We created a computer profile of him. Using our ship's AI, running an impersonation protocol, the ship spoke with his voice and presented his image as we'd seen it in the holoprojector.

The effect was startling. The AI was quite good at this. The effect reminded me of all the dead actors who'd been brought back to life in films recently.

"I warn you, Captain Blake," the simulated Fex said, "the full weight of the Empire is behind me. You will be subjugated."

The image vanished a moment later. I glanced at Hagen, but he shrugged. Apparently, that's all they'd had time to cook up.

"There you have it," I said firmly. "Fex as much as admitted he serves the Imperials."

"That is a great crime!" Captain Verr said. "But it hardly means I have to listen to your commands."

"You're wrong. Read your reactivation clause. Should hostilities begin again in your local star system, you are bound by your oath to resist."

"I'm not in my own star system, I'm—"

"You're in *my* system," I told him. "Therefore, I'm in charge of the local defense. I require you, as a point of honor, to aid me."

Captain Verr looked confused. I saw him turn and confer with a few of his officers.

"That recording," he said. "Is that the only—?"

"Captain Verr," I said sternly. "You are obviously fearful. I understand this, but you shouldn't let your terror of Fex cause you to dishonor yourself. Time is of the essence, and you have your orders. I will await your arrival at Mars."

After this little speech, I waved for Chang to cut the signal, which he did immediately. Hagen breathed a sigh of relief. I don't think he was the kind who enjoyed elaborate pretenses.

"Display the Terrapinian ship," I said, and the AI did so immediately.

We all watched to see what they would do. At first, nothing happened.

"They didn't take the bait," Hagen complained. "They're smarter than that."

"They're dumbasses," Dalton said with certainty, "but they might have smelled a rat this time."

For several minutes, the alien ship did nothing. I began to worry, but I kept up an expression of easy confidence.

"Perhaps, Captain," Chang said, "we should contact them again. Perhaps your rapid cutting off of the channel offended them."

"I've got a better idea," Hagen said, "let's get the AI to create another damning scene starring Fex. That first one looked pretty good, but—"

"No," I said, thinking they were both amateurs when it came to bluffing. "Just wait."

A full ten squirming minutes later, our patience was rewarded at last. The Terrapinian ship turned and followed our course.

I dared to grin. They'd taken the bait. They weren't happy about it, obviously. Maybe they'd reviewed their Rebel Fleet contracts as I'd suggested. Maybe they'd held a meeting of the commanding officers and discussed it.

Whatever the case, their ship was following mine, and that was all that mattered for now.

=24=

By the time we reached Mars, I'd explained everything to Earth and the local dockyard people. For some reason, none of them were happy with my solutions.

"You *lied* to them?" Admiral Vega demanded. His voice was incredulous.

"That's right, sir. The Terrapinian captain said Fex was on his way back soon. We have only my ship, and a few phase-ships in the system. With their vessel fully repaired, we'll have double the—"

"This is a diplomatic breach! I can't be responsible for a fresh shit-storm today. I'm not covering you this time, Blake. I'm sorry."

"I'm sorry you feel that way, Admiral. Maybe I'll die in the upcoming defensive action, and you'll be relieved of any embarrassment I've caused you."

He snorted at me. "That might not be a fast enough solution. I'm considering putting your XO, Commander Hagen into the captain's chair."

That surprised me. I felt a pang—not of regret, for I felt sure I'd done the right thing, but I didn't want to lose command of this ship. I'd only just gotten out into space.

"You're of course free to do so," I said.

Standing up, I began to pace in my office/cabin. There wasn't really enough room to do it, and I cursed all the Earth designers— Abrams most of all—for having condensed our living space. My knee bumped my bunk twice before I gave up.

"Consider this," I told Vega, "Captain Verr only respects one human: me. I'm an official Rebel Fleet officer, and I beat him in combat one-on-one. My hold on his loyalties is therefore stronger than anyone else's in this system."

"Objection noted," Hagen said tersely and closed the channel.

At Mars the repairs began, but they didn't go quickly. The alien ship's subsystems weren't fully compatible, even though both of our vessels used rebel design. It wasn't a full match. Every power coupling needed a custom adapter, and our computer system didn't want to connect to theirs at all.

As a result, we took to cannibalizing whole systems from our newest light cruisers, sister ships to *Devilfish*, which were still under construction. That would slow down their completion by months, but I figured that Earth might not have months left.

Even though Captain Verr maintained it was a waste of time to repair the life support system, I insisted we do so anyway. That, plus a number of power generators, formed the bulk of the repairs.

The weapons, propulsion and navigational systems were all in reasonably good shape. The Terrapinians were most happy about the new generators.

"This will make a difference," Verr admitted. "But I don't like that you will now behave as my lord."

"We're part of an allied force," I told him. "I'm not your lord— I'm your comrade. Fex is the common foe. How shall we defeat him?"

Captain Verr turned to stare at me. He looked, after a fashion, to be surprised. "You ask an underling what to do? Why struggle so hard for command then?"

Gritting my teeth to hide my irritation, I answered him evenly. "I'm following your tradition. Don't you consult with your top officers before making a key decision?"

"No," he said, "I might ask them for information—but that's not the same thing. Their opinions are nothing. Only their knowledge is of value."

"Right... What knowledge do you have that might help us defeat Fex?"

"It is simple enough. We must gather all our ships into a single fist. We shall strike him with that fist, and if he breaks, we shall win."

"That's an excellent piece of advice," I lied. "Thank you."

"You thank underlings for answering questions? Your day must be filled with trivialities."

"Dismissed," I told him. I was starting to lose it.

That, he understood. He left my presence without another comment.

Hagen walked up in his wake. He lowered his voice and shook his head. "What an ingrate," he said. "We fixed his ship—half wrecking two unfinished vessels of our own to do it—and what does he do? He spits insults at you."

"I'm sure he doesn't see it that way. He's only being honest about his thoughts and feelings—painfully honest. Many of the Rebel Kher are like that. They don't appreciate politeness—really, they consider it a form of lying. They understand honor in battle, but they feel no urge to protect anyone else's feelings."

Events took a fresh turn when the Terrapinians flooded our Mars base. It was only natural for them to want to get off their own vessel. They'd been cooped up without life support for weeks.

Unfortunately, a large number of suspicious, impolite and rather stinky aliens didn't blend in well. The local yard-dogs weren't happy and fights inevitably broke out.

This sort of thing was to be expected among the rebels. They weren't easy-going, tightly organized people. They were mean, and they were violent. That seemed to be a universal constant among the Kher—vicious in-fighting.

Our yard-dogs were surprised, but they didn't run for help. They brawled.

It was the local base commander who had a conniption and came to talk to me about it.

"Captain," he said sternly, "this is a military facility. These aliens are barbarians. You must control them!"

I looked at him with raised eyebrows. "Me? Haven't you got MPs or something?"

"Not enough to police seven hundred additional stinking aliens! We've only got a crew of a thousand, with fifteen assigned to security. They're overwhelmed."

"Well... I wouldn't worry about it too much, Major. These things happen."

"We've had a *death*!" he said, his voice cracking high. I didn't think he was used to dealing with an officer like me. Most wanted strict discipline. "Did you know that? A *death*!"

"Theirs or ours?"

"Theirs. One of the Terrapinians somehow found himself spinning in space, tossed out of an airlock."

I stirred a cup of hot caf and shrugged. "He probably got lost," I said mildly. "Accidents will happen in space. The Terrapinians will understand."

The base commander was wide-eyed. "So, I'm taking it you plan to do nothing? Is that correct? Very well, you leave me no choice. I'm contacting Admiral Vega as soon as—"

"Really?" I said. "You're that worked up about this?"

"A *death*, Captain. Did you hear me?"

"Yeah... I've seen lots of deaths, Major. But all right, I'll think of something. To start with, I'll give you twenty security men armed with shock-sticks."

Grumbling, the base commander retreated. With a heavy sigh, I contacted my security chief and ordered him to put patrols on the station. After that, I donned my full dress uniform and applied my old rank pins from the Rebel Fleet to my lapels. They sat next to my earthly insignia. I knew they would give me more creditability with the Terrapinians.

On the way to the station air lock, I stopped by Abrams' lab.

"Hey, Doc," I called to him. "Are you busy?"

"Not at all, Captain. I was hoping someone would come by and begin to chatter pointlessly."

While he said these sarcastic words, he remained bent over a block of ticking equipment.

"Okay then, never mind," I told him and walked out.

I didn't get ten paces before I heard a tapping sound behind me.

"Captain?" Abrams said. "You might at least explain your reasons for interrupting my critical research."

"We shouldn't even talk about it, Doc," I said. "You'd only be tempted, and I'd feel bad about getting you off-track."

Turning my back on him again, I kept walking. Abrams stood still for a few seconds, fuming, but at last he had to come running after me.

I grinned, but I made sure the expression was gone before I turned back around to face him again.

"I *insist* you tell me what's going on," he said. "It's unfair to leave me in the dark."

"Well, since you asked, the base commander has a discipline problem."

I quickly explained the situation aboard the station. As I did so, Abrams look increasingly bored. He flapped his hand at me dismissively before I'd finished.

"A single death? Seriously? The man is hopeless. He should resign and take up farming."

"I agree, but I came to ask for your help."

"A bunch of reeking reptiles who like to start fights on our station... That sounds like work that's cut out for you, Blake. What assistance can I possibly render?"

"Normally, I'd agree, but I've got an idea. Tell me what you think."

After explaining what I planned, he went back to frowning, but this time his attitude was speculative.

"I don't know... it will take a day or two. I'm currently involved in something *much* more important."

"Of course you are," I agreed. "I get it. I thought you might be exhausted and needing a rest. If you're not up to the challenge, I can accept that."

"Well, I didn't say—"

"Forget about it," I told him. "I'll go back to the base commander instead. Maybe his boys can cook something up."

He made a snorting sound. "Absurd. These rubes couldn't weld a joint closed without consulting the manual."

"But you're clearly not up to this, so I—"

"I'll do it," he said suddenly. "In fact, I *insist* on it. Clandestine alien experimentation—that's something that should only be performed by an expert. It could cause a diplomatic flap if botched—by the way, you *do* have permission to try this, don't you?"

I gave him a big smile. "Of course I do, Doc. Glad to hear you can help out. Let me know when you've got a prototype working."

"I won't know that without testing..."

I paused. I hadn't thought of that. He was right, he had to be allowed to run tests.

"Yeah..." I said. "Okay, let me know when you think you've got something working. We'll try it out."

Walking away before he could ask any more questions, I escaped his level of the ship and headed up to the safer levels.

Before I went to bed that night with Mia, I took the time to reconsider my plans. They were bold and somewhat dangerous, but I figured the end result would make it all worthwhile... probably.

=25=

brams worked all night long. That's the only way I could explain it. By morning, while I was still groggy and standing in the shower, he was buzzing my sym with messages.

"I've got it," he sent. "I'm *certain* I've got it."

I almost messaged him back *got what, Doc?* But I managed to stop myself. He had to be talking about the gizmo that had been only a thought in the back of my mind the day before.

Surprised and elated, I washed up, and after checking with Hagen on the bridge, I raced down to his lab. I hadn't even had breakfast yet.

What he showed me was a small, unimpressive device. It looked like a pistol, but with twin forked antennas instead of a gun barrel. The trigger mechanism was still intact, however, and I naturally curled my finger around it.

"Don't!" Abrams said urgently.

I looked at him in surprise. "You think this thing is dangerous?"

"Of course it is."

"But it only sends out a jamming signal, right?"

"Only a jamming signal? We're talking about sentient minds here, Blake. Wouldn't you panic if that dormant organ of yours suddenly misbehaved—that is, if you even noticed?"

Sometimes, Abrams could annoy even me. I was used to his bullshit, but he kept on pressing buttons until he pissed you off— he was a master at it.

Tossing the thing in air in his direction, I watched him scrambled to catch it. He cursed at me and glowered.

129

"Fine," I told him, "we'll do it your way. We'll conduct a controlled test aboard the station. Now is as good a time as any. Let's go."

He followed me muttering about negligent fools and incompetence.

I didn't want to call attention to myself, but I wanted to make sure we weren't walking into trouble. Accordingly I brought along a trio of security men. They were all muscular, thick-jawed guys who didn't seem to know how to smile. They were the human equivalent of Terrapinians, in a way.

We headed first toward the local bar—but it was closed. Even on a space station, crews weren't allowed to drink until at least noon. We headed to a lunchroom next, where they were serving a late breakfast.

The patrons eyed us with a mix of alarm and suspicion, but no one said much. They all knew about the crackdown. They probably assumed we were looking for someone in particular to arrest.

The group might have contained our guinea pigs, but they were all human. There wasn't a Terrapinian in the bunch.

"This is a pointless waste of time, Blake," Abrams complained. "You might have at least have identified a suitable group of targets. I spent all night building this prototype for nothing."

"We'll find them, Doc. Don't worry."

I soon resorted to doing a database search on personnel. That would flag some people's screens, but it couldn't be helped.

"Ah-ha," I said, eyeing the results. "They're down in the construction area. That makes sense, I guess. They're working on their ship."

"But that's a useless test area. We have to have a mix of human's and Kher."

"Right... I'll send a team down there from our own engineering department."

After pulling some strings, I sat down to eat. Abrams watched me in disgust.

"Seriously?" he asked. "You're going to stuff your face while I'm standing here with nothing to do?"

"Take a seat. I'll pay."

Still grumbling, he took my offer and gulped a few eggs. That was about all I ever saw him eat. Eggs, and maybe a cup of coffee now and then. Maybe that was how he stayed so thin.

At last, we got the signal. My engineering team had sent a group to deliver another power coupling unit. It was timely, as I guess the last one had shorted out due to overuse.

"Let's go, and keep that thing handy."

We marched down to the bedrock under the station. Mars' space dock was located on the larger of the two moons, Phobos. The real reason was one of gravity. The small moon had enough to facilitate construction, but not enough to make a trained man become fatigued. Better still, with no atmosphere and a low escape velocity, our new ships were easier to launch.

Under the base itself we found the icy-encrusted black rock the station was built upon. The area was pressurized, and we kept our faceplates open despite the bitter cold.

The Terrapinians were there, suspiciously watching everything the human workers did. To my surprise, they did nothing to help. Maybe they weren't familiar with our equipment, or maybe they were just too good for it. Either way, their scrutiny seemed to irritate my yard-dogs more every minute. No wonder they'd gotten into fights down here.

"You know," I said, "maybe we can solve this without—"

But Abrams wasn't listening. He had his toy out, and he lifted it as I spoke. He pulled the trigger.

Nothing seemed to happen for a moment. There was no hum or sparks. Nothing.

But then... the Terrapinians stopped moving. They'd been walking around the human workstations—not helping, but observing. They'd been inspecting each piece of equipment with vast suspicion.

One such inspector froze—then all of them did it.

"Hey, hand that back," a machinist told a Terrapinian.

The Terrapinian didn't react. He just stood there, unblinking. His black eyes were like marbles of obsidian. He didn't move. He didn't even seem to breathe.

"*Hey!*" the machinist said, grabbing the equipment from the alien harshly.

The Terrapinian lurched slightly when the device was removed from his grasp, but his hands remained frozen in the air in front of him.

"There's something wrong here, Doc," I said.

"What was your first clue?" he asked in a bitter tone. He was already tapping away at a programming unit. He shook his head and sucked air through his teeth. "It has to be the code... why is it *always* the code?"

The Terrapinian who'd had a box-like unit of equipment plucked from his fingers had never quite recovered his balance. He toppled right then, doing a facer into to a carton of heated rivets.

Wispy vapor came up from the alien. Could he be burning his face off?

A few of the yard-dogs, concerned now, moved to help, but they couldn't stand the rigid alien up again. Others circled around the other Terrapinians, snapping their fingers in their faces. Some laughed, others commented on how weird the situation was.

Reaching toward Abrams, I grabbed hold of the transmitter he'd been toying with. He squawked and tried to hold on—but it was an unfair contest.

I wrenched it away from him, and the trigger he'd held down all this time snapped back.

That was when everything changed—all hell broke loose.

=26=

The Terrapinians came alive again—but they didn't just stagger and blink. They all flew into an instantaneous, insane rage.

Making mindless grunting and choking noises, they attacked whatever was closest to them. In most cases, that was a curiously staring human being.

Even the poor bastard that had fallen on his face in the carton of hot rivets went mad. His face was smoldering and black where the metal had branded his thick hide, but he didn't seem to care or even notice. He grabbed the nearest man by the throat, someone who'd simply been trying to help him up.

With powerful arms, he forced the man's head into the hot rivets, and a screeching sound began. The sound was grim, but it was quickly drowned out by a dozen similar cries of shock and pain.

All around the big construction chamber, Terrapinians were attacking everyone—even each other. They smashed down foes with tools, fists and even workbenches plucked from the ground. They drove power drills into men's guts, crushed helmets with picks and shovels, and generally behaved like murdering automatons.

The mayhem was kicked up a notch moments later when the yard-dogs got over their shock and began to fight back. They'd been taken by surprise, but they weren't soft people. Snarling with the simmering rage they'd been feeling toward these outsiders all along, they attacked them just as brutally as they'd been dealt with themselves.

My trio of security people surged forward, but I put up a hand. "We have to handle this carefully," I said. "This riot is not a natural one. Just try to save the badly wounded."

They did as I ordered, darting in to retrieve fallen bodies that were in danger of being trampled or worse.

"Blake!" Abrams called out. "You have to stop it—they'll kill each other."

I grabbed him by the skinny neck and pointed at the mess. "You said it would work!"

"It *is* working—too well. When we cut them off from their syms, they went catatonic. The sudden reconnect threw them into a berserk rage—that was your fault."

"Why would they go ape just because they couldn't hear their syms for a while?" I demanded.

"I don't know anything about these creatures. Perhaps they've been conditioned, perhaps they've been listening to their syms whispering in their minds since they first hatched—how could I know?"

I let go of Abrams and turned around. Blame didn't matter now. As the captain, *everything* was my fault. That's how it worked.

For about three full minutes, the melee raged. That's a long time when you're getting your ass kicked. We got involved only when someone appeared to be seriously injured. We pulled helpless combatants to safety and let the brawl rage on.

When it looked like it was winding down, I put my fingers in my mouth and released a blasting whistle. Several of them looked at me—not all, but several. Everyone was exhausted, swaying on their feet or trying to crawl away.

"This exercise is over!" I announced loudly. "Security will fire on anyone who doesn't disengage right now!"

They looked at me in confusion. Most separated, but a few continued to struggle. I ordered my bewildered security men to use their disruptors on low settings. They burned the diehards repeatedly until they were on the deck, writhing and whimpering—or, in the case of the Terrapinians, hissing incoherently.

"Yes," I said, marching among the fallen, "this was an exercise. The Rebel Fleet has been reinstated. We're operating on Rebel Kher rules now—and I've got to say, I'm proud of what I just saw."

This last statement, possibly more than any of the other lies that had been dribbling from my lips over the past minute, seemed to stun everyone.

"That's right, *proud!*" I told them. "You fought like demons. Like real warriors. I'm awarding rank points to everyone. One point per fighter, two for those who are still standing at the end."

"How is this permitted, Captain?" a wounded Terrapinian asked.

Turning, I recognized him. He still had burnt holes in his face in the shape of rivets.

"I have the authority. I'll award status points from my own personal score if I must. Congratulations—you've earned three."

Strangely, this pronouncement calmed the Terrapinians. The humans still seemed confused and in shock—but I wasn't as worried about them.

Twenty minutes later the wounded had all been picked up from the ground and given at least basic first aid. There had only been six deaths, three on each side—a drop in the bucket by Kher standards.

Beginning to think I'd pulled off my ruse, my face fell when I received a call. It wasn't Admiral Vega, or the base commander—it was Captain Verr.

"Blake," he said, "what fresh idiocy is this I'm hearing about?"

"It wasn't all that bad, Verr. Some of your boys lived. Those who did got extra status points. They seem pretty happy about that."

"You aren't authorized to hold such an event without consulting me first!"

"Wrong. I'm in command of the local defenses for the Rebel Fleet. I'm—"

"You are *not*," he said with certainty. "I contacted Rebel Command using a message probe. I questioned Secretary Shug himself. He said Fex is *not* in league with the Imperials."

"Huh..." I said. "That doesn't fit with my sources."

"What sources?"

"You just heard Fex himself confess."

Verr made an odd, snorting sound. "I've figured out that bit of trickery. I was hatched over four centuries ago, after all."

My heart sank. All my bluffing was turning into sand in my grasp.

"What trickery?" I asked, putting the best face I could on it.

"Fex did this. He told you he was working for the Imperials to cause terror. It worked, too. Look at us, scrambling to defend this backwater planet against an imaginary enemy. I'm taking my ship home the moment it's serviceable."

"Fex did this... sure," I said, unable to come up with a better reply.

He soon disconnected in disgust, but first he took the time to blame me for overreacting and mishandling the situation.

"Trouble, Captain?" Dr. Abrams asked.

He'd been standing nearby, listening in on my side of the conversation. His lips were pursed tightly. His expression was part anger and part smirk.

"Nothing I can't handle," I told him, and I walked out.

Behind me the wounded groaned, and the dead stared at the rough-hewn ceiling. The day had been a thorough disaster.

It didn't take long for news of recent events to reach Admiral Vega. He contacted me promptly to ream me out.

"This is incompetence, Blake. Straightforward failure. I want to hear how you're going to fix this mess."

"That's too harsh, Admiral," I told him. "Abrams was only doing his best—and I'll think of something."

I waited for the response to travel home to Earth and come back again.

"You'd better," the Admiral said. "And by the way, we're not going to get away with blaming this disaster on Abrams, much as I'd like to. If Captain Verr leaves Earth behind with tons of our equipment in his hold, I'm giving command of your vessel to Commander Hagen. Vega out."

So that was it then. The Admiral wasn't handing out any more second chances. He wanted the Terrapinians manning the walls along with *Devilfish*, or I was being removed from command—again.

136

=27=

Thinking it over, I decided I was going to have to contact Captain Verr again. The key would be convincing him to stay without letting him know how much I needed him.

The plan went wrong almost before it got started. The moment I contacted him, using my sym to connect to his, he brushed me off.

"I've got no more time for you, Blake," he said. "I'm removing my crew from your station as we speak. The repairs have gone well, and we—"

"—are a bunch of ungrateful cowards," I finished for him. "Full of tricks and underhanded behavior. I'm surprised you don't have a tail as long as Fex's—oh wait, you *do* have a short one, don't you?"

There was a sputtering sound that reminded me of static, but it sounded too angry.

"Now, you go too far. Has your sym gripped your mind? How can you—?"

"No," I said, cutting him off, "how can you run out on a friend? I've fought with your kind before. Never have I met one so anxious to evade a fight and ditch his comrades on the eve of battle."

"Clearly, you've gone mad," Captain Verr said.

"No, I don't think so. I think I'm just starting to figure things out. You came here to Earth for help, and you got it. Now, you're running. In fact, I have evidence that indicates you started that fight between my troops and yours on our base. That was your best trick—manufacturing a convenient excuse to leave."

"These words are foul. You have no evidence and no couth. My people are anything but cowardly, we—"

137

"That's right..." I said, sounding suddenly thoughtful. "It doesn't fit that you'd piss yourselves and tremble in fear like this—can it be treachery then? Are you actually in league with Fex? Or the Empire?"

A hand closed around my arm. I looked down to see Gwen. She'd come out from Earth to check up on me while we were docked—effectively, she was spying for Vega. I knew that.

Gwen's eyes were big and round. She gave me a slow shake of the head, indicating I should tone it down.

But I couldn't. It was this or nothing. If Verr pulled out, I'd lose my command, and we'd probably all die when Fex came back anyway.

"You *are* insane," Captain Verr said in my ear.

"I've been called worse. But you can explain this to me: why would a brave, honorable warrior race run like this? After agreeing to fight at our side? I refuse to believe it has anything to do with a few scuffles aboard our station. I know your kind. Your people have never been so weak."

Verr paused. By praising him, I'd put him in a tough spot. He couldn't run off now without proving all my accusations true, and all my compliments false.

"You are, of course, correct," he said at last. "We would never leave a comrade. We would never take gifts and return nothing. We would never flee because we'd failed to defeat another in a fair fight."

"Good!" I said. "We're going on maneuvers in the morning. Are you ready? Your ship and mine need to train together."

"What of the rest of Earth's Navy? Why isn't it here? We've scanned the skies, and we haven't—"

I cleared my throat, interrupting him. "That's something I wanted to talk to you about. You haven't detected the approach of Earth's fleet because most of them are capable of stealth."

"Stealth? In space? How can you cast out an exhaust plume the width of a planet and maintain stealth?"

"Well... we do it through phasing. That's a secret, but you might as well know the truth now."

"Phase-ships!?" he demanded in horror. "The ultimate dishonor! Never has a rebel world built such abominations. No wonder we've had our doubts about you—you dishonor yourself and all other rebel worlds by deploying such monstrosities!"

I gazed at the steel roof and took in a deep breath. Phase-ships were considered dirty weapons by the Rebels. Only the Empire deployed them. But Earth, starting off with no fleet of her own, had built them in order to have a fleet in space very quickly. Of all the ships we could have constructed, phase-ships were the most effective given their relatively low production cost.

"We'll see if you feel that way on the field of battle," I told him. "You might like knowing there are invisible ships all around you when we face Fex's fleet."

"That's still a matter under review," Verr said, but he sounded like he lacked conviction.

"Don't worry about your weaker officers," I said. "Sometimes the young are cowardly, and they will make up all kinds of excuses to evade a difficult fight. But you'll convince them. Your iron will must prevail."

"Yes..." he said unhappily.

I got out of the call as soon as I could after that. Gwen was standing next to me, her face almost white with worry.

"Did you hear that?" I demanded. "I nailed it—I nailed him. He can't weasel out now."

"I heard you all right. It made me physically ill. You don't believe all that bravado, do you?"

"Well... sort of. Terrapinians are tough. I just need to shame them in to staying and fighting with us."

"Why is that so imperative?"

I took a few minutes to explain the situation to her. The grimmer details about Admiral Vega threatening to remove me from command slipped out of the story, but the rest of it was accurate.

"Hmm..." she mused. "This is serious. Do you think you managed to shame Verr into sticking around?"

"Maybe. He's wily for one of his kind. He's been around long enough to have heard bullshit before. You don't get to be four hundred years old by fighting to the death all the time."

"Yeah..." she said, thinking it over. "That's true. He likes to survive. No matter what he says about honor and honesty—he's got to be a survivor."

Gwen walked away, and I thought about what she'd said. It was a good insight. I'd have to keep it in mind.

Soon I was back on the bridge of my ship. Now that the Terrapinians were pulling out, there was less need for my people to patrol the base—besides, for some reason the locals were tired of us.

Just as my shift was ending, Chang made an odd, humming sound.

"What's that, Chang?" I asked.

He didn't look at me. Instead, he kept frowning at his instruments.

"An anomaly, Captain. I was plotting our patrol path, taking us near several likely spots an enemy might open a rift in this system."

"Yeah?"

"And I—I saw something, sir."

"Roll back the stream and play it for me."

I'd been bored for hours, as had most of my crew. The shift was about to end. They were yawning now, looking forward to grabbing something to eat and hitting their bunks.

But that could wait. Dalton, in particular, seemed put out. He slumped in his harness and let his chin rest on his chest.

"Play it," I ordered Chang again. "Let's see what you've found."

Nothing was quite as dull as watch-standing in a peaceful system while docked. I appreciated everyone's desire to change shifts, but I didn't feel like taking any fresh chances today.

We watched a slow scan of the skies. To make things less interesting, the scan wasn't even in the visible spectrum. It was reading X-rays and gamma rays. Splines and flashing, meaningless arcs of color shot across the stars. The stars themselves were black, the void of space white. It was hard to make out what, if anything, was going on.

Then, I thought I saw whatever it was that Chang had noted. A spot on the visual data went dark, with a brilliant center—then it went dark again.

"What the hell was that?" Dalton asked. His hooded eyes snapped wide open. He was suddenly alert.

"What does it look like?" I asked.

"I don't know... A rift, maybe? A fast one, opening and closing like a blinking eye."

"Yeah..."

"The stream is moving forward at ten times normal speed," Chang explained. "Let me slow that down and replay it."

We all watched, and we were amazed.

"That's a breach," Samson said. "A small, fast breach. No way around it."

"Yes..." I agreed. "Someone has just entered our system. Why didn't the computer flag it?"

"I did," said the AI. "That's why, out of sixty trillion gigapixels, Lt. Chang was able to spot this anomaly."

"You didn't report it as a rift. No one said anything about an invasion when I started this shift!"

"It fell below the profile thresholds," the AI explained. "I shall adjust them."

"Do that. When was this scan taken?"

The AI caused the time and date stamp to loom up in green numerals.

"Last night..." I said, thinking hard. "I don't believe it. We've been sitting on our thumbs while they arrive and assemble."

"Who?" Hagen demanded. "Who do you think it is, sir?"

"Probably Fex. But it could be someone else. We've been like Grand Central Station around here lately. Whoever they are, they're hostile. Why else would they arrive so far out? Isn't that past Saturn?"

"Yes sir. In Saturn's shadow, in fact, from the point of view of Earth."

I nodded. "That's why they chose that spot. From here, we've got a better angle. Someday we've got to get defensive probes built and placed all around the Solar System."

"All our space-based construction is tied up in building new starships, sir."

"Right..."

Even as I spoke, an alarm went off. It was a proximity warning.

"AI? Is that you? What triggered that warning?"

"After being scolded," it said, "I've lowered my threshold for significant events."

"Well? What is it?"

"It's Captain Verr's ship, sir," Chang answered. "The Terrapinians have disconnected from our docks. They're drifting away slowly now, falling behind us in the Mars orbit."

I glanced over at Hagen. Our eyes met.

"That's an amazing bit of timing, don't you think, XO?"

"It is indeed, sir," he said. He checked his chrono. "We're supposed to have gone off-duty just ten minutes ago. Do you think Verr knows that?"

"I would bet on it, Captain."

Staring after the retreating ship, I made a fateful choice.

"Plot a parallel course," I ordered. "When he's slipped around to the far side of Mars, undock and pursue."

=28=

I'd really started to believe I'd lost Godwin. He hadn't showed up and talked to me since I'd left Earth suddenly. In a way, it'd been a welcome relief. He was like the ghost of some ancient relative that just wouldn't stop haunting me.

But he finally found me again—if I'd ever really managed to shake him—the day we left Mars.

"Captain Blake?" a voice asked in my cabin. "Do you have a moment?"

I froze. It had been weeks. Somehow, down on Earth, Godwin's appearances were easier to take. Your mind could convince itself that it was all a matter of quick feet. That *no one* could slide into existence and out of it again—not in reality. That it was all some kind of trick.

But not here. Not aboard my own starship. I knew every bolt aboard by this time. There was nowhere to stow away. The AI would never have permitted it, even if there had been such a spot. It tracked every micron of oxygen consumed, counted the heartbeat of every crewmen aboard, and generally mothered us every moment we were aboard *Devilfish*.

Even more convincing, perhaps, was the fact I'd been in my cabin alone for an hour. The voice piping up from behind me hadn't come from the bathroom, or the doorway. Both hatches were firmly shut.

I turned slowly.

Godwin smiled at me. He was stretched out on my bunk, with his hands laced behind his head.

"Get up!" I ordered. "Have some class, man!"

Looking surprised and amused, he swept his papery boots off my bed and stood. As he did so, he gave the mattress a thump.

"Such hard butts you humans seem to have. Nomads live in luxury by comparison."

He was remarking upon the austerity of the cabin—which was entirely due to Dr. Abrams and his miserly designs. But I didn't feel like talking about that.

"What are you doing here?" I asked him. "What do you want, really?"

"I thought that was abundantly clear by now. I'm trying to help you—to help Earth."

"As long as our goals align, I'll believe that."

He chuckled. "Who's been abusing your trust? I know it can't be me."

"The list is long and distinguished," I assured him. "Now, what do you want?"

"To help! I understand you're in pursuit of an enemy vessel."

"It's not an enemy ship, she's crewed by another type of Rebel Kher—Terrapinians, they're called."

"Ah..." he said, and he walked around my cramped cabin. He toyed with a picture I had on the wall that depicted sailing warships from centuries past. One finger righted it slightly. "Are you sure they're really your friends?"

"The Terrapinians? They might be difficult and stern, but they have honor."

"There, we'll have to agree to disagree. I have a very different view of those people."

"You know them?"

He shrugged. "No more than I know your people."

"Look, Godwin, I'm getting sick of these visits. Why don't you appear before the Council? Earth will surely recognize you as a foreign dignitary. You can play Ambassador down at Geneva whenever you feel the urge to visit our star system."

He turned at last and looked at me. "I'm hurt," he said. "Don't you value our visits? Don't you get something out of them?"

"I guess..." I said. "But I'm busy running one of Earth's finest warships now. I need to focus on that. I'm not a diplomat."

"I'm not either. I would hate such a task. Imagine, spending all your time trying to talk people into giving up their sovereignty—

that's the point of the whole thing, you know. Alliances, deals, treaties—all ways for planets to restrict one another."

I figured he was probably right, but I didn't care.

"Isn't there anyone else you can haunt?" I asked.

"Haunt? An odd choice of words... but it is apt. I told you last time how I travel from star to star, didn't I? Of course I did..."

Grunting impatiently, I put my hand on the door panel. It lit up, but the hatch didn't open. Not yet.

"Is there anything else you'd like to say?" I asked. "Because I'm late to my watch. I've got to go."

Godwin met my eye. "Just this: blow the Terrapinians out of the sky. Don't hesitate. Don't let them talk you out of it."

That surprised me. He wasn't beating around the bush—not this time.

"Why?" I asked him. "We just armed them and repaired their ship, you know."

"I *do* know that. I've been busy—but I came back to warn you. Now, you've heard the warning. I'll be going again. Perhaps we'll meet again, Captain. *Bon Voyage.*"

What happened next was the strangest thing. He sank down toward the floor. He melted, sort of. It was very weird.

I stepped close to watch, and I thought to turn on my sym's recording systems. Body-cams caught the end of it, even though the process was quick.

"So strange..." I said, watching. "He just committed suicide, of a sort. I can still smell a faint tickling odor."

I coughed and felt disgust overwhelm me. He'd done something to disintegrate his corpse, but it wasn't complete. There was a stain—a wet spot that was already drying up. I was reminded of a spill of cleaning fluid.

A freaky way to go, I thought. Would instant interstellar travel be worth such a sacrifice? I didn't think so. Not for me.

Taking the evidence to the one person I knew who might be able to comprehend it, I marched down to Abrams' lab. I knew he was in there, even though he seemed reluctant to open the hatch at my knock.

As the captain, I had the key codes to every hatch on this ship. I used them now to open Abrams' lab.

There, I found him. He was alive, but only barely.

"A Terrapinian," he croaked when I gently turned him over. His face was bruised and clawed. Blood ran over his clothing in a slow oozing stream. "One got in here somehow and struck me."

"What? How?" without waiting for an answer, I broadcast the alarm over the ship. "Security! Get to lab, and bring a medical team."

Turning back, I knelt to check his vitals.

"How did a Terrapinian get in here, Doc?" I asked him. "Where did he go?"

"I can't answer that—the beast was here, then it was gone. It asked me no questions. It merely struck me repeatedly until I fell. Then it continued beating me. Perhaps it sought status points."

"You're not worth much in the way of status, I'm sure of that."

Abrams gave me a flash of annoyance, but I ignored him. I stood up as the security people and a medical team arrived.

"He'll live," said a nurse with curly hair. "But barely. This had to have just happened. He's got open wounds that are still bleeding freshly."

Abrams had lost consciousness, so we couldn't ask him about it. The whole thing seemed odd. Very odd...

As a lifelong scammer, I didn't believe in timely coincidences. I'd created my own too many times to be anything other than highly skeptical. I recalled that Godwin had just appeared and vanished again in my own cabin. He'd given me the hard sell on attacking the Terrapinian ship—then this happened.

Could all this be a series of freak occurrences? Or was it a setup?

I asked myself how I might have proceeded, if I'd been tasked with pushing the captain of one starship into attacking another.

Nodding to myself, I became convinced of several things all in a rush. One, Godwin was trying to pull a fast move. Two, he had to be desperate to try it on me. Three, and most importantly, he'd managed to convince Captain Verr to buy the bullshit he was selling.

Why else was Verr pulling out and running right now, without a word?

=29=

Feeling sure that Godwin had been playing with Verr's head just as surely as he'd tried to mess with mine, I contacted the Terrapinian Captain in a new way. Instead of opening a dialog, I transmitted a vid file. It was a simple document—sort of an exposé.

"Here, we see the stain a Nomad leaves behind when he dematerializes. Apparently, some of the liquid in his form is too resilient to be dissolved away into the air. We've noted that the humidity level is considerably higher after such a vanishing trick is performed."

I used the recording I had, and chemical analysis of the stains— both the one in my cabin and the one I'd found in Abrams' lab.

As a nice touch, if I do say so myself, was the demeanor with which I narrated this hit-piece. I made sure to sound bored. I wanted it to seem as if I was delivering information I believed Verr already knew—as if these details were so obvious that any moron with a nickel's worth of brainpower already understood it to be true.

"Yeah, these Nomads think they're so smart," I said. "They think of us Kher as fools. Dupes, to be manipulated like children. One day I plan to find their base and exterminate a few of them in retribution. Can you imagine the dumbass fools who must have fallen for this kind of trickery in the past?"

I played it up to the camera, working hard on the "dumbass dupes" angle. The more incredulous I was at the gullibility of unnamed others, the angrier any Terrapinian would become at having been fooled.

147

When I was finished, I transmitted the file and slouched in my captain's chair. A few crewmen eyed me strangely. It wasn't my shift, but I wasn't budging.

"Sir?" asked the off-hours pilot. She was young, bright-eyed and nervous about everything except steering a starship. "Aren't we supposed to be catching up to the Terrapinian ship?"

"Negative," I said. "Maintain course and speed. Shadow her without appearing to do so. The cover story is that we're both heading out to that anomaly which Chang discovered yesterday. I don't want to get there before they do, but I don't want them to feel pursued, either."

The pilot and the navigator looked at each other and shrugged. I couldn't help but notice they were both nice-looking women. Thinking about that, I began to frown. Could it be that Commander Hagen had a predilection toward selecting a certain kind of personnel?

I shook my head, erasing the thought. Just because the bridge was about half full of eye-candy didn't mean Hagen's judgment was at fault. Even *thinking* what I was thinking would have been offensive to some—but I couldn't stop wondering, as I knew Hagen had hand-picked his own team...

"Captain?" bright-eyes asked me.

I forced myself to look at her nametag.

"What is it, Lt. Rousseau?"

"The Terrapinian ship is altering course—do I continue to follow her?"

"That's what I said."

"But... it's shifting away from the anomaly."

"I see... Navigation? Plot their most likely new course. Helm, stay with them."

There was a pause as the woman at the navigational computer worked silently. At last, she conferred with the AI before giving me a verdict.

"They're wandering, sir. They aren't aiming anywhere special— no single point in space can be identified. They're changing their course every thirty seconds or so, but only slightly. Each time, the new course is nonsense. It's like their dodging in slow-motion— but they're still headed in the general direction of the anomaly."

I frowned at that, then I nodded to myself as I thought it over.

"It's a test..." I said. "Helm, belay my last order. Lock onto the anomaly and head directly there. Keep our speed at a matching pace with the Terrapinian vessel."

Lt. Rousseau made the adjustments and for a time, no one spoke. We were all feeling tense.

A moment like this was precisely why I was standing watch on the bridge in the middle of the "night" aboard our ship. The Terrapinians probably knew our schedules. Unless something big happened, they knew my crew was unlikely to awaken their captain to see if their orders should be changed.

Therefore, this simple test was an easy way to know if the bridge crew had been ordered to follow their ship, or to head out to the anomaly in space. With my adjustments, they couldn't be certain.

As old Sun Tzu had said, warfare was mostly a matter of deception.

After an hour or so of drifting around and randomly altering their course a degree or two, the Terrapinians finally gave up. They proceeded directly toward the anomaly, allowing us to stop worrying about it. We coasted at a safe distance, and I went to bed after leaving orders that I was to be awakened if anything changed.

Just when I'd reached the state of REM sleep some two hours later, the contact came.

"Sorry sir," Commander Hagen said, "but you left instructions to the effect that—"

"Is this an emergency?"

"No sir—I don't think so. The Terrapinian ship is trying to open a channel, but they refuse to talk to anyone other than you. Arrogant bastards. If you want me to—"

"I'll be right there. Leave them on hold."

My sym switched over to the pending channel. My reality grayed and shifted, even though I kept walking along the passages. This was a dangerous trick, recently made illegal while driving or even walking near traffic. It was too easy to get lost in a conversation with a person you could see and hear right in front of you.

"Captain Blake," Verr said. "You *are* awake. How was your hibernation?"

I knew the Terrapinians didn't sleep much, and they thought of themselves as superior to monkey types who needed six to eight hours every day.

"Unlike most humans, I never sleep," I said, giving him a blatant lie.

His black eyes blinked in surprise. "Interesting... perhaps that explains your rise to power. In any case, I'm contacting you in regards to your previous message. Our science crew was amused, and our xenopsychologists delighted. Neither could comprehend such an elaborate hoax."

"It's no hoax. You must have checked out my data and found similar chemical traces on your ship. You wouldn't be contacting me otherwise."

"You maintain that this Godwin person—a being unknown to us—is capable of transmitting himself aboard a moving starship?"

"Yes—and I'm willing to bet he's done the same thing to you. What did he promise you to get you to fly out here, Verr? Tell me the truth."

Captain Verr hesitated. "I'm in a quandary," he admitted at last. "There have been... visitations. I'd assumed I'd been uniquely chosen to experience them. The fact that this entity has apparently revealed itself to you as well forces me to question what it has said."

"How did Godwin appear to you?" I asked him. "Was he a sultry female of your species? Or a long-lost friend?"

"Godwin... it never provided me with a name. Instead, it appeared as a living plant from our homeworld. A plant that is sacred, something none of us would dare uproot and take into space."

"A talking plant?" I asked.

"There are legends... The truth is embarrassing now. Perhaps it is as the younger members of my crew say. Perhaps I'm too old to be commanding a starship. My mind is easily misled."

Privately, I agreed with his junior officers, but that wouldn't do me any good now. "That's nonsense!" I stated flatly. "You should reduce them in rank and give them the worst assignments. They're nothing but jealous rank-climbers."

"A pleasant thought... In any case, what should we do about this duplicitous being you call Godwin?"

"We're going to play along with his game for now," I said.

"Play along?"

"Yes. Let's fly out there to the anomaly point. Let's see what awaits. But, we're not going to fight. We'll be secretly cooperative."

His dark eyes flashed. "Ah, I understand now. You hate this being as I do. Your vid file indicated you were barely interested—but I see the truth now. You're angry. He must have fooled you in the past just as he fooled me. I understand, and I share your blood-rage."

"Damn straight. Is it a deal?"

There was a hesitation, but it was brief.

"Yes," he said at last. "It is a deal, Blake."

The connection closed. Smiling, I walked onto my bridge and relieved Hagen early. It was good to have a plan—even a vague plan.

My ship would face her next challenge with an ally at her side.

=30=

A s we drew closer to the point where an anomaly in the space-time continuum was registered by our deep scanners, the tension aboard ship heightened. We had no idea what we would discover, and when we thought about that it put everyone on edge.

When we were about six hours from our destination, and we were already braking, we were close enough to see an idle ship in space.

"Anything?" I asked for the hundredth time.

"Still nothing on our scopes, Captain," Chang answered. "At least, there's nothing out here the size of a cruiser."

"They could be phase-ships," Dalton suggested. "Running quiet way out here—just as we'd do with our own stealth vessels."

I glanced at him, but I didn't say anything. He was right. Besides Earth, the only known fleet of phase-ships belonged to the Empire.

Could that be the answer? Were they lying in wait out here, after having baited their trap with anomalous readings?

"At least we know it's not Fex," Samson said.

"How so?" I asked him.

"If it was Fex out here, he'd be grandstanding. He'd let us know it was him, just to flash his own giant ego."

"Hmm..." I said. "You have a point."

"That's the way, Samson!" Dalton said. "A few more ideas like that, and nobody is going to mistake you for a dolt."

"Belay that shit, Dalton," I said as I saw Samson begin to get irritated. I couldn't allow Dalton's fun to interrupt the smooth operation of the ship.

Dalton glanced my way like he was detecting a bad smell, but he shut the hell up all the same. That was good enough for me.

"I want to shoot something," Mia complained. "It's been weeks."

"Less than a week—but you might get your chance."

"Not if you visit their ship and talk to them sweetly—again."

She was somewhat bitter about the ending of our last encounter with the Terrapinians. Diplomacy, deal-making and alliances were all considered sinister by the predator races. They'd evolved fighting for territory and dominance on their home worlds. For most of the Rebel Kher, there was no room for nobility out here among the stars. Enemies were to be killed—or they killed you. That was that.

Ignoring my crew for the next hour, I studied what little data we were getting from the region as we got closer. More and more sensory equipment managed to get a reading on background radiation, drifting particles of mass and other vital info.

Unfortunately, it all painted a vague picture. Something had opened a rift here, that much we could be sure of. Had a ship glided into the star system then glided back out? It was perfectly possible.

It was also possible they were still here, cruising silently. At great distances, ships detected one another by their exhaust plumes and radioactive trails. But if a ship came in coasting and didn't turn on her engines—well, there was no way to detect a small dark object at this distance. Earth didn't yet have a comprehensive set of sensor buoys out this far. We had no idea what had happened, only that a rift had opened and closed.

Conversely, if any ship was lurking out here, they had almost certainly spotted us by now. We were flying under power. That meant we had a plume of exhaust and plasma trailing us like a torch. We would look like comets to them, and we were just as hard to miss.

On impulse, I used my sym to contact Captain Verr.

"Captain," I said, "are you seeing anything we aren't?"

"We've detected residual ripples in this region of space. There has been a rift formed here recently."

"Yeah... anything else?"

"No. Not yet. Perhaps they hide like your evil ships."

"That would make them Imperials. Do you think the Imperials would come here?"

"No—not yet."

That made me pause and frown. I'd never gotten even a suggestion from the Terrapinians that they thought the Imperials were coming. It had all been about Fex and his supposed armada of ships.

"Uh... when *do* you expect the Imperials?" I asked off-handedly.

"When this matter is done, of course."

"What 'matter' are we speaking of?"

The connection, which was audio-only and essentially connected one aural nerve to another, went quiet for a time. He was either thinking, or consulting with others. Either way, I didn't like it. He might be hiding something.

"I misspoke," he said when he came back online at last. "I have no knowledge of the Imperials."

"Yeah... right," I said, and I broke the connection.

My ally was screwing me already, or at least that was my impression.

The last few hours dragged. When we finally got there, we arrived pinging away with every piece of detection equipment we had.

"Captain?" Dr. Abrams said, buzzing in my ear.

"Yes, go ahead. What have you got, Abrams?"

"There are no phase-ships in the immediate area. I'd stake my reputation on that."

"How do you know?"

"I've studied them intensely, as you must realize. They tend to leave particles when they phase-in or phase-out. None of those particles are within a million kilometers of this location."

"That's good news, Doc. But what if they glided in, without power? What if they didn't use so much as a chemical jet to alter their course? Could they be here—phase-ship or not?"

He hesitated. "You're using the term 'here' too loosely for me to answer."

"Let me be more clear then: if they were within ten million kilometers of us right now, could we detect a ship?"

"While it was running silently? No emissions?"

"Correct."

Again, he hesitated. I got the feeling I was blowing up some of his presumptions.

"That seems highly unlikely, Captain."

"And your answer seems evasive. It's no more unlikely than the idea a starship popped in here then performed an immediate U-turn and went back out through the same rift."

"I can think of a dozen scenarios where—"

"Don't bother," I said, cutting him off. "Keep analyzing the data incoming from the sensors. Blake out."

He was in mid-squawk when I closed the connection.

I had to think. If the Terrapinians were playing us... we were in trouble. Could they possibly know more than they were letting on about this breach of the star system? Godwin had suggested as much.

"Godwin..." I muttered, thumping a fist lightly on some steel tubing. The next time I got ahold of that guy, he was going to give me some solid answers.

A few hours later we arrived at the point where the rift had opened. It was in the middle of nowhere, even by interplanetary standards. There were no significant bodies of mass within fifty million kilometers of us. Nothing bigger than a beach ball was drifting in all that volume of space.

At least, nothing was there that we could detect.

Sixteen long hours inched by. I went off-shift late, slept badly, and came back on-shift early. It was all for nothing. Local space was as empty as it could be.

Finally, I lost patience and contacted Captain Verr again.

"Captain," I said, "please tell me what's going on. I know you have information I don't."

"Naturally," he said. "We aren't even the same species. Our minds have a differing number of layers, sub-processors, and—"

My fist thumped down again. "Forget about that! What's happening? You don't even sound quite the same..."

"There is no true audio transferring between us," he said. "You realize that, don't you?"

"There it is again. A certain snottiness... Captain Verr was never like that."

"I have no idea what you're talking about."

"Let's talk about what you do know," I said, pressing. "You told me Godwin appeared to you as a bush, or something. A sacred plant."

"I did? Oh, yes..."

Frowning, I ran my hands over my control plates. Our ships were near to each other now, in relative terms. If I'd been standing on the outer hull, I might have been able to see Verr's ship with binoculars—if there had been light reflecting off the skin of his vessel.

All his engines were stopped. He was drifting, not even running stabilizer jets.

"Why are we here?" I asked suddenly. "Why did you lead us out here?"

Another hesitation. "I did not 'lead' you. We came together of our own accord."

"Initially I thought that was the case, but now, I'm not so sure."

"You're not making any sense, Captain Blake."

"Let me talk to someone else. Your exec, perhaps."

More quiet, then: "That would be impossible, I'm afraid."

"Why?"

"I'm sorry, Captain. Please be patient. Everything will become clear soon."

He cut off the connection. Cursing, I got up with a lurch that caused me to bounce into the air due to the low gravity. I had to push off the hull to drift back down again and land on my feet.

"What's wrong, sir?" Samson asked—his hands poised over the controls.

I saw that Dalton had the engines warmed. Mia was wide-eyed and rolling her turrets around to pinpoint the nearby mass of Captain Verr's ship.

Waving them all back down, I paced the deck with light steps. "I don't know what it is," I admitted, "but something's wrong over there on that Terrapinian ship."

=31=

We made a series of attempts to contact Verr's ship over the next several hours. Each was blocked. They were unresponsive. As time passed, my entire crew was becoming increasingly worried.

"The Terrapinian ship is drifting, Captain," Chang announced just as I was giving up for the night.

"What do you mean?"

"She's off her position."

"Wasn't she stable before? What exerted force to propel her?"

"There are a variety of possibilities," he said. "She might have been struck by a meteor, for example."

I waved my arms for emphasis. "Do you see anything like that out here? We're becalmed in space terms. There's a bit of Solar Wind, but—"

"That's been accounted for. It can't be the source of the drift."

Squinting, I eyed the hull of my ship as if I could penetrate them by sheer will. After a moment, it seemed to work. I used my computers, sensors and my sym to reach out and grab a visual of the drifting derelict ship nearby.

I could see the Terrapinian vessel clearly. It was distant, but distinct. There was no visible damage. No jets streaming from her sides—why was she drifting.

Returning my perception to the bridge, I glanced at Chang. "Get Abrams up here."

A few minutes later, Dr. Abrams walked onto the deck. His nose was about a mile in the air. He had the miffed look of a girlfriend I'd once had in college.

"Abrams, I've got a mystery for you."

His hands were clasped behind his back, but one of them lifted up high and his finger fluttered dismissively. "It's already been solved."

"You know what's wrong with the Terrapinian ship?"

"Well, I know why it's drifting. There's a gravitational force being exerted. In time, it will affect us as well."

I squinted at him. "You mean there is a mass out here? Something we can't see?"

"No, not exactly. There's a gravity-well—but not a large volume like a Moon. The object is small, but dense."

"Ah..." I said, catching on. "Where is it?"

"I'm employing gravimeters. If you allow me to toss out a few probes equipped with similar devices, we can triangulate and pinpoint the collapsed matter."

My crew was wide-eyed. Some were clueless about what we were discussing, but those who did understand it were even more alarmed.

"We aren't talking about a black hole, are we?" Dalton asked, breaking the ice on their fears.

"No, no, no," Dr. Abrams chuckled. "Don't even dream of a true singularity. We'd all have been extruded into particles and energy long ago if that were the case—Earth included."

"What then?" I asked.

"Collapsed matter. Neutronium, if I don't miss my guess. Something perhaps a half-meter in diameter."

We stared at him. "What is it? Why didn't we detect it previously?"

"I should think that was obvious," he said.

"Humor me."

"We didn't detect it previously because it wasn't here. It's been moving closer. That's why the Terrapinian ship is now drifting, where before it was stable."

"And... *what* is it?" I demanded.

"A ship, of course. A tiny ship of collapsed matter."

That threw me. It shocked everyone. A tiny ship? No bigger than a beach ball?

158

"How's it moving?" Chang demanded. "We can't see any engine plumes, or radiation trails."

"There are more methods of propulsion possible than throwing mass overboard to create a primitive, Newtonian reaction."

As usual, I found Abrams both haughty and uninformative. In this case, however, he was making sense. If there was a tiny ship out here, one with mass sufficient to tug a starship off course, it couldn't be using traditional engines. We would have spotted the emissions if it had been.

"Okay," I said. "What do we do?"

"I believe I mentioned my requirement for two probes equipped with—"

"Yes, of course. Give him the probes, Samson—whatever he needs."

No one argued. We all worked and soon the probes were launched on diametrically opposed trajectories.

"Do you think this thing is dangerous, Doc?" I asked.

"I would assume so—if it wants to be. The technology is beyond our own."

"What's it doing here?"

"I can only conjecture on that point. Since we've never seen a vessel like this before, and the technology is advanced, I would assume it was built by the Imperials."

I exchanged glances with my crewmen. "Mia, keep those weapons hot."

"Opening gun ports!" she said happily.

I hadn't directed her to do so, but I didn't argue. Perhaps it was a wise precaution.

Abrams was already consulting an incoming data stream. After a few moments, he displayed his findings on our holo projection system.

"There," he said, pointing at a red dot and making it pulse. "It's very small... Definitely under a meter. Spherical, moving through gravity manipulation..."

"Gravity manipulation?"

"Yes... but the findings are embarrassing," he said.

"How so?"

"My earlier hypothesis might have been premature. I'd assumed it was dense—but I'm not certain it's so extremely dense now. The propulsion system is what's affecting the Terrapinian ship."

159

I looked at him, then the approaching object.

"It's a probe of some kind, then? Or a bomb?"

He sniffed. "I would call it a stealth missile. Or a mine. I'm heading to my lab to work on the analysis. Something that's attracted to mass the way a magnetic mine is attracted the hull of a ship by—"

"Mia!" I shouted. "Blast that thing out of space!"

Dr. Abrams threw up his hands in exasperation then hurried below to his lab. He probably thought we were overreacting—but I didn't care.

Mia made a happy, snuffling sound. "Helm, line me up!"

I realized she wanted to use the center-line main batteries. That wasn't what I'd figured, but I didn't want to countermand my gunner now. I nodded to Dalton, who swung us around.

Devilfish's main batteries aligned with her hull, permanently aiming forward. They could swivel in about a thirty degree arc, but more than that would cause the released force to throw us into a spin.

Already, secondaries and point-defense cannons were going off all over the ship. As the primary gunner, Mia was by no means our *only* gunner. She coordinated the fire of all the ship's weaponry.

Mia's people were uniquely qualified as gunners, as they possessed a greater killer instinct than humans did, coupled with faster reflexes. The truth was, she was only truly happy when she was in the middle of a hunt.

"Are we getting any hits?" I asked.

"The probes show the target is still moving closer and intact," Chang pointed out. "We haven't stopped it yet."

It was strange to be battling such a tiny opponent with entirely unknown capabilities—no, strange was the wrong word. It was frightening.

"Keep firing," I ordered. "It's small, and we don't have it pinpointed. We'll have to get lucky. Still nothing on radar?"

Chang shook his head. "It's not registering. Active sensors are all telling us there's nothing there."

Another minute passed. The ship shuddered and rumbled as guns fired into the dark. We were throwing a great deal of ordnance downrange, but hitting nothing.

I stabbed the intercom button. "Dr. Abrams to the bridge!"

He contacted me via my sym instead.

"What's the problem now?"

"I'd say it's the same problem, Doc. We can't seem to hit this bogey. You're detection equipment must be faulty."

"Hmm..." he said. "That's almost impossible. But I don't blame you for the confusion. The enemy must have countermeasures."

"What kind of countermeasures can a gravity-propelled basketball have?" I demanded in exasperation.

"We have to assume it was built by a technically advanced people. They've obviously built subsystems to defeat our relatively primitive technology."

"All right then... so the target is fooling us as to its exact location. We'll lay down a pattern of fire."

Before I could relay the order to Mia, she was already on it. Instead of pouring away beams and kinetic rounds down a narrow shaft of space, she spread it all out. She peppered the region with explosives too.

"Ah," Abrams exclaimed.

"What? What?"

"Look at your display, Captain. The object has shifted its influence."

"Did we hit it?"

"Either that, or it's dodging. A third possibility is that it's continuing on in a straight line, but the deception system that's giving us a false reading decided to *pretend* it's shifting course. That might indicate were getting close."

"Which one is it?" I demanded in exasperation.

"I really don't know. It's your call, Captain."

Taking about three seconds to think about it, I turned to Mia. "Go back to your original pattern. The one you were using right before it seemed to move."

She looked baffled for a second.

"It's hiding, Mia. It's a trick. Shoot the area of space that scared it."

She got that, and her field of fire went back to a previous pattern. She widened her cone of fire slightly, and I understood that. As the target got closer, it's range of possible locations was widening too. Fortunately, it was going to be hard for it to hide if we'd guessed right.

"Contact Captain Verr again," I ordered. "Tell him his ship is under attack."

161

"I've been trying, sir—no response."

"Damn..."

We watched for another tense minute. The target—whatever it was—kept getting closer.

Suddenly, I felt a tug. It was slight, but it was undeniable. I swayed on my feet.

"Was that the enemy—thing?" I asked.

"Yes," Abrams asked from near at hand.

I turned to see him standing at my side. He was studying the situation with a gleam in his eye.

"It's within range of *Devilfish* now. I have several new theories concerning its methodology—just conjecture, of course."

"Give me your best one."

"All right... I think their 'engine' reaches out to objects of significant mass. By falling toward them, it's able to propel itself in the direction it wishes."

"But wouldn't that mean it would crash into the first thing it got near?"

"No, as it seems to be able to control what gravity source it is magnifying. Like a mythical ape swinging on vines from tree to tree, it lets go of one support and grasps another. In between, it coasts on a steady trajectory until the next viable target gets close enough."

"That's all very interesting... but it seems overly complex. Why not just use a rocket jet and go where you want?"

He flipped up a single long finger like a flag. "Ah-ha! There, you have stumbled like a drunk onto the intriguing point. What advantages does such a system have? One, it doesn't leave a plume and so is therefore difficult to detect. Two—"

"Captain!" shouted Chang.

I looked up, my eyes swiveling to the holoprojector.

What I saw there made my mind glass-over. I didn't hear Abrams any longer.

An expanding cloud was growing in an uneven spheroid shape on the far side of the Terrapinian ship. In comparison, Captain Verr's ship looked small.

The probe, ship, weapon—whatever it was—had exploded.

=32=

The region of released energy grew with great rapidity. Without an atmosphere to block it, the expanding field became a blob a thousand kilometers wide in a second.

"We're dead," Dalton said in a bleak voice.

No one argued with him. No one had time.

Samson was working his board in a frenzy. He shuttered every port, camera pod and hatch with shielding. Even Mia's weapons were shut down and enclosed in rolling clamshells.

Mia whirled on him, snarling, but he took no heed. His job was defensive coordination. Over the years, he'd come to take his role to heart, and I'd learned to trust him.

When push came to shove, survival of the ship won out. Mia would have to wait to sate her bloodlust on her distant prey—besides which, it appeared to me that she'd already nailed the thing she'd been targeting. Either that, or it had calculated it was close enough and gone off like a bomb.

Sampson's controls overrode every other panel on the ship when it came right down to it. He'd taken over, and I hadn't even given him the order to do so—there just wasn't time.

"Hull battened down—brace for impact!" he announced, his voice rolling out of every speaker on the ship.

Everywhere, crewmen scrambled for a safe berth. Most of them had already been at their battle stations, but now they took cover, assuming the worst.

Everyone struggled during the final moments with their breathing apparatus and suit-seals. It was probably futile. All of us were fated to die or survive the following seconds, regardless of

163

what we did, but it was human instinct to try to determine our own destinies.

Dalton buckled himself in with a crisscross of smart straps. Dr. Abrams landed his tail on a fold-down jump seat and stuck his skinny arms through the loops—there was no time to buckle it securely.

"I didn't think the plasma cloud could reach so far..." I heard him say aloud with puzzlement.

For my own part, I did nothing. I stood on my feet, staring at the globe of shifting energy and particles as they first swept over the Terrapinian ship, then touched ours.

I was knocked from my arrogant feet before the antigravity kicked in, at which point I began floating.

That respite only lasted for a moment. The ship lost power, and when the antigravity died we were all thrown around. I quickly wished I hadn't made a brave front of standing firm on my deck. I was thrown high, then low. I learned what a mouse might feel like in a washing machine. *Devilfish* was tumbling in space.

From the moment the bogey had detonated until *Devilfish* was knocked out had taken perhaps twenty seconds. There had been so little time to react.

The ship righted itself violently when the power flickered back on. Her autostabilizers had kicked in with a vengeance.

Getting up and suppressing an urge to vomit, I groaned aloud. Forcing my numb fingers to grasp anything I could reach, I crawled toward the soft webbing of my seat. It felt like a featherbed compared to the hard bulkheads and decking.

Samson was up with an emergency kit. He swept me up like a baby and cinched me into my chair. Straps snaked over my sweating body.

"Are you broken up, Captain?" he asked.

"Uh... not too bad," I lied.

He nodded, looking me over critically. He lowered his big head and his voice.

"You should have buckled up, sir," he said.

"I think you're right."

Chuckling, he walked off to check on others. Casualty reports began rolling in. Engineering had been hit the worst. There'd been a chemical spill—something radioactive. The main hold was venting, the seals had blown. There was more, but my eyes were blurry.

Mia came to put her hot hands on me.

"You stood proudly on your deck," she said. "A Ral captain would have done the same. Don't listen to these tree-people, Leo. Honor is all that matters. Everyone aboard ship will be talking about your stand by the end of this hour."

I wondered if she was right. I also wondered if I was going to get any nursing from her—but I didn't. She wasn't that kind of girl.

Mia went right back to her gunnery station and unlimbered her weapons again with relish.

"Stabilize this bitch, Dalton!" she shouted. "We're still locked in a slow roll. I need a solid deck to fire from."

"Working on it, she-devil."

My crew was operating the ship without me. I felt like my bell had been rung. My thoughts weren't confused, exactly—but they were fuzzy. I found it difficult to speak, so I just sat back and breathed deeply for a minute with my eyes closed.

A heavy hand landed on my shoulder what seemed to be a moment later, making me wince. I looked up and saw the concerned, craggy face of Commander Hagen.

"May I relieve you, Captain?" he asked. "You've been on the bridge for two shifts straight."

I thought about telling him no. I almost sat up stubbornly, holding in my guts with one hand—but then I relented.

"All right. Have someone carry my ass to sick bay."

Commander Hagen immediately took command, shouting for orderlies. I was hauled away like a sack of grain.

Hours passed, and countless medical procedures, salves and slathered tickling nanites did their magic. I woke up tired but functional.

Groaning as I struggled up onto one elbow, I found there was only a single human watching over me. It wasn't Mia, or Hagen, or Samson—it was Commander Hagen's hand-picked pilot, Lt. Rousseau.

Blinking at her with bleary eyes, I made a croaking sound. After a moment's effort, I cleared my throat.

"Lieutenant? How long have I been in the morgue?"

"About six hours, Captain."

"Did Hagen send you down here to check on me?"

165

She hesitated. "I... I wanted to see how you were doing."

"I'm fine," I lied reflexively, and I tried to get up. I failed and almost fell on the floor.

"Captain," she said, "you're not in any condition to—"

"Help me into my uniform—that's an order."

Rousseau complied. A few minutes later I managed to stand up, swaying only slightly.

I leaned on her heavily, and she grunted and strained. She wasn't very big.

"I'm okay," I said, lifting my arm from her shoulder.

"Are you sure?"

"Yeah... I'm good. Let's keep moving, or I might stiffen up."

Further progress down the passage way hurt a lot, but my pride was involved now. I couldn't let this girl see how bad I felt. I walked unaided—with a limp, sure—but I walked.

When the hatch opened, Commander Hagen was clearly surprised to see me. He didn't look angry, but he might have been a little disappointed.

"You were in a bad way, Captain," he said.

"Yeah... but I always heal fast."

"Captain on the bridge!" he announced. "Captain has the watch!"

He backed off from the command station, and I took over. Slowly, painfully, I settled into the chair.

"Any change? Any more shots out of the dark? Maybe we should get out of here..."

"Funny you should mention that, Captain," Dr. Abrams said from behind me.

I glanced back at him. "Hold on a moment, Abrams." My attention shifted back at Hagen. "Something happened?"

Hagen shrugged. "No sir. Not really. We've been hanging out here in space wondering what hit us and whether there's anyone left alive on the Terrapinian ship."

My eyes roved over the holoprojector. Captain Verr's ship was still there. It looked like it had weathered that last attack better than we had, despite the fact it had been closer to the detonation point.

"Play back the sensor readings of the blast," I ordered.

Chang was gone, and the new sensor man had one leg in a tube-like cast. But he seemed functional enough. "Playing the file, Captain."

We watched as the explosion swept outward with alarming speed. There was nothing we could have done.

But the vid did show that the Terrapinian ship wasn't flipped over and spun around like a bug in hurricane. It drifted and rolled, but it didn't utterly lose its grip.

"Maybe they've got better stabilizers than we do," Hagen speculated.

"Or maybe..." I said, "maybe they knew this attack was coming. Maybe they knew a way to avoid the effects, or at least mitigate them. Maybe *we* were playing the part of the fool in this story. We thought we were saving them, but we might have been duped."

Dr. Abrams cleared his throat loudly. I glanced at him again.

"Do you have some sort of speculation to make, Doc?"

"Speculation? That's offensive. I hypothesize on the basis of available data. I never speculate."

"All right, whatever. Tell me what you're thinking."

He made a puffing sound. "I will share with you those elements of my thoughts which you *might* comprehend."

"That's mighty big of you, Doc."

"Just so. I believe something else is here. Something lurks... Something which fired that weapons system in our direction."

I stared at him for a moment. "Have you detected any other vessels?"

"No."

"What leads you to believe this dense ball of matter wasn't just a mine, or a sophisticated drone, left behind here to destroy us?"

"That is a strong hypothesis," he admitted, "but I've rejected it."

"Why?"

"Because a second device, similar to the first, has been found. Several others lurk as well. We are, in effect, surrounded."

Glancing around at my crew, I saw they looked just as shocked as I did.

"And when were you going to share this finding with me?" Commander Hagen demanded.

"I thought it inappropriate," Abrams said in a huffy tone. "You aren't the captain, and you never suggested we should leave the area. As there was no immediate danger, I worked to confirm my data—and I've just completed my analysis."

We all looked at him. "And...?" I prompted.

"Well... I was right. All along. We *are* surrounded by devices similar to the one that struck our ship six hours ago. There's a globe of them stationed at about a million kilometers out in every direction."

"How many?" I asked, with my heart sinking.

Dr. Abrams took control of the holoprojector, and the sensory officer grumbled. I shook my head at him.

The display came to life. Hundreds of dots like red stars appeared all around our position.

"There are approximately six thousand devices," he said. "The exact count is difficult to make, as I'm using inferred data rather than empirical evidence. We can't 'see' these objects, or pinpoint them with active detection systems such as radar. Only our gravimeters, used in a coordinated array, have been able to pinpoint them and count them."

He sounded pleased with himself, like any academic displaying a successful experiment to his colleagues. He droned on, explaining his methodology at length and praising his own cleverness with every sentence.

The rest of us, however, were feeling differently. We were glum and stunned.

We were trapped in a small pocket of space. The big question in my mind was: who had done this?

=33=

"The answer has to be aboard the Terrapinian ship," I told them, interrupting Abrams' long-winded speech. The truth was, I hadn't heard anything the scientist had said for at least a full minute.

"Answer?" Abrams said. "What answer?"

"The answer as to who is behind this. What's the purpose? How can we get out?"

He made a puffing sound again.

"Such conceit," he said. "There's only one way to get out. We must form a rift and jump."

I slewed around painfully in my chair to look at him.

"Really?" I demanded. "That's your answer?"

"I thought it was obvious from the start. There's no other way."

"We'll scatter. We scattered badly before on a short jump. You'll fly us off to nowhere. Getting back will be almost impossible, because we'll just scatter again."

"We don't know that. One anomalous test—"

"Is all you're going to get, Doc. Think about it. Last time, the only way we made it back to the Solar System was by going through the same rift we'd just created. If we do that again today, we'll be right back here in this mousetrap."

Abrams looked sour. "Perhaps we should report back to Earth Command and see what they say about this."

"I've been making hourly reports," Commander Hagen said. "They know we're in uncharted waters. They're letting us call the shots—but with that said, leaving the star system would be a big step. We'd have to ask Vega—"

169

"We're not doing that," I said. "Not yet. First, we're boarding the Terrapinian ship to find out what happened over there."

They all looked surprised at this idea.

"What can possibly be gained—?" Abrams began.

"I'm the captain here, Doc," I told him. "There's a lot we might learn."

"But they might repel any such invasion with deadly force."

I shrugged. "You've got me there."

"Sir," Hagen said, stepping forward. "Allow me to lead the exploration team."

I glanced at him. I knew immediately he was right. I was the captain, and I was banged up. He was the best candidate if I was going to send a senior officer at all.

"The trouble is," I said, "they only respect me. I'm a bona fide Rebel Fleet officer. None of you have any recognized status as the Kher see it."

Hagen sighed and shook his head.

"I've got status," Samson interjected.

We all looked at him.

"I'm an officer in the Rebel Fleet," he continued. "The equivalent of an ensign. I could put on my old insignia and lead the team."

I glanced at him approvingly. "Yes... all right. I'm not in any condition to argue. Hagen will be in command, but Samson will do the introductions and appear to be in charge. Do you think you're up to that, Samson?"

Dalton gave a rude laugh. "Samson fooling someone? Will there be a live feed? I want to watch this cock-up in the making."

Samson gave him a dirty look, but then he turned back to me. "I can do it."

"All right then. Hagen, saddle up your team."

He looked upset. "Captain, this is absurd. If I'm in command I should be in command, period."

"Normally, I'd agree with you. But these Kher don't think the way we do. Have you read up on the Age of Exploration on Earth?"

He shook his head.

"I believe I recommended a reading list weeks ago."

"I'm sorry sir, we had to get up to speed very fast..."

"I guess that's true... Well, when the entire world was mapped out by people from Europe over a period of several centuries, there were many cultural conflicts. The explorers and missionaries of the past became adept at learning local customs to avoid disastrous misunderstandings."

"Excuse me, Captain," Hagen said, "but I don't think this is the time or the place to—"

"Then you're thinking incorrectly," Abrams said, interrupting him. "Listen, for all our benefits."

Hagen shot him an unpleasant stare, but Abrams seemed immune to such things. He either didn't notice when he annoyed others, or he didn't care. Either way, the effect was the same—most people hated him. I was glad for once, however, that he was actively supporting me.

"Anyway," I continued, "explorers learned to use interpreters and guides, and they always arrived with gifts for chieftains. The point is, they learned to fit into the expectations of the people they were trying to impress. We're going to employ some of that guile now. We're going to play the part of Rebel Fleet personnel."

"I don't like it," Hagen said, "but I know how to follow orders. I'll take Lt. Rousseau with me. She'll be our tech. Just the three of us."

I felt a pang at that. I kind of liked Rousseau.

"Is she really the best choice?" I asked.

"Of my shift crew? Yes."

At that moment, for some reason, I glanced over my shoulder and saw Mia staring at me. She knew I had a small thing going on for Rousseau. I wasn't sure *how* she knew—but she knew.

Without so much as a nod in Mia's direction, I turned back to my screens. "That will be fine, Hagen. Three will fit easily in the shuttle. Proceed."

Commander Hagen grumbled about Samson all the way down to the airlocks. I understood how he felt. This was his first boarding action, his first chance to lead a party in space of any kind, and I was having him play second banana to a junior officer.

But I didn't care about his feelings. This mission had to succeed. *Devilfish* was in danger, and I wasn't going to let her be destroyed by a flock of gravity-drones without at least making an attempt to find a way out of this trap.

When they'd gone, I turned to Chang. "Set up a feed from their body-cams. We'll monitor their progress from here."

"On it, sir."

Then I turned back to Abrams. He looked irritated.

"In the meantime, Doc," I told him, "I want you to work on a jumping strategy. If you opened a rift now, check to see if you could target it more precisely than you did last time."

"That was a miscalculation, not an error," he complained.

I failed to see the distinction, but I let it slide. Dr. Abrams didn't handle criticism very well.

We got down to humping and bumping after that. The away-team loaded onto a shuttle and began the short flight toward the Terrapinian cruiser.

"Any sign of a reaction?" I asked Chang. The scopes and boards were quiet, but his sensory data was much more in-depth than my overview screen.

"Nothing yet, sir. No energy readings, no defensive measures—the ship looks as dead as ever."

Glancing over at him, I pulled up a screen full of numbers from his station. He was right, the ship did look dead.

"These life support numbers," I said, "I've paged back, and there's been no venting for hours."

"We did just repair their systems," Chang said.

"Yes, but even our systems, using carbon-scrubbers designed for this ship, occasionally puff out a little gas. The heat numbers, the energy readings... So flat for so long... Wouldn't a normal crew operating a ship for days cause fluctuations?"

Chang shrugged. "I would suppose so, but we're new to examining alien ships and studying their behavior. Maybe the crew or their ship is more efficient than ours."

"Hmm..." I said, unconvinced.

What I was sure of was that something was wrong over there. I couldn't even get a contact point with Captain Verr anymore. I'd tried every hour or two for a long time. He hadn't spoken to me since he'd given me an oddly vague reply about the Imperials.

Feeling tense, I watched Commander Hagen float toward the other ship. I had misgivings about the entire mission. I even felt an urge to call it off—but I didn't.

At last, they slid up close and gently nudged their way through the overlapping force shields. That was a trick you didn't want to try at home. The slightest adjustment by a single crewmen could cause the shields to shift, and the tiny shuttle would be torn apart.

But nothing changed. They slid through and drifted in close until they touched the hull. There was no welcoming main hold to yawn open and swallow them. Instead, they had to mount the hull directly next to an external hatch.

Climbing out manually as we watched, the team worked tools and tried to break in. I thought I saw Samson's form among those on the skin of the ship, and after checking the individual feeds, I realized I was right.

"Careful out there," I said. "There's no telling—"

A gush of vapor shot up in the midst of my men right then. One figure was lifted up, his magnetic boots having broken free. He did a flip, but Samson's arm grabbed him by the fabric of his suit and hauled him back down again.

I wanted to shout orders and encouragement, but I kept quiet. They were on the spot, dealing with the situation. Distractions could be deadly.

After a few moments, the venting stopped and they climbed into the airlock. Apparently, they hadn't managed to get the ship to cycle the air out of the chamber, but they'd at least gotten the outer hatch open.

Stuffing themselves into the space inside, the trio shut the outer hatch over themselves.

"They're going to die," Mia said in a flat tone.

No one else argued or agreed, and she might well be right.

For a few moments, the vid feed went dark. The signal was blocked by the ship's hull. Then, it flickered back into life.

"...getting this, *Devilfish*?" Hagen's voice asked us.

Video came in after that. The video frames were stuttering and blurring, but we could make it out—barely. The ship's interior was dark, but at least it wasn't glazed over with frost like the first time I'd entered.

"Try that passage," I said, "the central one. That should lead to the bridge."

"Let's go," Hagen said, his breath blowing over the audio pickup.

The body cameras moved and rolled as I watched. The cameras turned as they turned, moving slowly and hampered by their heavy suits.

Another minute passed—and then they found their first body.

173

=34=

Samson knelt to examine a slumped form on the deck. It was surrounded by a black stain. The shape was undeniable, as was the state of the victim.

"Terrapinian's bleed black, don't they sir?" Samson asked me.

"Yeah... you should know. We've fought with enough of them."

Samson gently rolled the figure onto its back. It was a low-caste member of the crew. No spacesuit, only a harness full of well-used tools adorned the body.

"Get your weapons out," Commander Hagen ordered.

Samson looked up. "I guess I'm not in charge anymore."

"You never really were," Hagen told him.

Samson nodded and got up with a disruptor in his hand. He cranked up the charge to maximum and let it cycle up for a hard blast. I couldn't blame him. Something had killed the crew on that ship.

"Are you getting all this, Captain?" Hagen asked me.

"I can see enough. Proceed. If things look dangerous, pull out. It's your discretion."

"Roger that. We'll try to get to the bridge."

They walked another dozen paces before Lt. Rousseau spoke up. "Commander? I'm getting a reading... There's a heat source ahead—through that hatchway."

"Let's check it out. Samson, take point."

Samson walked ahead of the rest to the hatch and tried to open it. He couldn't get it to budge.

"The bolt's jammed."

"Try the wheel."

The Terrapinians believed in redundancy. I thought that was wise of them. If one system gave out, they always seemed to have another, even simpler way of doing things.

Samson's gauntlets came away from the wheel. They were smoking. "No dice, sir. The wheel is too hot. It's expanded."

"Let's get a crowbar or something."

"Uh..." Lt Rousseau interrupted. "I don't know, sir. Maybe we should try another passage. If there's that much heat, there must be a fire or something on the other side."

"A fire? How could it burn for days in spaceship?"

"I don't know," she admitted.

"Are you getting any residual radiation readings?"

"No... nothing big. No spikes."

Dalton was watching with the rest of us. We were in a tense circle a hundred kilometers away, glued to the feed. I noticed he'd been fidgeting more and more as they got deeper into the alien ship.

"Hagen is a madman," he said at last. "You should pull them out of there, Captain. He's only trying to prove he's got a big dick."

"What are you talking about, Dalton?"

"I'm saying he's not taking precautions. He saw a body, he found a burning room sealed behind a hatchway—it's time to get out. It's clearly a dead ship. Fly a drone through the rest of the ship if you have to see more."

"A drone would have trouble with that jammed hatch, don't you think?"

Dalton stared at me. "You could pull them out if you wanted to," he said. "It's your call."

My jaw worked. Mia was looking at me. So was Chang. They all seemed to want me to abort the mission.

Leaning back, I crossed my arms. "We're trapped by a swarm of gravity bombs. Just one or two might take us out—and there are thousands. We have to take risks. We have to have answers."

Dalton sighed, but he didn't argue. He hunched over the monitors and frowned.

I thought it was ironic that he'd started off this mission eager to see Samson in trouble, but now that he was, it seemed he wasn't happy about it at all. As friendships went, theirs was a strange one.

175

Time crawled, as did my away team. They made it through the ship via an alternate route. At last, they found their way to the bridge.

By that time, they'd found a dozen more bodies and a pile of empty harnesses. These last were a mystery to me. Terrapinians liked it hot, and they wore little in the way of clothing on their native world. The harnesses were like full sets of clothing to us.

I could understand the dead. Something had killed them, something unknown. But where had the harnesses come from? They were lying in abandoned poses all over the decks. Could they have all gone mad, some ripping off their clothes and killing the rest in a frenzy? The evidence was inconclusive.

When they reached the bridge, the situation was even stranger. Every seat had a harness draped over it, as if they'd been at their stations when the calamity struck.

"No bodies?" I demanded. "No fire?"

"The fire seems to be contained in a neighboring compartment," Hagen said, panning slowly so I could make out the scene. "As to the bodies—no sir. There's no one home here."

"Move to Verr's station. Let's have a look at it."

He did so, and I stared at the scene. Like the others, he appeared to have vanished without explanation. There was only his harness and his badge of rank.

"What's that?" Samson asked. He reached down, off camera, and brought up something in his hand. It looked metallic and circular.

I knew right off what it was. I'd seen one before.

"That's a piece of gear from a Nomad," I said. "Godwin had one of those—get Abrams up here immediately."

While they searched the rest of the bridge, I waited impatiently for my chief scientist. At last, he made an appearance.

"I predicted this," he said sternly when I showed him the still video of the circlet.

"How so, Doc?"

"The Nomads are not our friends. They're independent players. Who's to say they even oppose the Empire as we do?"

"Well, the Imperials do seem really anxious to kill them," I pointed out.

"Yes, but just because your enemy hates sharks, that doesn't mean you should make one into a pet."

176

I nodded slowly. "Point taken. Godwin has been playing his own strange game from the beginning. Did you examine the first circlet we found back on Earth?"

Abrams flicked his fingers at me. "I wanted to, but no one gave me the opportunity. They assigned the task to another team, saying that I was stretched too thinly. Absurdity."

"Right... Well, how'd you like to get another crack at a circlet? No rules this time, either."

For the first time in a long time, I saw Dr. Abrams smile. It was a real smile, the kind that a predator displays when it's given a tender baby animal to consume.

"I'd like that, Blake. I'd like that very much. Stretched too thin... fools. I'm glad you're a man who's capable of intelligent decision making—upon occasion, at least."

"Thanks, Doc. That's the nicest thing anyone's said to me all day."

=35=

I pulled out the away-team out after that. We'd all seen enough. The whole trip back to the airlock and their tiny ship was stressful for the onlookers. We kept expecting something to nail them—but they made it out eventually.

Everyone aboard the Terrapinian cruiser was either dead or had vanished. On a hunch, I had them bring back samples of any wet spots they'd found where the harnesses lay, along with a few of the harnesses themselves.

They bagged and labeled everything like evidence at a murder scene. Getting back to *Devilfish* took them two full hours.

When their tiny ship bumped up against ours at last, and they eased it into its berth, I headed down below to greet them. I was proud of them. They'd handled a dangerous mission perfectly.

When the hatch opened, Commander Hagen stepped through first. He looked pleased when he saw me.

"Captain! You came down to give it the personal touch, huh? That's a good sign. I was worried we'd be placed in quarantine or something."

"What's the point?" I asked. "We're all as good as dead if we don't figure this out, anyway."

"We could still run, sir," he said seriously. "Jump *Devilfish* out of here and let Abrams work his figures until he can get us back to Earth."

"That's possible, but have you ever considered that someone might want us to do exactly that? Why else would they have set up this elaborate trap in empty space?"

He looked troubled. "No sir, that hadn't occurred to me. You're saying this is some kind of test? Or some trick to get us out of the way?"

"I'm hoping we'll figure that out soon."

Hagen gave me the circlet then, and before I even got a good look at it, Abrams appeared at my elbow.

"You wouldn't mind if I relieved you of that, would you Blake? It will only confuse you in any case. The control system is quite alien."

I glanced at him, but held onto the circlet. "I don't know..." I said. "I'm the only one who's seen it in action. I recall Godwin using it... I wonder if—"

Flipping it over in my hand twice, I was startled by Abrams. He snaked out quick fingers and snatched it away.

"That's not a toy, Captain," he scolded, clucking his tongue. "It's dangerous."

Annoyed, I grabbed it back from him. He tried to pull away, but I was stronger and faster.

"You're making me reconsider," I said, deciding to torment him for a while longer. "Perhaps another team would be best suited—"

"Really, Captain! You can't be serious!"

"Oh, but I am. I've already got you working on your calculations for creating a rift to get us out of here safely. It makes no sense to assign you two critical projects at once."

He squirmed visibly. It did my heart good to see it.

Glancing at Hagen and Samson, I noted that my XO was frowning. My old friend, however, was grinning ear-to-ear. He knew me better. He knew I was enjoying myself.

Finally, after listening to Abrams wheedle and complain for a few minutes, I grew tired of the game and handed the circlet over. He ran off with it to his labs before I could change my mind again.

Hagen and Samson headed to the upper decks, but I examined the other artifacts they'd brought back from the dead ship. I became aware of scrutiny by the only other person nearby—Lt. Rousseau.

"Yes, Lieutenant?"

"Nothing, sir."

"You were on a dangerous mission—one that was highly successful. I'd like to hear your thoughts."

179

She frowned, then nodded. "Very well. I think it was mean and counterproductive for you to mistreat Dr. Abrams that way."

This took me by surprise. First off, I didn't think she'd noticed. Secondly, people rarely stood up for Abrams in my presence.

"Mean, huh? How so?"

"You know how driven he is to experience alien hardware. You didn't want the artifact yourself, so there was no purpose in toying with him."

"That's where you're wrong, Rousseau."

"How so?"

"Have you heard of the Nomads? The one named Godwin in particular?"

She shrugged. "Vaguely. I know you've had odd personal relationships with many aliens."

That line made me blink. Could she be complaining about my girlfriend, Mia? I couldn't think of anyone else she might be referring to.

"I am experienced with xeno-behaviors, if that's what you mean," I said. "Teasing Dr. Abrams amounted to a purposeful test."

She put her hands on her hips. "Really? What did you get out of it?"

"Information. The Nomads have the power to appear as other people—every time we see one he's in various human forms, at least. To make sure Abrams wasn't compromised, I gave him a behavioral test."

"Really? You made sure he wasn't an alien? How'd you do that?"

"Mannerisms. Behavioral twitches gave him away."

"Gave him away...? So, he's an—?"

"No," I said. "He's clean. He acted just the way Abrams would have if I'd hinted I might not give up the circlet. Threats, whining, outrage—it all fit his usual personality. The key to understanding a person's character is in their behavioral patterns."

She blinked at me, and slowly her face transformed, becoming prettier as it went. Her hands came off her hips, and she lowered them to her sides.

"So... you think an alien might be aboard our ship?"

Now, we were getting into uncharted territory. I'd been bullshitting about Abrams—I'd just wanted to irritate him a little.

But now I couldn't back off of my story. I was the captain, after all. I had to play it all the way.

"Um... it's possible," I admitted, thinking of Godwin's last visit. "Something strange is going on out here, you have to admit that."

She nodded slowly. "Thank you for sharing that, Captain," she said, heading past me and into the passageway. "I'll be sure to keep this to myself."

"Yes... it isn't general knowledge."

As she brushed by me, I sensed the heat coming up from her spacesuit into my face. She'd taken off her helmet, and she'd spent tense hours in space. Her scent was hot, but not unpleasant. For some reason, I found it intriguing.

My eyes lingered on her form as she walked down the passageway. Despite her suit being basically a bulky protective bag of fabric, she seemed quite feminine in her movements.

My mind wandered for a few seconds. She'd probably head to the showers next. I couldn't help but wish I had an excuse to join her.

Giving myself a shake, I followed Abrams' trail to his lair instead.

He'd already set up what they called a "glove box" and inserted the circlet. It was a large box made of lead-impregnated glass designed to handle hazardous materials.

With his arms thrust inside the long gloves, he handled the ring delicately, connecting wires that led to a variety of test equipment.

Stepping up and looking over his shoulder with interest, I gave him no warning of my presence.

"Hey," I barked loudly. "Any breakthroughs yet?"

He jumped, and his glasses slid on his nose to hang askew. Inside the glove box, the circlet toppled to the bottom of it with a rattling sound.

"Good God, man!" he complained. "Of course there aren't any results! I only just got hold of the thing!"

I sniffed. "All right, Doc. I'll check back soon and often. Carry on."

Walking out, I grinned as he carefully set the circlet up again. He muttered unpleasant comments under his breath in a steady stream, and it did my heart good to hear them.

=36=

nalysis teams all over my ship churned for two solid days after the away-team had returned. *Devilfish* was as much a vessel of science as of war, so there were nearly a hundred folks with doctoral degrees in something prowling our decks.

Generally, the overload of nerds had seemed like a waste of O_2 to my regular crew, but they were showing their value today. They analyzed everything that came back from the Terrapinian ship. Air samples, remains samples, equipment samples—the works.

Data flowed into the computers and the AI did most of the raw briefings for me. Higher up the food-chain, human teams were working on assembling the picture of what had happened over there into something coherent.

"So there's nothing toxic in the air other than smoke—that's confirmed?" I asked the AI.

"Correct," it said patiently.

"How did the dead ones die, then?"

"There were a variety of causes. Physical trauma, smoke inhalation, and injuries sustained in combat."

"You mean from the shockwave? When the gravity bomb hit?"

"Insufficient evidence."

"But you said physical trauma and signs of combat."

"That's correct. Most of them were either beaten or strangled to death."

I don't know why, but that thought chilled me. The idea of hundreds of beings all going berserk and beating each other to death—

"Hold on," I said to the AI. "End session."

Wheeling around, I beckoned for Chang to follow me. He did so without a word. He was heading up an analysis team, as he was a medical doctor. The only man of science in my crew who'd spent an extended time in space among the Kher.

"Sounds like someone jolted their syms to me," I said to him.

He nodded grimly. "I've come to the same conclusion. They appear to have died killing one another."

My eyes narrowed as I turned it over in my mind. "We found a Nomad circlet—on their bridge. We also found evidence that a Nomad had teleported in and out. Possibly, some of the Terrapinians went with him—or them."

"Let me postulate a theory," Chang said. "What if your friend, Godwin—"

"He's not my damned friend. He's like a ghost that haunts me."

"Sorry sir—an important distinction. In any case, Godwin knows about the syms. Godwin knows how to move among us undetected—why couldn't he do the same thing Abrams device did to the Terrapinians back at Mars Station?"

"Right..." I said. "I've been thinking along those lines. Worse, that circlet of his—he could erase memories with it."

"More mental manipulation. Influencing emotion through the syms, memories through the circlet..."

The more I thought about it, the more it seemed likely the Nomads, or someone with similar powers, had done this.

Armed with new information, I headed down to Abrams' lab to confront him. He was holding a meeting with a score of lab coats when I got there.

"...entirely unsatisfactory," he declared to them. "This team is being downgraded. No, no—I don't want to hear any whining. This circlet has been in our possession for nearly forty-eight hours, and we haven't gotten back so much as a blip from it."

I stood with my arms crossed in the hatchway until his team slunk away. They looked dejected, and they grumbled as they passed me.

"Doc?" I said. "Have a moment?"

He threw his hands high in a dramatic flourish.

"Why not? Everyone else has pestered me and failed in every particular today. Feel free to join in, Captain Blake."

"Thanks."

Walking up to the much more elaborate setup he had going now, one in which the circlet appeared to be enclosed in a compact particle accelerator, I picked up an instrument and toyed with it.

"What is it, Blake?" Abrams asked, sounding pained.

"Are those calculations ready?"

"What?"

"For a quick exit. I don't want to wait around if we see the encircling gravity bombs begin to fall."

He waved at me dismissively and snatched the instrument I was toying with from my hand. He set it back on the workbench and fixed me with a level stare.

"Of course," he said. "I've run the calculations a dozen times personally. If any drones approach, they will be detected. We'll have ample time to escape."

"Assuming they take as long to fall on our heads as they did the first time."

He blinked at me. "Your usage of the word 'fall' is incorrect in this instance—"

"Right—whatever, Doc. Let's talk about the circlet. I take it you've gotten nothing out of it?"

"Nothing. No energy pulses. No indication whatsoever that it's anything other than a piece of metal."

"Did you try X-raying it?"

He rolled his eyes at me. "Oh no, that never occurred to me!" he said sarcastically.

"Okay, okay. So, you did your best and failed. That's okay, not everyone can figure out an alien mystery in two days."

His face reddened. "I want to try it on a human subject," he said.

"Hmm... we went over that, Doc. I can't risk—"

"The memories of a crewman? How about a volunteer?"

"It wouldn't be right. What if it gives them total amnesia? What if it drives them mad?"

His tongue darted out, slid over his thin lips, and then vanished again.

"I'll do it myself," he said.

I stared at him, shaking my head. "No way. You're much too valuable for that."

This pleased him, and I realized I'd been tricked into giving him a compliment. He relaxed a little and even smiled with the left corner of his mouth.

"You really think it would be worthwhile?" I asked, staring at the circlet.

"More than that. It's a necessity. We can't figure out what this thing does without attempting to use it."

I rubbed at my jaw lightly. "You could be right... but I've got another plan."

Turning to leave, I heard Abrams raise his voice. "It won't work."

"What won't work?"

"You'll never get what you want out of Godwin, even if he *does* come back to haunt you again. He's too smart for that. I think he's been outsmarting you all along."

"What do you mean?"

"The Terrapinian Captain said he was after Godwin, didn't he?"

"Yes."

"And Godwin has been following you. Once we got out here, and we followed their ship for a time, Godwin seems to have preempted the bounty hunters."

"You mean... he struck first?"

Abrams nodded.

"That is possible... I just don't know what else I could have done."

"You could have let them go home. You could have left them with their honor and not shamed them into staying here."

I frowned at that, and I thought about it. Was Abrams right? Had I gotten the Terrapinians killed? Or was he just tweaking me now, the way I liked to tweak him? I looked at him, and I decided he wasn't just trying to make me feel bad. He wasn't like that. He wanted to feel smarter than everyone else. That's all that moved him to do anything.

There was a quiet moment in the lab. Abrams turned back to his tests and fiddled with settings. But I could see the defeat in his slumped shoulders. He was going through the motions. He couldn't get the circlet to perform any tricks—not without wearing it.

* * *

185

The next morning—it was very early in the morning—I awoke with Mia's fuzzy ears in my face. I was having a pleasant dream, but the universe had other plans for my day.

The ship's klaxons began to wail.

It was no drill. I knew that right off, and not only because there weren't any drills scheduled for today. I rolled out of bed and stumbled around the cabin, bumping into things and pulling on my uniform.

Both my sym and my traditional intercom were demanding attention. I assured everyone who cared that I was on my way to the bridge.

Commander Hagen's was the one call I took and conversed with him directly, without just giving an instant affirmative response through my sym.

"Captain?" he said urgently. "The mines are falling."

That was all I needed to hear. "Open a rift immediately."

"The generators are already winding up, sir."

I could hear them now as I strode down passages and bunched my legs before shooting up vertical, gravity-free tubes. The generators had started off with a deep thrum, but they were winding up now to a higher note every second.

Reaching the bridge, I felt the guns begin to swivel and fire. Mia wasn't there operating the weapons station—instead I saw one of Hagen's hand-picked women performing the task. She had a rough look, and she was only mildly attractive compared to the rest. Her hands worked the controls like she meant business, and the ship shuddered as her guns lashed out toward the incoming targets.

"How many targets do we have?" I demanded of Hagen.

He turned to me, his face whiter than I'd ever seen it. He looked sicker now than he had when I'd beaten him down to the ground in the final exercise of my seminar back on Earth.

"As far as we can tell sir—it's all of them."

"Helm," I said, stepping up to where Lt. Rousseau sat at her post. "The second that rift opens, you get us the hell out of here."

"Will do, Captain," she said, sounding out of breath. Her eyes never left her console. She didn't even glance at me, and I was glad for her dedication.

After taking command formally from Hagen, I sat in the center of his team. There was no time to switch the watch now. I figured we'd just have to chance this maneuver with a green deck crew.

No one talked much other than to relay information. Sensors tracked dozens of objects—then hundreds. They were all moving toward us.

The gunner worked her station with consummate skill. I was impressed. Mia perhaps had a more natural aptitude and superior speed, but this woman was smooth and practiced. She zeroed in on one target at a time, destroying it with mechanical efficiency. The fact that it was hopeless never impinged. She destroyed a score of mines before the rift appeared, all at great range. Quite possibly, she'd bought us a dozen more seconds during which we could freely draw breath.

The gunner was benefiting from our superior sensory technology, I could see that right off. Abrams was to be praised. No matter how irritating he might be, if we survived this experience, I knew I owed him a beer.

Suddenly, *Devilfish* lurched into motion, swinging her nose downward and toward our port side. A spiraling rift had formed there, nearby, but not directly ahead of us.

"You're spoiling my aim!" the gunner said, making her complaint sound bitter and heartfelt.

"Can't help it," Dalton told her. "The rift didn't appear squarely ahead of us."

"That's not—" her words cut off.

I never did find out what she was concerned about, because we plunged into the spiral of luminescence and left normal space.

Behind us, still visible as if through a circular window of blackness, I saw the Terrapinian ship. It was struck repeatedly.

The first mine made the shields spark and flash. The second strike caused that same shield to buckle and die like a snuffed flame, but still, the ship was unscathed.

That all changed a fraction of a second later. More and more mines rained down. The ship was utterly destroyed as I watched.

And then, as if it had all been a horrid dream, the iris in space behind us faded, and a new one opened up directly ahead. We plunged through, helpless to stop ourselves. We were committed now.

It occurred to me that I hadn't even bothered to ask anyone where the new rift went. I wasn't sure that it mattered, but I felt that as the captain, it was something I really ought to know.

=37=

"What the hell is this?" I demanded as the holoprojector began to display our surroundings. "This isn't Alpha Centauri!"

Alpha Centauri looked like a single point in the sky from the perspective of Earth, but it was really a triple-star system. Two of the stars, Alpha and Beta Centauri orbited one another in a tight embrace. They were both yellow stars like our sun, and they had a third companion that swung far out, a dim red dwarf.

None of this relationship appeared on the holoprojector. There was only one star, and it was big, white and hot.

"I... I don't know, sir," Commander Hagen said. "Navigator? Are these the coordinates you were given?"

"Yes, Commander. There was no deviation, no mistake. We used Rigel as a beacon this time, as Dr. Abrams suggested. I don't know what happened."

"We scattered again, that's what," I said. "Badly. Worse than before."

"But sir," Commander Hagen said, eyeing the layout of the system as it grew ever more distinct. "The odds are low we'd land in another star system. If we'd scattered, we should have—"

"It doesn't matter," I snapped irritably. I took a dubious glance at the rift as it still smoldered on the screen behind us, knowing it was a lousy option to use it again right now.

At this rate, I'd never see Earth again. Engaging my sym, I connected to the ship's network and hunted down Abrams. He was in his lab, still playing with the circlet. For some reason, this threw me into a rage.

189

"Abrams!" I roared, commandeering the PA system near his balding head and cranking the volume to the maximum. The speaker crackled and distorted, but I didn't care. "Get up to the bridge on the double. We've got a disaster on our hands—one of your making."

I didn't bother waiting for a reply or a complaint from the good doctor. I returned my perception to the bridge, then reached out to the holoprojector. Connecting my full sensory input to it, I drank in all the data the ship was feeding us and had a good look around.

One tricky power of the sym I was better at performing than most humans, was the ability to build a virtual environment using a vast body of information. Rather than having the AI depict the star system graphically, then process that with my eyes and brain, I used the sym to change my point of view.

In an instant, it was as if I stood alone in space where *Devilfish* coasted. Off to my left and up high the single large sun sat burning. It was white, and hot, tossing off more rads than old Sol did back home. The planets were there too, circling in a plane that appeared to be at an angle to our position. There were ten planets—no... I perceived more now—there were sixteen...

"Captain?" someone said, impinging on my new reality.

"Leave me alone unless this is an emergency," I ordered.

In reality, I stood on the deck of *Devilfish*'s bridge, eyes shut and mind wandering. But to anyone else, it probably looked like I was having some kind of an episode.

The disrupting presence left me alone, and I was glad for it. Space was much more peaceful, roomy and clean without them.

One at a time, starting with the innermost planet and working my way outward, I drove my perception toward each sphere. I examined the first six in quick succession, finding little that was of interest. They were all rocky, hot and small. None of them could support life nor had a single ship in orbit. The intense radiation from the star would have fried anyone daring to get so close.

The seventh planet had an atmosphere, at least. But, like our own Venus back home, it was a vile world of caustic dense clouds and intolerable heat.

Next up was a planet that was almost livable, but it was too big. A chunk of rock so large it pulled with four gravities, it had a grim atmosphere like thick soup comprised mostly of carbon dioxide—no, it was hopeless.

190

The ninth planet, after the first eight, came as a shock. It was lovely. Blue-brown, green at the poles and belted around the equator with a wide stripe of desert hotter than the Sahara. I could tell she was like a hotter, slightly larger Earth. There were no ice caps, but there were oceans. Presuming there was more than just jungle-like vegetation, all life had to exist huddled at the two poles.

It was there, in orbit over this strange world, that I saw ships. There was more than that—stations. The planet was definitely inhabited.

"Sir!"

I snapped my eyes open. For a dizzying second, I existed inside the ship and out among the stars simultaneously. I sucked in a breath and held it until the illusion passed.

"Sir?"

It was Lt. Rousseau. She had a hand on my forearm. Her brown eyes looked up at me, full of concern.

"What is it, Lieutenant?" I asked.

"Sir, we've detected electromagnetic disturbances."

I nodded slowly. The images that I'd seen in my head—they still lingered. "Right," I said. "The ninth planet. It's inhabited. They have a fleet—ships and orbital stations."

Looking down at her again, I saw a mixture of wonderment and worry in her face.

Giving her a flickering smile, I shook my head. "Don't worry. I'm good at casting my perception into space. Better than our AI, if I'm correct."

"That's unlikely," the AI complained. "I haven't gotten to the ninth planet yet. I've been thoroughly examining each of them in turn. A full analysis takes—"

"Too long," I said, finishing the computer's thought for itself. "I used a heuristic algorithm. If the planet I examined looked unlikely to support life, I immediately moved to the next."

"That's not an optimal approach."

I smiled. "What planet are you processing now, *Devilfish*?"

"The fourth," it said stubbornly.

"Abort that process. Proceed immediately to the ninth. Perform a full diagnostic on that world. That's an order."

The ship stopped talking. I got the impression it was peeved with me. That was surprising to me, as Dr. Abrams hadn't helped construct it.

I'd no sooner thought of Abrams than he appeared on the deck as if summoned.

"What is the emergency, Blake?" he demanded.

Turning to him, I walked close and threw an arm around his shoulder.

The gesture was unwelcome. He eyed my limb as if I'd wrapped a snake around his neck. He made a half-hearted attempt to remove it, but I pulled him close like a drunk might his best friend.

Stepping toward the central holoprojector, I gestured with my free hand.

"You see this? Sixteen planets? A single, white-hot F-class sun? Where are we, pray tell, Doctor?"

His eyes darted over the scene. The look of indignant outrage on his face faded, replaced by perplexity and wonderment.

"Where's Alpha Centauri? No... this isn't possible!"

He whirled then, wriggling free of my arm and approaching the pilot. He made a strangled sound of anger.

"What did you *do*?" he demanded.

"Nothing!" Lt. Rousseau said in a hurt tone. "I flew through the rift your software created!"

Abrams whirled toward the navigator next.

"I gave you *specific* coordinates. Advanced formulations. The vectors were *perfect*, every detail was calculated a hundred times over!"

"And I didn't touch your software," she said. "Look at my station. See the checksum here on your file? You didn't even give me the password, so I just loaded the file blindly. I won't do that again!"

Abrams angrily addressed her console. He tapped at it like bird pecking up seeds. After a full minute, he straightened and looked baffled.

"I'm at a loss..." he said. "There's been an error—a *gross* error—but I can't find it. Someone has tampered with my work, Captain Blake."

My lips twisted into an annoyed grimace.

"Dr. Abrams," I said gently. "Isn't it possible—*remotely* possible—that you royally screwed up?"

The very thought seemed to shock him. He shook his head.

"No," he said emphatically. "There was no mistake. I'd stake my reputation on it."

This last statement gave me pause. Dr. Abrams usually knew when he made a mistake. He often tried to cover up these incidents, using bluster and obfuscation to lower their importance—but for him to stake his reputation on an error? That was a departure.

"All right," I said, "I believe you. Obviously, you have a new project. Forget the circlet. Forget everything else. Find out where we are and how the hell we can get home."

Abrams narrowed his already narrow eyes.

"I'll do exactly that," he said. "The culprit will pay. I won't stand for this sort of thing. I won't stand for it!"

Then, he stormed off the bridge. Every eye followed him. None of us knew what to think.

After he'd left, Commander Hagen came close and leaned against my station. "You know, if we didn't need him so badly, I'd toss him out an airlock."

"You wouldn't be the first to think of that," I assured him, "and I'm pretty sure you won't be the last."

A relatively slow period followed our exciting brush with death. After escaping a hail of gravity mines, most of the crewmen aboard ship were in an upbeat mood. Sure, we were lost in an unknown system, but we were still breathing.

Only the lab coats and bridge people seemed upset. They worked hard while the others relaxed.

I shared their worries. I knew we weren't safe—far from it. Worse, we'd left Earth behind. Who knew what was going on back home while we lingered out here, lost among the stars?

"How long will that rift we made last?" I asked my pilot.

She glanced at me. "I've been monitoring that—we should have another thirty minutes at least."

Thirty minutes. Not long to make a fateful decision. Should we head back through again? There was no way of knowing if all the gravity mines had fallen, or if they'd stopped when we'd slipped away. Possibly, they were just floating around where we'd vanished, programmed to wait for our return to unleash their payloads. Should we chance destruction, or some other cruel trick, by placing ourselves back into that cage?

Our other options were no more inviting. We could linger here in an unknown system inhabited by technologically advanced beings who may or may not be friendly. We could try another blind jump into the stars—but that possibility didn't seem too inviting, either.

Unfortunately, the choice was mine to make. Sometimes, the burden of command weighed heavy on my shoulders.

=38=

Things went from bad to worse as time crawled by. The inhabited ninth planet detected us somehow, despite the fact we were hours away at the speed of light. We didn't have a chance to understand that, until they were upon us.

"Captain!" the sensors op called out. "We've got another rift—only a hundred thousand kilometers off."

"How—?" I began, but more bad news flooded in to cut me off.

"Six rifts now, sir—twenty. At least twenty."

Lights began to spin. The AI had put up an emergency alert. A fleet was arriving. That could be good—but it was probably bad.

"Any ship configurations yet?" I asked.

"Nothing. None of them have poked their noses out into sight."

We waited, and I was so tense my shoulders felt wrapped in wire. My eyes darted from the collection of new rifts to our own, and back again a dozen times.

"Helm," I said at last, "come about. Head back into our rift."

Lt. Rousseau worked her controls, and the ship slid around in an arc. She looked over her shoulder at me. "We don't know if it's safe to go back, sir."

"True, but I'm willing to bet we're being hunted by Imperial phase-ships right now. Look at the newest data coming in from the ninth planet."

Every eye swiveled to review it. The AI was drawing a grim picture. It had taken time, due to the distance, but the Imperials were clearly the owners of the world in question. The resolution of the optics, analysis of the electromagnetic radio traffic and a dozen other clues had all led inexorably to the same conclusion. We were in an Imperial system.

Worse, some of the ships in orbit were phase-ships. Such vessels were masters of stealth. Until recently, we'd thought only our ships could slip out of a rift point without leaving a wake or any other recognizable trace, but now it seemed the Imperials could do the same.

"Phase-ships," Lt. Rousseau said in a quiet, fearful tone. "That's why we can't see them. They're stalking us, but how did they know we were here? We've only just arrived."

"FTL travel is possible, why not FTL communications?" I asked her. "Besides, the evidence is overwhelming. The odds an enemy fleet would show up here by chance are astronomical."

"You're right, Captain," Commander Hagen said. "They have to be Imperial phase-ships. Should we employ countermeasures?"

I glanced at all the predictors and arcing red lines between the rifts and our ship. "We should have ample time to slip away," I said, "but I don't trust the predictions. Nothing Abrams' computers have predicted has come true today. Employ countermeasures."

The ship shuddered as dozens of drones were unloaded in our wake. They immediately began broadcasting various jamming signals, and the scene depicted on our holoprojector wavered and froze.

"Our jammers are messing up our sensors?" I asked.

"Yes. They've upgraded them—but they have unpleasant side effects now."

I didn't mind. If they saved our bacon, losing track of the enemy was a problem I was willing to deal with. They were already here, stalking us. What difference did it make if we blinded ourselves? At least the enemy couldn't see us either.

We were picking up speed, and I dared to allow a tiny smile flicker over my face. We'd soon get out of here and head home.

As if they could read my mind, the enemy crews finally took action.

"Incoming channel request, sir," my comms officer said.

I turned and made eye-contact. "Patch it through."

The face that loomed on my screen was a surprise to me. I'd expected an Imperial to call, mind you. What I hadn't expected was to recognize her.

"Lael?" I asked. "Captain Lael?"

"Leo Blake..." she said in response. Her face registered disgust. "I might have known you were working for the Nomads. Who else would have the right mixture of bravery and bestial ignorance to bring our enemies to our doorstep?"

"Enemies?"

"The Nomads, Blake," she said, speaking as one might to a small child. "You can't tell me that you didn't know they were coming through the rift behind you."

Confused, I looked at my sensor op, and she shrugged. I stood up and strode to the holoprojector.

"Ship," I said, "drop the long-range sensory data. Show me our immediate vicinity."

The image wavered and went dark. There was our own ship, depicted with a green wire-frame in the center of the map. Ahead of us was the dying rift. There didn't seem to be anything else—

"Ship!" I said, alarmed at a sudden idea. "Deploy Abrams' gravimeters. Scan local space."

Suddenly, a swarm of red contacts appeared. They were small, the size of beach balls. They weren't moving, just drifting out of the rift in a steady stream.

I felt a sick, cold lurch in my stomach. These were the same gravity-drones we'd thought we'd left behind. They'd followed us.

Worse, I realized now. We'd opened the way for them. We'd brought them out here to an Imperial star system. We'd deposited them on Lael's doorstep.

How could such an act, intentional or not, do anything other than reignite the smoldering war between the Imperials and the Rebel Kher?

Turning back to Lael, who was a floating head and torso above the scene, I let my mouth drop open, and I shook my head.

"I'm sorry. We didn't know. They chased us, trapped us, and dropped bombs upon us until we ran."

"And you ran straight here? Directly into the arms of your most dedicated enemies? An unbelievable tale even coming from you, a consummate liar."

"I—I don't know how this could have happened. We were navigating toward Alpha Centauri—not whatever star system this is. We scattered, and we—"

"No, Blake," she said. "Try to expand your limp mind. You did *not* scatter. You did not target a local star. You came here directly and without deviation."

"It would seem you're right," I admitted. "We've managed to commit a grave error. We'll shoot all these drones. Perhaps if we set one off, we can destroy the rest in the plasma cloud. They're tightly bunched now."

"Self-destruction?" she said, and she cocked her lovely head, which resembled a flower on the long stalk of her neck. She studied me for a moment. "Ah—of course. You fear our righteous revenge. You fear our wisdom, which dictates that animals that have been proven dangerous must be put down."

"Not at all," I lied. "As a friendly peaceful power, Earth wishes to right what has gone wrong. We can't stomach the thought of a single civilian death due to our mistake."

Lael chuckled. "You are amusing. We have an animal, a small thing we call a *tonch*, which can be taught to dance on its hind legs for hours when the sting of a nerve-whip is correctly applied. You remind me of a *tonch* now."

Her insults and threats had no effect on me today. I was too horrified at what I'd done. Somehow, we'd been duped into bringing this armada of gravity-drones to an Imperial system.

We were dupes, it was true. The patsies of the Nomads. I vowed to bring up the topic with Godwin, should I be so blessed as to live long enough to meet that snake again.

"The enemy phase-ships are getting closer, sir," the sensory ops officer told me quietly. "We still can't target them, but the signal is getting stronger. If you can keep her talking..."

I nodded to the officer and turned numbly back toward Lael. I knew she must not be within range yet, or she'd be firing.

"There was one Nomad among us," I admitted. "It took us months to figure out that's what he was. He's been appearing and disappearing for a long time. We thought—we thought he was some kind of envoy."

Lael laughed aloud. Imperials, in my experience, rarely did that.

"You're too stupid to be allowed to breathe," she said. "I'm recommending eradication for your species after this."

The screen went blank. We all stared at it for a moment, as if caught up in a spell.

"Well, that could have gone better," Commander Hagen said, sighing.

For a moment, I looked at him, my mind whirling with plans. Most of them were pointless and dangerous. At last, I selected one of the worst.

My eyes and my face hardened. I turned to Lt. Rousseau, who'd almost managed to wade through the gravity drones to the rift again.

"Helm," I said gently, laying a hand on her shoulder. "Come about to a new heading. Target the enemy ships—wherever that signal came from."

She did as I ordered, then looked up at me with fear in her eyes.

Opening a general call channel, I summoned new crewmen to the bridge. I needed my best at my side now—this might well be our last stand.

"Chang, Samson, Dalton, Mia—and Dr. Abrams. Everyone report to the bridge on the double."

"You don't trust us, sir?" Lt. Rousseau asked.

"It's not that," I said. "I need a crew that trusts *me* implicitly."

She didn't argue. When Dalton showed up, she stood down, relieved of duty. She walked off the bridge without a look back.

Mia, I noticed, tracked every step of her retreat like a cat watching a snuffling mouse slink down a hole.

"Permission to stand the bridge, Captain?" Commander Hagen asked.

I nodded to him absently. My eyes were riveted to the local display. The number of bombs floating around our ship—it was like being in a sea of ball bearings.

"Mia," I said, "as soon as you get lined up, lay down a pattern of fire toward the approaching phase-ships."

"We can't see them, sir."

"I know that. Do your best to hit them anyway. Use your instincts. They're out there, rushing into range. If we can hit them before they can shoot back..."

"Target area selected," she said. "Pattern programmed. Locked and ready to fire."

"Fire at will."

Mia didn't hesitate. She rarely did. The ship began to shiver as the big mains unloaded into what appeared to be empty space.

It had begun. We were fighting, and this battle was already hopeless.

Even as strikes were being tallied against open expanses of space ahead of us, I ignored all that action.

Staring at the river of floating metal surrounding us, I could not help but wonder what they would do. Any single one of them could get it into its tiny artificial brain to light itself up and finish us. There was nothing we could do, however, other than look like we were on their side.

=39=

For a time, the battle was rather sterile. We were hammering away at empty space, hoping for a lucky strike. Around us, spreading thinner by the minute, was a vast armada of smart-bombs that were apparently seeking targets just as we were.

"Captain?" Dr. Abrams said, being the very last to make his way up to the bridge in answer to my summons. "What is it now? Do you want me to man a gun or something?"

"It might make you marginally more useful," I admitted. "But no. I want you to answer a few questions for me before we die out here in a vain flash of glory."

He looked at the tactical situation and blanched. "It looks like you've got too much on your hands to bother—"

"No," I said firmly. "You're staying up here with me. Now, did you or did you not interact with the Nomads recently?"

Abrams hesitated. "I'm not sure I know what you mean."

"I, on the other hand, am sure that you do."

His features took on a stubborn cast. He crossed his arms and lifted his sharp nose into the air.

"I see what this is," he said. "The blame-game. When things go badly, the need for a scapegoat often becomes critical."

"We're far past that now. Doctor, we're not likely to survive another hour. In that light, let me ask you a simple question. Did you, or did you not, have contact with the alien known to us as Godwin?"

Abrams fidgeted. "This is some sort of witch-hunt, isn't it?"

"I'm trying to ascertain the truth, Doctor. You came up with an astounding number of discoveries in a relatively short amount of time. One of them, for example, was the drive we used to open that rift at our stern."

Abrams' eyes slid toward our stern, and his expression shifted to one of alarm.

"We're not heading back to the Solar System? Have you gone mad yet again, Blake?"

"Yeah, probably," I admitted. "Now, answer my question."

"All right," he said. "If it will stop you from killing us all in this Quixotic manner. I was visited by Godwin several times. During those meetings certain... items of value were exchanged."

"Such as... the plans to build an FTL drive?"

"I might have been provided with a little guidance," he said primly. "A helpful hand when certain technical restraints arose. You have to understand, I took such design suggestions in an advisory sense only. I was on the verge of breaking through on every one of them."

"Right..." I said in a heavy tone. "So, Godwin fed you the design for our engine. What else?"

He sputtered for a moment. "There might have been some help with the ship's control package..."

"Let me guess. He gave you a software toolkit to build our AI. Did it ever occur to you that Godwin's navigational package caused us to scatter the first time? That you should never have taken its recommended settings?"

"YES!" he boomed suddenly. "Of *course* it occurred to me! The first time we jumped, I examined the AI settings and rejected them. They made no sense. I came up with my own equations and used them instead. I didn't trust Godwin implicitly. Quite the opposite."

I looked at him, thinking back to our first foray into interstellar space. "But we scattered that first time. Your numbers were no good. So, the second time you created a rift, you trusted the AI?"

"What choice did I have? We were about to be blown to bits by those damnable mines."

"Right... it was all a setup. We were led out here like dupes. The Nomads must have had a ship fly here and deposit thousands of these drones. Then, they needed a delivery vehicle. They got us to do their dirty work for them. We transported their weapons to an Imperial star system—this one—so they didn't have to."

Abrams peered at me, thinking hard. "It seems plausible," he admitted. "But in the name of all that is Holy... why?"

"I can answer that one, Doc," Hagen said, stepping closer to us. "You nailed it two minutes ago. They wanted a scapegoat. A patsy to deliver their bombs. Or maybe, they just wanted us out of the way. In either case, we're involved in a diplomatic disaster out here, and I don't know if we can do a damned thing about it."

"Abrams," I said. "You're a liar. A court might someday decide if you're a traitor as well, if we're lucky. But for right now, you're all I have. Use the facts we have. Use the knowledge that the ship's computer has been compromised in your next set of equations. Try to map us out a safe route home."

He nodded and hurried off the bridge.

"Are you hitting anything, Mia?" I asked.

"Negative," Chang answered for her. "She's pounding empty vacuum and filling it with radioactive particles."

"I'm firing blind!" she complained. "It helps if you can see your prey."

I noticed that as she said this, she was looking at me. I wasn't sure if that was significant or not.

"All right," I said. "Helm, ease off the throttle. Slowly begin to brake."

Dalton looked at me and smirked. "Trying to lose all these little steel doggies, eh?"

"Something like that."

At first, my gambit appeared to work. The spheres that were orbiting around us pulled ahead. They no longer formed a swirling cloud, but rather a vanguard.

But then, things took an unexpected turn.

"Captain! They're on our stern!"

For just a second, I thought Samson was talking about the spheres. But I realized as he hit the emergency dump of decoys and shielding, it had to be something else.

"Evasive action. Random course, Dalton."

He had us all standing on our heads a moment later, sending our ship into a slowly corkscrewing plunge. It was all relative, of course, but it *felt* like we were moving downward.

There were three smaller vessels on our stern. Phase-ships. They'd come out of hiding and fired immediately.

The enemy's first salvo went wide. We'd pumped out obscuring crystals, aerogels and decoys, but their software made rapid adjustments. Negating our defensives the second time around, they nailed our flank shields several times.

The ship shuddered and there was a horrid electrical ripping sound, as if we'd been struck by lightning.

"We've lost our port side shield," Samson informed me.

"Mia, get some fire on those phase-ships!"

"I'll have to cut through the gravity drones to do it."

I looked and saw she was right. Dozens of our companions had broken off, and they were now plunging to intercept the enemy ships.

"Hold your fire!" I ordered her. "Let's see what the drones do first. Dalton, accelerate away from the point of impact—if they're going to go off, we don't want to be here.

The phase-ship captains had the same idea, it appeared. They broke off and moved away—but the spheres pursued them. The chase lasted about a minute, and then the spheres caught up and went off in unison.

"Did they phase out?" I demanded.

"I don't think so," Chang said. "I think they couldn't get charged up fast enough to escape. There's debris... Sir, I think they've all been destroyed."

I slammed my hands together in triumph. "Then Nomads are on our side so far."

"Well," Chang said, "at least they're programmed not to destroy us just yet."

His description was far less positive, but I didn't argue with him. There was no reasonable way that I could.

"Dalton, swing back down into that swarm of drones," I said. "I think we're safer there."

"I'm way ahead of you, Captain."

We did a looping barrel-roll and plunged back into the mix of spheres. They grudgingly bumped out of our way.

"Any sign of the Imperials?" I asked.

"Negative," Chang said. "They're maintaining stealth. Apparently the Nomad drones can't find them either. They only attacked when they came back into normal space."

"Right... if we stay here in this bee-swarm, we should be okay. Where are we headed, Chang?"

He worked his numbers for a few seconds before looking up. A glittering yellow arc of light lit up the screen, and the holoprojector zoomed out to show more of the star system.

"The ninth planet..." I said. "I'm not surprised."

"Captain, we've got another trio of contacts."

I swung my view to the region specified. A triangular formation of three ships had emerged a thousand kilometers off our flank. They were pacing us.

"Can we fire through this cloud of marbles without hitting them?" I asked.

"I'm not that good," Mia complained.

"Then I suggest we fall back and bring our main batteries to bear on them, sir," Commander Hagen said.

I looked at him thoughtfully. "No. They're just hanging out there. They want us to come out to play. They want us to either shoot one of these drones by accident, or to leave their protection to attack. Remember, Captain Lael has plenty of other ships out here, hidden on this battlefield."

Hagen stepped up to my station, rubbing at his chin. "This is tricky," he admitted. "Tactically complex. We're fighting ghosts, and relying on alien smart-bombs that we can't talk to with only guesses to guide us on their behavior."

"That's right," I said. "It gets worse when you're dealing with twenty different species all running around a battlefield at once. The Rebel Kher are anything but tightly organized."

He nodded slowly and didn't offer any more suggestions. That was a pity, as I could have used a good one about then.

=40=

"**O**kay," I said, "this can't last forever. Lael is trying to trick us out of our nest of drones, but she can't wait until we hit her world. She has to make a decision soon."

"We don't know that, sir," Samson interjected.

"Why not? You don't think she wants to protect fellow Imperials?"

"I don't think we know for sure who lives on that world. What if it's a Rebel Kher planet?"

That thought did give me pause. Could we be riding herd on a deadly swarm of intelligent bombs? Taking a force of fantastic destructive power straight into the waiting arms of an ally?

Heaving an uncertain breath, I came to a decision: I needed more information.

"Contact Lael."

"She's not answering, sir," Chang reported.

Leaning back in my seat, I pondered my next move. After a few moments, I came up with an angle. I opened a channel myself and broadcast a message.

"To the new commander of the Imperial task force. We present you with Earth's sorrowful regrets at the death of Captain Lael. We found her to be a capable adversary, even if she tended to make many tactical errors. Hopefully, you will do better and bring less shame to the Empire for which—"

That was as far as I got. I rather regretted the quick success of my tactic, because I had a lot more backhanded compliments to hand out—they were lined up and ready to go inside my head.

"This is Captain Lael!" said an angry voice. She appeared then, a ghostly form superimposed over the depicted star system. "What do you want, Blake?"

"Captain?" I exclaimed in surprised. "I had no idea—who led that brave assault on our stern if it wasn't you?"

"If I'd been leading the assault, your ship would have been destroyed!" she assured me. Calming down with a visible effort, she continued speaking a moment later. "Flora was a capable second," she said. "She had promise, but that potential will never be realized now."

"A pity..." I said in a vague tone. "Tell me, if you've lost the will to fight, why are you still following us at all? Perhaps you'd best race ahead to your homeworld and work to mount a superior defense."

Lael made an odd noise. It was something between hiss and a gargle of rage.

"I've heard enough of your insults. Your ship will never reach Diva. Of that, I can assure you."

She closed the channel, and I laughed out loud. "She named her planet! I wasn't even going for that much. Where does that leave us, Chang...? Navigation?"

The navigational team huddled around a few consoles for about ten minutes before they were willing to make the call.

"It's Diva—a star system near Pollux."

"Yeah, I heard that. It's Imperial, right?"

"We've got no reliable charts from this far out. The Rebel Kher maps fade away at this distance."

That made me blink in concern. "We're *way* out? As in more than a thousand lights?"

"Yes, Captain. It's more like two thousand lights."

I winced visibly. For some reason, being so far from home always made me feel a little faint. I didn't like being someplace where my home star couldn't be picked out by the naked eye on a clear night.

Two thousand lights... At this range, it would be hard to find old Sol with a telescope.

"How'd we get out here so far, so fast?" I demanded. "Normally, a long jump takes time, and you usually scatter when you do."

"Why don't you think we scattered?" Hagen asked.

207

"Space is too big. If you lose your target-lock on a beacon star, you'll probably hit the open void, not a populated star system."

"Yeah... I knew that."

"When you apply classroom knowledge to a real live voyage, you find out it's all different don't you?"

"Reality is always a deal-breaker, Captain."

My thoughts brought me back to Abrams. I hadn't checked on him lately. I was interested in a report on his progress, but I didn't want to leave the bridge in a volatile situation.

Deciding to ride things out for a time, I spent half an hour in my command chair, monitoring everything. During that time, Lael didn't attempt to kick us in the ass again, but we hadn't yet dared to fall out of formation with the swarm.

"How long until we reach the ninth planet—the one she called Diva?"

"About fifteen more hours, Captain."

"That gives us some time to think. I want my senior staff all coming up with scenarios. Commander Hagen, you have the watch. I'm going below."

Hagen looked surprised, but he didn't comment. I left him in command and headed down to pester Abrams. I knew from experience I wasn't going to get anything useful out of him by just calling.

There was an impressive huddle going on when I got down to the labs. At least fifteen lab coats were humping over figures and simulations. They had a full-fledged holoprojector of their own, and they'd worked out countless scenarios.

"What's the verdict, Doc?" I asked aloud.

A few eyes flicked to me, but no one answered. It took me a second to realize Abrams himself wasn't in the midst of his team. He was, in fact, nowhere to be found in the planning rooms.

One woman with a strange haircut and glasses caught my eye with a waving finger. Wordlessly, she pointed me toward the swinging doors in the back.

Striding that way, I straight-armed the doors, sending them flying. Somehow, I already knew what I was going to find.

There, sure enough, was Abrams. He was crouching over a shiny object in a glove box.

The room was dark, but not pitch-black. The primary light source was from inside the box, where his hands and his attention were directed.

Crossing my arms, I cleared my throat loudly.

"What is it?" Abrams demanded without looking back. "Is that clown down here again? Am I to have no peace?"

"No," I said. "There's no rest for the wicked, Doc."

He slid his hands out of the glove box and straightened. "Ah, Captain Blake. I was wondering when you would return to check on me. I'm sure you're satisfied, no?"

"No," I said. "Why would I be satisfied? I've gotten nothing from your team, and it's been an hour."

He spun around with a look of sudden rage. "An hour? Those cretins!"

He charged past me and began shouting in the labs. Soon, I heard the thudding of feet.

"You'll get your report. We came up with a new formulation perhaps forty minutes ago. I approved it and moved on."

"Why didn't I hear about it?"

He shrugged. "I told them to check the numbers. Perhaps, they are timid. Or perhaps, they have difficulty with so many variables at once."

"I don't know what you're talking about. I charged you with finding out why we couldn't jump wherever we wanted to. Why were your calculations so far off?"

"The answer is so simple even you can understand it," he said. "The swarm threw us off."

When he said that, my face froze. I did the math in my head— not the advanced calculus, mind you, I'm talking about the basic addition.

Creating a worm-hole was a tricky business. Getting a rift started was relatively easy. You aimed a device at a point in space and ripped a hole in it. That wasn't much more than an application of intense warping to very tiny region.

The real trick came when you were placing the end-point of your tunnel at the precise coordinates in normal space that corresponded to where you wanted to go. It was like firing a rocket at an angle—lighting the thing off was easier than getting it to land exactly where you wanted it to.

What we used to perform this trick were guidelines, mostly large gravity-wells. Big stars served this purpose in most cases. We weren't interested in their radiation output, brightness, etc. We were only interested in their gravitational pull. That recognizable constant could be used to guide our placement of an end-point across the lightyears.

Knowing all this, I immediately understood what Abrams was talking about.

"Gravity-drones..." I said. "Of course. They were all around us, not close enough to distort our ship's position, but plenty close enough to ruin our calculations."

"Exactly," Abrams said, nodding. "The first time we jumped, I ignored the data the AI was feeding me. The computer's numbers made no sense—however, the AI clearly knew about the spheres and had compensated."

"Right," I said. "It all makes some kind of sense now... but the second time—we didn't come out on target then, either."

"Oh yes, we did."

I frowned. "But we weren't targeting the Diva system. We didn't even know it existed."

Dr. Abrams gave me a thin smile. "No... but the AI did. The truth was, if I'd taken the numbers the first time, or the second time—or the tenth time for that matter, we would have ended up right here."

"The AI is compromised," I said. "It's programmed to take us right here."

"Yes, we've discussed this before."

"But it's conclusive now—can she hear us?" I said, looking around at the dim-lit walls of chamber.

"No. I took the precaution of banning the AI cameras and sensors from this deck."

"Well done. I'll do the same on the bridge. What do we do now?"

He shrugged. "We form a rift, fly through it, and head home. What else?"

I thought about it. "You've done the math on that—without the computer?"

"Now that I've compensated for these gravity-warping spheres, yes. We can go wherever we want to."

My lips compressed into a hard line. I felt that a hard decision was on my shoulders.

We could bug out. We could leave Lael and her handful of phase-ships at will. They could deal with the spheres plunging down toward the ninth planet.

I knew that option wasn't going to leave a satisfactory feeling in my gut. Sure, the Imperials had wiped out hundreds of our worlds. Why shouldn't we do the same to them when we got the chance?

But still, I was having a hard time with the concept of killing a planet full of civilians. Lael's ships—they weren't going to be able to destroy this swarm. They just didn't have the firepower, or the numbers.

The Nomads had used me. They'd used me as a tool to strike a hard blow, probably a deadly one, against an Imperial world. What's more, they knew Earth would be blamed for the attack, not just them.

We'd been manipulated. We'd been tricked into playing the part of an ally, rather than the safer role of the bystander. We were being dragged back into this war on their side.

With every passing second I spent thinking about it, I became increasingly pissed off.

=41=

Abrams had gone back to his work. After a few minutes he turned to find me still standing behind him, and I was still cursing under my breath.

"Godwin, you alien prick..." I said to no one in particular.

Abrams gave me a crooked smile. "It is difficult to accept the fact one has been played, is it not, Blake? On a number of occasions, I've felt the same way you do right now."

"I bet you have," I admitted.

"You may not realize this," he continued, "but I pride myself on my intellect."

I almost choked, but I managed to change it into a cough. "You don't say, Doc?"

"Yes, it's true. It is a sin, you know—pride, I mean. The Christians would call it the greatest of all sins."

I nodded, only half-listening. Most of my mind was focused on a heavy decision. Should I let the Nomads destroy Diva, or should I try to stop them?

"Pride leads to downfalls. I would only give you one word of advice: don't let pride be your guiding light."

With that, he turned back to his box and continued toying with it.

"That's real helpful, Doc," I told him, approaching his box. "What are you doing with this thing now, anyway?"

"Idle foolishness," he said without looking at me. "Do not be concerned."

My frown shifted. When Dr. Abrams told you to calm down, it was generally way past time to panic.

"Hmm…" I said, examining his work. "Why not just put the damned thing on your head and activate it?"

"I value my brain more highly than you do, apparently."

"That might be true…" I admitted. "Tell me, what are the most likely effects one would suffer?"

He looked at me speculatively. "Your recent memory may vanish."

I nodded. "I know about that one. What else?"

"You might die."

"Die? That's it? You just fall over dead?"

"No, not exactly. You would become a puddle of strange chemicals on the deck."

We stared at each other for a second. Suddenly, I was beginning to get what he was saying. "You think this thing—this circlet of metal—is how the Nomad comes and goes? What evidence do you have of that?"

He shrugged. "There must be a way. There must be a receiver. The technology is very advanced, but even a fusion reaction needs a generator to contain it. I know he used our transmat system on a number of occasions. More recently, when he visited us repeatedly—including on this vessel—there was no transmat available."

I stared into the glove box. The power that gleaming circle of metal might have—it was amazing.

"Why are you telling me this now?" I asked him, suddenly suspicious.

"It was something you said. About not caring too much about your brain."

I looked at him, aghast. "You want me to put it on and test it, don't you?"

"I did not *say* that. What you suggest would be a reckless act."

"Damned straight it would…"

"But…" he continued, "it would be highly revealing. I've done everything I can without a human subject."

"Why not try a housecat or something?"

He didn't say anything. I looked at him accusingly. "You already tried it, didn't you?"

"Non-human subjects have been fruitless. Possibly, it will not work at all for anything other than Nomads. We just don't know."

213

"But you still want me to try it. Why not one of your lab coats? You seem to have plenty."

"They have proven disloyal in this instance."

I chuckled. "You mean they told you to fuck off and try it yourself, right?"

"That is a crude representation—but essentially accurate."

"Hmm..." I said. "I'm the captain. I can't risk my life. To do so would be irresponsible."

"Good point," he said smoothly. "Perhaps you could find a volunteer among the crew. Surely, they can't all be worthy of their keep."

"Wow, you are an ice-cold prick, you know that, Doc?"

"Again with the pointless insults. I'm a man of science. Without me, you would not be standing on this deck. You would not be making these decisions. Earth would have no ships to send into space at all."

"Yeah, yeah... you and some sneaky aliens are owed a great deal. But that doesn't change what you are."

He fell silent, and I stared at the circlet. At last, I sighed. "I can't do it now—probably never. I've got critical decisions to make. Help me make the right calls, Doc. What would you do?"

"About the swarm and the Imperials? That's an easy one. Fall back from the swarm a little. When they get close to the ninth planet, form a rift and jump back to Earth. With thousands of bombs zeroing in on their world, the enemy will not have time to worry about us."

I shook my head. "That's some cold shit."

He shrugged. "They *are* the enemy. They will not rest until they're tired of killing us. Perhaps, if we kill a few of them now, some of their bloodlust will drain from them."

Leaving Abrams behind, I walked back to the tubes. I was more disturbed and uncertain than ever. What was the right move to make? I didn't feel certain about any of my options. Abrams' advice was sterile and horrid—but he was right. The Imperials *had* killed countless Rebel Kher. Had the situation been reversed, they probably would've slaughtered every human on Earth without a qualm.

But being a human, I was plagued by doubts and worse—hopes. I dared hope for a real peace, for an end of hunting parties coming out of the Empire to wantonly destroy lesser civilizations.

When mercy was shown, it could sometimes change the nature of a relationship between peoples. Perhaps this could be a new beginning...

There was more to my thinking than that, of course. There was the other side of the equation, the negative side. If Earth was seen by the Imperials as hostile, we were more likely to be targeted the next time they came to our stars for adventure and sport. But if we'd done them a good turn, well... maybe they could be convinced to go elsewhere.

Even that solution was grim to contemplate. We'd be hiding, ducking low, hoping the bear ate the next guy. Was that really all we could do?

The situation was maddening.

I was so lost in thought I didn't even notice a huddled shape at my feet. I almost stumbled over the body of Lt. Rousseau. She was motionless, stretched out on the deck in an empty passageway.

=42=

Immediately, I knelt to check Lt. Rousseau's vitals. Her heart was still beating. There were four matching red lines on her face, and they told me the story: She'd been attacked.

Drawing my weapon, I looked around. The passage was quiet.

Kneeling again, I tried to rouse the lieutenant.

"Sarah?" I said softly. "Are you all right?"

It was the classic, inane question people always asked when they found someone who'd been knocked flat. Obviously, she was *not* all right.

She rolled onto her back and moaned softly. Her hand came up, pressing her wrist to her cheek. It came away bloody, and she looked at the blood with bleary eyes.

"Captain?" she said.

"I'm sorry about this," I said. "I should have seen it coming..."

"It was Mia," she said, still looking dazed. "She attacked me... She told me I had to be—to be your second girl. I didn't understand what the hell she was talking about, and she became angry."

I nodded. "Right... So she hit you harder?"

"That's right. My confusion threw her into a rage."

I heaved a sigh. "She's not human. Sometimes I forget that."

Lt. Rousseau lifted herself up on her elbows. I tried to help her, but she pushed me away.

"I'm not going to be your sex-slave," she growled.

"I wouldn't suggest it."

"Especially not with that fuzzy bitch of yours around..."

That comment made my eyebrows rise speculatively. Was she saying that she *might* be interested in the post if Mia wasn't involved? I decided this would be a bad time to ask for a clarification.

Trying not to admire her form as she got to her feet, I apologized again and told her I'd discipline Mia for this.

"No," she said. "That wouldn't be right. She's Rebel Kher. We're effectively at war with the Imperials again. Like it or not, getting brained by a rival is part of the game now, right? You said we had to get used to this sort of thing, didn't you?"

"Yeah... but... where are you going?"

"To the gym. She's not going to sucker punch me like that again."

Lt. Rousseau stalked off, and I watched her go. Sometimes, I felt like I missed human women. This was one of those times. Mia was fantastic, but... she caused problems. She was different.

"That one *cannot* be first girl!"

Whirling around, I saw Mia standing in the passage behind me. She was better at sneaking around than any human I knew of. I guess that was part of her heritage.

"Dammit, Mia. You can't go around attacking bridge officers out of jealously."

"Why not?"

"Because I said so, and I'm the captain of this ship."

She pouted for a moment. "I will *not* be second girl," she repeated. "Never again. I will fight for my position."

"Mia, you're not going to have to share me with anyone. That's not expected of you. I've explained this before. Human males—"

"Human males are just like Ral males," she finished for me. "You're Kher underneath. Kher males all have the same instincts. Don't lie! I've been watching you. I'm *always* watching you."

"That's not—"

"You called her Sarah. When you touched her—you called her Sarah. That is a term of endearment for that one."

"It's her first name."

"Right. But you never call Dalton by his first name. When have you ever touched his cheek gently, as if caressing an infant?"

"Well... but..."

"So *don't lie!* Ral has a different ratio of males to females, but the game is the same. I just want you to know that I *will not* be second-girl. I would return to Ral first. If you take her, and I am still first-girl, I can accept that—but I will not be happy. I will

217

mark her face whenever I want to, just as I've done today. That is my right."

After this little speech, she marched off as well. I wasn't sure what to say, so I just watched her stalk away. At least she'd gone in the opposite direction that Sarah had chosen. I didn't think this would be a good time for these two to meet up again.

Sarah...

Mia was right. I was using Lt. Rousseau's first name in my thoughts now. I felt something for the girl, and she felt the same way about me. I'd often noticed there was a certain light in her eyes when we looked at one another.

Heaving a deep sigh, I pushed all these distractions from my mind and headed toward the bridge again. I told myself firmly that my personal life would have to take a backseat. I had much bigger problems to deal with.

Reaching the bridge, I pondered my immediate problem. The swarm of gravity-drones still surrounded us, and together we were plunging toward the ninth planet like a pack of gleeful hounds. The drones clearly meant to destroy the target world.

There were a few options I could think of. I could fall back, as Abrams had suggested, and try to escape. If we timed that move to coincide with the final approach of the drones, the Imperials would be too busy trying to save themselves to worry about one human ship full of cowards.

We had four hours left, so I decided to try another more palatable option: diplomacy. I figured it couldn't hurt to try to talk to the Imperials again.

"Lael," I said, transmitting in the clear. "We have to discuss the fate of the local Imperial world."

There was a hesitation, but it was less than a minute long. I'd been just about to repeat my words when she answered me.

Lael looked harried and angry. Her voice tones matched her appearance.

"*You...*" she said, spitting out the word. "Why do you insist on gloating like this? Isn't a billion deaths enough to sate your lust for glory?"

"What...? Hold on, it's not like that. I'm trying to figure out a way to get out of this situation."

"Ah... the blood-bargaining. My staff has been wondering if you'd try some last minute extortion before the final moments. Apparently, the more pessimistic members of my crew were right."

"No, they weren't," I said firmly. "I'm just contacting you to let you know I'll help if I can."

"Help? How might you help?"

"I don't know... maybe we could divert the spheres before it's too late."

"Divert? All you need to do is change course. They follow you like their mother."

I shook my head. "It looks that way, but that isn't what's happening. The spheres—"

"They are protecting you! They do not strike you, even while you are in their midst. Don't pretend and lie, Leo Blake. I know you. I know you are in an alliance with the Nomads."

"We were used," I said patiently. "These spheres struck a Terrapinian ship we were flying with before they forced us to come here."

"What do you mean, forced you?"

"We had to create a rift to escape. Our navigation was compromised, and we ended up here."

"Why would the Nomads bother with such a complex plan?"

"Well, they needed my ship to open the rift for them to begin with. The spheres can't jump between the stars on their own."

"All right," Lael said in a purring voice. Her tone had shifted dramatically, and that put me instantly on edge. "Let's say I believe you. Let's try an experiment. Fall back from your little friends. Let them move away from you, and you'll have proven your words."

She had a good point. How could we work together if I couldn't demonstrate I wasn't in control of the swarm?

Commander Hagen slid up to my station and gave me a slow, definite shake of his head. The message was clear—he didn't want me to try it.

"Helm," I said, "reduce speed—gradually. Drop back, reducing our velocity by ten percent."

Dalton gave me a strange look, but he did it. We began to fall away from the swarm. It soon moved ahead, looking like a giant school of silvery round bubbles.

"How far are we going to let them—?" Dalton began, but he never finished his question.

"Enemy vessels, phasing-in at our stern!" Chang called out.

Red contacts began to appear behind us. Every second, the swarm moved ahead and away, while the phase-ships drew closer. There were five of them—then seven.

"All power to our stern shields," I said calmly.

"We can't survive a strike from that many of them, Captain," Hagen said, "the shields will go down in the first barrage."

"I know..." I said quietly. "Keep falling back, Dalton. Let's see what they do."

=43=

I have to give Lael some credit, she didn't fire on us right away. She contacted me first.

"What kind of a vicious ape-trick is this, Blake?" she demanded.

"There's no trick, Lael. Not this time."

"You're hoping we can't catch up. You're hoping your spheres will get to the planet unimpeded. But you should know we have enough acceleration to catch up with them. We can destroy you and still run down your swarm."

"I'm sure you can," I said. "That's not what I'm trying to do. I'm trying to prove to you that—"

Something out of the corner of my eye caught my attention. I broke off and turned to look.

There, to my shock, I saw Dalton walking onto the deck. Normally, that wouldn't be unusual, but this time was different. Dalton was already at the helm, flying the ship.

"Godwin..." I said, knowing immediately that one of these two had to be an imposter. "Hagen, arrest that man!"

"Sir," said the Dalton who'd just arrived. He pointed an accusing finger at the man at the helm. "That *thing* took my place. He brained me and left me for dead!"

As evidence, he lifted a bloody hand from the back of his scalp. A flap of skin and hair hung loosely there, and blood ran red down the back of his uniform.

The Dalton at the helm turned at last and did a double-take when he saw himself.

"Bloody hell..." he said. "What kind of bullshit is this, now?"

221

My eyes went from one Dalton to the next and back again. The bleeding version walked slowly forward, eyes locked on his double. He looked as stunned and freaked out as the man at the helm did. From their voices, behaviors—I couldn't tell them apart.

"Blake!" Lael shouted. "I've had enough!"

"Lael, here's your Nomad. He's right here. Godwin is playing games on my bridge right now. I'll arrest him and hand him over—"

"I *knew* it!" she shouted, looking at the two Daltons. "Your species is diseased. Riddled with the enemy! You're probably not even the Leo Blake I once knew."

"Now, hold on!" I shouted, but she didn't listen.

"All ships, advance and engage," I heard her say.

In the meantime, events aboard my bridge had taken a further turn as the two Daltons lunged at one another. Both moved like wicked fighters. Dalton had always been a mean man in a duel, and today was no exception.

Disrupters came up, but each gripped the other's wrist. They struggled and butted heads —cracking their skulls into one another. Blood and curses flew.

"Commander Hagen, take the helm!" I ordered. "Samson, take them both out."

Samson advanced and shot both of them repeatedly with his disrupter. Burns and swollen flesh left an acrid smell in the air. Raging and gouging at one another, the two went down on the deck and Samson had to subdue them with blows.

In the meantime, Commander Hagen sat at the helm controls. He tried to alter our course—but nothing happened.

"Captain... we're accelerating. We're moving back into the swarm. I can't—I can't seem to unlock the controls."

Rushing to my chair, I tapped at my own console and tried to regain control over the helm—it wasn't responding.

"Samson," I said, "that second Dalton, the one with the bloody scalp, I think he was telling the truth."

"He's already unconscious—or maybe dead," he said. "What do we do now, Captain?"

"Sir," Chang said, "the spheres are slowing now, falling back to our position. We're still speeding up and closing with them—and the phase-ships are beginning to rake our stern."

I looked down at the two Daltons, both of whom were now slumped in an ugly embrace on the deck.

"He suckered them in," I said. "Godwin must have wanted the Imperials to attack us again..."

As I watched, one of the Daltons began to melt away. He collapsed in on himself, turning into sticky fluid that ran and dripped like hot wax.

How long had Godwin been aboard our ship, moving among us? I had no idea.

The first salvo from the phase-ships hit us in the fantail a moment later. Our aft shields flared and buckled. The impact rippled through the ship.

"Captain," Mia said. "What are your orders? Do I return fire?"

"Yes," I said, "fire everything we've got. Try to get them to hang back to play it safe. Chang, get Lael on the screen again."

"She's not answering, sir."

"Damned, stubborn, arrogant..." I chanted a litany of unflattering terms as the Imperials continued to close on us.

Mia let loose with a dozen beams and missiles. It was an impressive barrage, but it had gone off too early. Most of the ordnance was never going to reach the targets at this range, but it might make them duck.

"The enemy are spreading out, staggering their formation, but they're still coming."

"Did we hit anything?"

"No sir. Nothing."

We watched after that, bracing for the worst. We couldn't even turn around to face them with our best weaponry and armor.

Another barrage from the Imperials lashed our rear, and one of our engines flicked out. We weren't going to live through the next.

"Abrams," I said, speaking through my sym. "Open a rift. I'm praying you can do it fast."

"I anticipated this precise request," he said primly. "I even took the liberty of withholding an emergency pool in the main capacitor."

"You what—?" I began, but I broke off. Sure, he was a prick and he rarely followed orders—but today, he may just have saved us.

"Open the rift. Now."

Less than thirty seconds later, a swirling cloud appeared ahead.

"Hagen... have we got any kind of helm control?"

"No, we don't, and we're going to hit that rift too early. It's not fully formed yet, sir."

I gestured toward the spheres. They were all around us now, as we were passing through them. Faster and faster, they dropped away to our stern.

"Are we accelerating...?" I asked.

"Yes but... so are they—in the opposite direction. They've locked onto the Imperial phase-ships. Lael got too close."

We all watched a fantastic disaster unfold. The gravity drones homed in, and they began to pop off. An expanding cloud of plasma consumed three of the phase-ships—four.

"Are we going to make it?" Mia asked as we plummeted toward a sickly-looking rift. It was yellow, and there weren't even any stars in the middle of it to give us hope.

"Of course we are," I said, giving her a confident smile.

"Thanks for lying, Leo," she said as we all watched our doom close in from behind and zoom up to meet us from the front at the same time.

=44=

To the best of my knowledge, no one from Earth had ever tried to navigate a premature rift. It generally took a few minutes for a wormhole to form. Why? One astrophysicist's guess was as good as another's, but the theory I'd heard was that the two points in space had to find one another, like two strands of spider's silk fired by two different spiders striking one another in mid-air. FTL travel was tricky business, and it was a miracle every time it happened.

While phase-ships darted around behind us, forgetting about shooting at our stern and just trying to survive the wave of deadly gravity-drones, we hit the rift at a dangerous pace.

We entered the rift, and I felt a ripple of illness go through me and my ship together. It was like having your stomach do a slippery little flip in your guts.

The feeling was more intense than it usually was, but I was glad I was feeling anything at all. We hadn't just slammed into some kind of celestial brick wall. We were in hyperspace, and on our way... to somewhere.

"Abrams? Dr. Abrams? Where are we going?"

Even as I said those words aloud, I knew it was a mistake to do so. My crew, who was already semi-panicked and holding onto their harnesses for dear life, certainly didn't want to hear that I had no idea where we were headed.

Abrams didn't respond anyway. That kind of pissed me off. He'd gotten his way and yet he couldn't even bother to answer a simple question from his commander.

"Son of a bitch," I muttered and exited the bridge. I headed down through the ships tubes to his lair and tossed aside a nerd who tried to get in my way.

"I don't care if he's busy," I told him. "I'm talking to him right now."

I knew where he was. He'd moved back into his inner chamber. He was probably dry-humping that circlet by now, having turned off his com system so he wouldn't be interrupted.

"Abrams!" I boomed as I pushed open the door.

There was no answer. The room was dark, except for the glove-box, which was lit up inside.

Striding to the box, I frowned as I saw it was hanging open. There was nothing inside. Just instruments, and limp rubber gloves.

Looking around, I saw Abrams. He was stretched out on the deck. He had the circlet on his head.

"Oh my God..." I said. "You *did* it. You really did it..."

Touching his neck, I found no pulse. I needed him alive, so I called security and medical, ordering them to send an emergency team to the labs.

Before they arrived, however, I saw something unexpected. The body—it was getting smaller. Shrinking. How could...?

Almost without a thought, I reached out and grabbed the circlet. I ripped it off the dead man's head. A moment later, the melting process accelerated and Abrams was no more.

Standing up, I was pretty freaked out. I had no idea how this had happened. Abrams had been working up a calculation and creating a rift. He'd been right here—and now he wasn't.

Either Abrams hadn't been Abrams, he'd been a Nomad, or there was another...

"Captain Blake?" demanded a familiar voice from behind me. "What are you doing here? Why can't you leave my equipment alone?"

Turning slowly, I saw Abrams standing there looking pissed. His sycophantic science team was behind him, their mouths gaping like baby birds. They didn't know what the hell was going on, either.

"He tried to get it back..." I said, piecing things together.

"Who?"

"Godwin. He was right here, looking like you."

"That's such total nonsense I'm not even going to entertain you by pointing out the countless flaws in your lie."

"No..." said one of the sycophants.

I recognized her. She was the girl who'd given me a steer before when I'd come down here to find Abrams. Her name was Theresa, and I realized I'd been seeing her around a lot lately.

"What do you mean *no*?" Abrams demanded in a sudden fury. "You're dismissed. If we ever get back to Earth, I'll see your pay is docked for the precise amount it took to give you this joy-ride into space."

"Hold on," I said, looking at the girl. "You saw him come in here, didn't you?" I asked. "You thought he'd still be here."

"I won't have you abusing my staff this way with your fables, Blake."

"She's not your staff anymore, you just fired her. Now, let's have a look at the cameras in the main lab. You record everything don't you?"

"Naturally, but this is a pointless exercise. I was in the engine room, checking on the rift creation. You must recall that I said I'd withheld a certain portion of the ship's energy capacitance for just such an emergency."

"We can talk about that protocol violation later," I said. "Let's have a look at the video."

We scrolled back in time on a tablet, and the video played out as I expected. About five minutes before I came down from the deck, Abrams barged into the lab, passed the girl who'd witnessed the whole thing, and entered the inner chamber.

"A few minutes after that I came down here and found you, dead on the floor. You were wearing this circlet."

Abrams frowned fiercely at me, the circlet, and the girl who'd gotten involved.

"I'm at a loss..." he said. "He's obviously trying to retrieve the circlet—but why? It seems inert. I've thrown every test I could at it. Radiation, heat, particles, wavelengths, code-breaking signals..."

I nodded, looking at the circlet in fascination.

"I'm starting to get some ideas," I told Abrams. "Godwin has been behaving rather oddly on this journey. He's sort of like a poltergeist. He comes and goes, but rather than being calm and collected, he's not playing the part of a diplomat. He's been actively trying to trick us and avoid us."

Abrams bit one of his nails and stared at the empty glove box in thought.

"Hmm..." he said. "I've been thinking about what he told you about their mode of travel. The Nomads aren't teleporting—not exactly. They make and remake bodies to inhabit."

"That's right. They can make them look like anyone they want, too."

Abrams walked past me, flapping his hand in my face like my words were irritating him.

He knelt beside the puddle of chemicals on the floor.

"Even the clothing disintegrates..." he said. "Very strange... I have a theory."

"Let's hear it."

He stood suddenly, but he didn't speak. Instead, he drew out a thin, wand-like disrupter and aimed it at the lab girl. The point glimmered, and it was clearly charged.

"What's this?" Theresa asked, gaping in surprise.

"Are you Godwin?" Abrams asked her. "I know Blake is Blake. I know who I am... but *you* are a virtual stranger. You have somehow inserted yourself into this situation. That's exactly what Godwin would do—in order to get close to the circlet again."

The girl made choking sound. "Don't shoot me! You're crazy. Captain, stop this crazy old coot. No one likes him. No one can stand him. He drives us all mad."

I was pretty sure she was speaking the God's-honest truth there, but that didn't let her off the hook entirely. She still might be Godwin in disguise.

"We can settle this," I told them. "Let me pull up the ship's roster."

I used the ship's roster system to check on her location, and it showed she was right here with us.

"That proves nothing," Abrams argued. "Godwin is more sophisticated than that. Perhaps he murdered the real Theresa and disposed of her body."

"That sounds so crazy," she said, crossing her arms and looking pissed off. "I'm glad you're firing me. Captain, can I go now?"

"No," I said, squinting at her with suspicion.

"Oh—you can't think—*really*? I don't believe this."

"We have to be sure," I said. "If Godwin is aboard ship, he can look like anyone. He switched from being Dalton to being this old coot here in the matter of a few minutes."

"What's more," Abrams said, "I'm now convinced that Godwin is stuck onboard our ship. He's made many appearances in various guises. He hasn't moved his agenda forward much—why not just leave? Maybe he can't."

I didn't quite agree with Abrams, but I didn't argue with him. I couldn't help but think of the fiasco we'd left behind in the Imperial system. He'd done quite a number on their phase-ships. For all I knew, he'd taken out one of their worlds with our help as well.

"Is there some way you can prove you're the real Theresa?" I asked.

She thought about it for a second, then she smiled. She reached for the tablet in my hands. I gave it to her warily, and she scrolled back through the video files.

"There," she said, replaying the scene where Abrams rushed past her into the room with the circlet. "How could I be Godwin, watching him walk by—when *that guy* was Godwin?"

I nodded. "That does seem conclusive," I said. "Godwin was imitating Abrams. He died right in front of you, and I'd just talked to you a moment before... Yes, I'm willing to take your word for it."

So saying, I snatched the weapon from Abrams hands and gave it to Theresa.

Both of them looked startled.

"Keep that weapon trained on his chest," I told her.

"What's this nonsense?" Abrams demanded, sputtering at me.

"You said yourself that he's probably right here, trying to get to that circlet. You must have made a new body—however you do that—and come back in here to see if you could get the circlet and try again."

"Preposterous!"

"Come on, Godwin," I said. "Let's stop fooling around. Talk to me a bit. I might even let you go."

A strange look came over Abrams' face when I made that offer. In that single instant, I knew I'd guessed right. This wasn't Abrams at all—it was Godwin again.

=45=

D r. Abrams had a hunted look on his face. It wasn't anger, or self-assuredness. This was significant because those were pretty much the only expressions the real Abrams ever wore.

"What do you want to talk about?" he asked me.

Slowly, I smiled. "I wasn't sure, but I guessed right at last."

"Proud of yourself, are you?"

"Yeah... I guess I am," I admitted.

He sighed. "All right, I'm Godwin. Now, either shoot me, or give me that circlet."

Lifting the item in question, I tossed it into the air, letting it spin for a second before snatching it back again.

"This little thing, huh?" I asked. "That's what this is all about?"

"No, not at all. This about war, revenge, extinction and glory— but I need that right now, Blake."

"My first question is: why do you need it so badly?"

He glanced at the girl, looking pained.

"She won't tell anyone," I said. "Will you, Miss?"

"Doctor," she corrected. "I'm Dr. Theresa Williams—but sure, I can keep quiet."

Godwin laughed. "She's a scientist. A xenobiologist who'd love to dissect me, if I don't miss my guess."

"Well..." she said, "you do keep fading away into a puddle of spit. It's very frustrating."

"Are you going to answer the question or not, Godwin?"

"Not with her standing there rubbing that weapon so eagerly."

I glanced at her, and I took the pen-like device from her fingers again.

"Outside," I told her. "Go try to find the real Abrams." I glanced at Godwin. "You didn't kill him, did you?"

"I should have... but no. You need him to form rifts, remember?"

Theresa left reluctantly.

"Right..." I said. "She's gone, so you can start talking."

He hesitated. "Why don't you just shoot me again?"

"Because you'll come back as someone else. You can't get off this ship, can you? We were right about that."

"Yes... There's no reference point. I need to die with the circlet on AND fade away with it. That's all. You removed it before it could leave this squalid sector of the galaxy along with my body. If you allow me to complete the process, I can go home. My consciousness will be broadcast and this mission will have ended."

I nodded slowly. "You've been popping up all over my ship. How can you do that? How can you form a body out of thin air?"

"I don't," he said. "It's just tech. If you showed a TV set to a primitive, it would be a magic box, right? It's the same thing here."

I wasn't satisfied. I shook my head. "So evasive—even now. What's the point? If you're so far advanced, you can tell me what you're doing. It's not like we could easily figure it out and copy your tech."

Godwin shifted uncomfortably. "It's not that. You might be able to interfere with the process if you knew more about it. That's why I'm reluctant to discuss it. Consider: we're talking about my very existence."

Thinking that over, I decided to let it go. He might have built a device and hidden it somewhere in the ship. Or, it might be that the circlet allowed him to reform in a localized area—he had said something about an anchor... Or, he might even have an accomplice aboard. I might be dealing with a team of Nomads under deep cover.

Whatever the case, I could understand why he was willing to die to protect a secret that was so critical to him. Since we didn't have that much time before we were going to come out of hyperspace, I decided to let it go.

"Okay," I said, "we'll drop that one. What are you trying to do?"

231

"Get off your ship. My mission has been accomplished."

That pissed me off. I frowned at him. "You mean because you managed to wreck a squadron of Imperial ships and embroil Earth in a fresh war?"

He snorted. "It's more than that. You'll be blamed for genocide."

I froze for a second. "All those gravity drones didn't double back against the phase-ships? Or follow us into the rift?"

He shook his head slowly. "No. Most of them continued on. Think about how that sequence of events looked from a distance. You came in with a swarm of bombs trailing you. Using them cleverly, you destroyed the defending fleet, then fled. Behind you, traveling in your deadly wake, a cloud of death homed in. Diva is gone—but the way the planet died was recorded and transmitted by countless sensory devices."

Nodding, I began to pace the deck. "I get it. You've been playing Earth all along. Making mysterious visitations, sizing us up, figuring out an angle and a plot... but you've got to know that the Imperials know who their *real* enemy is. They'll blame the Nomads, not Earth."

The strange amalgam of Abrams and Godwin shook its eerie head.

"Yes and no," he said. "They'll know we were involved, but they'll also know you were my ally."

"What the hell is the point, then?" I demanded. "Why drag Earth into this? You could have done the same thing without me at all."

"There are details," he said. "For one thing, all starships leave traces where they've been. Signatures that can be tracked down to the builder's star system. Did you know that the source material for a nuclear bomb can be identified after it has gone off? Even you Earthers have mastered that process. You can tell from particulate matter what nation manufactured a given weapon and trace it back to them. So, you see the problem? We didn't want anyone tracing anything to our home cluster."

"You came to Earth, helped us build a starship, and then you used that starship to deliver this attack without giving the enemy any way to trace it back to you."

"Oh, they'll try," he said conversationally. "After Earth's been reduced to a floating cinder, they'll search for signatures. I doubt they'll find anything useful, however. We were very thorough."

I thought about the lonely spot in deep interplanetary space that was chosen for the trap. Clearly, they'd tried to do their dirty deeds in an area so remote not even the best forensics crew could figure it out. On top of that, the gravity drones had gone off—doubtlessly obscuring any tracks that had been left behind by the Nomad ship which had dropped them off in the first place.

"Used..." I said, "Earth has been used again."

"Of course," Godwin said. "Did you honestly expect anything else? Think of yourself as a tribe on an island. A primitive people who've only just been introduced to the rest of the universe. You're not much good to anyone—other than as pawns. That's how these meetings between civilizations always go, even in your own history."

Heaving a sigh, I straightened up. "All right then. You've answered my questions. For that, I thank you. As to the rest of it..."

Breaking off, I stepped up to him, slammed the circlet on his head, and shot him with the beam.

It was a tight, hot laser. Stabbing and burning through his left eye socket and into his brain, I was pleased to see his ephemeral body could feel pain. Far from an easy death, I got to watch him writhe, shiver, piss himself and die shaking on the floor.

The entire time, I kept that beam cooking. I had to drop the beamer in the end, though, as it had become too hot and burned my hand.

"Until we meet again, Godwin," I said to the corpse.

This time, when the body melted away, the circlet melted with it. Soon there was no sign he'd ever graced our ship, other than a stain of clear sticky liquid.

Abrams was located about an hour later. Theresa herself found him in a storage locker filled with waste-baggies and one pissed-off scientist. For many hours afterward, Abrams and his pack of followers searched every inch of the ship, but they never found the circlet, Godwin, or any other trace of our friend, the Nomad.

=46=

The hyperspace journey was still going on six hours later, and that by itself was frightening. We could be going anywhere— or nowhere at all. Not even Abrams dared to guess where we would come out.

"We were surrounded by gravity-drones when we launched," he said in an accusatory tone, "and you didn't even give the navigational people time to lock onto a beacon star."

I shrugged. "Would you rather be dead?" I demanded, my eyes sweeping a resentful group of officers. "That was the other option. We could have driven our ship right into Diva with a pack of gravity-drones riding with us, or maybe we could have fought it out with a dozen phase-ships and died that way."

For a moment they were quiet, but it didn't last long.

"You could have let the drones destroy the phase-ships," Dr. Abrams suggested. "We might have lived through the blast... After regaining control of the helm, we could have left the swarm at will, creating a rift without interference."

Glowering at him, I shrugged again. He was the ultimate backseat driver.

"We *might* have lived—but when we get out of this hyper-spatial tube, we might live through that, too. It was risky either way."

Abrams pouted, but he shut up.

"All right then," I said. "What's done is done. I need status reports on our repair efforts."

Samson chimed in next. Support systems and defensive armament were his *forté*. Some of the other officers complained he didn't have enough formal engineering training, but he'd pulled me out of grim circumstances many times, and I liked having him around.

"We've got full helm controls again. The starboard drive is at seventy percent. I doubt we can fix that before hitting home base. Our shield generators are operating again—but they're weaker. We've lost some aft power cells. The phase-ships did a number on our stern, and some of those sections are still airless and open to space."

He displayed some scenes. The aft chambers crawled with suited spacers. They were patching the small holes and welding big plates over the gaping ones. Beyond their glowing faceplates, I could see a backdrop of swirling light. It was hyperspace.

"There's a lot of radiation out there," Commander Hagen said. "Those men are too exposed."

"We're monitoring each man's dose of rads," Samson said. "When they hit their monthly limit, we take them out and switch in a fresh spacer."

Hagen looked less than satisfied. "How long does it take them to hit that?"

Samson shrugged. "Twenty... maybe thirty minutes."

Hagen laughed ruefully. "Good thing we've got a big crew. Is medical smart enough to be shooting them up with potassium iodide?"

Samson assured them the crewmen were being cared for, and we moved on.

"Dr. Abrams," I said, turning to him, "Godwin got away, right?"

"As far as we can tell," he said. "I've taken the liberty of reprogramming the ship's AI to stop hiding Nomads in the future. Instead, it will now give our key personnel a private message warning us that a duplicate crewmember is aboard."

"We should have had that software working all along. Have you tested it?"

"It's still a work in progress," he admitted.

"Great... what about navigational questions? Any clue where we're headed?"

He threw his hands in the air. "I've been working on the Godwin problem, but in my opinion our destination is unknowable anyway. You didn't follow any procedures when you opened this rift."

"As you keep pointing out... but we have to come out somewhere, don't we?"

Dr. Abrams squirmed a little. "Maybe..." he said.

Frowning, I turned fully to face him. "What do you mean, 'maybe'?"

"Just as I said. The odds are this hyper-spatial tube has an endpoint within our local region of the galaxy... however..."

"What? Spell it out."

"Theoretically, a wormhole can terminate anywhere within the known universe. That's quite a big domain mathematically. If we, for example, are on our way to a distant galaxy several million lightyears away, it could take us a period greater than our natural lifespans to reach the endpoint."

We all stared at him in shock. No one said anything. Usually, I could put a bright face on just about any bad news—but this one had me stumped.

"Uh..." I said. "That's why you wanted me to take plan B, isn't it?"

"Yes," he said firmly.

"I don't recall hearing any talk of this circumstance back in our astronavigation courses. I had no idea a blind jump might really be so dangerous..."

"Of course you didn't hear of this option," he snapped. "It's always assumed crews will follow directives. Many other suicidal acts were similarly not covered, such as flying your ship into a star, or—"

"That's enough," I said. That, along with a fierce glare, shut him down. "Well then, we'll make the best of it. Hagen, rotate the watches as usual, but work in an extra shift of trainees to give our core bridge teams a break."

"Will do."

We adjourned, and I headed for my quarters with a lot on my mind. Mia was there, waiting for me. She hadn't been in the command meeting, so she was bright-eyed and upbeat.

"When do we get home?" she asked.

"Soon, I hope."

"Good. When we do, I don't want to go on another trip until we're forced to. No more volunteering yourself, Leo! Let's just hang around in space waiting for Fex... On second thought, even that will be tiresome. Do you think we can arrange a few days of shore leave?"

"Um... sure," I told her, giving her a wan smile.

"What's wrong?"

"Nothing!" I lied. "It's just been a long, long day."

She looked me over curiously. I could tell she was trying to figure out what was going on. She immediately leapt to the wrong conclusion.

"I know what it is," she said, creeping behind me and putting hands on my shoulders. "You're sad about that Sarah-person. You expected her to move into our bed, didn't you?"

"Uh..."

"Well, she must have rejected the offer. When I saw her at the gym, she showed me her longest finger... strange. I didn't think she'd refuse to become your second-girl. After all, you *are* the captain."

"That's not exactly—"

"No, no," she said, shushing me. "It's very sweet. I told you how I felt, and you chose to keep me over a new girl. That's a compliment. It's her loss and my gain. Now, I'd like to make it up to you."

"Yeah?"

At first, I wasn't positive what she meant. But then she started to pull off her clothes and mine.

There are a lot of things I don't know about women, but one of them I do understand is that when they're in the mood, you seize the opportunity—and you keep your damned mouth shut.

=47=

We came out of hyperspace nine days later. By that time, some of us had given up on surviving the experience.

The rift opened, big and green-white this time. To me, it looked brighter than they usually did, but that could have been an illusion.

It turned out that it wasn't.

"We're passing through, Captain."

"All hands to battle stations," I ordered. "We don't know what we'll encounter. Hold on for the transfer into normal space."

My eyes squinched up tightly when we broke out of the hyperspatial tube. It was one thing to be targeting a given system, only to find yourself lightyears off-target. It was quite a different experience to come in *cold*—completely uncertain where you were about to emerge.

We broke through and immediately began scanning our environment but within seconds we knew something was wrong.

The ship slewed and my crew all fell against the port side of the hull. Many were strapped in, but those moving around were thrown off their feet and slammed into the walls.

"Get everyone to a seat!" I ordered. "Samson, flip on the anti-gravity, man!"

"Sir—it is on. We're in a strong gravitational pull."

"Source?"

The crew worked, and the computer began drawing out our surroundings.

The image on the holoprojector looked strange. We were in a body of moving debris, gas clouds, matter, radiation and violently released energies blurred everything around us.

"Our sensors aren't working," Chang said. He was at a loss.

"Dalton, assume we're crashing into a gas giant. Use the pull to our port side as a point of reference and turn our jets against it."

"Working on it, Captain."

I could tell he was already fighting the controls. Over the last week he'd made a good recovery after his vicious combat with Godwin. We heeled over and the deck was the deck again.

People slid around again as we slewed into our new orientation. A few victims had been knocked senseless, and they flopped like ragdolls over the hull onto the deck.

"Dr. Abrams? Do you hear me? I need an evaluation of our status."

There was about a seven second delay, and then he finally spoke. "We're in a strong gravitational field. Our anti-gravity systems are unable to overcome it."

"How strong?" I asked. "Are we near a planet or a star?"

"Neither," he said, "if this kind of power was being exerted by a star, we'd have burned up by now. If it was a planet—well, no planet can pull this hard. Anything of sufficient mass would have lit up due to internal fusion and begun burning by now."

"All right then, give me a theory."

Abrams hesitated. "Captain, I believe it's a singularity."

My mind froze over. For some reason, I hadn't considered such a grim possibility.

"You mean a black hole?"

"Yes, that's the colloquial term."

"Can we escape? Are we near the event horizon?"

"I'm still analyzing. I'll get back to you the moment I have an answer."

"That's very helpful. In the meantime, what do we do?"

He hesitated again. "We could form another rift. A blind-jump due to the interference."

"Set it up. We might have to try it."

The connection closed, and I looked around my bridge numbly. We were all going to die. It was just a matter of time.

"Captain?" Chang asked. "I'm getting a signal. A faint signal."

"What are you talking about?"

"Radio, sir. From outside the ship. Sir... they're using an Imperial code."

"Open the channel," I said, figuring we had nothing to lose.

A voice came into my mind. It was a familiar voice, and it was extremely angry.

"...did you *know*? You're a sorcerer, Blake. A rodent with a dozen lives to live, all the while tormenting your betters."

"Lael?" I asked, shocked. "Is that you? Where are you?"

"Playing the ignoramus to the last, Blake? Well, I don't believe it now. You brought us here on purpose. You lured us into following you into that rift, and flew straight into a black hole. How can you be so cruel?"

"Um..." I said, trying to think. "So, you followed us into the rift?"

"Of course we did. We had no choice. Most of my captains didn't make it, naturally. Good women all. The Imperial Kher owe you a thousand bloody deaths. You've harmed so many with your unscrupulous tricks."

I tried to visualize the situation. Lael had to be close by. She'd followed us through hyperspace, much as smaller ships in any fleet followed a designated starship. We'd opened a path, and she'd taken it to avoid the gravity-drones. She'd made the same split-second decisions we'd made moments before her.

"You should be glad," I said. "We could have left you to die in the Diva System. The gravity drones—according to Godwin—would have destroyed all your ships."

"Just as they destroyed ill-fated Diva," she finished for me. "We know that. That's why we're here. But to call this a favor on your part—that's a stretch. You must know there are only two of us left, and we're in no condition to fight you."

I glanced at Chang, who was listening in. We traded surprised glances. Our sensors weren't even operating this close to an event horizon, and we couldn't see Lael. We were effectively flying blind.

"Of course," I said. "Are your drives strong enough to escape the pull of the black hole?"

"It is a losing battle. We're gratified, however, to see that you're losing ground as well. You'll soon fall into the abyss of time and space with us. Hell will make us good neighbors, Blake."

"I don't think so," I told her. "We'll be gone by then. We're charging up for another jump."

"A blind jump? Insanity... but I guess you have no choice."

"Hmm," I said, thinking over the situation. "You can't escape. You can't do battle with us—it would seem that you should be very polite to us, your human hosts."

"Why?" she demanded. "For your further amusement? I will not grovel. I will not beg. I would rather cease to exist than do so."

"Very well," I said. "I respect your decision. You're an honorable foe, and I'll write a suitable epitaph to your memory when I get home. Possibly, if peace is ever reached between the Empire and Earth, I'll be able to inform your people of your chosen fate."

"We chose nothing!" she raged. "We were tricked, taken out into a field to be shot like meat-animals!"

"Of course you are making a choice," I told her. "I said we're leaving. I informed you of this, but you've clearly stated you're not interested in salvation. I respect that choice utterly. I wouldn't dream of asking you to—"

"What do you want?" she demanded. "I draw the line at slavery. I would never submit to it."

My eyebrows did a speculative up-down motion. Chang grinned at me.

"That's too bad," I said. "I was rather looking forward—well, never mind. You've made your choice. As I said, highly respectable."

"You monster!" she howled. "Very well, I will become your captive again. I knew that would be your requirement. You're smitten by me, like your crewmen before you. I have some shred of pride left, I want you to know. I'll never—"

We went back and forth bartering like this for quite a while. Each cycle she'd construct a barrier which I accepted immediately, then expressed my regrets at her imminent doom. That move immediately caused her resolve to collapse all over again.

I was simply enjoying myself at her expense, of course. I wasn't planning to enslave her—for one thing, Mia would never allow it. She could understand a human rival, but to share our bed with an Imperial? No, that would be asking too much.

After five or ten minutes of wrangling, I almost had her down to begging me. That was a fine thing. She'd personally overseen the deaths of millions of Rebel Kher. She was callous, selfish and downright evil at times.

241

At last, I grew tired of the game. Dr. Abrams came to my rescue, signaling me that he'd recharged our drives enough to allow for another jump into the blue.

"Use all your thrust," I told Lael. "Get as close to my vessel as you can. You can sense our hull, right?"

"Our sensors are built by Imperial workers. They are in every way superior to—"

"Right, got it. When the rift forms, we'll have to take our chances together."

"You'll allow us to enter with you?" Lael said in a near whisper. "You will not fire upon us?"

"You've offered me such a fine deal that I can't refuse. As I know, you're a woman of your word, and I've decided to allow myself to be persuaded."

At this point, Mia stepped onto the bridge and came stalking across the chamber to her station. Turning to face me, she slithered into her harness. The look on her face made me clam up. Had someone ratted me out?

I didn't know how much of the exchange she'd heard from the doorway, but it was enough. She stared flatly, and her tail was twitching. That was never a good sign.

I cleared my throat. Perhaps I'd overplayed the slave-girl angle with Lael.

"You will have to die a thousand times over to pay for today's sins, Blake," Lael said, and she signed off.

"The moment Abrams is ready," I ordered, "open that breach."

A few minutes later, the ship began to shake. The shields were buzzing too, as if they wanted to flicker and die.

"We're losing power, Captain," Hagen said calmly. "We've got to go soon. The event horizon is becoming increasingly hazardous."

"Radiations levels are spiking," Samson said unhelpfully. "Soon, we might begin to stretch."

I looked at him, then Chang. "Is he right?"

Chang shrugged. "The gravitational forces are extreme when you're circling a black hole. We might not survive much longer. A critical point will eventually be reached, after which we'll be extruded into component molecules, a phenomenon punctuated by a large release of energy."

"A release of energy... as in an explosion?"

"Yes—maybe. It might be more like a contained conversion of a mass into energy. A compression that isn't allowed release."

"Huh," I said, "Dalton, when that breach forms, drive us into it."

"Will do, sir."

We waited after that, sliding around uncomfortably in our seats. We were getting heavier, that much was obvious. We had to be under two Gs of force or more. We were supposed to be weighing nothing, but the gravity repellers weren't able to keep up. We were sinking closer and closer to total annihilation.

Before we reached three Gs, Abrams gave us the signal. We opened a rift and slid toward it.

The experience was a strange one. I felt a sick twisting sensation inside my guts.

Was Lael following us? Maybe. There was no way to tell. The bridge crew could barely hear one another anymore, and our vision was blurring. Gravity waves were rolling through our bodies, making us ill, as our antigravity tried to do battle with the fantastic forces outside the hull.

It was a losing struggle. Each minute that passed felt like it had to be our last.

=48=

We never did learn where we'd been. There was no way to know which black hole we'd visited, although we estimated it had to have been within the boundaries of our own galaxy. We hadn't traveled in hyperspace long enough to reach another, such as Andromeda.

The lack of detailed information was due to the fact our sensors hadn't operated properly at the edge of the black star's event horizon. That was something no one found surprising, but it was disturbing to think about. We hadn't just been at the edge of death—we'd hovered dangerously close to nonexistence.

"So that was really a black hole, huh?" Commander Hagen asked me when things settled down. "I'd kind of expected to see something."

"They don't really show up as a dark star," Chang explained. "Their gravity is so great they warp even light, sucking it up. They can only be detected by the whirlwind of stellar material that orbits them. As it is drawn in and destroyed, the swallowed mass emits a great deal of radiation and warps everything around it."

"Yeah..." Hagen mused. "I took the classes, but descriptions in an astrophysics textbook are nothing like the real thing. It's terrifying to experience one in person. It was like riding out a hurricane in a rowboat."

"Agreed," I said. "Hopefully, we'll have better luck this time around."

Hagen turned and looked at me with wide eyes. "You're not saying we can justify trying to jump blind again, are you Captain?"

244

"Well... if you asked Dr. Abrams that question, he'd assure you we couldn't. But I know better. There was no good way to navigate out of that singularity mess."

"Right... Our instruments weren't working—I'll tell him that when he complains."

"Our options may not have improved much. That's the nature of jumping blind. We have no way to know if we'll have a point of reference, like a beacon star, until we hit the endpoint. Essentially, we may be as lost as ever."

"Great..." Hagen said, and he wandered back to his station.

I'd never seen him so resigned to a grim fate. He was brave beyond the norm when it came to combat, but these random jumps into the darkness seemed to have put him on edge.

Shrugging, I went back to going over the damage reports. In a way, none of them mattered. We were free again, flying through a tube of radioactive hyperspace. We'd suffered some systems damage, particularly to our delicate external sensors—but that hardly mattered. Who needed to know where you were or where you were going? We were blue-jaunt travelers. We'd flown off all the maps and were hoping for the best.

The jump was much shorter than the last one. We came out almost abruptly.

"The tunnel is breaking up—we're breaching, sir!" Dalton called out.

I sounded battle stations, ordering everyone to strap in. After the last disastrous exit, we were ready for anything—or so we thought.

This time, we could see at least. Our sensor arrays still weren't in perfect order, but they functioned.

A panoramic view of stars formed. We were in the middle of a tight cluster, if I didn't miss my guess.

"Are these all red giants?" I asked. "So close together?"

The navigational officer gaped. "There are... six of them within a lightyear. All dying suns, and a lot of gaseous debris."

"Sir, Lael is trying to contact you."

After a moment's hesitation, I opened the channel privately. I let her come through visually, not just by voice. I wanted to see her face.

Honestly, I'd expected to see her wreathed in smiles. She was a lovely woman, and after discussing all the personal duties and services she was willing to provide an hour earlier, I'd been daydreaming about her.

Unfortunately, she didn't look happy at all.

"Is this some kind of cruel joke, Blake?" she demanded. "We're near the center of the galaxy."

"Is that bad?"

She made an irritated sound. "It's not good. It's not the home of any Kher. These stars are too close together. They have few planets and those they do have are burnt to ash."

"Hmm," I said. "Well, we escaped the black hole as I offered. Our bargain is almost complete."

"Ah-ha!" she shouted, wagging a long finger at me. "I understand now. You brought me here to abuse me. To make certain I'd uphold my end of the bargain before you take us anywhere near our home region of space. What do I have to do to get back to the Perseus Arm of our galaxy, Leo?"

She stared at me in irritation.

"Hmm..." I said, unable to flatly deny her offer. Why were women bent on tormenting me lately? Was it because of my new rank of captain? "We should meet in person," I said aloud, and I immediately regretted it.

Mia stood up from her post. Her shoulders were hunched tightly, but she didn't turn to face me.

"Permission to leave my post, Captain," she said. "I need a break."

"Permission granted," I said, and I summoned her replacement.

She stalked past my chair and I lifted my hand toward her in farewell. She didn't even acknowledge the gesture.

Lael, in the meantime, had never stopped talking.

"...and I want it in writing," she finished up. "There will be no agreement, no sexual favors—nothing without a written document."

"Wouldn't such a thing be unenforceable?" I asked her.

"Possibly," she said. "But it will give me a personal excuse for this fraternization to give my superiors."

"Ah," I said. "Covering your ass, are you?"

She frowned and blinked. "Is that a requirement?"

"Um... certainly not. It's an expression. Never mind. Will you come aboard now?"

"I have no choice. I will do as you demand. There are no starships for a thousand lightyears, as I'm sure you're well aware. If you leave us, we die in sterile space. My sacrifice will be recorded and presented as evidence at my hearing."

"Recorded?" I asked. "Hearing? I'm not following you."

She sniffed loudly. "Imperial Kher aren't rutting beasts like you Rebels. We require documentation to prove these acts you've demanded are indeed carried out, and that no additional abuse was applied."

"Uh..." I said, thinking to myself that things had gone too far. It was my own fault, of course. Imperial Kher lacked a sense of humor, other than the joy of laughing at another man's discomfort.

"All right," I said, "come to the main hold alone. I'll meet you in there."

"I will do so—because I must."

With a regal air, she got up and headed for the exit. The camera pickup lingered on her moving form, and I felt my heart quicken. Could I go through with this? I told myself no, I had to stick with the plan. Lael was attractive, but she was also very dangerous in a dozen different ways.

When I met her at the docking bay, I was surprised to see she wasn't alone. A half-dozen large Imperial troopers exited the tiny shuttle boat in their powered armor. I wondered for a second if this was some kind of trick. Did she think a handful of troops could capture my ship? If she did, she was in for a surprise.

A full squad of suited marines met her ship and her little entourage. I watched as she exited behind her troops—and one other person walked softly behind her.

This last person was a young woman. She had a wand of rank as most female Imperial Kher did. She was as lovely as Lael herself, but younger and shorter.

Lael watched me, and she glanced down at the stranger. "This is my underling, Elsa. She will serve in my place. Just because she is of a lower rank, you're not to abuse her beyond our agreed upon—"

Elsa looked at me with a mixture of frank curiosity and a little fear as Lael spoke. Her eyes widened when I interrupted angrily.

"Hold on," I said. "This is a classic bait-and-switch, and I won't stand for it. We had a deal."

Both the women looked startled at my outburst.

"Indeed..." Lael said. "I hadn't realized... I'd assumed you merely wanted to sate your beastly lusts upon an Imperial female. I didn't quite understand that you're obsessed with me personally."

Clearing my throat, I felt a little embarrassed. The marines around me were casting odd looks to one another. Fortunately, no one laughed aloud.

"That's a very rude way to put things," I said. "The point is that, you, Captain Lael, are to be my prisoner. Not Elsa, or your ship's cook, or anyone else."

"Absurd," she said. "My ship and crew need me. Who will command in my absence?"

"I don't know. Your second officer, I guess. You can put Elsa in charge if you want to."

"An obsession..." she said, frowning. "I hadn't realized... This puts an entirely different light on things."

I put my hands on my hips and stood firm. "Well?" I asked. "Are you coming along or not? My ship is ready to jump again. Will your ship be accompanying ours, or are we leaving it behind?"

Elsa looked up at Lael seriously. "An acceleration of our time schedule is in order, I think," she said.

"Agreed," Lael said, and she touched her thumb to her wand.

Instantly, my marines and I were jolted with a nerve-shock. We were flattened onto the deck like dead fish.

=49=

Fortunately for both me and my crew, we'd dealt with Imperials before. There were no more arrogant, double-dealing creatures to be found among the stars. Not even Godwin and his Nomad buddies could come close in duplicitous behavior.

Knowing this, I'd taken certain precautions. I hadn't been certain Lael would try to pull a fast one, but I'd understood it was within the realm of the possible.

When Lael pulled her little power-play, it worked—for a few seconds. After that, Samson opened the side hatches at both ends of the hold and emerged with two more full squads of marines.

These men had their weapons out and their shielding active. Lael's nerve-shock pulse wasn't going to reach that far, nor was it getting past their shields even if it did.

"Drop your gear and surrender," Samson boomed. "I've got orders to shoot you all down if you don't."

Lael looked at him sourly. She aimed her wand at my face.

I'd fallen on my back on the deck, and therefore I could see the scene despite the fact I'd stiffened up as if rigor mortis had already set in.

"If you fire upon us, I'll kill your captain."

"I repeat," Samson said, "disarm yourselves now, or I'll kill you where you stand. We have lots of officers on this ship to replace Blake. I have my orders and I will carry them out."

I had to give him credit where credit was due. Samson didn't sound like he was playing around. Knowing him, he probably wasn't. He was a hard man to bluff, as he rarely backed down. You had to beat him unconscious or damn near kill him to get him to switch tracks.

Lael studied the situation, then put away her weapon in disgust. Her tense escorts did the same, as did Elsa.

Samson approached cautiously.

"Drop them," he insisted, "or I'll shoot one of you every ten seconds until you comply. One... two..."

If I could have, I would have grinned. Samson would have made a fine parent.

Samson got to the count of seven before they obeyed. With poor grace, the Imperials abandoned their arms. Samson sent one squad in close to secure them while the second stood ready to fire. It was like a tactical overwatch operation, and he made it all look well-rehearsed.

When the Imperials had been disarmed and surrounded, I began to wake up. I choked, spitting and cursing. I could move my lips, but not my limbs. Not yet.

"You okay, boss?" he asked.

"Right as rain," I whispered. "Arrest Lael. Send the rest of them back on the shuttle."

Samson grinned and turned to face the haughty Imperials. He relayed my orders. There was a considerable amount of sputtering and squawking, but at last he managed to herd the majority of the party aboard the shuttle and get everyone else out of the hold.

I could walk by then, although I was wobbling on my feet. Lael sullenly followed me. For once, she wasn't talking much.

Perhaps I should have left that gift horse alone, but I couldn't help myself. I was a bit annoyed with her after her stunt in the hold.

"I recall a similar situation once," I said. "What was it you said to me when I attacked your guards? Something about displaying a deep barbaric viciousness that you appreciated. Well, I'm feeling the same way about you now."

She flashed me a look of hate.

"There's no similarity," she said. "Your low, animal cunning bears no resemblance to—"

"Oh, but it does!" I insisted, giving her a grin. "I took a chance, the same as you did just now. And I was put down on the deck, the same as your team was. It must be hard, surrendering to a Rebel Kher. Sort of makes you think..."

"Think of what?"

"Of what you might have done differently. Of regrets for past sins. Of—"

She threw herself at me. I was surprised, as were her guards. They weren't even watching. Her hands were bound behind her, but she didn't care, she charged up and jostled me in the shoulder, snarling.

"Whoa!" I said, laughing. "That's the fighting attitude I like to see! I'll have to take my body-cam recording and pass that one around. My own spacers could use an example of Imperial ferocity."

Suddenly, she was embarrassed and sullen again. She stalked after me, beaten but still scheming. She'd never stop doing that.

Deciding maybe I'd pushed her too far for the sake of personal entertainment, I cleared my throat and took on a more conciliatory tone.

"Well, Captain, welcome aboard your first Earth-built starship. This is *Devilfish*, and I want you to make yourself at home here."

"That will never happen," she said.

"You'd rather go home?"

"Of course, fool."

"That's of course, *Captain*."

Lael didn't answer.

"Anyway," I said, "this is my office. Let's head inside and have a little talk."

She marched inside and I followed. My security detail looked mildly concerned, but I left them outside the door.

Heading to my desk, I stopped. Lael was standing in the middle of the chamber, staring at my bed. It was big enough for two, and I hadn't had time to call a service bot to smooth out the blankets yet.

"Uh... about that," I said.

"So..." she said. "This is how it is to be? No questions, just depraved behavior? My worst fears are realized."

"No, no," I said, feeling a little embarrassed and cursing Dr. Abrams for the hundredth time. "The ship was designed with efficiency of space in mind. My office and my quarters are all in the same chamber—this one."

She looked at me warily. "Why bother to lie now, Blake?" she asked. "I can't resist you."

"You won't have to. I only touch willing women."

Lael snorted in disbelief. "Is that part of our deal? Must I pretend to enjoy myself?"

My face was reddening. Dr. Abrams had done it to me again.

"Just come over here to my desk," I said, taking a seat behind it.

She walked slowly to stand in front of my desk. "I would remove my garments, but my hands can't reach the clasps."

I sighed. "Okay, look, just answer my questions."

Her eyes drifted down from the ceiling, where she'd been studying a star chart with resignation.

"What will happen to me if I don't answer? Will you mete out your special punishments then?"

"Maybe," I growled, becoming annoyed. "First question: why were you stationed at Diva?"

She stared at me for a second. "I guess I can answer that without giving away a vital secret. Diva was a world known to be under surveillance by the Nomads. We deployed a squadron of phase-ships there to catch them."

I nodded, believing her. "How did you know the Nomads were interested?"

"They spy on us all the time. They use advanced techniques, but we have ways of detecting their agents if they spend too long in corporeal form among us."

"Ah... So they visit you Imperials the same way they do us? Duplicating individuals and moving unseen in your midst?"

She blinked, and then she nodded. "I see you have learned something about them."

"I know more than I want to about those miserable sons-of-bitches."

Lael squinted at me. "Children of dogs?" she said, questioning the translation. "Is that a good thing? It doesn't sound positive."

"It isn't. I hate them. I especially hate the one called Godwin that got us into this mess."

Lael narrowed her eyes at me, as if suspicious. "You're claiming you don't work for the Nomads."

"We don't. They are as much our enemy as the Imperials ever were."

"You're doing this in hopes of absolving yourself from the genocidal crimes that occurred in the Diva system."

I cleared my throat. "I don't know what happened there. I ran, and I hope the people of Diva survived somehow."

"If you cared so much, why didn't you do something to save them?"

She'd come forward now, and she was standing with her thighs pressing against the far side of my desk. She was quite attractive in that stance—hell, she would have been pretty in any position—and I ran my eyes up and down her person once, quickly.

She caught that, unfortunately. She backed up and stood tall again, almost at attention.

"Why do you look at me like that?"

"Um... you're a lovely woman."

"I'm not a woman. I'm an Imperial Kher. Still, I'm impressed that you've managed to contain your natural lusts this long. You must really want whatever information you feel I have."

"I do. I mean—it's not like that at all. Uh... let's just keep talking. You don't like the Nomads. We don't like the Nomads. That might be a basis for an understanding."

Lael paused thoughtfully. "What kind of understanding?"

"An alliance against a common foe, perhaps?"

She laughed. "Absurd. An alliance requires two participants. You're unthinkable in that role. It would be like a mouse teaming with a lion."

"Let's not call it that, then," I said, staying upbeat with difficulty. "Perhaps we can cooperate in some small way to bring down a common enemy. Nothing more."

She thought that over. "It could only be a temporary arrangement."

"Right. Let's say we have the joint purpose of capturing the Nomad that caused Diva to be attacked."

"Capture? You can't capture a Nomad. You can only destroy its vessel so it can't immediately return to plague you again."

"Vessel? You mean those circlets operate like ships for them?"

She looked at me speculatively. "I'm not sure who is being manipulated here," she said. "But I now believe you truly want information about the Nomads."

Unexpectedly, she turned her hip, aimed her shapely rump at my desk and sat on it. She looked at me with pursed lips. "Remove this offensive slave-bracelet and I will become more cooperative."

I thought about it. She'd been searched for weapons, and without them she wasn't very dangerous.

Standing up, I came close and stood behind her. I removed the cuffs and dropped them on the floor. She rubbed her wrists, and I found myself lingering near her.

She had a nice scent. It wasn't quite like an Earth woman's perfume, or just a clean, soap-smell. It was more delicate than that.

"You plan to force yourself upon me now," she said. "I can see the intent in your eyes."

"Uh... no, no," I said, retreating behind my desk again.

Lael frowned and looked confused. Possibly, she was even a little disappointed.

"I don't understand. Have your genitals been injured?"

I laughed. "Not at all."

"Then you find me unattractive?"

"No... it's not that, either. I'm just trying to question you."

"Then continue. I will cooperate."

"I'd asked you about their circlets. We found they use them to return here, and must die with one on their heads to leave permanently."

I played a short vid on my desk. Godwin as Dr. Abrams died and melted away at the end.

Lael stared, breathing hard with her nostrils flaring. "You... you put that circlet on him and executed him!"

"Yes," I said. "I found him annoying. He was interfering with the operation of my ship."

She looked up slowly, and she had a strange look on her face.

"Nomads are far more than annoying. They are a form of artificial life. They never give up on a plan once it has been set in motion. Clearly, you are at the center of one of their monstrous schemes. I can only imagine what they have planned for you and your planet."

"They can't be much worse than you Imperial Kher," I pointed out. "You've planned to exterminate us for some time now."

She shrugged. "It would be a clean death at least. The Nomads will take you like predators from the darkness. You'll never know when the end is near, and you'll end your lives in abject terror."

Trying to digest this, I blinked a few times in thought. "You said something interesting there—that Nomads are artificial life forms? What do you mean? Are they machines?"

"They are biological. But they are designed, not born. They are therefore something in-between a living creature and a machine."

254

"Where did they come from?" I asked.

She spread her hands wide. "Here. This galaxy. This space where we stand."

"If they're designed, who made them?"

Lael looked surprised. "I thought that would have been obvious by now. They were created originally by the Kher. They were our slaves, our servants. But they rebelled many centuries ago. They've been banished from our stars—but they want to come back to their home."

This was a stunner to me, but it answered many questions. It also indicated there could never be peace between Kher and Nomad.

How could you strike a bargain with a race of creatures so different from yourself? A race that called the same stars home that you did?

=50=

After talking to Lael a little longer, I had a security team escort her to the brig and lock her up. This seemed to surprise her as well.

"I'd assumed I would stay here—in your quarters." She indicated my still-unmade bed with a nod of her head.

The two marines froze. Their eyes widened, but they didn't say anything.

"You were mistaken," I said. "Take her below."

They led her away and no sooner had the door shut than it opened again. Mia stood there with her hands on her hips.

"That took a very long time," she complained.

"She had a lot of interesting information to share."

"I bet."

Entering, she stalked around our shared quarters. I noticed her pawing suspiciously at the unmade bed, then wrinkling her nose in the bathroom area, but I pretended not to notice.

"Her scent is here, lingering—but it's not on everything," she said.

At last, completing her inspection, she climbed into my lap and kissed me.

"Mia, this isn't the time—"

She pulled away, squinting at me. "Her taste isn't there... How did you do it?"

"The taste...? Oh, Mia, we didn't have sex."

She lifted my fingers and ran them near her face. I knew she was sniffing them. She had a better sense of smell than any human I'd ever known.

"Here, I catch her scent," she said. "But only that of her skin. You touched her?"

"I removed her handcuffs," I said, indicating the bonds on the deck.

"Why would you do that? She's a prisoner."

"To make her more cooperative. I was questioning her."

Mia stared into my eyes. "I want to believe you, but it's difficult..."

"What will convince you?"

She began pawing at my clothing. I could have resisted, but the truth was all of Lael's hinting around had gotten me aroused. I let her do it.

She sniffed me all over, and finally smiled. "You didn't mate with her."

"I told you I didn't."

"Are you feeling sick?"

I laughed again and hugged her. "Human males can control their instincts—sometimes."

"That's strange... what are you feeling now?"

That was it for me. She was in my lap, and I didn't care anymore if I was on duty and behaving unprofessionally. I took her right there on my office chair. It swiveled and creaked loudly, but I made no effort to be quiet. I'd been teased long enough.

Afterward, she left with a smile on her face and a lighter step. I sighed and leaned back in my chair, knitting my fingers behind my head. For some reason, I nodded off.

"Boss?" Samson asked sometime later. "Captain, are you really sleeping?"

I lurched awake with a snort. Samson's looming face was unwelcome. I'd been having an excellent dream.

Adjusting myself and sitting bolt upright at my desk, I shook myself all over.

"You okay, sir?" Samson repeated. "Commander Hagen sent me to find you... you're late."

"Perfect," I said. "I'll be right there."

Samson looked at me strangely for a second or two.

"Dismissed, Ensign."

He left then, shaking his head. I washed up quickly and headed for the bridge. I was late for my watch—that never happened. Everyone on the command deck stared when I came in.

257

Taking my chair like I owned the place—which I did—I began demanding reports and giving people extra duties. That made them all relax. They forgot about wondering where I'd been.

All except for Commander Hagen, that was.

"Sir," he said quietly while standing next to me. "I hope your interrogation went well."

I glanced at him. "What's that supposed to mean?"

He shrugged. "Did you... ah...get anywhere with the prisoner?"

He looked at me so deadpan, I couldn't help but laugh.

"Actually, she told me quite a bit."

Proceeding to relay all the details Lael had let slip about the Nomads and their relationship with the Kher, I was gratified to see my smug XO slowly become impressed.

"That's quite a technique you have there," he said. "They told me you led her into your quarters tied up, but she came out with her hands free."

"She's not dangerous without her wand, or some other weapon."

He looked at me seriously. "That's not what I heard, sir," he said. "I've read the files on your prior missions—and I've interviewed surviving crewmen. According to them, Lael had inappropriate relationships with a number of her jailors."

"So... that's what this is about. I'm not a hard-up spacer, Hagen. I got her to talk without any physical contact at all."

"No abuse?"

"None."

"No... entertainment?"

Getting angry, I shook my head firmly. "No."

"All right then," he said. "You understand, as your first officer, I need to know if my captain is in danger of becoming compromised."

"Got it. Case closed."

I felt like telling him he was more jealous than Mia, but I withheld such comments. He was right, in a way. It was his duty to know what was going on with the ship's captain.

"One more thing, Captain," he said before turning away. "There's someone I'd like you to talk to... a xenobiologist."

"What for?"

"She'd like to study Lael. I think she could help advise you on handling this prisoner."

I narrowed my eyes. "I get it," I said. "You'd rather have a woman in Lael's cell—instead of me. Are we talking about Dr. Theresa Williams?"

"The same, sir," said a voice behind me.

I turned to face Dr. Williams. "You're timing is impeccable," I told her, and I saw her exchange meaningful glances with Hagen.

Commander Hagen stepped quietly away at this point. He'd done his work well—I'd have to keep my eye on him, just as he was so obviously watching me.

"I haven't seen you on the bridge before," I said to Dr. Williams. "In fact, I haven't seen you at all since we faced down Godwin together."

"I'm sorry Captain, but Commander Hagen said—"

"—never mind, I've got it... and I'm in agreement. You can interview Lael, or test her reflexes, or whatever else you want. I'll sign the order."

Grateful and excited, Dr. Williams left the bridge with signed orders. I knew how she must feel. She'd been close to the Nomad, Godwin, but gotten nothing out of him. Lael represented a second shot at exercising her skills.

Abrams came through about an hour later with a coordinate estimation. It was hard to do, so close to the center of the galaxy, but he'd managed to get a fix.

"We're about here," he said, stabbing his fingers into a cloud of dust on our charts. "There are several quasars with measurable output pulses in the region. That helped me triangulate our position."

"How close are your guesses?"

He looked offended. "They're hardly *guesses*, Captain. They're based on empirical data which—"

"Okay, okay. What kind of precision do you have?"

He shrugged. "Within a hundred lightyears."

I nodded, impressed. "That's hardly pinpointing it, but I'll take it. Have you got a good beacon for a jump?"

"Yes. We'll make three short hops, no more than a thousand lightyears each. This will take us out of this clouded region to where we can clearly spot our home stars. With luck, we can be home in less than a week."

My teeth bared themselves. "Not good enough."

"What, Captain?"

"We've been gone for days already. I want to get home as quickly as possible. I'm willing to take some risks to do it."

He eyed me thoughtfully. "Really...? Such as?"

"Assume you're right about our current position. Take the biggest leap in the right direction that you can. We'll come out somewhere easy—like near Rigel. Using that fix, we can get home in one more jump. I want two jumps, not three or four."

"Why take a risk now?" he asked me. "We have time. We have control. We've lost the gravity drones, and we should be able to prevent all risk of scattering if—"

"We're taking the risk," I said, turning away from him. "Run the numbers, and give them to me."

Frowning, he side-stepped until he was within my field of vision again. The man could be incredibly irritating at times.

"Captain?" he asked. "Can I inquire as to your reasoning? We took a risk before because we were under fire. What is the excuse on this occasion?"

"No excuses, this is a precaution. Think, Doctor: What if Fex returned to the Solar System yesterday? Or the day before? What's he doing to Earth right now while we're out here roaming the stars and sightseeing?"

He stared for a second, then nodded. He clasped his hands behind his back.

"I see. I'll do what I can, Captain."

With that, he left the bridge. I hoped to hell and back he could come up with good numbers this time. I didn't trust the AI, and his science team was made up of smart people—but they weren't quite geniuses.

Sometimes you really needed a genius... no matter how big of an ass he was.

=51=

The next jump went well. We hauled Lael's phase-ship with us successfully. All her others seemed to have been lost, either to the Nomad drones or to the maelstrom surrounding the black hole. Once again, I was impressed with her ability to out-survive her own underlings. I suspected this was due to her habit of sending others into harm's way first. Lael's crew didn't seem to be happy about their status as our sidekick ship—but it was better than having been left to die in a radioactive dust cloud at the center of the galaxy.

"Where are we now?" I asked the moment we came out of the rift.

"That's uncertain..." Chang said as he tried to get fresh readings.

"We're in the Rigel system," the AI said.

Several of the bridge crew whooped, and I joined them after the assertion was confirmed. Immediately, I contacted Dr. Abrams.

"I *knew* you had it in you, Doc," I said. "They said you were a crackpot, past your prime and winging it—but I *knew* you could do it!"

Abrams made a choking sound. "Who uttered these slanders?"

"Ah, you know... pretty much everybody. But they're eating crow now. You got us into home space."

"—beyond the pale," he was saying. I'd caught him in mid-complaint. "I've explained countless times that any previous errors were unavoidable. The gravity drones—"

"Oh, now, hold on, Doc," I said seriously. "Are you admitting you contributed in some small fashion to the errors the last time we jumped?"

"Not at all!" he sputtered. "I did the best anybody could. *No one* could have sorted through thousands of tiny gravitational pulls to distinguish a beacon star. It simply couldn't be done."

Mia walked up to me and put a hand on my arm.

I looked up at her and grinned, but she shook her head. I got the message then: even she thought I was having too much fun with Abrams.

"You're right, Doc," I said. "You did great. You did it right. You saved us all."

"—simply unacceptable that... uh... thank you, Captain Blake. I'm glad you're clear of heart and mind today."

A compliment. That was all the guy was looking for. Was that too much to ask after he'd brought us into home space again? I decided it wasn't, and I spent a few minutes verbally patting him on his bald head.

Finally, when I'd had enough, I signed off and lounged in my harness.

"How long until we jump again, Captain?" Samson asked.

"An hour or so, that's all."

"What about... the Imperials?"

I glanced at him thoughtfully. "I'm trying to see how they might fit into our near future, but I'm having trouble visualizing it."

Commander Hagen approached with his hands clasped behind his back. "Are we ditching them here, Captain? I'd recommend it. This is borderline space, in-between Imperial territory and the Rebel Kher frontier. If we leave them here, they might eventually be picked up by an Imperial ship."

"Yeah..." I said. "But eventually could mean years. Or, a Rebel force with a harder heart might find them and destroy them."

Hagen nodded. "These are realistic possibilities... what are you going to do?"

"I'll talk to Lael about it. After all, it's her fate."

Getting out of my harness, I was surprised to see Hagen standing between me and the hatchway.

"Uh, sir? Do you think that's a good idea?" he asked in low tones.

"I just said it was. Step aside!"

He did so, and I marched down to the detention facility. This time, there had been no conduct unbecoming with the guards. She sat sullenly in her cell, and she didn't look at me when I entered.

"What do you want?" she asked. "It can't be sex, you're a eunuch."

"A what?"

"A previously male creature that has been deliberately—"

"Yeah, yeah, I know what a eunuch is. Why are you calling me names?"

She sniffed. "All that talk about my personal duties was a joke to you, wasn't it?"

I didn't answer right away, as it *had* all been a joke, at least to me.

"Just as I thought," she said. "Well, if you've changed your mind then so have I. I won't be abused in this dungeon of yours—"

"That's not why I'm here. We've arrived safely at Rigel. I wanted to know if you would like to be returned to your ship now."

She perked up and got to her feet. "Of course I would!"

"Good," I said. "We'll make sure you have supplies enough to last quite a while. There are no local planets, as they must have been consumed by Rigel's last expansion ages ago."

"What? Wait... you're leaving me?"

"Of course," I said. "What did you expect? To be chauffeured to Imperial space and dropped off at your uncle's palace?"

She blinked in confusion. "I can go back to my ship—but in exile. There are no regular patrols here. It might be years..."

"Right," I said, "like I said, plenty of supplies. Are you ready to go now?"

Lael didn't budge. "No," she said. "I'd rather stay on. Take me to your quarters. Make me your woman if you must. I can't be left here to die aboard a cramped phase-ship."

This surprised me. I hadn't considered the idea that she'd refuse to be dumped here.

"Uh..." I said, trying to think.

"You know you're leaving me to die," she said. "I'm inconvenient now that you've gotten information from me."

"You won't die—"

"Rebel ships come here much more often than Imperial ones. Most are unfriendly."

263

"You have burned down a number of their homeworlds..." I pointed out. "Hmm, I seem to be making your point for you. Well, what are we to do with you then?"

She stared at the bulkhead, crossing her arms.

I wasn't used to being in charge of a prisoner. Her life was in my hands, and it felt odd to know that. I didn't want to kick her out, but she would be hard to explain back on Earth.

"We're jumping to Earth next," I told her. "I don't think you'd like it there."

"If it's full of humans, you're probably right. Make your decision, Captain."

Lael still didn't look at me. I took in a deep breath and let it out with a sigh.

"All right. I'll jump with you one more time. If we reach Earth, they can decide what to do with you. I would warn you, however, you might end up as a prisoner of war on my homeworld."

She shrugged and seemed unconcerned. I found her attitude somewhat baffling, but I left her in her cell and returned to the bridge.

"Captain?" Chang asked. "Could I have a word?"

"Is it important?"

"No, just a local sensor anomaly."

"Well then, for safety's sake, it's time to move out. We're jumping again. Abrams has coughed up the numbers and recharged the coil—any reason we shouldn't leave?"

He shook his head. "No, sir."

Less than twenty minutes later, we entered a fresh rift. It felt good this time. Every other time we'd jumped in this ship, I'd had my heart in my mouth.

About an hour after we were underway and relaxed for what should be a two hour journey, Chang approached me again.

"Ah yes, your sensor anomaly," I said. "What have you figured out?"

"Well sir... I've been working on it ever since we left Rigel. I've isolated the problem."

"What is it?"

"A chemical trail, sir. Particulate matter, slightly radioactive. I haven't come up with the exact composition, but I have identified the source."

"What source?" I asked him, frowning.

"It's Lael's phase-ship, sir. She's trailing something. It could be innocent, of course. They were damaged and haven't had a chance to dock safely for repairs. But..."

"But what?" I demanded, becoming increasingly alert with every word he spoke.

"Well, it might not be innocent. What if it's some kind of signal? I'm not sure how it could be anything useful... I mean, what could you encode into a radioactive cloud?"

I stared at him, and I suddenly recalled Godwin's words about tracing radioactive isotopes to their source.

"A message..." I said. "Or just a simple trail of radioactive breadcrumbs to trace us. It could be the Nomads—it could even be the Imperials."

"Or," Chang added, "it could be nothing."

I shook my head slowly. "No... Lael wanted to jump again. She really wanted me to take her to Earth. She insisted upon it... Why?"

Getting up in a hurry, I left the bridge and trotted down the passageways. My magnetic boots clanked and snapped as I ran.

I had a sick feeling in my gut, the kind of sensation I'd learned to trust with my life while traveling among the cold-hearted stars.

Straight-arming the door, I barged into Abrams lair.

"How long has this been going on?" I asked him, breathing hard.

"About seven seconds," he responded crisply.

I blinked in confusion. "What?"

"That's how long it's been since I've felt a sensation of irritation with you as its source," he said.

"Same here—listen, we might be in trouble."

That got his attention. "The radiation leaks?" he asked unprompted.

"You knew about that? You didn't say anything."

He shrugged. "I assumed the rest of the crew was doing their jobs. How foolish of me."

"Right... well, Chang thinks it might be a traceable amount of leaked radiation. He said something about a message."

Abrams squinted at me. "Really...? A message? What an intriguing idea... There is some support for the hypothesis. The Imperial ships we've been dragging along in our wake with such merciful intentions have been trailing radiation of a peculiar sort, in a peculiar pattern..."

"A pattern?"

He showed me diagrams. There were indeed pulsing patterns. The radiation wasn't just dribbled out at a regular rate. It was cutting in and out periodically.

"That's odd..."

"Not if you're trying to leave a message behind."

I thought it over. "How did you get all this data? I only just got down here with the news."

"Chang forwarded his findings to me approximately two minutes before he brought up the matter to you. He made no characterization of the data showing a message—but now it seems obvious."

"Oh... he wanted corroboration."

"Before he tried to explain it all to our physics-challenged captain, yes."

Trying not to get mad, I looked over the data. It looked serious.

"This *could be* a message..." I said. "A trail. Godwin said ships could be identified by traces like these. That's why the Nomads set up their trap so far out from Earth and lured us out there—at least, that's according to him."

"Will there be anything else, Captain?"

I looked at him again. "Yeah, stop acting snooty."

He blinked at me. "I'm not sure what you mean."

Could he really be that clueless? As a good judge of bullshitters, I figured he really didn't get it. He lived in his own world.

"Forget it," I said. "How long until we reach Earth?"

"We'll be there very soon, ten minutes to an hour, I should think. The jump from Rigel to Earth is only about eight hundred lightyears."

"Right... and there's no way to tell if this wormhole is a straight-shot or not?"

He snorted at my imprecision.

"Wormholes tend to dilate or contract time," he said, "and they're never straight lines. That leaves some wiggle-room concerning our perceived departure and our perceived arrival at the end of a given hyper-spatial tube. Sometimes it takes minutes, other times hours—rarely, even days."

"I know all that," I said. "I want to hear your best guess on the exact duration of this trip."

"Twenty minutes, give or take."

Jumping up, I headed below decks again. I went ever deeper, down to engineering, and farther down still. At last, I found Lael's cell.

She seemed surprised to see me.

"What is it?" she asked, studying my face.

"We found your trace—the trail you've been leaving behind."

Lael froze for a second, and I saw her eyes widen. Then, she got herself under control again and studied the bulkhead.

"I don't know what you're talking about."

"I don't believe you. Who or what are you leading to Earth? For what purpose?"

She didn't answer for a few moments, then she suddenly stood and smiled at me. "I've maintained this charade for too long, it's unbearable. I don't care anymore... Your *doom*, that's what's following!"

Nodding, I looked her over. "Playing upon my pity. Begging for mercy. All to get a little revenge, is that it?"

"I lost my command because of you," she said. "Didn't you notice? I was flying *Splendor* last time we met. They gave me a squadron of phase-ships instead. It's been like piloting a swarm of gnats in comparison to my starship."

"Hmm," I said. "Whatever you've done, you can be sure you'll suffer the same fate we humans will."

She snorted. "It'll be worth it. I'd rather die than have it said Lael was defeated by a ship crewed by apes."

I left her then, slamming the hatch behind me. Traveling the passages, I felt a familiar tremor run through the ship.

We'd exited the rift and arrived.

For once, I really hoped Abrams had screwed up and navigated us right out of the galaxy.

=52=

We came out of the rift, and I knew right off we were screwed.

"Captain!" Samson called to me jubilantly. "We're home! We made it! Tell Doc Abrams he nailed it—we can't be more than ten million kilometers from Earth."

"I'll tell him," I answered, trying not to sound glum.

I was in the main passage, but I halted in my tracks. My mind was whirling. We were home. If anyone had managed to trace our tracks, they'd be coming here too. Soon.

What should I do?

A lovely ensign sauntered by as I stood there. She waved at me with her fingers and gave me a sweet smile.

"We made it back to home space, Captain," she said. "I knew you guys could do it."

I didn't even nod to her for a second—but then I realized it and stopped frowning.

"Is something wrong, sir?"

Giving myself a little shake and forcing a smile, I turned to her. "No, Ensign. Not at all. Carry on."

She walked off, but I didn't even have the spirit to stare after her.

Performing a U-turn, spinning around on my heels, I headed back to Abrams' lab. He was surprised to see me again so soon.

"Barging in again? It's only been a few minutes!"

"That's right. I want you to charge the capacitors again. We'll jump out again as soon as possible."

"Really? Did you think that up all by yourself?"

I squinted at him. "What are you talking about?"

He worked a console, and the power systems began to hum with a rising pitch.

"I'm doing it, I'm doing it—I just don't think it will work."

"What won't work?"

"Come now, Captain. It's obvious you're panicking. You think we're being followed, and—"

"Lael confirmed it. She told me our doom is on our trail. Furthermore, it's her doing."

Abrams nodded appreciatively. "Impressive bit of work on her part. But in any case, if you think jumping out before this 'doom' of hers arrives... I'm telling you it's pointless."

"And I'm asking you why?"

"Because they'll scan the system the moment they arrive. They'll see no evidence of our presence and then become curious..."

"About Earth?"

"Of course. Why would our ship come to this system? Why would it pause so briefly, then flitter away again?"

"You think they'll investigate?"

"I would—wouldn't you?"

I thought about it. Whatever this doom was, if they were Imperials or Nomads... they'd want to know why we'd stopped at Earth. And if we left our world behind, she'd be defenseless.

"Damn..." I said.

Abrams gave me a smug smile. He lifted a finger to the panels, and raised his eyebrows high. "Should I kill the power-recharge?"

"No," I said firmly. "Keep charging. I'm going to contact Earth for orders."

Exiting, I moved back up to the bridge. Normally, I would have tried to slip away without checking in with Space Command—but this was too big, I'd never get away with it. Besides, I didn't know what to do. I thought I'd let them share in the good news.

I spent the next twenty frustrating minutes making my report to Admiral Vega and some of his flunkies. They didn't seem to grasp the urgency of the situation.

"So..." Vega said. "You think you might have been tailed back to Earth?"

"That's what I'm saying."

"Hmm... since you first reported this, Blake, about fifteen minutes ago, we've run it past all our techs. They don't think it's possible."

Closing my eyes to keep from cursing, I tried to speak in a civil fashion. "We believe the threat is real, sir. What are your orders? Should I try to lead them away, or should I stand my ground here?"

"Lead them...? You mean run from your phantom force? You only just got back, Blake."

"That's true, sir. But I'm hoping that if they come to Earth and everything looks quiet, they'll keep following me, rather than attacking our homeworld."

"Attacking our homeworld? What else did you do out there in space, Blake? I think I'm going to need a full report."

"Admiral, there's no time—"

Vega crossed his arms, and his face took on a stubborn expression.

"We'll make time. All our sensors show that local space is empty. If you jump again, you might be gone for months. Every member of the brass down here wants a full report—and possibly, they'll want blood as well."

"Yes sir," I said, "we'll stand here and wait."

"Wait for what?"

"For whoever is following us to show up."

"You'll do no such thing. Bring *Devilfish* home. We need to work on her—and we'd like to interrogate Captain Lael as well."

"Returning to Earth orbit then..." I said, full of misgivings.

"Blake out."

That was it. I ordered Abrams to stop charging the coils for another jump. I had Dalton fly us toward Earth, but we didn't move at top speed.

My foot-dragging didn't go unnoticed. Within a half-hour, Vega contacted me again and ordered me to come home at flank speed.

Relaying the order, I felt sick. We'd reach home orbit in less than an hour.

Accordingly, I took up my seat on the bridge and sweated it out. Most of my crew was overjoyed. Our home stars and planets were quite a sight for sore eyes. I got the impression many of them had done the math and assumed we'd never see home again.

"Samson," I said sternly as I checked his console over. "Our shields are at half-strength—why is that?"

"Uh... to divert power to our engines, sir."

"We're not in a safe-zone. Put them back up to one hundred percent. That goes for all our defensive systems—and Chang, I want you to ping away like we're hunting phase-ships."

"Speaking of which, sir," he said. "Our companion vessel is still following us like a puppy. What are we going to do about Lael's ship?"

It was a touchy question. Lael had admitted to treachery. I had no orders to destroy her ship and crew—but then again, I hadn't asked Vega about that.

"Maintain course," I said. "I'll contact Earth again."

For some reason, it took several minutes to get through to Vega. When I finally did, he was frowning at me.

"What's wrong, Admiral?" I asked.

"You haven't seen it? Maybe we have more local probes out there in the right position—anyway, you were right after all."

My blood chilled. "Right about what, sir?"

"About someone following your Imperial friends."

"Their ship is a captured prize, sir. Not an ally."

"Clearly, you're right. Two rifts opened up behind you. They're both spilling out ships."

"Chang!" I said, whirling around to look at him.

He looked up from his console. His face told me the story. He'd detected the enemy in our wake now, too.

"How many ships, Admiral?" I asked.

"We're still counting... twenty at least. Maybe thirty now."

"Configuration?"

"They're Rebel Kher—not Imperials. A mix of light cruisers and light carriers. Nothing else so far."

"That would seem quite sufficient."

"Yeah... We're pretty much screwed..."

"What are my orders, Admiral?"

He didn't answer right away. "You're to maintain course. We're going to try to talk to them. It might be Fex and his promised armada, or it might be someone else. About our earlier discussion, Blake—I don't want you to feel bad about leading them here. It's too late for feelings. I need your head in this game."

"What about *Devilfish*'s two sister ships?"

"We cannibalized critical components as you might recall. We might be able to get them underway, but they won't be fully operational. You're the only serious ship we have in local space."

"I understand, Admiral. *Devilfish* will not let you down. We'll fight to the death."

"As will we all, Captain Blake. Vega out."

He signed off, and I felt fully sick now.

There was no getting around this fight, I had that feeling. They were coming out of the rift still, but they weren't approaching. They were setting up an attack formation.

The worst part was we were trying to communicate, but they weren't answering. We pinged, hailed, made formal statements and demands—but every message was met with dead air in response.

=53=

O nce they'd gotten organized they rolled forward in a silent wedge-shaped formation.

"They're taking their sweet time about it," Dalton complained.

"They've got all the time in the universe," I said. "Target count, Chang?"

"Thirty-one ships, Captain. Eight carriers and twenty-three light cruisers."

"Do they match Fex's ship designs?"

He hesitated. "I've been going over that with the AI. We're pretty far out—but I'd say that they do not, sir. Wrong silhouette. Wrong electro-magnetic signature. Even spectral analysis of their exhaust plumes is a failed match."

"Okay, so this isn't Fex's Armada."

Commander Hagen cleared his throat, and I looked at him expectantly.

"Begging your pardon, sir," he said, "but we don't know what Fex meant by his 'armada' in the first place. It could be this is some kind of auxiliary or allied force."

"Hmmm," I said, "that might explain the quiet treatment. Fex likes to talk—not all Kher do. In fact, if I had to guess, I'd say they're acting like predators instead of primates."

"Is that significant, sir?"

I glanced at him. "Not really... not when there are thirty of them. The point is that a hungry bear who finds a camper with a broken leg probably wouldn't talk much either. He'd move in very intently, thinking of nothing other than the coming meal."

"You paint quite a picture, sir."

273

I stopped talking, as I realized I was psyching out my own crewmen. They hardly needed defeatist talk out of their captain when they were facing hopeless odds to begin with.

It was time to start thinking. After a full minute of watching what truly did look like our doom on the scopes, I came up with something.

I contacted my security people. "Get me the brig commander."

A moment later, I ordered Lael to be brought up to the bridge. She arrived soon thereafter with two men half-carrying her.

Sullenly, she looked around the group. Mia bared her teeth for a moment, and Lael chuckled.

"You brought that absurd creature from Ral with you?" she asked. "They must make better slaves for humans than they do on Imperial worlds."

"You're the slave now," Mia hissed back at her. "Who is standing in bonds on this deck, and who is free?"

"And who is shortly going to be dead?" Lael demanded in return.

"Ladies, ladies," I said, "settle down. We're *all* as good as dead. No one will survive this onslaught. Just look at them. They won't even answer my calls."

"Of course not," Lael said, "they've traced my vessel. They know you brought it here. They will not hesitate to destroy you."

"I must hand it to you, Lael," I said. "You did a wonderful job tricking me into rescuing your vessel. I never would have known what you were up to if you hadn't admitted to leaving a trail behind to get the rebels to follow."

"That's right, fool," Lael said, but then she stopped. She frowned at me. "Just a moment, you figured that out on your own. What are you trying to pull, Blake?"

I made a desperate cutting motion to Chang. He stabbed a button on his console.

"Did you get that?" I asked him

"All of it, sir."

"You haven't transmitted any of it yet, have you?"

"No sir. You said to wait for your go-ahead."

Lael followed this interchange with growing concern. She made a wild cry as realization dawned on her, and she tried to lunge at me. The guards caught her arms, but her foot came up and grazed my hair.

274

"That's good enough, take her below," I ordered.

The guards removed her as she howled about my devious ape-nature and how none of my plans would work.

"This force is only the spearhead," she insisted. "The armada is still coming!"

I waited until she was dragged out, then I turned to Chang. "Edit out those last few seconds, then send it to them on every frequency we can, in the clear."

"On it, Captain. Let's pray they listen."

"What's going on?" Mia demanded.

"I'm engaging in a little old-fashioned primate trickery."

"Oh..." she said, looking disgusted. "Can't we just fight them?"

"We'd be blown from the sky, girl."

"Yeah... too bad. It would have been glorious."

"Well, don't worry," Dalton said. "They're still approaching in lock-step."

It was true, they were. They didn't reply to my messages, or the video.

"Keep sending it," I said.

"They're not acknowledging anything, Captain."

My lips were a tight line of stress. It was hard to think clearly, but I had to try.

"How long until they reach Earth?"

"Less than an hour, sir."

"Okay," I said, taking in a deep breath. "We have no choice. We're going to eject the Imperial phase-ship from our shielded area. Dalton—plot out a rapid maneuver to that effect."

"Working on it..." he said, punching at his console. "Ready to let her rip, Captain." He grinned at me. I think that he, alone among my crewmen, knew what I was going to do next.

"All right," I said, "Mia? This is your lucky day. I want you to target that phase-ship the second she's no longer hugging our belly. You're going to destroy her. No mercy, no hesitancy—do not disable, destroy. Do you have that?"

Mia grinned, and her big eyes lit up. She looked excited, and I thought I heard a tiny purr of joy escape her.

"Finally!" she said, turning to her console joyfully. "We should drag that Imperial bitch back up here and make her watch."

"That won't be necessary," I said. "Dalton?"

"Course programmed in."

"Mia?"

"Opening gun ports now."

"Okay... Execute on my command... Execute!"

Our ship rolled over and away from the Imperial vessel. For a few seconds, they didn't react, but then they began to shimmer.

"They brought up their shields!" Commander Hagen said. "They're slowing, Captain... looks like they're planning to fire into our stern point-blank."

"Mia...?"

She worked her gun, swiveling it around to get it lined up. Our ship's main weapon wasn't meant to be used at such close range.

"I can't get them into my field of fire!" she said.

"Dalton, come around broadside for a sweep. Mia, we're going to have to use our secondaries. All batteries, fire at will on the phase-ship."

The gunnery crews were awake, at least. They opened fire about one second after I gave the go-ahead. The computer painted lavender lines on the displays, showing where our beams were lancing out by the dozens to stencil the smaller enemy ship.

Then, the Imperials returned fire. We bucked, caught amidships.

"Flank shields down," Samson read out. "Minor hull damage. No decks breached."

"Dalton, the secondaries aren't doing it," I said. "Bring around the bow to give the mains a shot."

The phase-ship knew exactly what we were doing. I'd half-expected to see her vanish—but she didn't. She fought on.

"Damn you..." Dalton muttered as he swung past the phase-ship. He was trying again to get the center line of our ship lined up with the enemy vessel. "The pilot knows his shit, Captain. He's cutting angles on me..."

"Got it!" Mia shouted, and she released a powerful shell point-blank. Our main guns spoke, and at this range, there was no missing.

The phase-ship exploded in a gush of released energy and gasses. Particulate matter splattered us a moment later, sparkling all over our shields.

"I nailed them!" Mia said gleefully.

I looked at her, and I saw how flushed she was with excitement. Her species lived for the hunt.

=54=

It didn't bother Mia at all that the Imperial crew she'd just slaughtered had followed us for days. They'd depended on us to save them from the gravity-drones, then to transport them among the stars. After all that, what had we done? We killed them all in a surprise attack.

Thinking about the situation *did* bother me, but I harshly suppressed my natural feelings of guilt. They weren't innocent beings. I'd been forced to do it to save Earth.

"You destroyed them..." Hagen said. He looked shocked. "Can I ask why, Captain?"

"I had to," I said, watching Dalton swing *Devilfish* back around to face the closing line of Rebel Kher ships. "They have to believe Lael tricked us. They can't think for a moment that Earth is on the Imperial side."

Hagen nodded slowly, but he still looked stunned.

"Life is cheap in space," he observed. "Just staying alive in our little steel cans of warmth and air is hard enough under the best of circumstances. I guess that lesson is sinking in today. You people from the original crew—you must have seen a lot in your first voyages."

"We did," Samson said.

"Chang?" I said. "Hook me up with the approaching fleet. Tell them I wish to discuss terms of surrender."

Everyone looked at me, and I shrugged in return. "Nothing else has gotten their attention. What have we got to lose?"

Disgruntled, they turned back to their stations.

"Captain...? They've opened the channel. But it's audio only—and no one is talking on the other end."

"So they want to listen to what I have to say, but they don't care to identify themselves? Fine."

I used my sym to tap into the feed and sucked in a deep breath.

"Fellow Rebels," I began, "this is Captain Leo Blake, commanding *Devilfish*. We've discovered the Imperials we captured have tricked us. We've destroyed their ship. Please respond."

There was a long moment of quiet. I began to think that they were going to keep stonewalling us—but they finally spoke up.

"Captain Blake, we don't believe you. No being can fool a primate like you."

I shifted in my seat, trying to think. It took several seconds, but I soon came up with an angle.

"It wasn't the Imperials who tricked us—not originally. We were manipulated by the Nomads. An agent of theirs, Godwin, came to Earth and promised us an alliance against the Imperials. He gave us gifts, such as the engine that allows this starship to open a rift. It was he who led us down this path to destruction."

"You are indeed about to be destroyed," the voice said. "Your continuous spouting of fantastical tales won't save you. We know you brought the Imperial ship with you willingly after they performed the worst of crimes against our world."

I frowned. "What crime, specifically?"

"As if you don't know. Your every word is a falsehood—but I will play along so all can see the depths of your dishonor. The Imperial phase-ships you've been escorting destroyed an unarmed colony ship—a ship bearing two million civilians."

Hagen and I exchanged worried glances. Lael had never mentioned what she'd been up to that might have gotten people so upset with her—now we knew.

"I understand your anger. Those aboard the last of the phase-ships have perished. The *Devilfish* has finished your mission for you."

"As slippery as an oiled worm," the voice said, and for a second, I thought I recognized it. The voice was female, but deeper than the norm. Where had I heard that voice before?

"Listen, old friend," I said, hoping they knew me as I did them, "I'm sorry for your loss. But we didn't help these Imperials do anything. We destroyed the Diva system with the help of the Nomads. We—"

"I doubt the Nomads are involved. Their fleets were all destroyed centuries ago. I don't even understand why you're convinced you've met them, Blake."

"They'll be in range in five minutes, sir," Chang said quietly.

"Listen," I said in the calmest voice I could muster, "how could Earth build a starship in just a few years? There's no way we could have done it without help."

"That proves nothing. You could have had help from a dozen different Rebel Kher worlds. The Nomads? It's too much to believe."

"All right then, we will send proof," I said, and I ordered Chang to send multiple brief recordings to their ship. The channel balked at the upload at first, but then whoever was running the boards on the other side decided to relent. They allowed us to transmit our data.

A full minute went by before they spoke again.

"This is surprising," the voice said. "I don't think even a human could fabricate so many details..."

"Then stand down your ships," I said. "Close your gun ports and I'll close mine."

"No," she said. "You will shut down *your* ship. You will submit to being boarded and searched. You will do this—or I will be forced to destroy you, Leo."

Just then, finally, I knew who I was talking to.

"Ursahn?" I asked in surprise. "That's you, isn't it? Ursahn, you have to listen to reason. We didn't know the Nomads were as bad as the Imperials. All we knew was that they were the enemy of our enemy, and they gave us technological help."

"I opened this channel, Blake," Ursahn said, "because you indicated that you were willing to surrender your ship. If you're telling the truth, a peaceful finish to this day is possible—but I can't guarantee anything."

I was left with a terrible decision. Mia looked at me, her head turned so I could only see one eye. She whispered in a harsh voice.

"Let them come close," she said. "I'll shut our gun ports, and we'll play dead. But when they come very near—I'll tear them apart. I promise you three kills—maybe as many as five."

"There are thirty of them, Mia."

She snorted. "I'm not a god. Five kills—that's amazing! Doesn't your heart thrill at the prospect of such a glorious finish?"

"We can't win," Commander Hagen pointed out.

"Of course not," she said, "but at this moment we can decide *how* we die. Isn't that the best thing any Rebel can say? No one lives forever."

I took her council seriously. If we could destroy five of them by suckering them in, playing dead... Earth might stand a better chance. But they would still outgun everything else our planet had. Worse, they wouldn't be in a merciful mood after our treachery.

"No," I said at last. "We'll play it straight. I'm going to have to talk to them and get them to see reason."

Mia was disappointed. She sagged in her harness and shook her head.

"To captain a starship you must be born a predator. You lack the killer instinct that war in space requires."

It was insulting, but she could have been right, so I didn't argue. The truth would become clear soon enough.

"Stand down," I ordered. "Everyone drop shields, cycle down our weapons."

My orders were met with reluctance and groans all over the ship. But my crew obeyed. I was proud of them, no matter what our fate was to be. They'd all proven Earth ships had good discipline at least.

=55=

Ursahn herself came aboard *Devilfish*. She had a squadron of her heavy marines at her back, big hulking figures with thick necks and even thicker arms. They marched onto my ship as if they owned it.

"Welcome aboard *Devilfish*," I greeted her. "Let us meet as friends."

Ursahn regarded me with suspicion. We'd once been friends, but now—I wasn't so sure. She had a cold glitter in her eyes.

"You surrender your ship?" she asked.

"I'm here to be boarded and inspected. Let us make our case. Let us become friends again."

"No," she said. "Not so easily. We've brought detection equipment—old tools that we haven't utilized since long before I was born."

Blinking in confusion, I tried to keep my attitude upbeat. "Fine," I told her. "We've got nothing to hide here."

"That will be determined."

She then ordered her troops forward. My own team ruffled at their brusque manner, but I waved for them to let her spacers go where they wanted.

"While they're searching our ship," I said to Ursahn, "perhaps we can share some refreshment."

"I'm not hungry."

"Well then... perhaps you'll accompany me? I'm famished."

Ursahn eyed me strangely. "You do not eat before battle? Does this tighten your senses?"

"Yes," I lied. "It's a human trick. We stay hungry because that way, we're more focused on the kill."

"Interesting... I will allow you to demonstrate your hunger."

Playing it by ear, I led her down to the mess deck. Putting on a great show, I ate a pile of rare meats. She watched with a wrinkling snout.

"You have burned your food."

"It kills bacteria and enhances flavor."

She laughed. "On Ursa, we feed burnt meals only to cubs. Adult guts can tolerate any kind of rot. You eat like a baby."

I dropped my fork, and let it clattered on the platter. I looked at Ursahn flatly. I was getting tired of her disdain.

"Let's discuss the situation plainly, Ursahn. You'll soon find we're telling the truth."

"I have no way of foretelling the future."

"Well, I do. You'll find traces of the Nomad creature we chased from our decks. Isn't that what the devices you brought aboard are built to do?"

"No... not at all. The Nomads are almost legends, as I explained to you earlier. Our equipment is attuned to the spoor of the Imperial Kher. It's been a long time since we needed to locate one of them. They rarely hide and cower, but this is a unique occasion."

My alarm grew as she spoke these words. They were bound to pick up Lael. The people of Ursa weren't overly imaginative, but they were horridly suspicious. They'd assume that I was harboring Lael, and they'd take the situation as clear evidence that I'd lied to them.

"I have to admit," Ursahn was saying, "you have piqued my interest with these smells of yours."

"What?"

"That substance—you called it tri-tip? Would you permit me to try it?"

"Uh... sure."

My first instinct was to summon a steward and order more meat—but then I realized that might take too long.

"Take mine," I said, pushing the plate toward her. "I've eaten my fill."

She sniffed at it warily. "This is a good gesture. What man salts his own meat with poison and eats it before passing it to an enemy? Not even a human is so underhanded. I will try your portion."

Ursahn took my plate and began wolfing it down. Red juices ran from the corner of her mouth and down onto her fuzzy neck and chest.

"I must see to my ship as you feast," I said, "I'll be right back."

"Urmph," she said indistinctly. Evidently, tri-tip tasted good to her kind as well. She was eating with relish. "You have burnt it and salted it. So strange... it has an excellent flavor."

On the way out of the mess, I tapped a steward and ordered the kitchen staff to keep fresh platters heading to her table. They assured me the Kher wouldn't go hungry.

Once out in the passageway and out of sight of her staring guards, I began to run. I had to get below decks before they did.

I had to get to Lael's cell first.

When I arrived at the brig, I was out of breath. My heavy magnetic boots had clumped all over a dozen metal decks.

To my surprise, there was a group of them already circling her cell door. An emergency team from Medical was there as well.

They had the door open, and a figure lay draped over the deck.

"Dammit," I said, "what happened to the prisoner?"

"Nothing," a doctor said, looking up at me. "This is her victim—Dr. Williams."

Surprised, I took a better look at the person they were clustered around. I saw Theresa Williams. Her face was bloodied, and one eye was sealed shut. It looked like it had been gouged out. There was blood everywhere.

"What the hell...?" I demanded. "Guards, where's the brig officer?"

A man hustled up to me. He was stone-faced. "Captain?"

"How could you let this happen? Why was Dr. Williams allowed into the brig with a dangerous prisoner?"

He seemed prepared for this moment. He produced a sheet with orders written on it with a flourish.

"I believe that's your signature at the bottom, sir," he said.

"Yes... I recall now. She asked me if she could study Lael. She's a xenobiologist... but I never expected... What happened?"

The stone-faced brig officer opened his mouth, but Lael answered for him.

"I grew tired of her questions," she said. "She's weak, Blake. She doesn't belong on a warship."

Stepping over the fallen scientist, I faced Lael in her cell. She was restrained with cuffs. It occurred to me she should have stayed in bonds for the entire trip.

Her face told me a tale of hate. I'd kind of realized before that all of her sexual hints had been attempts of manipulation—but now I realized I'd been completely taken in. She'd used every trick she had to get revenge on me and my crew.

"Dr. Williams isn't a combatant," I told her. "She's a scientist. She was only trying to learn more about you."

"Well then, I gave her a good lesson, didn't I? Quit whining about it. She doubtlessly has another pen to take notes with back in her office, and I'm sure your medical people can grow her a fresh eyeball."

"Our medical technology hasn't progressed that far yet."

"No? How embarrassing for you... but I guess that's why you're born with two. She'll just have to use her spare."

I'd heard enough. "Get Lael out of her cell," I ordered the surprised guards. "Move quickly!"

By this time the emergency team had taken Dr. Williams to Medical. The guards threw the hatch wide and soon Lael was dragged into the passageway.

"So," she said, "is it time for my execution?"

I looked at her, and I almost admitted that it was.

If we shot her now, and we ditched her body in the waste tanks—they wouldn't detect it, would they? I couldn't know for sure with these Ursas and their sniffing machines.

"I see it in your eyes," she said. "You *do* mean to kill me. I'm surprised—I would have thought you were too frightened to execute a helpless Imperial officer. Perhaps it was the weakling I stabbed? Was she dear to you?"

Narrowing my eyes at her, I decided I could give her one last chance.

"The Ursas are aboard," I told her. "They're searching the ship, looking for any sign of you."

"Ah!" she said. "I understand completely. "You've been defeated in battle. The great Leo Blake now grovels before his own Rebel officers!"

"Look," I said, "if you want to live, you'll help me."

"Help you with what?" she asked. "Even if I shot myself, they'd still find the body."

284

"Is there some way we can fool their detection equipment? Some way we can cover your trail?"

She gave me an odd look. "Why would you bother? Are you so weak that you can't—?"

Taking out a sidearm and putting the barrel in her face, I made her flinch, and she shut up.

"You don't have long. If you help me hide yourself, you live. If you can't, or won't—you're dead."

"What you ask is dishonorable," she complained.

"To hide?"

"Not just that—it's where I must hide."

At last, I got it out of her. The Ursas detected creatures with a machine that sniffed for them. Lael, her clothing, and everything she'd touched in her cell had to lose her scent.

"But how can we—?" I began, but I caught her glowering at me fiercely, and I suddenly caught on. "Oh..."

It only took a few minutes. I contacted the maintenance crews. Plugging pipes, reversing them, flushing sewage into her compartment—the whole process was disgusting, but I thought it might just work.

The last thing I saw of her, Lael was floating in a pool of the ship's waste. Her whole cell was full of it.

When the inspection team got down to the brig, we told them it was a sewage holding tank. They wrinkled their noses and ran a forked instrument around for a moment which smelled nothing.

Nothing but shit.

=56=

Ursahn clapped me on the shoulder. The blow hurt, but I grinned at her and she bared her teeth at me in return. We were both trying hard to mimic the other's customs—and failing.

But it was the thought that counted. We were trying to reestablish our old bonds, our comradery from the wars with the Imperials.

"Tell me," I said, "now that we bleed again for the same cause, why did the Imperials attack your colony ship? Have they decided to begin the hunt again?"

Ursahn's bared teeth vanished under her dark lips. She looked troubled.

"We're not sure. The actions of the Imperials are unusual. They do like to kill wild Kher for sport, of course. But they performed this strike secretly. We almost blamed other Kher for it..."

"Really? Like who?"

She appeared uncomfortable, and I removed my hand from her shoulder. Perhaps long physical contact was too much for her people.

"You Earthers, for one. We knew it was done by phase-ships. The vessels were unmarked and stealthy. The captain managed to get out a report from the doomed vessel before she was completely destroyed."

"So... you saw a phase-ship and assumed it came from Earth?"

"No other Kher would build such a dishonorable ship. Not even Fex and his unscrupulous people would dare."

"Right..." I said, reflecting on the dangers we'd invoked by building phase-ships. Rebel Kher considered them dirty weapons, like chemical weapons back on Earth. But we'd been behind in the tech game and possessed no fleet. In order to rapidly build at least a deterrent force, Space Command had felt they had no choice. Phase-ships were cheap and quick to assemble. Since they cruised out of sight, the enemy could never be sure exactly how many of them you had in the region.

"It wasn't you," Ursahn assured me. "We know that now—but when we figured out it was the Imperials, we were still confused. They're acting strangely. We fear they've already launched a new campaign, but we're in the dark as to its nature."

Thinking it over, I came up with an idea.

"You're not going to like this suggestion," I said, "but maybe their plan is to sow discord among us. To get one planet to blame the next. To play us off like pawns riling up our populations until we destroy one another."

She struggled to grasp the idea. "Such a diabolical plan... How could you even *imagine* such a thing?"

I considered admitting that Human nations fought in just such a manner, through proxies and instigated bush-wars, but I quickly ditched that idea. She already had a dark opinion of my species.

How many times in Earth's past had a nation killed another country's leader and blamed a third, innocent party? I didn't know, but I was sure the practice was still going on my homeworld somewhere.

"I don't know how I thought of it," I told her. "It just seemed like something dirty that an Imperial might come up with."

"Exactly!" boomed Ursahn. "That's how I felt about it once I realized what had really happened. So... if you're right, our old enemy is out to destroy us from within. To think we came within a hair of destroying Earth's only legitimate starship. That would have been a shame."

"Agreed," I said, "but what are we going to do now?"

"Simple enough, we'll wait here on station for the rest of our fleet."

"Okay..." I said, keeping my pasted-on smile going. "There are more ships coming here?"

"Of course."

"Are these ships we're talking about coming from Ursa?"

"No, no," she said. "The battle-group you've encountered is the majority of what we've got. The rest of the armada is being led by Fex. Somehow, he's gotten control of the Gref crews, and they're quite loyal to him now."

My blood chilled, but I didn't let it show. Fex wasn't my friend. He never had been. At the very least, his imminent arrival meant that I was going to have to perform diplomatic judo all over again.

It didn't help matters to have our suspicions confirmed that his ships were all crewed by Grefs. If anything, they hated me more than Fex did.

"That's great," I said, forcing my smile to widen a notch.

She pulled back her dark lips to bare her teeth awkwardly in return. At least we were both trying.

Ursahn headed back to her own ship after that, and I relayed the good news to Admiral Vega. At least, I thought it was mostly good news.

"So you surrendered to them without authority?" he demanded.

"Would you rather I fought thirty warships, sir?" I asked.

I was discussing the matter from my office chamber. No one was there other than myself and the holographic image of Vega superimposed on the couch. My sym had starting doing that lately, working on my nervous system directly in order to facilitate communications and other functions.

"You could have checked in with us first, Blake. I know you— you like to do as you please. But I must remind you that you're driving around a trillion-dollar starship. It's a one-of-a-kind right now, and I don't want it broken."

"I got that, Admiral, but surely you'd agree that some level of autonomy is required in space. I'm nearly a light-minute away from Earth now. If you don't trust my judgment, have me removed from command."

Vega's next response was a bit slow in coming back, and I began to worry that he was going to say something that started with, "as a matter of fact, Blake..." but he didn't.

"You've got operational control," he said. "But I need a live-stream coming from your ship."

"It won't be live, sir," I pointed out.

"I'll take whatever I can get. As to the current political situation, you can offer your vessel to serve under Ursahn. That way, if Fex does fire on you she'll have no choice but to take it as an attack on her entire fleet."

Nodding appreciatively, I agreed and signed off. A few minutes later, I found myself on the bridge. I promised Ursahn I would serve as part of her task force for as long as her fleet was in Earth's home system.

Two days passed during which I drilled my crew. We got to fly in formation with Ursahn's battle group, a first for most of them. *Devilfish* was classified as a light cruiser—a step up in my mind—and placed at an outside point of their football-shaped formation. We were a screen, essentially, for the more important ships in the center of the fleet.

That was fine with me. We'd flown solo for quite a while, and it felt good to be part of a real fleet again.

It was at the end of the third day when everything changed.

We were drilling just past the orbit of the Moon when I got an urgent message from Ursahn. My own crew was on-duty, so I opened the channel personally.

"What is it, Captain?" I asked.

"Blake, you're falling behind."

"What...? Dalton, look alive!"

He was pondering our maps, and he sat bolt upright. "The fleet has shifted course—they're heading toward the outer planets."

"What's going on, Ursahn?" I asked.

"Ah yes... you're not fully integrated with the command structure of my battle group... in any case, we're heading out to your sixth planet."

"Saturn? What's going on out there?"

"We've picked up a disturbance. A rift has opened."

"So far out?"

"Fex is nothing if not cautious," she pointed out. "On the other hand, if it's the Imperials, they might be worried we'll fight to defend Earth."

I hesitated. My breathing had stopped.

Despite this, I managed to utter my next question without sounding panicked. "Ursahn," I said, "if it comes down to that— will your task force fight on Earth's behalf?"

She answered immediately, and without reservation. "Absolutely. Your ship is part of this fleet now. Your planet, therefore, is under our protection."

"Good to know..." I said, daring to relax a little.

=57=

Once we were tracking properly with our new sister ships, we swung around to the new course as a group and accelerated. I urgently gestured for Chang's attention.

"Captain?"

"Wake up Hagen—get him up here. Then connect me with Vega. I need to report this—I promised I would."

Vega beat my man to it. I'd forgotten that we'd set up a live feed on our bridge. A continuous channel transmitted our every word and action.

"Glad to see you're living up to your commitments, Blake," he said a few minutes later. He sounded as if he'd been dragged from bed.

Checking, I saw it had to be about four a.m. down there, and surmised he'd been sleeping very near the ops center.

"Glad to see you're observing us closely, sir," I said.

"You're following Ursahn's orders without checking with me first?" he asked.

"That's correct. There isn't time—"

"It's all right. Your maneuvers are pre-approved."

My eyebrows performed an up-down motion of surprise. "So... I'm preapproved to fire at will?"

"Never in Earth's home space! Not unless there's no choice other than losing your ship. What I'm saying is that if *Devilfish* is about to go into combat at Saturn with these new visitors, please let us know."

"Will do, Admiral. Blake out."

I dared to smile at his alarmed tone. I'd been messing with him slightly—I knew the rules of engagement we'd hammered out. I had orders to operate as part of Ursahn's fleet, but not to start any wars without explicit approval.

We sailed through the void for several hours after that. It took approximately half my normal watch to reach Jupiter, accelerating hard all the way. After that, we coasted toward Saturn.

The enemy—if it was an enemy—hadn't been idle. They were coming toward us on a collision course. They finally contacted Ursahn, and I was allowed to listen in.

"Ursa Task Force," a familiar voice said. "This is Admiral Fex. You're off-station and off-target. Earth appears to be quiet—did they surrender without a fight?"

"Not exactly, Admiral," Ursahn admitted. "We've discussed the situation with them. They were not responsible for the attack on our colony ship. They were also not responsible for transporting the Imperial phase-ships that committed the war crime."

There was a long delay, as our ships were still pretty far apart. The distance from Jupiter to Saturn was almost as great as the distance between Jupiter and the Sun.

"You're suppositions are not helpful," Fex answered, "and worse, they're false. Resume your original task: subjugate the armed forces of Earth. That's an order, Rebel Fleet Admiral Fex, out."

There followed several long minutes of sweating on my bridge after that. Fex wasn't messing around. He didn't seem to know my ship was among the group he was talking to—and I could only imagine what he'd say when he found out about that.

"We have to do something, Captain," Samson said to me. "Ursahn might turn on us."

"That's right sir," Dalton said, speaking in a low tone as if the other ships around us might hear. "I can plot an emergency escape course."

"What good would that do?" I asked him. "They'd rake our stern in a second."

"At least let me prime our shields and conserve some power, sir," Samson asked.

"Go ahead. Use Abrams' coil for the rift drive."

Dalton worked his boards, and so did the rest of the crew. I knew Dalton was devising an escape route despite my comments. I couldn't fault him for that. Maybe he'd prove to be the wisest man in the end.

Commander Hagen arrived on the deck a minute later.

"Still no word from Ursahn, sir?" he asked, straightening his uniform.

His eyes were red-rimmed, but he looked awake enough to me. Panic had a way of doing that to a man.

"Not yet, but I'm certain she'll contact us soon."

"Sir," Chang said, "I've detected a channel under the others—Ursahn's flagship is communicating with the approaching fleet directly."

"Can you tap into that?" I asked.

He shook his head. "Access has been denied."

Sweating a little in my chair, I squirmed for a moment. Mostly, I tried not to look nervous—it was a difficult task.

Ursahn wasn't the treacherous type. In fact, I felt I could trust her more than most humans. But that didn't mean she was entirely on our side. She could be talked into a wrong-headed course of action, convinced she was doing something honorable. It was quite possible she'd apologize to me profusely in the next minute or two before turning all her guns on us.

It was all a matter of whether Fex could fast-talk her better than I could. After waiting one more minute, I couldn't take it anymore.

"Chang, open a direct channel with Ursahn. Tell her it's urgent."

Chang worked his board for less than two seconds before he shook his head. He must have been ready for my request.

"We're getting the flagship's busy signal, sir. We've been told to standby."

"Break formation," Hagen said suddenly. "That's my advice, sir. They'll take a few minutes to react to that. We can get some distance, and either jump out or—"

"Or what? Fight to the death against overwhelming odds? I didn't like that option the first time it was offered. I still don't like it. Besides, breaking formation might give them the excuse they've been waiting for—proof that we're diabolical primates after all."

I spun around to find all my crewmen staring at me nervously. "Dalton, steady as she goes. Mia, keep our gun ports closed and cycled down."

293

She reluctantly removed her hands from her controls and crossed her arms in disappointment.

Time ticked by. It was only about three more minutes before someone talked to us—but it seemed like a lifetime.

"Sir," Chang said, with his board beeping at him, "I've got incoming orders from Earth Command."

My jaw jutted out in irritation. More interference from the ground. I could foresee the future for all Earth starship captains at that moment—if there were to be any in the future—they'd all feel irritated by the distant over-the-shoulder armchair commanders back home.

Historically, ship captains had enjoyed a very wide latitude in past centuries. A commander in the eighteen hundreds, for example, could do as he liked on the high seas. He might have to answer to a review board months later, but in the moment, he was all-powerful.

Radio had ended those freedoms after the Second World War, effectively allowing the Pentagon and others to directly control every action of their ships, even half-way around the globe.

Now, in the era of fleets in space, it was a mixed bag. Earth could interfere effectively, but only if we were close enough to our home planet. We were just about at the limits of our tether today, as we were more than a light-hour out.

"Blake," Admiral Vega's message said, "we've been monitoring your situation, and we've been examining that approaching force. Admiral Fex has seventy-seven vessels in his group. He's got nearly twice your firepower—that's assuming Ursahn's ships measure up as equivalent in battle. We've tried to contact both Ursahn and Fex directly, but they're ignoring us. How to proceed is up to you. Earth stands with you regardless. Godspeed, Vega out."

After listening to that encrypted audio message, I felt humbled. I'd expected fussy restrictions, demands for reassurance and hampering rules of engagement—what I'd gotten was almost worse, in a way.

It was all on me. I was in full command, and they'd taken off my leash. As the round trip for any messages between my ship and Earth was nearly a two hour cycle this far out, it was the only choice that made sense. No one could micromanage a warship at this distance.

Sucking in a deep breath and surveying the situation and my crew, I sat up straight in my chair.

"What are we going to do, sir?" Dalton asked, still talking in a whisper.

Who knew? Maybe he was right... maybe they *could* hear us.

"Steady-on, Dalton. Maintain formation. Samson, is that coil charged?"

"Half-way."

"Keep building it up—gently. We might need to divert the power in any number of ways."

=58=

It was Admiral Fex himself who finally contacted me to let me in on what was happening. He did it with a full holo-vid of his upper torso and head, and I relayed the imagery in all his glory into the middle of the command deck.

Like an imposing ghost, the lanky figure's upper half regarded us sternly. He was bigger than life and yet insubstantial in appearance.

"Captain Blake," he began in serious tone, "this situation is entirely your fault. I would expect you to feel ashamed—but I doubt you have the capacity."

"Welcome aboard, Admiral," I responded in a cheery tone. "I'm pleased you could visit us. This is a great day. Earth's forces have rejoined the Rebel Fleet in unison with your own, and I *know* that together we'll stop the Imperial encroachment—"

"What are you blathering about?" he demanded suddenly. "You're not a member of the Rebel Fleet—perhaps you were once in the distant past, as a minimal participant—but not today. In fact, no Rebel Fleet exists as of this date. It was disbanded years ago."

"That's all true, sir—the part about the past, I mean. But today events have moved in unexpected directions. Today, we face challenges we must all admit to. The Imperials are killing Kher again and—"

"Killing with your collusion!" Fex interrupted again. "I won't listen to any further weaseling. If you're too shameless to confess, I'll spell it out for you. This renegade ship of yours rescued a squadron of Imperial pirates. You transported them to safety, and then did their bidding afterward. I'm of the opinion that you were in league with them from the beginning, and that you still are right now."

"Sir, that's a devastating charge," I said. "What proof do you have?"

"Proof? Your own testimony is good enough for me. I've reviewed the recorded conversations you've had with Ursahn, and the so-called 'evidence' you presented to her to absolve yourself. It's all nonsense."

"Now, hold on, sir—"

"No, *you* hold on. A colony vessel was destroyed. Phase-ships did it. They were transported to the site and back to safety again by your ship. I wouldn't even be surprised, after we sift through your ashes, that Earthers built the phase-ships themselves and pretended they were of Imperial origin."

I glanced around at my officers, but I got no support there. They looked dumbstruck—even Dalton. Bluffing it through seemed like my only option, so I went with that.

"I have a solution, Fex," I said, deliberately dropping his rank. "Let's take this to Secretary Shug. He knows all the parties well, and he'll—"

"That's not going to happen. I'm in command here—and unfortunately, you've forced my hand. I'm only contacting you now in a final effort to make you see reason."

"Uh... about what, sir?"

"Surrender your ship! Surrender your planet! You'll be treated as well as any penal colony in the galaxy, I assure you."

"What's the alternative, Admiral?"

"There is none. Absolute destruction is the only other option. It sickens me to be forced to carry out this sentence, but only because Ursahn has refused to follow my orders. Possibly, her ships will even go so far as to return fire when we target your pathetic vessel. I would implore you to refuse her aid. Step aside from her formation and take your punishment like the proud, two-legged beast that you are. It's the right thing to do, Blake."

For a few seconds, I couldn't speak. I couldn't even think properly.

This was it. This was *big*. Fex's fleet was going to try to take us out. Would Ursahn really start a battle with Fex? Would she risk losing all her planet's ships in order to save Earth?

297

I wasn't absolutely sure, but I figured for our sake it was worth the gamble. After all, Fex might be bluffing as well.

Slowly, I shook my head. "I'm really sorry it had to go this way, Fex," I said in the most earnest tones I could muster. "I was wrong about you. Alpha Fleet will be in position shortly, and when you begin firing I won't be able to stop them. The carnage will be terrific."

Fex squinted at me. "Alpha Fleet? What are you talking about?"

"The worst thing is," I continued, "I assured the Alpha Fleet commanders you wouldn't push this charade so far."

"Blake, have you lost your senses as well as your decency? Speak plainly, like an intelligent ape."

"Certainly Admiral. You see, Earth's primary fleet is maneuvering in local space right now."

"I see a single ship. You speak of phantoms."

"Just like the phantoms that chased you out of Earth's orbit the last time you came here to our system. You *are* aware we have nearly two hundred phase-capable vessels, right? *Devilfish* is a cruiser and she's my command, and a fine vessel she is, but she's a recent advancement. We churned out a lot of phase-ships first for local defense."

"I don't believe it."

"Really? But isn't that what you just accused us of doing?"

Fex leaned forward, and his leering face almost seemed to protrude into my bridge with me. It was a disturbing image to behold.

"You're so full of excrement, Blake," he said. "Sometimes, I wish I'd expunged you and your disgusting crew the moment I saw you. I made a mistake that day—I permitted a weed to flourish."

"And now the weed has become a tree," I said, blinking mildly at him. "Listen, forget about Alpha Fleet. I'm probably going to be reprimanded for even bringing it up and losing our element of surprise."

"Shut up," he said. "Phase-ships don't have the range or the power to come out this far from your homeworld."

"Ah-ha!" I said, slapping my console. "Now I *know* why you appeared so far out from Earth. You didn't want to tangle with them again. Well, don't let the fact we've got a light cruiser with a working star drive worry you... Fex, you're absolutely right. Space around you is *not* teeming with phase-ships. You're all alone out here, and you've got the upper hand."

I was never quite sure if he got all of that final speech. His face disintegrated into pixels and vanished. He was gone.

"He didn't even say good-bye," Dalton said, snickering.

"Captain Blake?" Mia said, and I appreciated she hadn't called me "Leo" on my own bridge, "where is Alpha Fleet? I don't see them on any of the scopes."

"That's because he made them up," Samson told her gently.

Mia looked alarmed. Every human on that deck had known I was as full of crap as Fex suspected I was, but Mia had been completely taken in. That was a common result of interacting with the predatory Kher—they tended to be a little gullible. Xeno-psychs postulated that this was due to a lack of going through a phase of being prey themselves during their evolution. That theory could be right or wrong—but regardless, it was undeniable that the Ral and the Ursa were easy to fool.

Leaning toward Chang, I gave him a false smile. Underneath, I was sweating. I'd built a house of cards, and it could come crashing down at any moment.

"What are our friends doing out there, Chang?" I asked him.

"The enemy fleet is too far away to observe with certainty, sir. They appear to be flying in wedge-shaped formation, an arrangement which is both looser and larger than our own. If I had to guess as to their tactics—"

"Hold on," I interrupted, "I'm talking about our *friends*. Ursahn's ships."

"Oh... right. I haven't been tracking them closely. I've been directing all my sensors into a long-range array aimed at the approaching enemy."

I nodded, giving him my patented false smile.

"Well then, turn those dishes toward the Ursa ships. They're quite a bit closer—easily within range if they decide to start shooting at us, don't you think?"

He blinked twice. "I see what you mean, Captain."

"And another thing. I want you to make occasional transmissions in code. Direct them on tight beams ten or twenty thousand kilometers away from our position."

"Uh-huh," he said. "What should these messages say?"

"Transmit bridge-traffic, using our lowest encryption levels. Make sure you use the term 'Alpha Fleet' in every dispatch. Send something out in a burst every five minutes or so."

"They might be able to break our lowest encryption levels, sir— in fact, I would say it would just be a matter of time before they managed to do so."

I smiled at last. It was a real smile this time. "That's what I'm hoping for, Chang. Start transmitting, and keep doing it at random intervals."

Chang went to work. He seemed slightly confused, but I had no doubt he would follow my orders even if he thought they were insane.

He was that kind of guy.

=59=

The battle started off slowly. That didn't mean I was relaxed—far from it. We kept a nervous eye on the approaching enemy, and the Ursa ships floating nearby.

"Get me a line to Captain Ursahn," I demanded for the fifth time in two minutes.

Chang shrugged helplessly. "She's not taking any calls, Captain."

I chewed on the inside of my cheek until it started hurting.

Eventually, Dalton caught my eye.

"I've got that course laid in, Captain," he said. "We can spring out of here at a moment's notice—maybe when the fireworks start."

Frowning, I shook my head. "If Ursahn is going to fight Fex, we'll do it at her side. If she's thinking about screwing us instead, we're going to make it hurt her honor. We're not making the first move."

Dalton sighed and turned back to his console. He was a natural jackal, and I respected that. He'd survived a long time on quick wits and even quicker feet. But I was gambling at an even higher level. I was gambling on Ursahn. She was caught up in a moral dilemma, and she was trying to figure out what the right thing to do was. There was no point in making that decision any easier for her.

"Captain!" Chang said suddenly, "I've got her—private channel, or public?"

"Put it on the holoprojector—in fact, I want you to relay it all over the ship."

He worked his board and Ursahn's hulking image materialized in front of everyone.

"Captain Blake," she said, "we have serious business to discuss."

"We absolutely do," I agreed with enthusiasm. "Do you want me to coordinate my fire with the rest of your light cruisers, or are we to fight independently? We're not hooked up directly into your tactical feed, so I wasn't sure which way—"

"Captain Blake," she repeated, "I request a private audience."

There it was. She was going to screw me, and she didn't want to perform this shameful act in front of my entire crew.

Leaning back in my chair, I shook my head slowly.

"I don't think so," I told her. "If you've got something big to say, you can tell my entire crew. We're all part of the Rebel Fleet, after all. We're all one happy family now."

Her eyes flicked over the scene. Everyone on the bridge listened with stone-faced silence. Even Mia seemed cowed.

"Very well," she said at last, "your planet's actions have become too onerous for us to participate in the coming conflict honorably. We're pulling out. My flagship will open a rift and leave your star system—please don't attempt to follow us."

I felt a wave of sick worry. It was like my stomach was a stone, and someone had pitched it off a cliff.

"Captain Ursahn," I said formally, "can you explain why you're so willing to abandon allies in the face of battle?"

She blanched and squirmed. I couldn't recall ever having seen such behavior before. "This will be no battle—it will be a slaughter. All our computer projections point that way. Therefore, our presence isn't required."

"Not required? We don't have a chance without you! I thought the Ursa people were brave. I thought you never shirked in the face of a just fight."

Ursahn blinked and shook herself slightly. "Insults? Now? Do you feel so confident you can bully both my fleet and Admiral Fex's task force? I'm amazed. I never thought Earth could build up so rapidly. It took us a century to construct the vessels you see before you."

It was my turn to be confused for a moment, then I began to catch on.

"Uh... hold on. Let's talk privately. Follow me with my sym to my office."

When I'd taken a dozen steps, I was in my quarters. Ursahn looked ghostly, but she was still dead-serious.

"What now?" she asked. "We want no part of your abuses. Phase-ships are powerful, but no one has ever amassed so many in one—"

"Ursahn," I interrupted, "I have a confession to make. There is no Alpha Fleet."

She stared at me for a moment, dumbfounded. "But... what was all that about, then? Who are you transmitting secret dispatches to? We've located the angle and probable location of your fleet, but we can't detect them at all. We've even sent out probes. Our best sensor people are confused, wondering if you've come up with an ingenious improvement on Imperial phasing-technology."

I cleared my throat, feeling a little embarrassed. "Uh... right. You see, it's like this, Ursahn: I lied. I told Fex a story, just as he accused me of. We don't have any phase-ships out this far—not one. All the ships we do have are hugging Earth right now, except for this cruiser."

She chewed on that one for a few seconds, and she began to pace.

"A lie..." she said at last. "A primate trick. A filthy, underhanded, treacherous...!"

"No!" I said, cutting her off. "It's a tactic, not a shameful dishonor."

"So is destroying a colony ship. Are you guilty of that as well?"

"Ursahn, we're not traitors. We are mean in a fight—but we play fairly with our friends. We only lie to our enemies."

"Hmm... I'd like to believe that, Blake. I like you, and I've fought at your side many times. You're brave and fierce—but this kind of deceit... It's a difficult bit of gristle for my people to swallow. I'm not even sure now whether you have an Alpha Fleet or not. I suspect that you do. Regardless, dishonor is near at hand for both of us today."

"I understand," I said, standing up straight. "But consider this: I've told you the truth, and I've put a seed of fear and doubt in Fex's mind. Those two facts are all I could hope for today. If you feel you have to withdraw and leave us to fall before Fex alone, I'll understand your choice. Farewell."

So saying, I ended her connection. Her holographic image vanished from the deck of my ship. Effectively, I'd hung up the phone.

Was it the right move? Only time would tell.

=60=

U rsahn's fleet didn't withdraw. She kept to her original course, and she fed me some basic tactical instructions: we were to guard her flank, and not dishonor ourselves. That was it.

"Absolutely typical," Dr. Abrams complained. He was haunting my command deck again, as he had nothing serious to do but wait for the battle to begin. We were about twenty minutes out from contact at our longest range, and we were braking hard.

"What do you mean, Doc?" I asked politely.

"This business of vaguery and the complete lack of a battle plan. It's horrifying. How can these Kher expect to win conflicts without detailed strategy?"

I looked at him seriously. It was a good question, one I'd pondered myself on a number of occasions.

"Well, I think it stems from their early days. The Rebel Kher were seeded all over the local cosmos of stars in the Perseus Arm of the Galaxy. Once they became spacefaring, they found so many varied cultures they couldn't cooperate easily. In fact, they only do it at all when the Imperials fight against them."

"This fleet consists of Ursahn's ships and our single vessel," he pointed out. "We aren't running some kind of horde made up of a million babbling voices. Despite this, she's given you very little to do."

"She might not trust us," Dalton said. "If we know her plans, we could use that to our advantage."

What he was saying was true, and it troubled me. Could this be more than the typical lack of Rebel planning? Could Ursahn be relaying detailed instructions to her own ships, while keeping us in

305

the dark? I had to admit, it was possible. Even fighter crews like my old one had gotten more detailed commands when facing the Imperials in the past.

"There's nothing to worry about," I told them. "She's sticking with us. We've got thirty ships against Fex's force. Sure, we're outnumbered, but—"

"Salvo incoming!" Samson sang out.

We buckled in and reflexively hunkered down. Death could come at you very suddenly in space. The velocities were incredible. When something approached at ten thousand kilometers an hour, you didn't always see it coming at all.

"Abrams, get below decks. Samson, ready-up damage control. Boost the shields to one hundred percent—"

"Our lead ships in the formation have sustained a hit," Chang said, "two forward vessels at the nose of our group have been struck—they're falling back, and fresh ships are rolling forward."

"Are we firing yet?"

"No, but Ursahn is launching fighters."

My teeth gritted on their own. Fex's ships seemed to outrange us. That was bad in space combat—very bad. If you could kill an enemy before they could even shoot back, battles were pretty easy to win.

"We could launch some missiles now, sir," Mia said. "They'd have fuel enough to reach them."

"No, hold on. They'd only be shot down with such a long hang-time in front of a large fleet. If we fire at range at all, we'll do it as part of a general barrage combining our birds with Ursahn's."

Mia didn't complain, but she hunched over her controls intently. She was alive now, fully awake and in the fight.

No one fired on either side for the next full minute. Fex had tested his range, and he'd found he couldn't knock out one of our ships at this distance. Ursahn, apparently, had decided to hold onto her guns and their charging pools as well.

Finally, as if someone had blown a whistle, both sides opened fire at once. We were still at long range, but it was definitely effective range.

Our computers enhanced the visuals so we could see the invisible energies as they were released. Radiations swept out and stabbed through space. At the speed of light, they played over enemy shielding, defensive reflective aerogels and even simple chaff.

Tanks chugged out reflective material that formed a fog in front of our ship, but it was carefully shaped so as to not cover our gun ports or our sensor arrays.

"Prismatic chaff in place," Samson called out. "We can't make any sudden course changes now, or we'll be exposed."

"Dalton, hold our course. Mia, wait until a target looks wounded. Try to finish it."

Energies poured across the million kilometers wide abyss between the two opposing fleets. Each second took us closer, into a more deadly range.

"Formation point ship lost—second ship lost."

"Firing!" Mia announced.

She'd watched them all so closely, I hadn't even had a chance to register her target before she'd locked on and struck. An enemy ship, a battlecruiser by the look of it, collapsed inwardly and then released a gush of gas and light. Soon, it was a dark hulk tumbling in space.

"They're going to have to dodge that!" I said, "Mia, nail one of them when they come out from behind their shielding."

She fired again a few minutes later. My headset was bubbling with chatter. All over the vessel, secondary weapons were firing now. They'd been given a free hand to do so. Mia was only operating our main centerline battery.

"Missiles, Captain?" Mia asked again.

"Hold on. Ursahn seems to be waiting for point-blank range. We'll do the same unless we get hit hard."

I tried not to obsess over it, but the count wasn't going our way. We were taking out more ships than they were, but we had fewer to begin with. Ursahn's crews were superior to anything run by Grefs, and her vessels were well-designed—but they were outnumbered badly. We were taking down three for every two we lost, but we needed to do better than that.

"Chang," I said, "contact Ursahn."

"Trying... she's opening the line. Public or private?"

"Private," I said. "I need to talk to her privately."

He adjusted the channel, and Ursahn was there. She looked haggard and serious.

"Blake," she said, "I know what this is about."

"You do?"

"Yes—you're about to call in your Alpha Fleet, aren't you?"

I closed my eyes. Some part of me felt ashamed for my heritage. Those of the Kher who were like Ursahn—there was something more noble about them than my own squalid species. They trusted, they believed, they felt certain a friend was a friend and lies were only the domain of the devil.

"That's right," I said, "but we need to do something first."

"What? Anything. We're losing this fight."

"Come out from behind your shields. Go high, go low, dive around the central wedge of the enemy."

"We'll be destroyed..."

"Not right away. Get an angle on the enemy. Their shielding is directly in front of them. We'll be left with electromagnetics only—but we'll last for a time."

"What do we do when we're all scattered all over the field?" she demanded in exasperation.

"Fire everything you have at the hindmost ship. See him on your scopes? The one that's hanging back with two sister ships?"

"Which one of the three—?"

"The one in the center. The largest."

"All right Blake. I'm giving the orders—but you must tell me why I'm doing this?"

"Because that's their flagship," I said with absolute certainty in my voice and heart. "That's Fex's ship. We're going to destroy it—and him."

=61=

The maneuver seemed to catch the enemy by surprise, but that only lasted for a few seconds. They soon eagerly switched targets to what must have looked like a random swarm of fleeing vessels.

Rather than trying to hammer down the chaff between our ships and their guns, they took to firing stuttering beams at our exposed bellies and flanks. A thousand rays leapt out and many of them struck home. Three of our ships didn't even make it to a position where they could target the enemy rear.

But when we did get out and into the clear, the exposed flagship had yet to react. So far in this fight, it hadn't bothered to fire a single shot. To have done so would have been fruitless, as it had carefully and constantly maneuvered so as to place the bulk of the fleet between its hull and our guns.

Now, however, a dozen of our ships unloaded at once. The missiles we'd been hoarding up until now went with the beams—all of them. The result was dramatic and terrible to behold.

The two bodyguard ships slowly shifted to interpose—and they were both quickly destroyed.

"Mia, now!" I said. "Give him all you've got. Dalton, swing us around so we can get our big centerline guns into play."

We did this even as we began to take hits. *Devilfish* shuddered and the lights dimmed.

"We've lost generator six," Samson reported. "Two secondary batteries have been knocked out. Belly shielding—we're exposed, Captain."

"Dalton, level this ship off!" I called out. "Mia, take the shot when you get it."

"Captain..." Chang said slowly. "A rift is forming."

"Where?"

"Right in the middle of the enemy formation."

Stunned, I watched the truth of his words unfold. The situation was incredible.

"He's running," I said, "and he doesn't care who dies."

We all watched the greatest single act of treachery we'd witnessed in our lives. The enemy fleet was too close to deal with a rift now. The situation was magnified since so many of the enemy were in front of the flagship, and therefore were struck by the forming rift.

Like a scythe, a great curving oval of light and radiation opened in their midst. Taken by surprise and hemmed in by their formation, a half-dozen vessels simply plowed into the rim, slicing their hulls into strips. They hit the edges in a kaleidoscope of colors and kept going—half their mass in our universe and half of it sailing into hyperspace.

The ship in the center of it all accelerated into the yawning maelstrom it had created. It ignored all the carnage around it, and she never fired a shot at us in revenge. Instead, every beam, every ounce of power, was used to protect her own precious hull.

I watched as the enemy slipped away into hyperspace, along with perhaps ten others that had survived intact. A hundred missiles smashed down behind her, raining upon the confused mass she'd left behind.

After that, the battle was over. Ursahn ordered her ships to ceasefire when it was clear the surviving Gref ships were only trying to flee.

Mia wanted to shoot them in the fantails—but I didn't let her. We'd seen enough devastation today—all of it Rebel-on-Rebel. Somewhere, I knew, the Imperials and the Nomads were both laughing at us. We were barbarian fools too simple-minded to know who their real enemies were.

"Ursahn is contacting us, Captain," Chang said.

"Open it—privately."

Ursahn was all teeth and shaggy arms. She shook her clasped limbs over her head in victory.

"That was amazing!" she told me. "How did you know that was Fex? How did you know he would run like that?"

"An educated guess," I said.

The truth was, of course, I'd only wanted to go out in a blaze of glory. Figuring we were as good as dead, I thought it only right Fex should join us—the rest had been a combination of good fortune and selfishness on Fex's part.

"It's amazing..." she repeated happily. "But one thing I don't understand..."

"What's that?"

"Where did Alpha Fleet go? They never showed themselves."

I smiled at her. "You are the reason for that. Your people did so well, you fought so hard and gloriously, you exceeded all our carefully laid plans. The phase-ships never reached their optimal range before the battle had already been won."

Ursahn beamed. "That's the best news I've heard all day. This battle was won cleanly. We—none of us—need hang our heads in shame. We fought and battled until they destroyed themselves out of fear. There can be no better outcome."

"I absolutely agree with you. Congratulations Ursahn, and Earth thanks you for your help and sacrifice. We owe your world a great debt."

"No!" she boomed. "We served honor today. If anything, we owe you Earthlings for keeping our victory so pure."

"As you wish."

We signed off, and I seriously wasn't sure who was happier about the outcome.

Less than an hour later, when we'd all turned around and begun thrusting toward home again, a message came in from Earth Command.

I opened the channel wreathed in smiles. To share the moment with the rest of my crew, I relayed it to the central holoprojector. My crewmen hooted and cheered.

It wasn't going to be a conversation, we were too far out for that. But I expected to be praised mightily for the greatest victory ever recorded in the Solar System. It would be good for my people to share in the glory of recognition from home. After all, we'd saved billions of their asses out here in space.

"Captain Blake," Admiral Vega began in a serious tone, "this is an official message from Earth Command."

I toasted Vega, thrusting a victory beer toward his looming image and taking a swig. My faceplate was open and my gloves were off. Beer spilled down into my suit and cooled my chest, but I didn't care.

All over the ship, damage crews were working hard, but my work was done except for thoughtful management.

Behind Vega, I saw a number of dour officials. They weren't military people, they were suits—government types.

"From what we can see, your ship has survived the battle in space. For that valiant effort, we're all grateful to you and your crew. In fact, I want you to know, that I insisted this formal transmission be withheld until now. After all, we had no idea if you'd live through the battle or not."

Along about then, a portion of my mind began to understand this wasn't the message I'd been expecting.

"Chang," I said, "they love us back home, but I think this is private business. Switching the channel to my sym directly."

I clammed up, closing my faceplate, sitting back in my seat, and listening with my sym. It played upon my mind and created imagery. I was there, sitting among those who'd transmitted the message from Earth.

This way, I could look around at them. They couldn't see me, but they stared in my direction. To them, I looked like a video pick-up.

"...the nature of the crimes are too complex and detailed to go into now. Suffice it to say, you've been charged with murder by a member of the Nomad peoples. We all know him as Godwin. Another Nomad came to Earth to lodge his concerns, and our government has taken the issue very seriously."

Dumbfounded, I continued to listen. I wanted more beer, but I knew I'd have to open my helmet to drink it. Instead, I sat in stony silence.

"Now, I know you're a war hero and all, and nothing said today will ever take that away from you. Those of us in the chain of command wish to—"

Someone in the room behind Vega cleared their throat loudly. Vega broke off and looked sidelong. A moment later, he continued in a less conciliatory tone.

"As I said, you've been charged with the murder of a diplomat. Another of their kind came here to inform us, and to provide recorded evidence. Accordingly, I have no choice other than to remove you from command, effective immediately, pending a full investigation. Please inform Commander Hagen he's now the acting captain aboard *Devilfish* and confine yourself to your quarters."

Vega looked around the circle of unfriendly government suits defiantly, as if to ask whether that was good enough for them. None of them took the bait. They didn't say a word.

"That's it, Leo... I'm sorry, and I wish you all the best. Admiral Vega out."

The message ended, but I just sat there in my chair with my faceplate flipped shut. Finally, a big pair of knuckles rapped on the plastic.

I flipped it open. Samson was standing there, looking down at me.

"Here's a fresh beer," he said, taking my last one from my limp fingers. "Looks like you need one."

I took the beer, and I downed it. As I did so, I wondered how Samson knew what was up before the rest of them. They were all in party-mode, cheering and laughing.

Sometimes Samson could be pretty intuitive for a big, mean, oaf of a man.

=62=

The trip back to Earth was miserable. Not only did I have to spend the majority of the voyage squatting in my quarters, but I got to spend a lot of that quality time with Mia—and she wasn't happy.

"I don't understand humans at all," she complained for approximately the fiftieth time. "How can they do this to you? I have a solution. You should—"

"Yes, I know," I interrupted. "I should retake command of my ship and overthrow my corrupt, short-sighted government."

"It's the right thing to do," she told me firmly, putting her hands on her curvaceous hips. "Not just for you, but for all of Earth. They're fools. No warlord of Ral would put up with this treatment."

I recalled there were precedents in history. In ancient Rome, conquering heroes returning home from abroad were viewed with legitimate suspicion. Julius Caesar was the most famous example, deciding to cross the Rubicon River in violation of Roman law, taking his legion directly toward Rome herself.

"Such things have happened in the past," I admitted, "but I'm a loyal captain. I'm not going to start a rebellion."

Mia made a sound that could only indicate disgust. She continued strutting around the room, complaining and gesturing broadly.

I soon lost interest in her words, as I'd been forced to endure them for days already. Instead, I enjoyed the view and tried not to become angry.

Before either of us lost control completely, I received a call.

"Captain Blake?" Commander Hagen said in my ear. "We're sliding into high orbit right now. I thought you should know."

"Thank you, Commander."

Mia stared at me angrily. "You shouldn't thank him. He's probably in on it. He probably wants your ship permanently."

"Such things do happen," I admitted, "but Hagen isn't that kind of guy. He's just following orders."

Mia snorted again and went back to pacing. I left her there, touching up my uniform to its best, and then moved myself to the docking port. *Devilfish* had arrived at orbital station Zeta without more than a single phase-ship guarding us.

Seeing the lack of defenses, I was driven to wonder at how easily a coup could be pulled off...

Giving myself a shake, I greeted the four marines that appeared at my side.

"We're here to escort you down to Command, sir," their leader said. "Sorry, sir."

"Not at all," I said, "thanks for the color guard, boys."

At least they didn't handcuff me. As a peaceful gesture, I'd left my sidearm in my quarters, which made things easier for everyone.

Less than half an hour later, we were riding a golf-cart down into Cheyenne Mountain. Cold, rough-hewn granite walls rushed by. I couldn't help but wonder why they were holding the trial underground, rather than in the larger base outside.

No matter, I told myself. One way or the other, their message was the same: they were in charge, not me.

Once down in the cool depths of the mountain, I was left in a cell to await my fate. I stretched out in a provided chair and took a nap.

When someone tapped on the door, I didn't respond. It opened almost timidly—then was thrown wide.

"There he is—asleep!"

The voice was feminine and familiar. I tipped my service cap up and blinked. "Lael? What are you doing here? Did they arrest you, too?"

She snarled at me and stalked into the room. Her hands were shackled behind her back.

"I'm a slave now, the same as you," she complained.

"You're most certainly *not* a slave, Madam," a prissy officer said behind her. "This is a trial, not a punishment."

"They're all one and the same. Political prisoners breathe at the sufferance of their masters."

"Madam," the small man said severely, "again, you're *not* a political prisoner, you're a witness at this trial—not a defendant."

Lael released a nasty laugh. She waved her cuffed wrists at him.

"Then release me, worm!"

"Unfortunately, you've shown violent tendencies. We've been forced to—"

"Oh right, you've been forced to chain a female. Are Imperial Kher so powerful to Earthmen, so threatening, that they cause you to reek from fear and urine?"

"Please, Madam, just sit down. We need you as a cooperative witness against Captain Blake."

"*That* I can do," she said, setting herself down on a steel chair opposite me. The insult of recent events seemed fresh in her mind.

"You've cleaned up some since the last time I saw you," I remarked off-handedly. "I don't smell a thing."

Her face reddened. It probably wasn't the best policy to taunt a witness who's about to be used against you—but I couldn't help it. The doctors never had been able to repair Dr. Williams eye. The girl was going to have to wear a prosthetic one for life.

More and more people kept filing in after that. I didn't bother to remember their names or ranks, although they all provided them. Most of them wore uniforms, but they looked like suits to me.

At last, Admiral Vega showed up. He was to preside over this event as the lead judge. I gave him a nod, but he didn't return it.

Was that a bad omen, or just him being political? I wasn't sure.

A few members of my crew were there, including Hagen and—to my surprise—Dr. Abrams.

They kicked off with a listing of crimes I was supposed to have committed. It could never be enough to just say you killed a man—they always had to put all kinds of garnishment on it.

The small prissy guy sat next to me at my side of the steel table, and it took me about five minutes to realize he was my court-appointed lawyer.

"Hold on a second," I said when they'd finished with the charges.

"Do you have an objection already, Captain Blake?"

I jerked a thumb at the lawyer. "I've never met this man before. Aren't we supposed to have time to review the case and discuss a strategy and so forth?"

Vega gave me a cold stare. "The process has been altered somewhat in this special instance."

"Why?"

The lawyer put his tiny fingers on my sleeve, cautioning me to settle down. I ignored him. No one else answered me.

"This isn't due process then," I told the group, "and I can only assume the verdict is pre-cooked."

"You're out of order, Blake," Vega said.

Looking around the group, I saw people averting their eyes and fidgeting. I must have hit close to home.

"No, I'm getting railroaded."

"Further statements can only damage—"

I made a broad gesture, and the marines at the door flinched.

"It doesn't matter what I say here," I said. "I can see that. You've decided to put on a show-trial and execute me or whatever. What I'd like to know is what the Nomads offered Earth to do this...? What could be so valuable you'd dishonor yourselves and kill your best officer in the bargain...?"

Some of the suits were getting red in the face. They leaned forward and hissed in Vega's ear. He nodded reluctantly.

"As the defendant is uncooperative, we're going to remove him and try him in absentia. Guards?"

They stepped forward and grabbed my elbows. I was truly surprised by this—I'd figured they'd tell me to shut up and yell a bit—but this indicated I'd guessed dead-on what was happening.

"Wait," Lael said suddenly.

For some reason, the group looked at her. Vega lifted his hand.

"What is it, Captain?"

"Blake is right—he's a beast, but he deserves to be treated with honor. Imperials, Rebels—all Kher believe in a fair trial. Except for some of the worst primates, that is. What has the Nomad offered you? Whatever it is—it's a trap. A bargain with a phantom. You'll never collect."

Admiral Vega looked disturbed, but he waved his hand furiously. "Get them both out of here."

Together, Lael and I were dragged from the court by large armed men.

317

"Hey," I tossed over my shoulder, "for what it's worth—thanks."

"You're a rodent, Blake," she said, "but the Nomads are infinitely worse. They'll use your race. We kill for sport—but they whisper and promise and lie. Who's worse? The devil who abuses you honestly, or the one who convinces you he's your best friend first?"

We were dragged apart before I could answer. That was just as well, as I didn't have a snappy comeback to her words.

The truth was I didn't know what kind of devil I preferred.

=63=

Less than an hour later they came and dragged me out of a holding cell. I'd like to say I'd been able to break out, or fool the guards into letting me go—but I'd only managed to shout and bang on the door for a while.

When they finally came downstairs to my door and rattled at the old-fashioned locks, I was hauled out again without a word.

One of the guards took pity on me and spoke quietly. "For my sake, sir," he said, "I think this is all bullshit, and I'm very sorry to be a part of it."

"Thanks, Sergeant. It's not your fault. When governments get scared or greedy—they sometimes do awful things."

When I arrived back at the chamber where the court was to be held, I was met with a wholly unexpected scene.

There was a body on the floor. A thin, willowy female... she'd been shot in the head.

"You killed her?" I asked, running my eyes over the silent group. "You executed Captain Lael?"

"A choice had to be made," Vega said. "A deal was forged."

That was when I noticed the new member of the group. It was none other than Godwin himself, wearing the skin he'd worn when I'd first met him.

"There you are," I said, "I was wondering when you'd crawl out from under one of these rocks."

"Good to see you again too, Captain," Godwin said calmly.

"Am I to be executed next?" I asked.

"That's the deal," Vega said. "Sorry, Blake."

I nodded thoughtfully. "I'm trying to figure this out... Are you trying to blame Earth for the Imperial's execution? Trying to divert them here sooner?"

Godwin shook his head. "Unnecessary. You're already, as we say, on the menu."

I looked at Vega. "Then they must be offering weapons— something to defend our planet?"

"That's right."

The marines behind me were chaining me into a steel chair. I got the feeling I wasn't going to be getting out of it alive.

"Still..." I said thoughtfully to the Nomad, "executing me doesn't add up to a win for either side. Is it just that you wanted me dead in order to remove a competent officer?"

"How disappointing," Godwin said. "I would have thought you'd know better than that. How can you battle the Imperials without your best on the line?"

"Why then?"

He came close and leaned forward. "Because," he said, "you pissed me off back on your ship."

"Petty personal vengeance? Really?"

Godwin shrugged and made a gesture indicating the group. "We aren't above it."

I glanced around at the suits, none of whom I'd ever met before today—and then I got it. "You're all Nomads, aren't you?" I asked.

Godwin smirked. "What nonsense is this?"

"Duplicates... Are *you* for real, General?" I asked, turning to Vega.

He wore a troubled frown. He was running his eyes over the group.

"Let's get on with it," Godwin said.

The sergeant who'd spoken to me in the hallway drew his pistol. He wore a grim, fatalistic expression.

Commander Hagen stepped forward. He touched the guard's hand. "Hold on," he said. "Blake is one of our officers, and it's our custom that the execution come from an officer."

The guard looked bewildered, giving Hagen a "since when" look. He glanced at General Vega for permission, and Vega nodded. The sergeant shrugged and handed over his sidearm.

"Get on with it!" Godwin urged.

Hagen stepped forward, put the gun to my temple, and looked me in the eyes.

"Sorry about all this, Blake."

"A man's got to do what a man's got to do," I told him.

I didn't close my eyes—I wanted to, but I refused. Not until I heard the gun boom.

For just a second, I thought maybe I was dead, or maybe he'd missed—but then I saw the gaping hole in Godwin's chest.

Commander Hagen turned and faced him squarely. "No deal, alien," he said.

Making a shocked, gasping sound, the Nomad pitched forward.

The effect on the other suits, the people I'd assume all along were government stooges, was electric. They rushed forward, eyes staring, hands out-stretched like claws.

Hagen and Vega were startled, but they didn't hesitate. Vega drew his sidearm while Hagen used his to good effect. His gun boomed again and again. It was a standard old-fashioned .45, and it held seven rounds. He plugged one of the Nomads with each shot.

They came on anyway, tearing at him with their fingernails, biting his wrists. It soon became apparent that only Command Hagen, General Vega and the guard who had escorted me were human.

The sergeant threw one to the ground, but while he was stomping that Nomad flat two others rode his back. The lawyer who'd supposedly been sent to rep me beat at Hagen with his briefcase, screeching like a madman the whole time.

More guards came then, realizing an execution shouldn't turn into a brawl. They tried to restrain the lawyers, bureaucrats, decorated brass and the like—but that didn't work. They weren't calming down.

All I could do was kick at them. It was frustrating. A struggling knot of people all around me, and I couldn't even land a solid blow on my own.

At last, it was over. There were just too many humans in the facility. The ten or so odd Nomads couldn't compete. I learned later they hadn't been armed, as that was part of the bargain. It was their undoing in the end.

Several bloody minutes passed, and they were all melting away on the floor, headed back to wherever they'd come from.

Vega came to my side. His left eye was a bloody mess. Some of his fingers didn't seem to work properly—and I realized they'd been bitten half-off at the knuckle.

Still, he managed to unlock my restraints. I got up and snatched a gun off the floor.

That made the guards jump a little, but Vega shook his head, panting.

"He's ours. All charges dropped. Blake—I'm truly sorry I let it go so far."

I was relieved to be alive, but I couldn't help thinking about one member of the party who wouldn't be going home.

Squatting down, I looked into Lael's dead eyes. We'd had our moments, over the years. She was a true witch and a mass murderer on a global scale—but the last thing she'd ever done was to wish me well.

I didn't know what to think about that. Could it mean the Kher could pull together as a single people someday?

Or was I entertaining a fantasy? Lael would have told me there could only be one peace: the peace of the dead.

"Rest in peace," I told her, and I straightened up painfully.

=64=

L et me say first off that I can take a practical joke the
same or better than the next man. I don't mind getting
scared on Halloween or surprised at a birthday party—
but this was an extreme case.

"Sir..." I said to Vega after our injuries had been treated,
"you're telling me you *knew* what these things were? And
you played along?"

Vega shook his head and sighed. "I was beginning to
suspect. They can manipulate memories to some extent,
remember. But we've got precautions against that sort of
thing now."

"But... if you knew they were a pack of Nomads, why'd
you go along with nearly executing me? Why didn't you pull
the plug sooner?"

He shrugged. "Okay, I'm going to level with you: they
promised us some amazing tech. That's the story, plain and
simple. And they weren't just going to give us a ship to fly
around, either. They were going to explain it. The principles,
the concepts... but I began to smell a rat. I didn't think they
intended to deliver at all. They were insisting on executions
up front without giving us squat."

"Uh... a real transfer of knowledge... okay, that's pretty
cool," I admitted, "but I have to ask: would you have shot
me to get your hands on that stuff—if you thought they
would actually deliver?"

He shrugged noncommittally. "It didn't happen, did it?"

"You bastard."

"Blake, this is war. We're a pipsqueak planet in a
universe chock-full of aggressive powers. We're playing for
keeps, here."

"Why'd you kill Lael then?" I asked.

"To prove to them we were for real, of course... Wait a second—you weren't in love with that planet-burning princess, were you?"

"Hell no."

He shook his head. "You sure can pick them, Blake."

"Forget about that," I said, "let's get back to what the hell we're going to do now. The Nomads were upset before—but I think they have to be positively pissed at this point."

"Agreed."

"So, now we've got two enemies. Two galactic rivals that control fleets and planets we don't even have a name for. One is an ancient wicked empire, and the other one is made up of soulless, evil, artificial life forms..."

"You're making it sound pretty grim," he admitted. "But what was I going to do? Let them kill our best captain for nothing? That's not how Earth works, and it's best all these aliens learn that right now."

"Yeah..." I said, "they've got to know that they have to pay up if they want to murder Leo Blake."

"That's right."

There wasn't much of a formal briefing after that. They quietly cleaned up the puddles of liquid on the concrete floors and sent it to Abrams to be analyzed. The rest of the base personnel were told to forget what they'd seen—or what they *thought* they'd seen, because they damn well better not remember anything.

Going back up to my ship, I was given a surprise party. I jumped a little when my crew leapt out of the shadows screaming *"Surprise!"* but I managed not to have a heart attack.

Forcing a grin, I assured everyone I was okay. Mia was especially accommodating, and I learned a new thing about her: she liked status. When her man was losing it, she was truly unpleasant to be around. But when her man became captain again, well, she melted.

When the party was winding down, Hagen came to find me with a bottle in his hand. He had staples in his cheek, a split eyebrow and a sloppy grin on his face.

"I told everyone we had one of your famous trainings," he said, laughing. "They bought it completely."

"Of course they did, Commander. Because that's what happened."

"Damned straight, Captain."

He leaned close, and an alcoholic fog wafted over me.

"Captain... I feel bad about letting the sergeant shoot Lael."

I nodded. "You're thinking you should have intervened then, huh?"

"It haunts me... She was a prisoner, and we killed her in cold blood. No trial—not really."

"Well," I said, "don't worry about it too much. If you'd ever been a prisoner on one of their ships the way I have— you'd want them all dead."

He looked at me. "It's like that?"

"Absolutely. They're monsters. They all deserve to die, really."

"Okay," he said, and he stood up, swaying slightly. He handed me his bottle.

"I won't be needing this anymore. Goodnight, sir."

He left me then, and I smiled until he was gone. Taking charge of his bottle, I took a hard swallow and stared at the walls.

I was thinking of Lael, too. It was hard not to do. She'd been a real person to me, not just a target to shoot at a million kilometers away.

Knowing that I'd lied to Hagen didn't bother me at all. I considered it, in fact, to have been my good deed for the day. But somehow, as I sat and pondered, I felt like I'd taken on the burden he'd left behind.

Had I played it right? Had I played it fair?

The last thing she'd said to me was she was the better devil, because you could predict her behavior. After having dealt with the Nomads and the Imperials directly, I believed she was right.

But now, all that was a moot point. They all hated us— the most powerful two factions in this Galaxy.

Hell, someday they might decide they hated us so badly they'd team up just to come here and stomp out whatever life was left on our little blue planet.

I lifted Hagen's bottle again, and I drank until I stopped thinking and fell asleep.

Books by B. V. Larson:

UNDYING MERCENARIES
Steel World
Dust World
Tech World
Machine World
Death World
Home World
Rogue World

STAR FORCE SERIES
Swarm
Extinction
Rebellion
Conquest
Battle Station
Empire
Annihilation
Storm Assault
The Dead Sun
Outcast
Exile
Demon Star

Visit BVLarson.com for more information

52717421R00205

Made in the USA
San Bernardino, CA
28 August 2017